ATTACK OF THE KAIJU
Volume 2:
THE NEXT WAVE

I0678472

COVER ART: Gabe TKezilla
(https://www.facebook.com/gabe.tkezilla)

**COVER LOGO DESIGN: Elden Ardiente of
Lungga Creatives**
(https://www.facebook.com/lunggacreatives/)

EDITOR: Christofer Nigro

i

AUTHORS:

Matthew Dennion

Christopher Conde

Skip Peel

Dustin Dreyling

Cody Bratsch

Neil Riebe

Kane Gilmour

Alex Dumitru

Christofer Nigro

Nathan Marchand

Andrew Nguyen

Andres Perez

Kevin Heim

Zach Cole

John LeMay

D.G. Valdron

INTERIOR ARTISTS:

Elden Ardiente

John Opal

Ray Fromm

GabeTKezilla

Garayann

Frank Parr

Neil Riebe

Brion Halloway

Mortiphon

This titanic grotesquerie will have his prose debut in a near-future publication from Wild Hunt Press, so stay tuned with us!

Art: Elden Ardiente

© 2019 Wild Hunt Press. All Rights Reserved. No part of this publication may be reproduced, distributed, or transmitted in any form or by any means, including photocopying, recording, or other electronic or mechanical methods, without the prior written permission of the publisher, except in the case of brief quotations embodied in critical reviews and certain other noncommercial uses permitted by copyright law. For permission requests, write to the publisher, who can be reached at the following email address: WildHuntPress@gmail.com. All events depicted in this work are fictional, and any resemblance to real individuals and events are coincidental or with non-malicious satirical intent. All pictures used are copyright Marvel Entertainment, Warner Bros., etc., and are reproduced here for demonstrative purposes only and within legal bounds of fair use.

DEDICATIONS

This book is lovingly dedicated to my grandmother Gertrude "Trudie" Nigro, the wonderful woman who raised me, loved me more than anyone else ever has, and graciously dealt with my difficult side no matter how difficult it ever got. Her family, the community, and the world was truly blessed to have her for 95 years now and I love her more than anyone else. And to the memory of her sister, my aunt Concetta "Connie" Denisco, who always believed in me, and was always there for me and everyone else she knew whenever she was needed. I miss her terribly.

I also dedicate this book to all the kaiju-fans who have made this genre such a prominent part of pop culture and fantastic fiction for over six decades at this writing. The inspiration your writings and artwork have given me throughout the course of my life filled my creative side with endless possibilities. Giants truly do walk the Earth, but their incredible might is not tooth, claw, or beam weapons but the pen and the paintbrush.

Table of Contents

INTRODUCTION

You gotta love kaiju… as long as you can watch them thrash *somebody else's* neighborhood (preferably that of your boss, if it has to happen near your hometown). Has this amazing sub-genre of sci-fi and (sometimes) horror fiction really been around for over six decades now? So many generations of writers, artists, musicians, readers, cinemaphiles, and television viewers (is there an official name for them?) grew up reading about or watching imagery of these largest and most powerful of all monsters as they represented everything from the destructive nature of atomic weaponry, environmental malfeasance and nature's instrument of revenge, or even a titan-sized version of the heroic ideal. The latter archetype includes not only certain kaiju (e.g., Gamera; and Godzilla during the 1970s), but kyodai – super-heroes who grow to immense size to combat the threat of kaiju; and mech – gigantic robots built by human beings (or benevolent aliens, etc.) to enable them to (well, hopefully) stand up to kaiju and defend humanity's position as the dominant form of life on the planet.

Kaiju have come in a myriad and imaginative variety of shapes, with an equally dizzying array of special powers – as if their immense size & strength and near-invulnerability to humanity's most advanced military weaponry didn't make them powerful enough already. But no, many kaiju (though far from all) boasted exotic beam weapons, spewed flame (or concentrated radiation) much like their dragon predecessors in folklore, or came in a mechanized form holding an arsenal of offensive ordinance designed by advanced alien civilizations who constructed them to either conquer our planet or help protect it from conquest. The most popular phenotypes remain reptilian, but insects, mammals, fish, cephalopods, and even humanoids and (again) robots were well-represented among them. As were more exotic forms that it strains the imagination to identify with something spawned by the natural world around us or designed by humanity.

Many of them take the oversized form of animals we know, others boast a chimeric variety of physical traits, and others still are culled from the images given to their forebears in world mythology & folklore. Their antecedents not only first appeared millennia ago in mythology with the likes of Jormungand the Midgard Serpent (Norse mythology), Tiamat (Babylonian mythology), Typhon (Greek mythology), and Orochi (Japanese mythology) along with the entirety of dragon and sea serpent lore, but also those giants of the more humanoid variety, e.g., the cyclops. Their early reptilian phenotype was likewise represented in *The Bible* with the likes of Leviathan and Behemoth, so these colossal monsters certainly have an esteemed and ubiquitous pedigree throughout human history. Yes, kaiju – or, more properly, *daikaiju* – have been with humanity for as long as we were cognizant enough to imagine and have nightmares.

Their modern counterparts came to us in a rough prototype form during the 1920s and '30s in such early cinematic gems like *The Lost World* (1925) and *King Kong* (1933), and achieved the size and form we are now familiar with starting either in 1953 with Ray Harryhausen's giant monster epic *The Beast from 20,000*

Fathoms or none other than Toho's king of the kaiju a year later with *Godzilla* (1954). I'll let kaiju-fans decide this one for themselves while noting what a huge fan I am of both Harryhausen's entire oeuvre of work and that of the folks at Toho like Tomoyuki Tanaka, Ishiro Honda, and Eiji Tsuburaya.

Having navigated mythology/folklore, movies, TV, comic books/manga, and video games it was only a matter of time before kaiju invaded prose and showed the possibilities of depicting them in that medium. There were examples prior to the 1990s, of course, but that was the decade when it was first widely demonstrated in America that kaiju fiction works in prose.

American pioneers in prose during the '90s prominently includes the two series of Godzilla novels penned by Marc Cerasini & Scott Ciencin respectively when Random House had the license from Toho, and the great Godzilla fan fiction and other kaiju fiction written by Skip Peel for *G-Fan* magazine – all of which really showed what kaiju tales could do in prose lit. This continued unabated into the 2010s with the Nemesis Saga (starting with *Project Nemesis: A Kaiju Thriller*) by Jeremy Robinson and the great interior art by Nemesis co-creator Matt Frank, to the great folks at Severed Press who published the kaiju novels of many great authors, including Matthew Dennion's *Chimera: Scourge of the Gods* and *Atomic Rex*. The 2010s has been the best decade in ages to be a kaiju-fan and the explosion of kaiju prose is one of those reasons, along with a new era of kaiju cinema courtesy of Toho and Legendary Pictures.

And it was no less a personage than Mr. Dennion who did me the great honor of asking for a story from me for inclusion in his self-published kaiju anthology *Attack of the Kaiju: Age of Monsters*. And then came the even bigger honor of allowing my publishing outfit, Wild Hunt Press, to continue that series starting with this, the second volume.

This allows WHP and a crew of both established authors and newcomers to make their own unique contributions to kaiju fiction via the medium of prose. It is nothing less than a dream come true for me, and the opportunity to share such a dream with the public is one of the most awarding aspects of being a writer and publisher. I hope you enjoy what you read here and find at least some of the variety of tales and authors found in the following pages to your liking, and if you do, please do not be shy about saying so in a review for Amazon, Goodreads, your own blog, or, hell, maybe all of the above. It is the firm hope of the WHP staff – whose hard work I am indebted to here – to produce a lot more of this in the future, including a potential sister kaiju anthology series to *Attack of the Kaiju* and our own series of novellas and novels from an assortment of authors.

Christofer Nigro
October 2019

PART 1: STORIES

CHIMERA VS. BUBBLES

Matthew Dennion and Christopher Conde

Author's Note: The following short story is a non-canonical adventure of Chimera from Matt's novels *Chimera: Scourge of the Gods* and *Atomic Rex: Conquest of Chimera*, both available through Severed Press.

The Atlantic Ocean off the Florida Coast

The sun was beating down on the surface of the ocean and a hot breeze was blowing up the Gulf Stream. Seagulls were cackling overhead, as Alex wiped the sweat from his brow and plunged his bucket and his bare hands into the cooler that held the chopped up fish parts and other carrion that fishermen lovingly referred to as chum. Once the bucket was full, Alex pulled the receptacle out of the cooler and made sure to take only shallow breaths as the rancid odor of mutilated fish swept past his mouth.

He looked over at his friend JD and joked, "You sure you don't want a mouthful of this for yourself? I mean, it can't make your breath smell any worse!"

Alex laughed as JD sneered at his friend. JD shook his head and wondered why he had decided to let Alex talk him into an all-night drinking bender followed by a trip for bluefish on his boat. JD was fighting a nasty hangover. He had already vomited once, and the smell of the chum combined with the motion of the ship was making his stomach and head feel even worse. He was so drunk when he fell asleep the night before, that he didn't even realize he had fallen asleep on Alex's boat. When he first woke up, he planned to tell Alex that he was going to skip the fishing trip and sleep off the hangover; but when he tried to stand up, he was immediately thrown back onto the bed.

JD had thought that his lack of balance was due to the hangover, but he groaned when Alex opened the door to the cabin and let the sea air in. He realized that he was already out to sea and that Alex was not about to turn back. Alex poked fun at JD for not being able to hold his liquor and it was in that moment that JD knew he was going to have to go fishing with his friend. He had been friends with Alex long enough to know that the fisherman would constantly be making fun of him and bothering him if he tried to go back to sleep.

Alex dumped the bucket full of chum over the side of the boat. The vile mixture had no sooner hit the surface of the ocean than dozens of small fish began swarming around the floating slurry.

Deep beneath the surface of the water, a pair of ravenous eyes stared up at the flurry of activity above. There was the strange sound of a gurgle as a surprisingly intelligent mind behind the ravenous eyes giggled with joy at the sight above him. Long red mechanical knees bent slightly and then pushed themselves off the ocean floor, thus propelling the huge robotic body toward the surface of the water. The creature that was both trapped in and controlling the robotic leviathan that was moving toward the surface of the water knew a feeding frenzy when he saw one. He also knew that where there was a feeding frenzy there were often fish food flakes.

JD was doing his best not to vomit as he looked down at all the sea life feeding on the dismembered trawl. Hundreds of small fish were darting in and out of the chum-filled water. But as JD stared down into it, he saw something much larger than the feeding fish approaching the surface. A huge, gold-colored fish was approaching the chum from the depths. JD had been deep sea fishing many times in his life and he was well acquainted with the fish that lived in the Atlantic. At first, JD thought that the enormous aquatic organism was a sunfish. As the creature rose closer to the surface of the water, it became clear that the beast was not something traditionally found in these waters.

As the massive creature continued to rise, JD began to think that it was the alcohol in his system distorting his perception. He called out to his friend. "Alex, get over here and tell me if you see what I see!"

Alex sighed and then started walking across the deck of the boat toward his friend. He saw JD looking over the side and joked. "If it's another mouthful of your puke, I can already tell you that I will see ..." Alex's declaration was cut short as he looked down into the water to catch sight of a massive goldfish swimming in a very tight circle. He peered closer and said, "Is that thing trapped in some kinda fishbowl?"

The bulging eyes of the monstrous fish known as Bubbles rolled over and stared at the carrion above him. He could see the dozens of ordinary fish feeding above him, but he was unable to detect any of the flakes that he craved. The aquatic monster moaned in agony as hunger pains rang throughout his body. His mind drifted back to the events that had brought him to his current state.

The monster/mech hybrid that had been dubbed "Bubbles" by his creator had once been a typical goldfish. The scientist known as Dr. Moor had been working on a shrink ray to help in the seemingly never-ending war between humanity and the kaiju. When the shrink ray was finished, Dr. Moor decided that he was going to test it on his pet goldfish. After the physicist fired the gun's ray at his pet fish he was astonished to see that instead of causing the goldfish to shrink, it had the opposite effect of causing it to grow to an enormous size. Dr. Moor soon realized that the creature's increased brain size resulted in a level of intelligence far beyond that of any typical goldfish.

Feeling that he had created something far more useful in the defense of the human race than a shrink ray, Dr. Moor immediately set to creating a gigantic battle suit with a huge reinforced fishbowl on top of it from which Bubbles could control the mech. The battle suit was bright silver, with a thick body and short powerful legs. In place of its hands, were two ominous weapons. Where the mech's right hand should have been, were three harpoons that Bubbles could fire at will. The mech's right arm ended in a long and powerful hook. The final two weapons adorned the mech's shoulders, in the form of twin old-fashioned cannons.

Once Bubbles was placed within the battle suit, the hyper-intelligent fish knew that it had found the means to acquire that which it desired most: fish flakes. With the kaiju's increased size, however, came a vastly increased appetite. Bubbles was driven by an insatiable hunger for

9

fish flakes. The former pet turned the mech toward its creator, and before Dr. Moor could say a single word in protest Bubbles swiped at the scientist and sent him flying. The hybrid then grabbed up the meager tube of fish flakes that his creator had on hand and dumped them into his fishbowl. The ravenous Bubbles quickly swallowed the miniscule amount of flakes before guiding his mech toward the safety of the ocean.

As Bubbles was entering the sea, he turned on the radio and heard an advertisement for SeaWorld in Orlando, Florida. The commercial boasted that SeaWorld housed the largest assortment of fish and marine life on the planet. A strand of large bubbles floated to the top of the fish's bowl as he laughed to himself. Bubbles was certain that a place which held the world's largest collection of fish would also hold its largest collection of fish flakes!

Bubbles had accessed the guidance system within his mech and set a course for Orlando. He nearly reached his destination when he saw the feeding frenzy occurring above him. As the top of Bubbles' fishbowl floated through the chum filled waters, he snarled at the lack of fish flakes to be found in the dispersed carrion. Bubbles looked up at the people on the boat above him and his eyes filled with anger.

JD and Alex could see the enraged fish monster and the mech it was connected to rising toward the surface. JD vomited over the side of the boat directly onto Bubbles' bowl, which infuriated the monster even more.

The sober and quick-thinking Alex ran to the deck of the ship and grabbed his radio. Ever since ancient gods and monsters had started attacking humankind, it was standard operating procedure that if a ship at sea saw a kaiju, the captain was to immediately contact the Coast Guard with the monster's location.

Alex grabbed his radio and called the Coast Guard, "Mayday! Mayday! This is private ship B.O.A.! We are just off the Coast of Orlando and we have sighted a kaiju! It appears to be some kind of a..."

Alex's words were cut short again as Bubbles lifted his hooked arm out of the water and then brought it crashing down onto of the B.O.A.! The colossal fish turned around inside of the dome that doubled as his bowl and then set his sights on the Florida coast. According to the guidance system within his suit, he was only a few miles from SeaWorld and the endless supply of fish flakes that he suspected were kept there. The monster commanded his mech suit to head toward land. As the robot carried the fish toward the shore, he could almost taste the fish flakes that awaited him there!

The sun was rising over the Atlantic Ocean, casting an orange glow over the horizon. The morning air was cool, and the breeze was covering the deck of the 30-foot vessel that was cruising off the shores of southern Florida with a fine mist. Luke Davis was the captain of this ship and today his crew consisted of his wife Melissa and their two daughters, seven-year-old Stacy and four-year-old Sally.

Luke was sitting on the second deck of the ship that was technically a naval vessel and what he referred to as his *work boat*. While the ship was given to him primarily to carry out his duties of training the most powerful creature on the face of the Earth, the Navy didn't mind if he occasionally used the craft for a joy ride. Today wasn't about work. Today was about Luke spending some quality time with his family... and *all* of his family. Luke looked down at the deck below him to see his wife standing behind the two girls at the bow of the ship jumping up and down and scanning the water.

Sally looked up at her dad and shouted, "Daddy, where is he?"

Stacy grabbed her younger sister by the shoulder and shouted, "I see him! He's going to come up over there!"

Stacy pointed her finger to the starboard side of the ship. Luke, Melissa, and Sally all followed Stacy's finger to a position roughly a half a mile away from the vessel. They could see a massive dark shape moving quickly through the water. The two girls screamed as the colossal monster known as Chimera breached the surface of the water to reveal his long sperm whale head with his lion like teeth poking out from inside his mouth. The head was followed by a shaggy lion's mane and then the powerful body and arms of a gorilla with the skin texture of a sperm whale. Its hind legs were like those of a lion, but they were covered by the smooth whale-like skin instead of fur.

Chimera roared as he reached the apex of his jump, then he turned onto his side and crashed back beneath the waves. The last thing that the family saw was the kaiju's thick sperm whale tail as it smacked down onto the surface of the ocean and sent a series of huge waves rolling toward the ship.

Luke turned the ship toward the wake left by the 250-foot tall monster. As Luke's wife and daughters cheered, the kaiju again leapt out of the water and plunged back beneath the surface. Luke smiled too as he looked at the giant monster that he now considered the fifth member of his immediate family. Two years ago, Luke was teaching students with severe cases of autism in a special services school district. He was a master teacher who utilized Applied Behavior Analysis techniques to teach his students the skills that they would require to be functional members of society.

Luke had finished teaching one day when two men dressed in black showed up at his school and asked to talk to him. Luke was known for successfully instructing some of the most aggressive and lowest functioning students in the state. Luke was offered four times his current salary to take his skills and to apply them to a special project that the government was working on. Luke was then taken to a facility in Virginia where he met three other individuals who would become important people in his life.

The first person was General Sam Parsons. Parsons was one of the head men in the US military and he was in charge of the nation's special projects. The second person was Diana Cain. Diana was a professor of mythology and folklore, and over the course of their adventures she would become his best friend. The third person was the head scientist of the military's special projects, Dr. Jonathan Toombs. Toombs was the genius who had created Chimera.

Parsons would inform Luke and Diana that humankind was under attack by the ancient gods and the monsters they controlled. Since Zeus, Thor, and other thunder gods were able to generate electromagnetic pulses capable of shorting out any weapons or machines powered by electricity, the only thing that humanity could use to fight back was Chimera. Parsons needed Luke to train Chimera and he needed Diana to use her expertise to keep them informed of the powers and weaknesses of the enemies they were facing. Luke led Chimera across the globe as they battled numerous mythological monsters and deities, and the kaiju had defeated them all. Since the end of the war, Luke had continued to train Chimera in preparation for any future threats from giant monsters.

Luke was watching Chimera surface once again to take a breath of fresh air when he heard General Parson's voice over his radio. "Luke, we have reports of a kaiju attack five miles south of your current position. The kaiju is named Bubbles, and we suspect that he is heading directly for Orlando and SeaWorld."

Luke shook his head as he replied. "Copy that, sir! Heading south now. Just one question though. What kind of mythological monster is Bubbles?"

Luke could hear Parson's sigh before replying. "Bubbles is not a mythological monster. He is one of ours." Parson was silent for a second before adding, "I have Diana researching everything that we have on Bubbles right now. I will have her contact you if she finds anything."

Luke smiled when he heard that his friend was looking into the monster's past. "Good. If there is anything that can help to defeat this beast, Diana will find it."

Orlando, Florida

Sirens wailed throughout Disney World, followed by instructions for people to quickly and calmly evacuate the park. The thousands of tourists who were visiting the Magic Kingdom were trying to decide what was the quickest way to exit the park when the ground beneath them suddenly shook.

Jamie Daniels was on his honeymoon with his new bride Jennifer. They had promised to cut themselves off from all distractions save each other and decided to leave their cell phones at home. Jennifer had convinced Jamie that there would be plenty of photographers in the park to chronicle their honeymoon. By simply purchasing the Disney Photopass, they could walk through the parks without a care of having to take a selfie with each character they ran into. They had just exited from beneath the famed Cinderella's Castle when the sirens went off.

When the ground shook for second time, Jamie turned to his wife. "Earthquake?"

Jennifer shook her head. "In Florida? I don't think so."

They were looking at the people around them checking their phones and yelling something about a fish when they heard a deafening screeching sound in the air above them. The newlyweds looked skyward to see three fighter jets streaking low above the park and over the fairytale castle. They followed the fighters' trajectory and then they both gasped in horror when they saw the jets fire their missiles at a target in the distance.

Jennifer screamed. "My god, are some kind of aircraft being used to attack Disney?"

The answer to Jennifer's question came not from her husband, but rather from the ominous form of Bubbles as the monster's shadow enveloped Cinderella's Castle. The top of his fishbowl-domed mech was still aflame from the last volley of the jets as he stared down at the people fleeing in fear of him.

Bubbles was filled with rage as he stared through the flames at Cinderella's Castle. Since he had come ashore, the humans had done nothing but attempt to prevent him from reaching the fish flakes that he so desperately craved. The monster fish heard the sound of the jet fighters turning around to attack him again and Bubbles blubbered in anger at their interference.

Jamie and Jennifer watched in disbelief as the mech lifted his clawed and harpooned arms into the air.

The flames were flickering out across the bowl that held the giant fish atop the mech and it only took one look from Jamie at the fish's engorged eyes to know what was coming next.

He grabbed his wife and yelled. "Quick! Into the castle!"

The young couple was running into the castle and toward the mechanical monster while everyone else was running away from him. Jamie had read about Disney before heading down there and one of the things that had fascinated him about the park was the fact that the Disney employees used a series of hidden underground tunnels to move around the park. It was through this method that Mickey and Minnie could pop-up anywhere in the park without being seen coming or going. Jamie found the tunnel that ran through the bottom of the castle and pulled his wife into it just as he felt the structure

16

shake and heard the sound of stone and mortar being torn apart. He glanced backward toward the front of the legendary castle to see several people being crushed by the steeple that once stood atop the structure.

There was a loud cracking sound as the ceiling above the tunnel at the base of the castle started to split in two. Jamie saw a door that said *staff only* and he quickly dashed into it, pulling Jennifer in behind him. The couple sprinted down a flight of stairs as the structure collapsed above them, filling the corridor they were in with dust.

Jamie closed his eyes and tried taking a breath, but his mouth immediately filled with particles of pulverized concrete. The young husband placed his right hand on the wall while he kept his left hand firmly clasped around his wife's wrist. The sound of more explosions reverberated throughout the corridor they were in and Jamie could only guess that the jet fighters had launched another attack on the fish robot.

He kept walking forward until he could no longer feel the dust from the crushed castle on his face. He then opened his eyes to see a long running tunnel with lights strung across the top of it.

He pulled Jennifer close to him and said, "I think we're safe now."

The walls shook from another explosion as Jennifer whimpered, "You saved our lives. If we had tried to evacuate the park we would've been crushed to death by that thing!"

The walls shook again as another explosion came from above them. Jennifer hugged her husband. "What do we do now?"

Jamie quickly kissed his wife. "I say we keep walking down this tunnel and away from what sounds like World War Three taking place above us. I think that if we reach the end of the tunnel, we should wait there until the fighting stops. Aside from that monster fighting the military, there is likely a human stampede of tourists running for their lives above us."

Jennifer nodded and then interlocked her fingers with her husband's as the two of them walked down a long corridor toward a future that mere moments ago was nearly taken from them.

Above ground, Bubbles reared back and drove his fish hooked arm through the remains of Cinderella's Castle. As the lower half of the former tourist attraction crumbled to dust the back of Bubbles' exo-suit was struck with a barrage of high caliber machine gun fire from the fighter jets as they renewed their attack. Bubbles looked up as the craft flew over him. The aquatic monster aimed his shoulder mounted cannons at two of the three jets and then with a sly grimace on his face, the colossal fish fired his weapons. Two round black cannon balls shot out of the shoulder cannons with a speed that belied the technology that had inspired them. The spherical projectiles slammed into two of the jets. The cannonballs tore through the outer hull of the jets, causing them to spiral out of control and toward the ground below them.

The last remaining fighter jet swerved around and locked his missiles on Bubbles. The pilot was closing in on the beast as he lifted up his arm with the giant harpoons sticking out of it. Bubbles aimed his arm at the approaching ship and then fired several of the harpoons at the oncoming jet. The skilled pilot was able to evade the first two harpoons but the third one struck the nose of the plane causing it to erupt into a ball of flames.

As the flaming debris crashed to the ground at Bubbles' feet, two more harpoons emerged from within the mech suit's arm to replace those that had been fired. After his weapons were finished reloading, Bubbles shifted his body in the direction of SeaWorld and he once more started walking in the direction of the fish flakes that he so fervently desired.

Florida Coast

Chimera was standing in the surf and waiting for instructions, while Luke and his family were standing on the deserted beach between two helicopters.

Luke hugged his girls then he kissed Melissa and whispered to her, "The helicopter on the right will fly you and the girls back to base where you will be safe. I will use the other one to lead Chimera to the monster that is attacking Orlando."

Melissa smiled. "Just stop that thing before it hurts too many people." She looked over Luke at the kaiju that she too had to come love and shouted, "And you make sure he gets home safely!"

Luke turned around to see Chimera still waiting for his instructions. "He always does. Doesn't he?"

Melissa smiled and kissed Luke again. She then grabbed their kids by the hands and led them toward the helicopter. Luke laughed to himself as he got a quick goodbye from the girls while Chimera got a loud, "Good bye, Chimera! We love you!" from them.

Luke ran over to his helicopter and yelled to the pilot to take off. He first instructed the pilot to fly by Chimera. When they were directly in front of the monster, Luke tossed one of the huge squid, beef, and bamboo cubes that he used to reward Chimera out of the helicopter. The cube had barely left the helicopter when Chimera's jaws lashed out and snatched up the treat. Having given Chimera a motivational reward before giving him any instructions, Luke had gained the monster's attention and compliance.

Luke grabbed the loudspeaker that was connected to the helicopter and shouted into it, "Chimera, follow me!" The slayer of gods roared in reply and then began lumbering after his friend as the helicopter flew toward SeaWorld.

As they flew over land Luke looked down at the path of destruction that Bubbles had left in his wake. When they first came ashore, the destruction was limited to a few structures and vehicles. However, as Bubbles met increased resistance, the scope of the death and devastation increased dramatically. When the helicopter had made its way ten miles inland, Luke could see the crushed remains of twenty-some police cars. He could see red stains on the ground near the cars that he was certain was blood and cringed when he thought about what a closer inspection of the sight might reveal. Fifteen miles farther inland, Luke saw an even more horrifying scene of death as he looked at the smoldering scrap heap of metal which had once been a tank battalion that had challenged Bubbles.

Luke shook his head in fear as the thought about what this monster could do if it reached a populated area

20

crossed his mind. Luke yelled to the pilot, "Where is Bubbles now?"

The pilot shouted back, "Latest reports have him attacking Disney World!"

Luke recoiled at the news that Bubbles had already reached the most densely populated theme park in the world. He screamed as he pulled the side door of the helicopter shut. "Take us to full speed now! We need to stop this thing before it reaches any of the other theme parks!"

The pilot looked back at Luke. "Are you sure the monster will be able to keep up with us?"

Luke yelled, "Chimera has the speed of a 130-meter-tall lion with the stamina of a sperm whale, which never stops moving! He could run past us and keep going for days if he wanted to!"

The pilot shrugged. "Copy that, sir! Sit down and buckle in."

As soon as Luke had secured himself to his seat, the helicopter shot forward at a speed of 315 kilometers per hour. When Chimera saw the vehicle flying away from him, the monster dropped to all fours and roared before taking off after it. Within seconds, Chimera had caught up to the quickly moving helicopter.

Luke was doing his best to avoid vomiting from the sudden acceleration when he heard his best friend's voice come in over his headset radio.

"Luke, this is Diana. I've found something that may help us to limit the destruction caused by a fight to the death between Chimera and Bubbles."

Luke knew that his faith in Diana would be justified. He smiled as he yelled back, "What do you have?

Bubbles is about to enter SeaWorld but we think that Chimera can engage him before he reaches the heart of the park where most of the civilians are!"

"Once you have Chimera engage Bubbles, you need to fly to the outskirts of downtown Orlando. The police and emergency service units are scouring every pet store in the city to put together a special package for you."

SeaWorld

Bubbles began to swim in a frantic circle around his fishbowl when he saw a sign with two huge orcas painted on the side of it. In the distance, the monster could see massive water tanks sprawling for acres around a theme park. He knew that he had finally found SeaWorld! More importantly, he knew that he had found the fish flakes that he yearned for!

Bubbles was about to take a step toward SeaWorld, when he noticed the water in his bowl was shaking. The fish beast was confused by this, since until now the only thing that had caused the water in his bowl to shake was his own footfalls. Bubbles turned his mech suit around and looked behind him to see a helicopter rocketing toward him and behind it was something much worse. For the first time in his existence, Bubbles was beholding a creature that rivaled him in terms of size and power. The creature was beyond definition, but when Bubbles saw its whale-like head, gray thick skin, and fluked tail he quickly came to the conclusion that the aquatic monster had come here for fish flakes!

Three long bubbles burped out of the goldfish's mouth as an overwhelming feeling of anger flushed through his body. Bubbles would not let this marine monster eat his fish flakes. Bubbles aimed his mech suit toward the charging Chimera and began advancing.

When Chimera noticed that Bubbles was charging him, the hybrid stopped for a brief moment. The monster shifted to a bipedal stance, threw his arms out at his sides, and roared a challenge at the approaching mech. Chimera then dropped back to all fours and ran directly at Bubbles.

The moment that Luke saw Chimera heading toward Bubbles he yelled out to the pilot, "Take us to downtown Orlando! There is some kind of special package there that we need to pick up!"

The two behemoths were in the middle of the SeaWorld parking lot as Chimera drove his spermaceti reinforced head into the mid-section of Bubbles' mech-suit. The blow knocked Bubbles off his feet and sent him crashing down on top of dozens of cars. The force of the impact was so great that inside of his bowl head, Bubbles' body was jarred and sent crashing into the side of his fishbowl. The dazed fish looked up to see Chimera standing above him with his jaws wide open and reaching down toward him.

Bubbles aimed his harpoon hand at the hybrid and fired one of the gigantic steel projectiles, which buried itself in Chimera's left shoulder. A stream of the hybrid kaiju's blood was sent spurting into the air. Chimera roared in pain as he backed away from Bubbles, affording the fish monster the chance to regain his feet.

Chimera was still trying to pull the colossal harpoon from his shoulder when he saw Bubbles preparing to fire another at him. Before Bubbles was able to launch his second harpoon, Chimera shifted his head forward and fired a high, tightly focused sonar blast attack at his attacker. The sonar blast struck Bubbles and while the monster's mechanical suit was unaffected by the attack, the central nervous system of the giant fish himself was temporarily disabled. This caused the huge fish to lose consciousness. Bubbles turned belly up and floated to the top of his fishbowl as Chimera pulled the harpoon from his shoulder and began advancing on the unresponsive monster.

Downtown Orlando

The helicopter that was carrying Luke began to slow down as it approached the outskirts of downtown Orlando. The pilot yelled, "Mr. Davis, I believe that I have a visual on the target!"

Luke unhooked himself from his seat and leaned out the side of the helicopter to see nearly twenty police cars surrounding what looked like a huge trash dumpster.

The helicopter was circling the site when Luke and the pilot heard Diana's voice over their radios. "The dumpster below you is your target. You need to attach a cable to it, fly it past Bubbles, and then use it to lead him back out into the Atlantic."

The pilot was already lowering a cable as Luke responded, "Copy that, Diana. Just one question. What's in the dumpster?"

Luke could hear a slight giggle from Diana as she replied, "Believe it or not, the dumpster is full of fish flakes and weightlifting plates."

Luke was looking down at the giant container of fish flakes as it was slowly being lifted into the air. "I hope the pilot can keep this thing steady. I would hate to have that crap drop on someone's home."

Diana laughed. "My ex-boyfriend lives outside of Orlando. If you happen to fly over his house and spill a little on his property, I think we could live with that. In fact, he has a pool in his backyard. Just imagine the look on his face when he walks out to see his pool has turned into fish flake-flavored oatmeal."

Luke finally laughed a little at Diana's last comment. He was fully aware that she knew he was concerned about Chimera, and despite the life and death battle that was taking place a few miles away from them a brief laugh was good. It helped not only to break the tension Luke felt at leaving Chimera in the middle of a battle, but it also helped him to take a breath and refocus so that he would be as helpful to Chimera as possible.

He was still smiling as the pilot spun the plane around and rocketed toward SeaWorld.

SeaWorld

Chimera had managed to pull the harpoon out his body just as he had reached the unconscious Bubbles. The hybrid roared as he lifted the harpoon above his head and then drove it through the center of Bubbles' harpooned arm, rendering the limb inert. Chimera then stared into Bubbles' fishbowl at the upside goldfish. Chimera roared as he lifted his right hand into the air and unsheathed his lion like claws.

25

Bubbles' eyes opened just in time to see Chimera's claw about to slice through his fishbowl. The giant fish righted himself then quickly shifted the front part of his mech suit backward, so that Chimera's claw swept passed his fishbowl instead of shattering it. Bubbles then brought his right arm up, smashing it into Chimera's chin and snapping his jaws shut. Bubbles continued his attack by first kicking Chimera in the midsection causing the monster to stumble backwards. As Chimera was trying to regain his balance, Bubbles slashed Chimera across the chest with his hooked hand causing a stream of bright crimson to fly across the parked and crushed cars of the SeaWorld parking lot.

Chimera grabbed his bleeding chest, then looked up at Bubbles. When he did so, the beast's eyes grew wide. Chimera threw his arms to his sides and unleashed a roar of pure rage at Bubbles. Chimera stepped forward with his left hand raised above his head. He then delivered a hammer strike to the top of Bubbles' right shoulder. This blow caused the knees of the mech suit to buckle. Chimera then stepped forward and connected with a right cross to Bubbles' fishbowl head. The blow was so intense that it sent shockwaves through the water in Bubbles' encasement, stunning the fish. With Bubbles staggered, Chimera charged forward and drove his head into the mech's chest, knocking the giant automaton to the ground.

Bubbles looked up to again see Chimera looming over him. The hybrid monster mounted Bubbles, raised his paws into the air, and began pounding on the center of the mech with the intention of cracking the fishbowl wide open and feasting on the animal inside of it.

Realizing that he would soon die if he did not act quickly, Bubbles aimed both of his shoulder cannons at Chimera's eyes and fired them. The act of having a cannon ball fired into each of his eyes at the same time was enough to disorient Chimera. The great hybrid kaiju was shaking his head from side to side trying to clear his vision as Bubbles used his hook arm to strike Chimera across the jaw. The blow was enough to dislodge the gestalt beast from his mounted position. With Chimera no longer pinning him to the ground, Bubbles was able to regain his feet.

The fish monster was about to reengage in the battle with Chimera when his olfactory sensors picked up something in the distance. Bubbles looked to the east, where he saw a huge box filled with the fish flakes he so desperately wanted and needed. Bubbles turned away from Chimera and took a step toward the floating feast.

Luke was watching Bubbles' movements through the windshield of the helicopter and when he saw the monster heading toward him, he screamed to the pilot, "We have his attention! Now head back out to sea at top speed!"

The pilot replied with a quick, "Yes, sir!"

The monster in the mech watched as the helicopter turned and started flying away from him. A short strand of bubbles escaped from the mutant fish's mouth as he blubbered his frustration at the sight of his prize flying away from him. Bubbles shot one brief glance at the quickly recovering Chimera and then he darted after the fleeing helicopter and its payload of fish flakes.

Chimera shook his head until his vision cleared enough to see Bubbles not only running away from him

27

but also running toward the helicopter that carried Luke. The thought of Bubbles attacking the one other creature that the hybrid creature felt kinship with enraged the kaiju. Chimera roared and began charging after Bubbles in an attempt to catch the fish monster before he was able to hurt Luke.

Luke's body was being pushed into the seat of the helicopter as the vehicle continued to increase its speed. He heard the pilot yell out to him, "I am going to have to gain some altitude! That thing is gaining on us!"

Luke felt his stomach drop as the helicopter quickly ascended farther into the air. He swallowed hard and yelled out, "How much longer until we reach the ocean?"

The pilot replied, "We will reach the shoreline in a minute! After that, it's about another fifteen minutes to the point of no return."

Bubbles nearly lost his footing as he took a step onto the beach. The monster righted himself and looked up to see that he had almost reached the fish flakes! Bubbles began bouncing up and down near the top of his bowl in a feeding frenzy as he swung his hook toward the dumpster full of fish flakes only to have the food supply ascend above his reach. Bubbles swam furiously around his fishbowl as he watched the frustrating helicopter fly out over the ocean.

Bubbles' mech immediately strode into the ocean after the elusive fish flakes. The robot was in hip-deep water when everything around Bubbles turned upside down and then went black.

Chimera had been running after Bubbles, but he had been unable to catch the fast-moving mech. The intelligent hybrid knew that he could stop Bubbles in his tracks with a focused sonar blast, but he also knew that such a blast would carry past Bubbles and strike the machine carrying Luke. The sonar blast would stun Luke and cause his helicopter to crash, killing his trainer and friend.

When Chimera saw the helicopter ascend above and away from Bubbles, the whale-like kaiju unleashed his focused sonar attack on his prey. The blast shook the monster's mech suit and once more momentarily shut down the fish's central nervous system. With Bubbles standing still in front of him, Chimera charged at the beast that was hunting his friend. Chimera struck Bubbles' mech suit in the back with such force that the blow sent the monster hurtling forward and far out to sea.

Chimera's blow managed to jar Bubbles back to his senses. The fish monster swam around his bowl to reorient himself. After he had finished swimming his lap, he looked up to once more to see Chimera moving toward him. Bubbles quickly spun around within his bowl to see that the fish flakes he was chasing were being flown farther out into the Atlantic. Bubbles looked back at Chimera to see the hybrid's fist a second before it crashed into his bowl. Chimera roared as he stepped forward and delivered another punch to Bubbles' chest. The latter blow caused the mech to step backwards in order to keep from falling down.

Chimera attempted to strike Bubbles yet again but this time the monster was ready for the attack and he took a half step back to avoid it. Chimera's hand shot past Bubbles' fishbowl, with the inertia forcing the hybrid to pitch forward off balance. Bubbles quickly acted on his momentary advantage by driving his hook hand into his opponent's shoulder and using it to pull Chimera to his knees.

Chimera's face was bobbing just above the waterline when he looked down to see the mech's knee rising out of the ocean. With Bubbles' hook hand still embedded in his shoulder, there was nothing that the monster could do to avoid the mech suit's coming blow. Bubbles' knee crashed into Chimera's jaw and knocked the kaiju's head backwards.

Bubbles pulled his hook hand out of Chimera's shoulder as the hybrid lolled to the side and dipped below the waves. Rather than press his attack on his opponent, Bubbles turned away from the monster and once again began chasing the fish flakes that he hungered for.

The pilot and Luke were both using the rear cameras to watch the kaiju combatants. When he saw Chimera dip beneath the waves, the pilot shouted, "Is your monster down for the count?"

Luke smiled. "No. Chimera is a hell of a lot tougher than that. He may have hit the canvas, but he's about to come up swinging."

As the salt water poured into Chimera's mouth it immediately revitalized the kaiju. Chimera's eyes grew wide and he unleashed a roar that shook the water around him. The monster surfaced and filled his lungs with air. He then stretched out his body and dove beneath the waves. He sent a sonar pulse through the water and a scant second later, the blast returned to him indicating how far ahead of him Bubbles was.

The fish monster had put some distance between himself and his opponent, and yet Chimera had no doubt that he could catch the fleeing creature. Chimera lifted his long fluke tail and then he swiftly brought it down in conjunction with moving his arms and legs. On land, Chimera could move extremely fast, but in the ocean, there was not a creature on the planet who rivaled his speed.

Luke's heart was racing as a result of the adrenaline pumping through his veins. He knew that the helicopter had almost reached the point of no return. Once the pilot reached that point, he would have to dump his cargo and head back to land or risk not having enough fuel to make it safely back to shore. Luke knew what would happen at the point. Bubbles would go after the quickly sinking weighted dumpster full of fish flakes, and Chimera would follow him.

Once they sank beneath the waves Luke would have no way of knowing if Chimera won or lost the battle. He had seen Chimera defeat opponents of unimaginable power. The kaiju had slain the Hound of Hell known as Cerberus, he had scaled Mount Olympus and dethroned Zeus, he had defeated the walking mountain of interwoven corpses known as the Colossus of Death. Chimera had even managed to defeat the thunder god Thor in a battle to decide the fate of the world.

Despite all these victories, Luke still worried about the final confrontation between Chimera and Bubbles. Bubbles was more than a monster from the past carrying out his master's bidding. He was a living creature that was simply looking for food. As a Master of Applied Behavior Analysis, Luke was well aware that there was nothing more reinforcing to a living creature than the pursuit of food. Bubbles had already proven himself a formidable creature and with nothing standing between him and his food but Chimera, Bubbles would not stop fighting until he reached his goal… or, until he was slain.

The thought had no sooner run across Luke's mind then the pilot yelled, "We've reached the point of no return, sir. I'm dropping the payload now and then I'm heading back to shore!"

Luke silently nodded in reply. He then looked out the side window as the dumpster splashed down into the water and immediately began sinking. As the helicopter turned around, Luke saw Bubbles swim to the spot where the fish flakes had fallen.

Bubbles saw the container fall into the water and sink to the bottom of the ocean. The helicopter that had been trying to keep the fish flakes away from him had finally given up. Bubbles' animal instincts began to take over as his mouth gulped furiously in anticipation of the feast that was awaiting him. When Bubbles reached the area where the fish flakes had been dumped, he slipped beneath the water and dove toward the goal which had eluded him for so long.

Chimera had nearly reached Bubbles when he saw the monster dive toward the bottom of the sea. The hybrid kaiju quickly glanced overhead to see the helicopter carrying Luke flying toward him. Chimera's mind was still consumed with the thought that Bubbles would attack Luke after he had recovered the thing that had dropped in the water. The hybrid took a deep breath, then he dove after the monster who had sought to destroy his friend.

Chimera could see Bubbles just below him. With a few powerful strokes of his fluke, Chimera managed to catch up to the mech monster. The whale-like titan opened his jaws and clamped them down on the mech's right leg.

Bubbles slammed into the side of his fishbowl as his forward momentum came to a stop. The giant fish turned to see Chimera attacking him. Bubbles' eyes flashed with anger at the realization that the hybrid creature was once more preventing him from reaching his fish flakes.

Bubbles shifted his mech suit toward Chimera and then he buried his hook hand into the monster's left forearm. Chimera roared in pain, expelling most of the air in his lungs. He then responded by delivering two thunderous blows to Bubbles' fishbowl, causing the exterior of the container to crack.

With the pressure from the ocean water pushing onto Bubbles' cracked fishbowl and Chimera bleeding badly and running out of air, the two monsters were engaged in a death struggle from which only one of them would survive.

Luke watched through the rearview camera on the helicopter as the spot on the ocean where Chimera had gone after Bubbles churned and foamed from the clash of the titans taking place beneath it. After several seconds, the water stopped churning and then became still. Luke looked down at the water and then he cheered when he saw Chimera rise out of ocean. The hybrid monster roared and then began heading back to shore.

Luke picked up his radio and called Parsons. "Chimera has emerged from the water and he is swimming to shore. There is no sign of Bubbles."

END

PARK ROT

Skip Peel

Editor's Note: The original version of this story was published in Robert Hood and Robin Penn's anthology _Daikaiju! Giant Monster Tales_ from Agog! Press. Many thanks to Skip and the editors of the above anthology for allowing it to be reprinted and re-edited here!

David Braggle, Vice President of Theme Park Operations, might have felt beauty in the touch of morning air, were he that type of man. Millions had stood in that same place every day and felt it. But Vice President Braggle had been hired in from the outside and never visited Thrill Acres before he found professional interest in it. He never parked in the main lot, only in his backstage executive space. He never entered through the main turnstiles but brought family and friends through hidden side entrances.

Standing there at 8 a.m. and spying the coasters and towers over the tops of trees offered him no excitement. To many the air outside a theme park is quite intense, but Braggle paid no attention.

For twenty years the main parking lot of Thrill Acres filled to capacity by mid-morning, but that day Braggle stood alone in the lot beside his car. He felt nervous, which suited his temperament, and grouchy, which suited him better. While waiting he turned over financial ledgers in his head and wondered how much longer the Company could afford to keep Thrill Acres closed.

A large industrial van sped across the lot. Braggle adjusted his tie, tried to look professional, and succeeded. Looking professional was probably the only thing in his career he was any good at doing.

The van pulled into one of thousands of empty spaces, and its rear doors flew open. Out from a den of scientific equipment stepped a slender Japanese man, much younger than Braggle. Behind him stood several even younger Japanese men, who remained quiet.

"Good morning," the man greeted with an accent, though he spoke English well. "I am Kazuo Tabuchi, Field Representative and Chief Case Handler for the Sekiyama Group's International Enterprises Division. I'm here to destroy a monster!"

Case Handler Tabuchi said the last part with business-like flippancy, yet there seemed a hint of pleasure in his intentions.

"You are the man we need," Braggle replied, eagerly shaking Tabuchi's hand, "I'm David Braggle, Vice President, Theme Park Operations here at Thrill Acres. Will you come with me please?"

Braggle proudly gestured to his car, but Tabuchi seemed unimpressed. He mentioned something in curt Japanese to his assistants and stepped into the vehicle. As Braggle drove across the lot, the assistants followed in the van.

"We appreciate Sekiyama for responding so quickly," Braggle began. "Have you been to our park?"

"Not in America." Tabuchi replied.

"Well, welcome to Thrill Acres, where over 100 thrills await you." Braggle said in the manner heard the park's recent commercials.

"You have 100 rides?" Tabuchi asked.

"We have 100 *thrills*, not rides." Braggle explained. "I'm proud to say that since I've been Vice President, I've been able to significantly reduce our operating cost by decreasing what rides we could. But yes, there are 100 thrills, including the thrill of eating a Misty-Twisty Pretzel, our newest Food item, or the thrill of this year's newest attraction, the Wild Daisy Gardening Spectacular!"

Tabuchi seemed further unimpressed and examined the perimeter of the park as they drove around it. "I've been to Thrill Acres Japan. They say it's bigger than the American one."

"The Japanese park may have more rides," Braggle answered, "but here in the U.S. we have more square footage. There's more acres in the U.S. Thrill Acres!" Braggle boasted as if he thought the American end of the deal better.

"You like red roller coasters," Tabuchi commented, as they turned down a street of industrial buildings behind the park. "Everywhere I see a red roller coaster."

"That red coaster is all *one* coaster," Braggle explained. "That's Tyranny, King of the Roller Coasters, Thrill Acres' premiere ride, the ruler of our dozen other coasters. Tyranny is the longest roller coaster in the world, covering the whole park and going through every section. Our designers say the ride lasts twenty minutes, but I've never been on it because I don't like roller coasters. But my office has a great plan going.

36

"Since most coasters top out at three minutes, we want to separate Tyranny into two coasters, what would be both the first and second longest roller coasters in the world, and then Thrill Acres could hold both records and have two rides. Don't you think that's a great idea?"

Tabuchi said nothing.

"For twenty years Thrill Acres has had the reputation for being an extreme park," Braggle continued, "with the most intense attractions in the world. We became known in this industry as 'The Dark Park,' because everything was creepy and weird here. Thrill Acres did start as a seasonal Halloween attraction, but we want to change our image. We want to continue two decades of success by becoming more kiddy friendly and lighthearted, fluffy and bright. Here's my office." Braggle pulled his car before an executive bungalow.

"So, Mr. Tabuchi," Braggle added as they left the car, "can you do what you've offered regarding our problem?"

"Yes, the monster." Tabuchi answered. "You stated in the initial call that it's some kind of mechanical weapon?"

"It's a robot, not a weapon," Braggle clarified. "Can your firm stop it?"

"Most of our contract work is with governments," Tabuchi explained, as Braggle led him into an office conference room, "but we'll take any client willing and able to pay, such as your financially lucrative company. Sekiyama Group contracts daikaiju elimination in and outside of Japan. We've many satisfied clients. I've just returned from South America, where for a nation which must remain contractually undisclosed, we eliminated a giant winged serpent that terrorized the countryside, some kind of devil or god come back for revenge they said. We destroyed it. What monster do you have, Mr. Braggle?"

Braggle placed a promotional poster on an easel while Tabuchi gasped in Japanese.

"This is what we're dealing with." Braggle said. The poster presented a green gigantic ogre. Rows of triangular scales hung over the body. Thick clawed hands extended from the muscular arms and shoulders. Green hair sprang all directions from the head like a monstrous Einstein. Its eyes glowed red, and the brutish mouth held perfect rows of silver metallic teeth. The rendering showed the monster lumbering through a swamp in the park where a castle and Tyranny, King of the Roller Coasters, decorated the landscape.

"This thing wasn't my idea at all," Braggle explained. "I only signed onto it to appease the designers and get their minds off making new rides. They called it an Automated Interactive Character. It could wander the park independent of any one place. They designed it for the park's Medieval Village and called it Grendel."

"Ah, Grendel!" Tabuchi exclaimed.

"You know it?" Braggle questioned.

"Don't you study World Literature in America?" asked Tabuchi. "Grendel was the monster in *Beowulf*. It ate men until Beowulf challenged it and tore off its arm."

"The designers said something in the proposal," Braggle replied. "I must've slept through that meeting."

"I'll be sad to destroy this fabulous machine." Tabuchi sighed. "Do you have any photographs, and I need to see original designs?"

Braggle fished out photos of the partially completed monster and other promotional sketches as he spoke. "We were beginning park redesign work during the slow season, when the monster, which hadn't opened to the public, appeared in the park and started trashing everything. We evacuated everyone and are settling lawsuits out of court. Security brought in guns, but they did no damage. The executive board was terrified that it'd escape and start real trouble, but it hasn't left the park. It stopped smashing things, but we have no control over it."

"Can't your military stop it?" Tabuchi asked. "That's attempted before anyone calls us."

"This is private property," Braggle explained softly. "We didn't report the situation to the local government or federal authorities. The political situation is delicate with our tax breaks and favored zoning. We decided outsourcing to your company would be best if we could stop the monster without upsetting governmental partners or ruining public image. The world outside believes Thrill Acres has closed for ride rehabs."

"I still need Grendel's designs," Tabuchi said.

"We haven't been able to uncover them." Braggle apologized. "For professional and financial reasons, we downsized our engineer and design staff, who failed to understand this is a business. The designers currently employed never worked on Grendel, and we found nothing in the files at Creative Content. The designs are misplaced. They'll turn up eventually."

"Mr. Braggle," Tabuchi sighed, baffled by the inefficiency, "as the company vice president, can you tell me about the Grendel robot? How is it powered and charged? What's the reflex speed and rotary torque of its joints? Does it possess significant tensile strength? As to operation, is it preprogrammed in sequences in a hard drive stored internally in its chassis, or is there a method of remote control by direct radio transmission or perhaps a GPS connection?"

"I wouldn't know." Braggle answered. "Those designers can never explain anything properly when they give a presentation."

"I'll have my crew," Tabuchi grumbled as he pulled out a two-way radio, "research your monster Grendel on the internet. You can find almost anything on the internet. Do you at least know where Grendel is now?"

"Sitting in the middle of Thrill Acres," Braggle offered, "like it owned the place."

"It seems he does," Tabuchi replied, "but not after my Exterminator arrives."

***

Vice President Braggle and Case Handler Tabuchi waited near the main turnstiles of Thrill Acres. Tabuchi was adjusting knobs on what he called a "High Frequency Transmitter" which controlled the "Exterminating Instrument" about to arrive.

"Couldn't this monster come in a truck?" Braggle asked.

"At 35 meters and weighing 75 tons, no truck could handle it," Tabuchi explained. "We ship him overseas in a cruiser outfitted for the purpose, but he must cross land himself. Don't be concerned, Mr. Braggle. Itara travels fast."

"Does it get feisty?" Braggle asked.

"No. Itara is docile, when I want him to be."

"I don't like your monster tramping across the state," Braggle said. "News might leak, and people will panic."

"Itara will be fine," Tabuchi assured. "He could run across your country in two days at top speed. Itara has never damaged any property or person while travelling. Destruction is only permitted during the extermination. Excuse me."

Tabuchi answered his buzzing radio in hurried Japanese. When finished, he beamed a smile.

"He's outside the park, Mr. Braggle, reported a mile away, and has succeeded in keeping public and governmental attention minimal. He'll be here any second. A mile is nothing to him."

Tabuchi adjusted his High Frequency Transmitter. Braggle felt the ground rumble as shaking trees parted open across the parking lot. A gigantic bipedal creature stepped through, lumbered across the lot, and skidded to a halt some hundred feet in front of them. With heavy hot breaths, it waited for a command, standing as tall as the coasters in the park.

The monster was a hulking amalgam of familiar yet bizarre flesh. Any child might have guessed its pieces, yet an adult would have been horrified by them. The thing was mad science at its most intense, as if the Sekiyama corporation of Japan had made a statement of revenge against the mad science so long ago visited upon its own people.

The creature's foremost impression was incredible strength; massive in the shoulders and back, having almost no neck, and a pack of muscle all down through the biceps and triceps of its long arms. The head was

41

feline, with ears drawn back fiercely, green cat pupils, and a whiskered muzzle. Long canines bulged from the black lips. The monster had opposable digits among its fingers, yet padded palms and long claws. Almost no hair grew from the beast's hide except bristly patches on its back. The skin was roughhewn like armor plating, reptilian and scaly. The creature had no tail. The rest of it was enough.

"This is Itara, Mr. Braggle," Tabuchi explained. "This is our daikaiju. Our Exterminator!"

"What is it?" Braggle asked, hardly comfortable.

"He's my own invention," Tabuchi proclaimed. "It took five years to design him. I can't explain the entire process, that's proprietary, but he is a clone. I combined benefits of three animals for maximum effectiveness. He has the sheer strength, foundational upright balance, and hand dexterity of a gorilla; his speed, flexibility, eyesight, hearing, smell, and general ferocious cunning all come from the genes of a tiger; and he needed a blind aggressiveness, a complete tolerance of pain, and a protective hide, which were answered in the dragon-like charm of an alligator. Itara is beautiful, is he not?"

"It's something," Braggle gasped, "but why'd you give 'It' such a boring name. That's it, It's just 'It.'"

"No," Tabuchi laughed. "He is Itara, or *Ita*. In my language that means 'pain.'."

"Nice," Braggle mumbled. "So, what do we do with it?"

"Mr. Braggle," Tabuchi said with a smile as they entered the main turnstiles of Thrill Acres, "I need you to clear your theme park of all personnel as a safety precaution."

"We got everybody out days ago," Braggle replied, "I cut the payroll and eliminated the chance of any lawsuits if our loose monster stepped on or tried to eat an employee."

"If Grendel is a robot," Tabuchi asked, "how could it eat anyone?"

"I don't mean," Braggle said with aggravation, "look, just do your job."

"You're certain there's no control center for Grendel's operation?" Tabuchi inquired. "It'd be easier if my Exterminator could storm that building and shut down the mecha, rather than having a direct conflict."

"All power to the main central computer is disabled," Braggle argued. "For whatever reason, Grendel is still running. We don't want any more damage. The robot has done enough."

While walking through the Main Entrance Plaza of Thrill Acres, Tabuchi adjusted a knob on his silent High Frequency Transmitter. The monster Itara took a wide step over the entrance turnstiles and began to follow, knocking an information booth into pieces as it shuffled past.

"Is your monster going to destroy much?" Braggle muttered.

"Have you ever seen a daikaiju battle?" Tabuchi asked.

"No."

"What will happen, will happen." Tabuchi explained with an almost respectful bow. "Take me where Grendel lurks."

And so, they entered the heart of the park, the cloned monstrosity lumbering behind them.

43

Thrill Acres remained a preeminent American theme park for good reason. It retained carnival and midway roots, but broke free of that cheesiness enough to be beautiful and inspiring in a quaint surreal way. In recreating Ancient Greece, the Amazonian Jungles, or Feudal Asia, the talent behind the park was distinct. It was no sprawling maze filled hodge-podge with rides. Everything made sense. As a theme park, Thrill Acres lived. With Tyranny, King of the Roller Coasters, rising above all, it was organic, an art in three dimensions.

Yet something seemed askew in the Medieval section of the park. Braggle and Tabuchi approached a gothic castle that stood foreboding on a craggy hill, the former Haunted Fortress. It might have been awesome and alluring, except most of the black stonework had been repainted an obnoxious yellow. Surrounding the altered castle were remains of three construction cranes, all twisted into shapes reminiscent of the park's pretzels.

"We can walk through the Fortress," Braggle explained, "but your monster must go around it. I want to be careful since the repaint cost 2 million dollars. Imagine if we had to fix a turret."

Tabuchi said nothing, adjusted the dials on his Transmitter, and followed his client through the archway. The Fortress seemed barren since all gargoyles had been removed in accord with the park's new image. Meanwhile, the mighty Clone slunk around through the moat.

Passing over a drawbridge, the Medieval Village, Classic Carnival, and Space Port Thrill sprawled before them, all with more rides than could be easily counted. Nothing operated in the eerie quiet. No music played.

No smells of candy and hot dogs graced the air. What looked like the more garish buildings had been smashed, handiwork of the monster Grendel. Far across a lake, a giant wooden roller coaster remained half standing. The portion that had lasted was a black color, while what lay splintered like scattered toothpicks was pink. More construction cranes were half sunk in the lake.

"What happened?" Tabuchi asked, pointing to the coaster. "More of Grendel's destruction?"

"Yes." Braggle sighed. "That was our only wooden coaster. It was called the Black Death for years, but it needed a makeover. It won't be opening again anytime soon."

"Quiet please," Tabuchi gasped, "I see Grendel, and since we don't know how it functions, it might detect us."

By the lake, amid a cluster of smashed trees, rising higher than the nearby tracks of the Tyranny coaster, the Robot sat hunched and still, as though it were shut down. Grendel seemed unreal with green hair standing out from its head, and serrated rows of metallic teeth smiling like two parallel saws glimmering in the sunlight.

"What do we do?" Braggle asked under his breath.

"Basic behaviors are programmed for Itara which give a trained, conditioned response," Tabuchi began. "I'll prompt him to shove the robot into the lake. If Grendel has delicate mechanics, the water should short circuit him with little other damage, shouldn't it?"

"I don't know," Braggle said, trying to hide behind Tabuchi. "Everything here is designed for the rain. Just do what you have to and get rid of that piece of junk!"

Tabuchi looked at his client with a cultural misunderstanding that in other places and times can lead to wars. Focusing back on his cloned monster, he pushed a Transmitter button.

An unearthly and deep noise came from the chest of the Clone. The energetic beast bounded from behind the Fortress and into the Medieval Village, snarling like a zoo of predators. Grendel did not move. Itara tore claws forward through some trees and into the lifeless Grendel. The Robot flew into the lake with a splash that sent water gushing to every shore. The Clone lingered, waiting to discover if more aggression was needed.

"On target!" Tabuchi cried, walking down into the Village while Braggle followed. "See, Mr. Braggle. Itara knows what to do. The robot hasn't moved and should stay down. It would pay to learn more about your own product, so you can fix problems like this and make upgrades. Inefficiency is as deadly in business as…"

Tabuchi stopped. The lifeless Grendel had risen and blocked the morning sun. The monster awkwardly moved with locked joints, the result of its mechanical skeleton. Water dripped from the scaly hide that rippled like lumps of carpet over its frame. A strange cry sounded from an implanted electronic speaker, and Grendel stood ready with glowing eyes visible even in the bright daylight.

Itara seemed naturally curious of its opponent, and received no orders, for Tabuchi stopped in awe of the Robot. With the noise of servos and hydraulics activating, Grendel strode through the water and brought both fists upward in a tremendous motion from the hinge of its shoulders. The torque sent the Clone smashing backwards through the track of the red coaster Tyranny and another black steel coaster. Itara roared as it landed in tent-top building in the Classic Carnival section of the park.

"We've not faced an enemy with such power!" Tabuchi cried. "If Itara is not mortally wounded, he will mount a fierce counterattack!"

"Watch out for the park!" Braggle shouted, for in getting to its feet the Clone had smashed a carousel and an arcade. Grendel approached swinging punches, but Itara crouched like a cat and scratched at the Robot's chest. Grendel fell back several yards but seemed unaffected. The Clone charged, but Grendel stood unmoving and grabbed its living enemy in a mechanical vice lock. The creatures spun in circles, stepping on buildings housing coin tosses and squirt gun races.

"What's happening?" Braggle demanded. "Why isn't your monster doing anything?"

"Give him opportunity!" Tabuchi replied. "He's very smart."

Still in a headlock, Itara lifted Grendel by the legs and ran, slamming into a tower called the Frenzied Free Fall or Triple F, twice as tall as either monster. A groan sounded like the foundations of the earth had cracked. The tower swayed, then fell, smashing through more of the omnipresent Tyranny coaster. Grendel stood up, a huge dent where its head smacked the tower. The Clone worked on catching its breath.

"The Triple F!" Braggle cried. "One of our top thrill rides! I wasn't planning on closing that! This is bad!"

The Robot then picked up the 200 foot tower in its arms and wielded it like some gigantic lance.

47

"Spectacular!" Tabuchi shouted with admiration of his robotic rival.

The Clone ducked under the Triple F tower as Grendel swung it. Before the Robot could counter-swing, the living beast grabbed the other end, and growling, wrenched the weapon from its enemy. Itara swung hard, and Grendel was unable to dodge. The blow sent the Robot skidding through a banquet hall and landing near a Gondola Skycab station.

Itara dropped the heavy tower and with deep breaths smashed through more rides to where his enemy lay motionless.

"Careful Itara!" Tabuchi warned aloud, as if his creation heard and understood. "The Robot has deceived you once, but you can finish him."

Itara's expression seemed half ape and half feline, as if puzzling how to kill the synthetic creature not even alive, when Grendel reached out and threw the Clone into some trees. Then with faster speed, Grendel pulled the metal cable holding the Skycabs out from its anchoring tower and power station. Electrical sparks flew, and everywhere the Skycabs ran in the park, they smashed to the concrete.

Grendel took the cable and wrapped it around the scaly throat of the Clone in a death choke. The living monster thrashed violently, yet Grendel held.

"This monster battles wisely!" Tabuchi said with solemnity. "There is genius behind it! Itara may not escape."

"If your monster dies," Braggle shouted, "the Company's not paying a cent!"

Gurgles came from the Clone as it struggled, yet it could not reach its enemy nor break free from the steel cable. With almost a smile, Grendel pulled back harder. Itara's eyes bulged, and its clawed feet kicked in death throes. By chance, one foot smashed into the transformer powering the Skycabs. With plumes of sparks and a terrific pop, both monsters quivered and shook, as thousands of volts went through the foot of the Clone and into both monsters. Itara bled at the ears, and one of Grendel's red eyeballs popped and shattered with a flash. Both monsters fell free of the transformer and landed lifeless on the ground.

Tabuchi ran to the battlefield. Careless of danger, he examined his Clone anxiously, avoiding the sparks that still flew out of the transformer.

Braggle caught up as Tabuchi turned with relief.

"It's okay. Itara's breathing without labor, so I believe he'll survive. No wounds seem mortal. His body can absorb that shock. And look at your Robot. It's defeated!"

"I guess I was going to close this Gondola ride anyway," Braggle sighed, "it's no premiere attraction and costs a lot to operate but look at all this damage! The CEO is going to kill me. I don't think..."

Braggle stopped, for he just noticed Tabuchi fall to the ground when he felt pain in the back of his head, and all went black.

***

Braggle's head hurt and his face was wet. As he woke, words rang in his ears.

"You idiot! Wake up! I want to talk to you!"

He sat upright but could not move. His hands were free, but something heavy gripped his shoulders and across his chest.

"Wake up!" the voice continued. It sounded familiar. He heard a squirting noise and his face felt wetter. He squinted and the water ran down his cheeks. A Thrill Acres Misting Fan was spraying his face.

"Vice President Braggle, are you awake?" came a voice. Case Handler Tabuchi sat clamped alongside him under the shoulder restraints of a roller coaster.

"Yes," Braggle grumbled. The jet black coaster car sat docked high in a scaffold launch station with brick stonework. Braggle failed to recognize the coaster, for he knew little more about his theme park than what he saw on the map in his office.

"Do you know this man?" Tabuchi asked.

Braggle gazed towards the ride's empty queue. A bright-eyed man stood alone, the misting fan in his hand, leaning against the railing. His forty-something graying hair flowed unkempt in the light breeze, yet his youthful countenance smiled as if his face were accustomed to it. His eyes, so bright and alive, analyzed everything with excitement. This man was always thinking. He could never stop thinking, stop dreaming, stop imagining. To stop was not in his nature, clearly.

Though Braggle typically noticed people about as effectively as he did his theme park, he did recognize this man. "I know you," Braggle began. "Don't I?"

"I'd hope so," the man answered. His voice was wonderful, full of character and experience, like some master storyteller, ready to weave a tale and mesmerize any audience.

"You're Skyler Blue, aren't you?" Braggle said, his head aching still.

"Yes," he said with a laugh. "I'm Skyler Blue, Senior Engineer and Creative Content Designer for Thrill Acres."

"Ex-Senior Engineer," Braggle corrected.

"Perhaps by your records," Skyler Blue replied, with a bit of frown in his smile, "but that doesn't make me any less than I am, any more than it makes you any more than you are, Mr. Braggle."

"What are you talking about?" Braggle asked. "What hit me? My head hurts. Get me out of this thing!"

"I'm pleased to meet you, sir," Skyler said, addressing Tabuchi and ignoring Braggle. "I've been to your country and you have some spectacular theme parks. And you do know how to run them. Tell me, is that fantastic monster yours?"

"The Itara?" Tabuchi answered, smiling though strapped to his seat. "Yes, I envisioned it, planned it, designed, grew, and trained it."

"My compliments," the Senior Designer said. "It's wonderful. It should be in a zoo. I'm sorry for attacking it, but you did strike first. That creature is a genetic creation isn't it? I noticed both cat and crocodile in it."

"Tiger, Alligator, and Gorilla," Tabuchi explained. "You must be creator of the Grendel mecha. A brilliant mixture of the new and the old. I'm impressed."

"Thank you," Skyler replied. "Grendel's my design. I've designed many things here."

"Enough crap!" Braggle demanded. "I don't care who made what. Mr. Blue, let us loose!"

"Sorry, Mr. Braggle," Skyler apologized. "I'm not going to do that."

"What?" Braggle exclaimed. "Release me now, Blue, or I'll fire…" here Braggle paused awkwardly.

"You'll fire me?" Skyler said with a grin. "It's a little late for that."

"Blue," Braggle argued, "as an ex-employee, you shouldn't have access to the park. Besides, we've had to evacuate. There's no one here but us and these monsters."

"Don't you understand?" Tabuchi interrupted. "This man created Grendel, and so he also controls it."

"That's right," Skyler agreed, holding up a device with knobs, two large levers, and a small screen. "This is my remote brain for Grendel. I designed it with complete override function, so even if the main control worked at computer central, I'd still have prime direction. Nobody working in Creative Content Division these days would know enough to do anything about controlling Grendel anyway."

"Why are you doing this, Blue?" Braggle asked snidely. "Sour grapes about losing your job? Still angry over our creative differences?"

"Creative differences?" Skyler laughed. "You never had anything creative to be different about! Your ideas of creating are to save a buck at all costs or unleash another layer of bureaucracy. Tell me, just sitting there, what ride is this?"

"It's one of our roller coasters," Braggle grumbled.

"*Our* roller coasters is it?" Skyler echoed. "Which one?"

"How do I know?" Braggle complained. "There's so many in the park, and one's as good as another."

"Can't you figure it out?" Skyler cried with a hint of madness in his strained temples. "Look! Notice the safety stops in the shapes of gallows! Here, replicas of medieval weaponry all painfully researched for accuracy! See the hooded dummy up in the monitoring station! What's that look like to you?" and here Skyler Blue got down in Braggle's face. "Can't you figure out, even if you never rode this thing, that this is the Executioner?"

"The Executioner, yeah that's right," Braggle mumbled.

"The Executioner!" Skyler yelled. "The first quadruple loop coaster in this part of the country! A coaster I designed to be 'the most sadistic coaster ever' in that it makes the rider believe his life is in constant jeopardy! A coaster consistently ranked in the top ten American coasters for six years running, last year at number three! A coaster which last year celebrated its 10th anniversary!"

"Okay!" Braggle shouted. "It's the Executioner, and I've never ridden it! Can you blame me if I don't like roller coasters? What about it?"

"You didn't know *what* coaster it was, and you're Vice President of the park!" Skyler cried, grimacing. "You sit in your office sipping coffee and making six figures, and you make life and death decisions for this grand park, but you're clueless! You don't care about any of it, yet you're in this position of power to take the heart of everyone who loves this place and trample it!

"People want to bring their grandchildren here someday, and take them through stuff they enjoyed as kids, like the Goblin Gardens, the world's greatest funhouse maze. But you turned it into a greenhouse. You take our beautiful Haunted Fortress and paint it tacky yellow! You take the Black Death and paint it pink! What sense does that make thematically or visually? Were you going to call it the Pink Death? Are you insane?"

"We were thinking Pink Thunder," Braggle attempted, "it's more gender inclusive."

"It's still awful!" Skyler shouted. "Redoing crappy rides, like replacing a Scrambler with a themed log flume, that's improvement. But you destroy things. You say a classic ride is too expensive to operate, so you gut it and make it a character greeting location. You turn masterpieces into garbage, like a tawdry tourist painting a moustache on the Mona Lisa.

"You may not respect the artistry of a theme park, but much of the world does. Talented people designed the 'breathtaking wonders' of Thrill Acres, but you've got those 'wonders' falling right and left. You took Ghouls of Hades, the greatest dark ride of all time -- did you ever see the animalistic architectural design in there? -- and changed it into the Family Fun Bears' Frolic! How could you? God save us all!"

Skyler Blue seemed at a breaking point, his voice rising higher into a raspy squeak. His eyes bulged, while his face turned bright red. Tabuchi sat open mouthed, dumbfounded by the enthusiastic ravings, but Braggle kept debating as if he were in a board meeting.

"All done to better the park's image and lighten things. Mr. Blue, you can't have a theme park attraction these days called Ghouls of Hades."

Skyler Blue stomped over to the Executioner's lost and found bin and pulled out a ragged plush toy of an infamous Family Fun Bear and looked it over with the disgust someone else might a diseased cockroach.

"You say that," Skyler growled, "because you think that up in your executive offices. You don't know what real people think. Ghouls of Hades was fine for twenty years, and none complained but Thrill Acre's corporate. In fact, none complained until you changed it. And boy, did they complain then, but you guys don't care."

"Look," he continued, holding up the Family Fun Bear, "you took a fabulous, fantastic ride that speaks to our subconscious; deals with our inner fears and shortcomings; a ride so spectacular in its timeless story and classical design elements -- it even had a killer soundtrack; well, you took it, and you exchange it for what? This, this…" and Skyler Blue stuttered as he shook the stuffed bear with passion, "you traded it for this crap! This absolute garbage!"

Skyler furiously tore the head from the Family Fun Bear. Stuffing flew everywhere as he shredded it to pieces.

"Mr. Blue," Braggle explained as the white fluff settled, "the Family Fun Bears represent an important merchandise sponsorship for the park and are the hottest thing for the under-five set these days. They may fade away tomorrow, but then we can cheaply change out the ride for whatever's next. The new Bear ride might represent a slight decrease in our base attendance and perhaps temporarily tarnish our perceived popularity with our main fan base, who will still come anyway, but it's great for profits. Those merchandise tie-ins are gold. Everybody wants a theme park tie-in these days. It's trendy."

"It's tasteless," Skyler replied.

"Your opinions," Braggle began, "cost you and your colleagues your jobs. If you'd taken pay cuts and minimized budgets, and made plans for financially responsible attraction makeovers, then you'd still work here, and you'd still have a voice."

"I have a voice now!" Skyler said. "I've stopped paint jobs and removed lesser abominations. I've saved the Family Fun Bears' Frolic, because I haven't the heart to destroy the former Ghouls of Hades building, but I think I'll smash that awful ride today. It'll make so many happy when the fans learn that the Family Fun Bears are gone. And that's what Thrill Acres is about, making people happy."

"There's nothing you can do to change my mind, Blue," Braggle barked. "Let us go!"

"No!" Skyler insisted. "There's much I can do. You may have tried to shut off the park's power, but I got this coaster running; my coaster, my Executioner."

Skyler hit a switch and the launch platform rumbled. Both captives heard clanking of an incline chain track in the distance.

"Are you going to ride us on this until we puke?" Braggle asked. "Is that your idea of torture?"

"Mr. Braggle," Skyler explained, kneeling beside the Vice President, "those fighting monsters smashed the end of the Executioner's track. I'm sad, because I love this roller coaster, but that circumstance gives the Executioner opportunity to live up to its name. I've disabled the automatic safety systems. This thing is going to run today, no matter what happens."

Braggle fell strangely silent and licked his dry lips.

"I designed the Executioner," Skyler recollected, "to look like it'll kill you, but it has a perfect safety record. No one's been injured on it. Today two people will spoil that record, and be, let's say, 'executed.'"

"To you, sir," Skyler added to Tabuchi, "I'm sorry, but guilt by association you know. Have a pleasant ride."

Skyler Blue hit the launch switch, and the coaster began to roll.

"Here!" he added, tossing a leg of the Family Fun Bear into Braggle's lap. "Take that with you!"

The Executioner headed towards the first incline to make its final run, slinking through a dungeon replica filled with torture devices. With a grunt Tabuchi pulled his shoulder and slid half his body out of the restraint.

"You're supposed to remain seated on these things," Braggle said, as the coaster locked into position to begin its steep ascent, and spears shot in and out of the stonework over their heads.

"I have an idea!" Tabuchi explained, twisting to reach in his hip pocket. "Mr. Braggle, how long is this ride?"

Braggle had closed his eyes, for at the apex of the incline stood a replica of a Guillotine. With each clank and lurch of the coaster, the blade shook and fell an inch, all safely timed to only look dangerous, while a bloody sign was marked, "Keep your head down."

"I see the end!" Tabuchi cried. "I must hold tightly!" As the coaster peaked some hundred feet in the air, he saw a loop, a corkscrew, another loop, and then smashed track. Tabuchi's back nearly hung outside the coaster, while he faced sideways towards Braggle.

"We're gonna die!" Braggle screamed, gripping the restraints, as the coaster plunged past an imitation wrecked coaster full of dummy skeleton riders, through a false door in the stonework, and into a cave.

"Banzai!" Tabuchi shouted, seeming to enjoy the ride in spite of circumstances as the coaster zoomed under swinging axes, swords, and other threats of decapitation. "Listen, Itara may be conscious! That man took my controller, but like him, I keep an emergency overrider spare!"

Braggle only shrieked as the coaster banked into its first loop. Tabuchi grasped his restraint with one arm, but the G-forces of the loop kept him planted in his seat. As the coaster settled into snaking through forest of hangman's nooses, Tabuchi spoke.

"I can set my controller to give Itara a mixed signal, both Call and Retrieve. If he's awake, he might save us before we wreck."

Tabuchi struggled with one hand in his pocket as the coaster spun into a corkscrew around a wicked-looking medieval machine, a giant drill of wood and rusted iron, filled with rotating spikes. The coaster appeared to collide with the machine, but, missed it safely, yet Tabuchi flew out of his seat. He held on to the shoulder restraint with all his wiry strength as they banked through the corkscrew. Tabuchi barely missed the spikes, and as the ride steadied, he scrambled to pull a leg back inside the coaster.

"Only one loop left!" Tabuchi gasped, "I must call Itara!"

Tabuchi pulled a smaller version of his Transmitter from his pocket and adjusted a few buttons with his nimble fingers. With such focused attention, he failed to notice the track bank sharply to the right. Tabuchi shouted in Japanese as he smashed against his seat and lost hold of his Transmitter. With the dumb luck that led him through life, Braggle reached out in blind terror and caught the device in a desperately clenched fist.

"Hold on to that!" Tabuchi cried. "It's activated, but I can't grab it now."

Braggle said nothing, his unblinking eyes dry from the wind. The coaster slowed momentarily as it passed through a mill between two gigantic buzzsaws, while a third buzzsaw from the roof spun at their heads! An accelerator in the track sent the coaster flying, and as Braggle screamed, the buzzsaw rose out of their way, and they charged into the last loop with the destroyed track beyond.

"Where's Itara!" Tabuchi cried, pressed upside down against his seat.

They felt a sensation unknown on any coaster as they flew off the broken track. Tabuchi saw the Transmitter still in Braggle's hand, the trees as a green blur, and then the motion of something brown and massive.

The coaster lurched to a halt with sounds of crunching metal. Coaster cars from behind them flew over their heads. Braggle snapped forward, saved by the shoulder restraint. Tabuchi held on, spared by his own strength, light weight, and some give that the coaster car had upon stopping.

They had not fallen to the pavement but hung suspended seventy feet in the air. Braggle whimpered, for on his side of the car, the mutated face of Itara glared at them with gigantic cat eyes. The monster had received the transmission and caught the car in its claws. Braggle held the transmitter, nearly crushing it, while the creature's hot breath stirred his hair. The coaster car rocked back and forth in Itara's grasp.

"Don't move!" Tabuchi said quietly.

"He's going to eat us!" Braggle cried.

"Don't touch any of the dials on the Transmitter!" Tabuchi warned. "He's been given a Call and Retrieve signal, but it could register an Attack Call. Itara is aggressive!"

Tabuchi crawled over to Braggle, as the Clone gave a gruff growl, watching. Caked blood clung about Itara's ears and head. Tabuchi wrenched the Transmitter from Braggle's frozen hand.

While Tabuchi adjusted a dial, Itara lowered the coaster onto the concrete amid the smashed cars, then backed away. Tabuchi slipped out of the coaster, which was covered with scratches and dents.

"Get me out!" Braggle panted.

Tabuchi found the safety restraint release lever near the smashed wheels. He pulled hard and with a clank, the shoulder restraints rose. Braggle slumped over and Tabuchi had to pull him free.

"I'm ready to leave," Braggle gasped, barely able to stand.

"No!" Tabuchi snapped. "We must find your employee. He tried to kill us, and I will not walk away without honor. The Grendel mecha may be operational. That man cannot escape with his robot. We have our weapon and must keep him from his. Come with me."

Braggle could barely walk but followed without argument. Itara's heavy footsteps thumped behind them as Tabuchi marched back towards the smashed Skycab station looking for Grendel's body. While passing through the Space Port Thrill section of the park, an object sailed through the air and landed at their feet.

"You might like that," came Skyler Blue's voice above them. He stood on a large neon sign reading "Mars Bazaar." Tabuchi's original Transmitter lay broken on the concrete.

"It's impressive," Skyler began loudly, "that your creature could withstand the voltage thrown at him. He's thickly built, but I bet he's hurting. Grendel's similar injures required work to get him going, but a Robot doesn't feel things like busted fuses."

The former Senior Engineer raised his Grendel controller. Looming over the building stood the Robot with one eye missing and wires hanging from its neck, but it roared an electronic challenge with enough feeling to seem alive. Skyler jammed the two levers of his controller in opposite directions, and Grendel's arms flailed outward in a fierce gesture.

Tabuchi kicked the broken Transmitter away and held up his spare controller. "We accept your challenge!" he proclaimed.

The hissing Clone charged, remembering its enemy. Claws and teeth tore into the polymer scales of the Robot as it stumbled backwards, making no defense, but neither falling. Snarling and shredding, Itara pulled a patch of skin from the Robot, revealing underneath a flat metallic surface.

Above the Mars Bazaar, Skyler's fingers poured over his controller. As the Clone chewed at the false flesh, Grendel grabbed Itara by the head and neck, and snapped it into a building labeled "Star Bumps."

Tabuchi raced ahead, trying to get a line of sight with his monster. He turned a corner and just dodged a bumper car that skidded across the concrete and into the glass window of a restaurant.

Itara was throwing Star Bumps vehicles at Grendel, pointless but impressive as each hit the Robot in the face. Cars piled at Grendel's feet, and Itara succeeded in exhausting itself.

"Don't leave me alone!" Braggle insisted as he caught up with Tabuchi.

"Since there's nothing you can tell me about the Grendel mecha, Mr. Braggle," Tabuchi said, "I'll aim for the head. There's significance in a head."

A giant rocket rose twenty feet above the tallest structure in Space Port Thrill. As Tabuchi spun a dial on his Transmitter, Itara leaped onto the building, wrenched the rocket from the construct which held it, and as Grendel charged, the Clone drove the rocket down in a stabbing motion. The durable steel split Grendel's head and lodged through like a stuck arrow!

Grendel's eyes, hair, teeth, and speaker system shattered away, and only some shell of its former head with the embedded rocket remained. Without pause, the Robot thrust its head forward and jammed the rear end of the rocket into its enemy. Itara's fangs cracked on one side, and it fell writhing to the ground, bleeding at the mouth.

Itara tried to crawl away, but the Robot threw punch after punch. The rocket still in its face and with mouth speaker smashed, Grendel made no noise other than the motors moving in its body. The radio still strapped to Tabuchi's belt buzzed, and he answered in Japanese.

"My assistants," Tabuchi said moments later, "have uncovered a bootleg schematic for Grendel off the internet. The hard drive for his computer function is housed in his torso chassis. Itara must aim for his chest."

Grendel kicked the bloody Itara into another part of Tyranny, King of the Roller Coasters. A loop of red steel crashed down on the Clone, breaking into three pieces.

"If I can prompt him to use a tool," Tabuchi said while spinning dials on his Transmitter, "and remain on that command, there's a chance of destroying that hard drive!"

The Clone grabbed a piece of the coaster track and drove the sharp edge of twisted steel through Grendel's chest. The metal pierced the hard plating and tore through the skin out the back side, impaling the Robot with a long piece of red roller coaster.

Grendel, unaffected, swung a fist, but the Clone dodged the blow. The Robot found the extra weight of rocket and coaster track awkward to its balance. As Grendel straightened itself, Itara drove another piece of the Tyranny coaster through the Robot's side.

Skyler Blue had designed Grendel with a CPU no bigger than a desktop computer. Even after a third piece of Tyranny was shoved into its mechanical guts, the

Robot fought on, taking no time to remove the pieces. It struck the Clone with both arms, but Itara pulled off a fourth coaster piece and shoved it into Grendel with a frenzy. The Robot kept coming.

"There's no stopping it!" Braggle cried.

"I will!" Tabuchi insisted. "There's not much chest that we haven't penetrated."

The Robot, looking like a red porcupine with a space rocket head, grabbed the frisky Clone in a vice grip by its neck. Crashing into the Alien Water Warp flume ride, the Robot shoved Itara's head into the main water reservoir behind the saucer vehicle loading station. As though exhaustion and wounds were too much, Itara relaxed and seemed to accept drowning.

"Your monster's losing!" Braggle cried.

"I know what I'm doing," Tabuchi answered.

The Clone no longer moved. With pieces of red steel protruding from its body, the Robot stood up and marched through several buildings. Braggle and Tabuchi then heard the gleeful voice of Skyler Blue.

"Sorry to kill your monster, but a winner is a winner. We should build an arena in the park, and have monsters fight in it. That was great. Hey, Mr. Braggle, I feel so good, that I'm going to have Grendel go smash your Family Fun Bears, right now!"

While Skyler raced from the roof to watch the destruction, Tabuchi slowly adjusted a dial on his Transmitter.

Itara stirred. The Clone, bloody and wet, stood up and blinked its angry eyes.

"A fake-out?" asked Braggle.

"Itara is part alligator," Tabuchi explained, "and can hold his breath longer than that."

With Skyler's attention directed towards Grendel and the Family Fun Bears, Tabuchi programmed his Clone to tear up another shaft of red roller coaster. Itara charged like the tiger it partly was, and pierced Grendel through the chest.

Grendel stood erect in a spasm as motors began firing, and its neck, arms, and legs began randomly contracting. With leg rotors out of control, the flailing monster tore through rides and shops. Then the Robot slowed, sparks flew from every joint, and with a lurch and a whine of failing engines, Grendel fell forward and collapsed before an exceptionally ugly building. A poorly painted, giant 2-D Family Fun Bear smiled down over Grendel's wreckage.

Tabuchi and Braggle ran to the scene of destruction and found Skyler hunched over, mumbling to himself.

"Fun Bears! I hate those stinkin' Fun Bears!"

***

At dusk Vice President Braggle stood chewing his thumbnail. Security, medics, and a custodial crew were in the park. The once Senior Engineer and Creative Content Designer Skyler Blue had been strapped to a gurney for his own safety. Thrill Acres First Aid did not have a straight jacket available.

"Please!" Skyler cried to the medic as they slid him into the ambulance. "Don't take me to those Family Fun Bears! Anything but them! I don't want to see the Family Fun Bears!"

As Skyler's cries faded into the distance, Braggle was startled by Case Handler Tabuchi, who had been conferring with his associates.

"Mr. Braggle," Tabuchi said, "I know you're busy with cleaning and repair, but on behalf of Sekiyama Group, it has been my pleasure to be of service."

"Thank you, I guess," Braggle answered, stunned by the day's events.

"And here," Tabuchi added, "is your bill. You will find it itemized."

Braggle grew as pale as he had been on the roller coaster. After studying the bill, which was in U.S. dollars, not Japanese yen as he first hoped, he stumbled over to Tabuchi in a daze.

"Excuse me, but this is the bill?"

"Yes," Tabuchi replied.

"Mr. Tabuchi," Braggle asked slowly, "what forms of payment do you take?"

"The usual methods," Tabuchi said. "Whatever you prefer as long as the amount is deposited in our account."

Braggle swallowed and imagined his next board meeting. He looked at the smashed trees, the twisted pieces of coasters, and the smoke rising from rubble which once housed a horde of fun and games.

"Tell me," Braggle finally asked, "would you accept a 900 million dollar theme park?"

END

NAUTILUS REX AND THE TERROR GRIFFIN VS. SAN FRANCISCO

Dustin Dreyling

Author's Note: This is but a snippet from my novel *Primordial Soup: The First Batch*, coming soon...

Golden Gate Bridge
San Francisco, California
North America

Traffic was flowing smoothly on the Golden Gate Bridge for a Wednesday afternoon. Vehicles of all kinds drove steadily back and forth across the gigantic landmark that was San Francisco's greatest claim to fame. Chunky cirrus clouds were in the minority in a blue sky that dominated the day, the rich hue bold and inviting to the eyes. A light, salty breeze continuously blew in off the Pacific, just enough to make the local seabirds work for the scraps they scoured the bridge and Fort Point for.

Erin Rasmussen and her boyfriend, Peter Anderson, were just beginning to drive across the bridge, heading back to the city from the Marin Headlands. Driving her blue Ford Taurus, Erin looked over at Peter, his bare feet propped out of the open passenger's side window. She momentarily lost herself gazing at his tan, muscular legs that she loved so much. Suddenly, he sat up and pointed out towards the other end of the bridge.

"What's that?"

Erin looked back at the bridge in front of her. Cars and trucks drove towards their destinations on the other side like normal, nothing out of the ordinary.

"Peter, what are you--"

Then she saw it, rising out of the water, right next to the bridge. It climbed out of the water and dug into the side of the rocky embankment. The creature climbed up onto the road and was greeting the traffic at the Cisco end of the bridge. It stood between the abutment and the toll booths just a bit further south down Highway 101.

Erin slammed on her brakes like the fifty other southbound cars, with only a few smashing into each other as a result. The exceptions were the few vehicles that had been just exiting the bridge when the... dinosaur, or whatever it was, stepped up onto the 101. A semi, several cars, and a couple of SUVs slammed into the massive thing's legs. This elicited a pants-wetting roar from the beast over so many vehicles crashing into its shins. The multiple impacts was nowhere near enough to take it down, however. One of the SUVs caught fire, burning the creature and further increasing its stress levels. A growl of pained rage reached their ears even on the bridge.

Erin and Peter, still a hundred yards or so from the giant monster towering above them at the end of the bridge, just stared helplessly at the thing. Standing at least 160 feet high, its head was as big as a small building and full of salivating, razor-sharp teeth. Drool dripped from a mouth the shoestrings quite visible in the sunlight. The couple both thought of *Jurassic Park* or those new Godzilla movies they had been making. It looked like a

68

velociraptor or tyrannosaurus, but the head and snout were longer, like an alligator or crocodile. Unlike any of those, however, wicked horns stuck out from all around the thing's skull, which was thick and armored... the kind of skull that rammed things.

The halo of bone thorns gave the impression of a crown. The thick layer of the skull that comprised the cranium ran forward on the monster's head to just before its eyes. There it tapered into symmetrical ridges that covered the both pair of eyes on each side of its head. Yes, this monstrosity had *a quartet of eyes.*

The first, side pair of eyes that were protected by the bony ridges were reptilian, their slit-like pupils tracking any and all movement in the chaos the kaiju's appearance had created. The second, front pair of eyes were set in the skull just below where the tapered ridges came together above its snout. These eyes were eerily mammalian, like a dog's. Almost human, but not quite.

The beast's body looked very much like a dinosaur as well: two powerful hind legs underneath a massive body and tail. Both body and tail were practically horizontal while it moved, as carnivorous dinosaurs were known to do for balancing purposes. However, instead of just two small claws, which there were three talons on a disproportionately spindly set of appendages; it had other limbs as well.

A mass of writhing tentacles, crazy long and too many for observers to count -- especially when in the beginning stages of shock in a car on the Golden Gate Bridge -- whipped and snaked all over the place. Some were grabbing car wreckage and tossing it into the bay or in seemingly random directions. Some also grabbed the tiny evolved apes that were trying to run for their lives from the enormous horror that had stomped its way into their Wednesday afternoon.

The incredible sight caused Erin to stare hard at the beast rising from the bay.

"Peter, why does it have four eyes?" She mumbled the almost rhetorical question, then looked at her beau, but his blank stare was all the answer she received.

Erin was too dumbfounded to care and looked back at the kaiju (*That's what they were called, right?*) staring them all down from the other side of the bridge. The makeup of the animal was mind-boggling, to be sure.

As the massive creature stepped up and blocked the entire south entrance to the bridge, a multitude of the dark green tentacles shot out and snared the sides of the bridge's viaduct. It was the strengthened beginning of the bridge that preceded the iconic, thick cables making up the suspension system. To Erin, it looked like an octopus latching onto a crustacean.

The kaiju began to pull at the viaduct with incredible strength. Erin and Peter could feel the vibrations a few seconds before the bridge under their car started to twist, and the vehicle began tilting and shaking with it. After checking behind her, Erin -- surprised to find a way out -- put the car in reverse and hit the gas.

The aging car lurched backward, throwing an unbuckled Peter forward. His face smashed into the dashboard and his forehead slammed hard into the glass. There was a crunchy crack, and a spot of red marked the spiderweb fracture where he'd hit after his body surrendered and mashed limply against the dash. Peter was unconscious before they passed the second set of

70

pylons on the south side of the bridge, returning north while still in reverse.

Driving erratically, Erin somehow managed to avoid the traffic entangled in pandemonium on the bridge, only scraping a truck and a small hatchback before breaking through the mass of stunned drivers that were quickly causing a roadblock. Miraculously finding the room to turn around, she did so quickly, spinning the car 180 degrees like a stunt driver. This sudden move tossed Peter into his car door with a meaty thunk as his head hit the passenger side window.

"Sorry, baby," Erin said through gritted teeth as she threw the car into drive and pushed the pedal to the floor. *I'll make it up to him later,* she thought with optimism.

The Taurus lurched forward again, something in the transmission making an ugly *ka-chunk* as it forced itself into the next gear before accelerating once again. Cruising past The San Francisco Bridge Tower and its steel licorice ropes, she stared down the other end of the towering construct. Erin kept her eyes trained on what she hoped would be the salvation that would deliver them from the horror roaring once again at the 'Cisco end. Pulling to the right and driving on the correct side of the bridge, she didn't dare risk looking back at the thing in her mirror as she sped forward. Far behind the distressed couple, where they had originally stopped before turning around, the whole viaduct of the bridge was starting to angle sideways towards the Pacific. The trusses underneath screamed as they started to bend, and stationary vehicles began to slide towards the sea while the beast wrenched on the bridge.

Then it suddenly angled back in the other direction as the kaiju's appendages pulled towards the bay, throwing traffic viciously to the other side of the northbound lane like stir fry tossed in a pan. As panicked people tried to head back north, they slammed into the tossed vehicles, flipping most of them into the air. A few of the lighter cars went over the side, tires revving uselessly as the people inside screamed.

Most of the commuters in cars closer to the creature had already abandoned them and run onto the bridge. Those people who tried to flee their vehicles in the wrong direction were either run down by motorists trying to get away, crushed by sliding or shifting cars, or propelled over the side of the bridge to plummet into the chilly waters below.

The more brazen people tried to run past the creature through its legs, but only one man and his young son made it past the attentive kaiju – the creature nicknamed Nautilus Rex by the monster's unknown creators, one of whom was watching the action from under a few thousand feet of ocean. The remaining people who were still attempting to flee were swiftly plucked from the bridge's surface, crushed in the serrated grip of a green tentacle, and mechanically fed to the gigantic maw atop the beast's neck.

"Its jaws never stopped chewing!" became a popular sound bite for the incident afterwards, for as long as the news was still a thing. The biased, joke of an information source – already diminished by the Internet – was seeing the start of their end of days. These heralds of destruction initiated that downfall as they made their mark upon the world… and it had only just begun.

Erin continued crushing the gas pedal to the floor, her adrenaline turning her fear into boldness as she weaved through the last dozen cars before the car was finally off the bridge. She drove a 1/4 of a mile further before stopping on the side of the road near where the elevated roadway came back onto solid ground.

Erin then leaned over and checked Peter's pulse at his neck. Her heart jumped with joy when she found one. She then leapt out of her car and began dialing 9-1-1 on her cellphone as the other cars fleeing from the bridge sped past her. The line was busy and a recording saying so was the last thing the woman wanted to hear.

She looked back at the shore across the bridge and the calamity that had befallen it in the form of a monster. Oblivious commuters going south continued to drive past onto the bridge. Most only got about halfway before turning around and zooming back towards her and the north side like bats fleeing Hell.

As far away as she was, Erin could clearly see the kaiju; the titanic monstrosity was extremely visible from even over a mile and a half away. With a deafening roar, followed by a loud, painful, metallic squeal, the beast's tentacles finally ripped the 'Cisco end of the bridge completely from its moorings. The viaduct lifted up in the grasp of Nautilus Rex's many tentacles and began to crumple and bend. Ear-piercing shrieks and groans filled the air as the tendrils flexed and ripped at the structure. People and cars were once again tossed over the sides of the bridge as if they had been on a rug that was violently shaken to remove the dirt from it.

An angry cry exploded from the beast as it dropped the bridge. The end it had held crashed into the Fort Point building located underneath, while the rest fell into the bay. The bridge was visibly destroyed all the way up to the northernmost set of pylons that marked the viaduct's end. Dozens of cars and people plummeted as well, pulled over from the bridge buckling and falling beneath them. Soon, a mass of vehicles and bodies were littering the shore and water like discarded refuse.

On the severed bridge, people left their cars, running to the edge and gawking at the destructive force towering over them on land. Cracks spider-webbed through the cement pillars where the fallen section had tried to take them with it as it fell.

The giant beast's jaws split wide yet again in a booming roar that sounded like a cross between an elephant and a lion's roar but split by a revving chainsaw. The visceral retort reduced the witnesses to its carnage to scared children. Children that instantly sank into shocked catatonia or raving lunacy.

Erin's bladder finally let go as she heard the sanity-crippling roar. Her bleeding, unconscious boyfriend forgotten, she did the only thing her smartphone-obsessed mind could do: she hit "stop" on her iPhone, ending the 17 seconds of death and destruction she had instinctively filmed instead of continuing to attempt contacting emergency services. She selected "share" on the application's top menu bar and posted it to her social media wall. Erin was an Internet star within an hour. She had done all of this on mental autopilot.

Numbly, Erin looked back at the car. "Peter!" she screamed once her memory returned.

She ran to his door and slowly pulled it open. Her paramour fell out into her arms. She caught him just as

74

the ground beneath her shook violently, causing them both to spill clumsily to the asphalt. The ground shook again, twice more, and then the sun disappeared.

Erin looked up and screamed as she saw a second kaiju as it stepped up and over Fort Baker atop the Marin Headlands next to the bridge. Its huge, cat-like paws cleared the monument on the other side of the hill and came down gracefully but thunderous as it dented the ground with each step.

The new kaiju continued up to the road, standing erect on its hind legs like a human. As it sauntered to the road like a hungry man to a buffet line, Erin continued to scream until her voice went hoarse and quit altogether. She couldn't see what it looked like very well, as it blocked the sun. However, it could be discerned that its head was shaped almost like a monstrous raven or crow, but the beak was tall and thick like one of those "terror birds" that she had seen at the La Brea Tar Pits.

The second kaiju bent down towards Erin, flicking back and forth as would a bird while checking out its dinner before it tries to flee. Suddenly it opened its beak and squawked at her, but instead of an ear-rupturing shriek it was a gurgled *squorrk!* This was accompanied by bright gouts of blue fire that blasted the unfortunate young couple and their car into charred nothingness.

The giant bipedal bird thing, satisfied with the blackened mess its fire vomit had created, turned to look at its fellow daikaiju across the bay entrance on the opposite bank. Screams reached its ears, reminding it of its purpose. With a savage jerk of its furry, feline body, two leathery bat-like wings unfolded and snapped into flight mode. Stretching out to a wingspan of over 400 feet, the extra-long finger digits that comprised the wings' frames flexed at the tips, where they stuck out like spikes.

It flapped several times to stretch them out, as a long tail flicked back and forth like that of an angry housecat. The Terror Griffin flexed the muscles on its humanoid set of second arms, just because it could. Then it took to the air with another *squorrk!* A second deluge of blue napalm vomit exploded from its beak and drenched the hillside surrounding the road, as well as the road itself, igniting everything it covered.

As it flew over the bridge and bay entrance and then towards its partner in destruction, the Terror Griffin made eye contact for the briefest of seconds with the tentacled dinosaur. Nautilus Rex roared at the gigantic newcomer with I recognition and turned back to chasing down the remaining people fleeing for their lives. The green whipping appendages snared and obliterated the helpless people with the countless hooks decorating the belly side of each tentacle before shoveling the results into its snapping jaws. Nautilus Rex then followed the flying monster towards the main part of the city, tearing through the bridge's toll gate like it was made during arts and crafts time at a nursing home.

***

The squadron of AH-64 Apache helicopters arrived on a scene out of a disaster movie. They were the main front of the Army's forces that had been stationed in the Bay area. Their main objective was to provide some anti-monster defenses to one of the country's major metropolitan areas.

This was beginning to happen all across the United States.

The rampaging monster on the ground had carved a wicked path of ruined buildings and landscape, straight through Presidio and the headquarters of a legendary sci-fi filmmaker's special FX company. The 15-acre expanse had been transformed into a smoldering pile of debris and wreckage, artificial and organic.

Laurel Heights had been the next stop on Nautilus Rex's tour, where its tennis-court-sized feet crushed the old Victorian and Edwardian houses lining the streets like little boxes. People ran everywhere, screaming ants attempting to escape the anteater. Some had tried to flee in their cars. Most were plucked from the road by the erratically snaking coils continuously striking out in all directions from the two-legged carnivore's horizontally aligned torso.

A white minivan was ripped up from the driveway it was trying to back out of and flung through the air. The poor people inside were treated for the scariest ride of their life as the van arced through the air and punched through an apartment complex in the Haight-Ashbury district three miles away. Miraculously, they all somehow survived with only some broken bones and a few minor injuries.

Hondas, Chevys, BMW's, Scions, Fords, and all kinds of automobiles were thrown, tossed, flung, and spiked into the asphalt by the writhing flurry of green, ropey, toothed squid arms. A Chevy Aveo tried speeding back towards the crowned kaiju terror, attempting to flee through its legs, a trick tried once before with little success.

With a growl, it shot a tendril-like arm out, wrapping around the small, bubbly hatchback. The arm came up quickly, rising just above the huge head of the monster, then hurtled the light green fuel-efficient car into the front picture window of a large Victorian house nearby. The car barreled into the structure, plowing through walls and people. The load-bearing supports destroyed, the second floor collapsed down on top of the car and the entirety of the first floor, only to be blown into sky-high bits as the gas line ignited. A huge fireball rose up into the sky.

Vehicles, humans, random objects, and pieces of demolished buildings sailed through the air in every direction as the beast had stomped on. It was ultimately heading towards the University of San Francisco to the south.

Rounding the west side of Lone Mountain and the USF's Lone Mountain campus that dominated its surface, Nautilus Rex tore through Beaumont Avenue and the neighborhood there. Several rows of houses that were crammed next to each other like sardines in a can went up in dust clouds, smoke, and flames as the mighty beast stomped through them purposefully. As it plowed through, its giant redwood legs and clawed feet crushed and carved jagged gashes through the clustered condominiums and houses like a child with overlarge snow boots walking through fresh snow with an icy crust -- each step meeting a small amount of surface resistance before crashing through as soon as just enough weight was applied.

Here people had been slightly more successful at evacuating, as most were already at work or school. Those unfortunate enough to still be home were obliterated without warning, their worlds caving in on them as their houses did as well.

Sondra Beverley had been one of the lucky ones. She had seen the chaos on the news, including the first images broadcast as Nautilus Rex had torn through Lucasland, and she actually felt the tremors from the destruction ensuing mere miles away from her. Sondra had quickly called her fellow network of daycare ladies, organizing a mass evacuation from their separate homes within a six-block radius. Within minutes, eight women had rounded up their daily wards -- 39 children in all -- loaded them into their kiddie cargo vans and drove east. They would eventually rendezvous at Lafayette Park sometime later.

As Sondra drove away from her house of twenty years, she saw the monster approaching in her rearview mirror. She swerved in a panic, and almost lost control of her Toyota Sequoia. This resulted in her sideswiping a parked Subaru and eliciting an outburst of frightened squeals from the already terrified children in the back seats. What Sondra had seen in her mirror had messed her up.

The green tentacles were thrusting themselves into every house surrounding each step the prehistoric thing took, retracting with tidbits about half the time. *My neighbors,* she thought grimly as her breath hitched twice in her chest.

"Don't look back kids, I mean it," she heard herself say, knowing full well it was a mistake.

In an obvious reaction to being told not to, all seven of her kids turned and looked back at the primeval terror stomping towards them even as Sondra sped away. Four of them screamed loudly, deafening her and causing a slight zig zag as she drove down Turk Street towards Cathedral Hill and Hwy. 101.

"Miss Sondra, there's a dinosaur chasing us!"

"Godzilla! He's gonna get us!"

"Kids, it's okay, we're getting away from the big, nasty dinosaur, and we're going somewhere safe, okay? Please try not to scream, it hurts Miss Sondra's ears and I need to pay attention to the road."

She tried to reason with them in her light, almost singsong, daycare voice. To her surprise, it worked. Whimpers and sniffling noses were still heard, but they sat and stared silently at the towering terror slowly getting smaller as it faded into the distance.

Tearing through the last of the residences in Sondra's neighborhood, the daikaiju's left foot slammed down into the parking lot of the University's soccer field, Negoesco Field. There had been a kid's game in progress, but they had fled already, leaving sports equipment all over the field. Also left behind was a small army of coolers and personal bags in the stands where players and spectators alike had dropped everything and gotten the hell out of there.

Leaving a couple of its trademark footprints across the field, the beast trudged towards the XARTS Lab and the neighboring USF buildings to the east of it. As it raised its right foot to step on the arts and agriculture labs building, a volley of Hydra 70 rockets exploded as they pummeled the daikaiju's left flank. The first flight of Apaches had arrived.

With an anguished roar from its elongated, tyrannosaur cousin's head, the towering brute went down, toppling to its right before crashing down hard and sending up a plume of dust from the instant rubble created by the fall. The second flight of choppers flew over, peppering the bloody flank of the monster with hundreds of rounds from the helicopters' 30mm M230 chain guns. A louder, higher-pitched roar was the downed thing's only retort, its wildly lashing tentacles unable to reach the attacking mechanical creatures plaguing it.

Suddenly, it was back on its feet, the army of cephalopod arms pushing it up in an instant. Nautilus Rex spun around with amazing speed and opened its maw at the third flight of choppers just as they were coming in for another attack. A jagged red bolt of what looked like lightning struck out from its throat and instantly connected with the three choppers closing in. For a split second, they seemed to freeze in midair as the bolt of unknown energy hit and surrounded them in its strange red glow. When it quickly dissipated not even a second later, the choppers dropped like stones, all signs of electrical or mechanical activity having ceased.

As the three Apaches crashed into the side of Lone Mountain, crumpling into mangled versions of themselves and starting on fire, Nautilus Rex turned towards the fourth squad of Apaches heading its direction. This flight of four choppers unleashed a second barrage of Hydra 70s, thirteen rockets streaking towards their target like angry snakes. A red bolt of the strange lightning was there to greet ten of them, dropping them uselessly onto the lawn of the University campus, leaving furrows in their wake.

The other three rockets hit home, however. Already bloody, the beast's left side again blew apart, chunks of flesh and bone scattering all over the area, covering most everything in thick, maroon blood. With a resounding crash, the beast fell once more, this time landing on the Church of St. Ignatius. It did not get up again.

The rotund chest continued to slowly rise and fall, but at a quarter of its normal rate. The choppers flew over once more per flight, blasting the gaping wounds with a fresh volley of gunfire before flying towards the downtown area. There they had a date with the bipedal, prehistoric griffin that was destroying everything.

Unseen by the Apaches as they flew towards downtown, the edges of flesh around the ragged wounds in the Nautilus Rex's left side began to take on a tarry, black appearance. The gooey coagulant slowly began to cover the mortal injuries. In the span of two minutes, thirty percent of the wounds had regenerated anew.

Unlike the original skin the beast had possessed, however, this new flesh was solid black. The epidermis had the sheen of an orca whale's skin fresh out of the ocean's depths. The black patches of skin also had some new features. Several eyes, gasping mouths, and dark tentacles of assorted sizes grew in its reformed flesh. Small tentacles writhed in the air for the first time like vines growing in time-lapse photography, as cat eyes blinked and human-like mouths gnashed crooked teeth and licked lips with discolored green tongues.

The black flesh rippled with each breath the prone animal took, decreasing in intensity with each subsequent breath. Soon, it was still once more. The huge barrel chest stopped moving as well. For ten seconds, the monster was completely immobile.

All at once, its four original eyes snapped open, darting back and forth. It roared, blasting the tiny, human gawkers who had accumulated nearby in a wave of audible agony. The Nautilus Rex rose again, propelled to its feet by its nest of boneless appendages once more. It charged in the direction of downtown San Francisco and the puny flying metal insects that had hurt it so much.

83

As the monster decimated the campus buildings, the new mouths on its left flank began to wail and shriek. The ungodly sounds tore at the sanity of those unfortunate enough to hear it. In the aftermath of the San Francisco attack, many of these victims would later have their causes of death be determined as heart attacks, puzzling morticians city-wide. A local newspaper claimed with a front headline:

CITIZENS DIE OF FRIGHT!

***

A group of seventeen Hydra rockets streaked towards the colossal form atop the "Tweezers Towers," or 345 California Center. It was the third largest building in San Francisco and was located in the financial district. The hotel/office building consisted of forty-eight floors, the top eleven having been built at forty-five-degree angles from the lower floors.

These two sections, originally designed for condos, had since become the Mandarin-Oriental Hotel. The nickname "Tweezer Towers" stemmed from the two spires reaching up to the sky from the middle of the 720-foot-tall building. They stood side to side like the simple medical tool of the same name.

The Terror Griffin was perched on the roof like an oversized feline gargoyle. Its front legs were on one of the hotel towers and its rear legs on the other. Immense bat wings were folded back behind it, the pleated chiropteran flight appendages looking like a pair of leathery antlers or horns protruding from the furry, striped back. The Griffin's ugly bird head -- with its prehistoric raptorial beak -- pivoted back and forth as it studied the surroundings and mass chaos on the streets below.

It heard the Hydras seconds before they struck, suddenly standing straight up in the air like a human and turning sideways like some gigantic action hero. The missiles all shot past the Terror Griffin save for one, where they exploded as they hit the buildings behind the monster, causing massive collateral damage. The one successful rocket struck the beast in its rear, the exploding result making the bird beast cry out in pain and lurch forward. A ball of blue phlegm reflexively flew out of its mouth and sailed through the city before slamming into the Transamerica Pyramid's tower.

The dunce cap-like cone tip on the tallest building in the city was splattered by the burning vomit ball. Already on fire, the excess splatter hit the ground below seconds later, engulfing everything. The helplessly massive traffic jam of panicked commuters and tourists, already tangled in an accident-ridden gridlock, was now a burning disaster. People abandoned their burning vehicles and ran any way they could to escape the potential explosions expected from all the Hollywood movies they had watched over the years. Several unlucky citizens and vehicles were hit by falling liquid and instantly self-immolated in a white-blue inferno.

Terror Griffin's rear end was already healing quickly, the black ooze covering the wound and transforming into the same shiny black skin that the tentacled dinosaur hybrid had sported. A single mouth was the only extra part that formed on this injury, however, and it began to shriek like a banshee immediately upon completion.

Two nearby Apaches instantly crashed into the buildings on either side of the 345 building. The shriek tore at the pilots' minds the second it penetrated their headgear. A mushroom-like cloud of non-nuclear smoke and flame billowed up from the smaller office buildings as the Apache exploded. This set off a chain reaction as the cluster of buildings ignited and soon become completely consumed by the resulting fires.

The other Apache, however, slammed into the top floors of the major bank building nearby. The rotor blades sliced through the windows as it cut into the front of the structure at an awkward angle before pushing through into the building itself. Smoke poured out like a fog machine. Flames soon followed.

As the fires found the leaking fuel tank of the chopper, it caught fire and even exploded. The resulting blast expelled chunks of the office building, white-collar workers, and helicopter scrap down to the street below and the buildings across the street. Some of the shrapnel rained down on the poor souls still remaining on Pine Street, while other pieces became missiles, propelling through the neighboring structures like hailstones through maple leaves. This started more fires that grew and soon raged out of control.

The remaining flights of Apaches flew at the Griffin one more time, the first firing more Hydras at the creature. Unfurling its wings quickly with a snap of its body, the daikaiju took flight from the building at the last possible second. Its huge wings caused the billowing smoke from burning buildings to curl up into a large cloud. The smoke also concealed the mighty monster's escape into the plumes as the rockets hit the roof of the Mandarin-Oriental.

In a series of explosions – each pronounced by a loud whump! – the Hydras took off the entire top five floors of the hotel, the Tweezer Towers being blasted to bits. The staccato explosions were followed by the cracking and splitting of most of the two hotel towers as burning rubble fell all around. Then both hotel towers suddenly collapsed inwards and crumbled down the sides of the building, taking out much of the front facade of the lower part of the structure on the way down.

What remained was a smoking, dusty ruin. Flames still burned in the exposed pockets that had been the building's uppermost floors. Charred furniture and decor littered the debris on California Street below. Alongside that was the gory remains of prematurely evicted hotel guests, strewn about the fallen rubble like squashed insects.

Emergency services began to arrive in droves to the scene, pulling up as close as possible before attending to the scores of injured and the dead. Firefighters arrived as well, brandishing water and foam rack and reel trucks and many wheeled fire extinguishing units on large inflated tires. They began trying to extinguish the burning blue-white flames, eventually finding success with the dry chemical-based wheeled units. The purple powder soon covered everything burning, smothering it and tamping down the smoldering flames quickly.

Suddenly the ground shook violently and everyone on the scene looked down California Street towards the noise's source. Buildings mere blocks away exploded, contributing to an expanding cloud of dust behind them as a tentacled horror burst forth through the obscuring dirt and debris. The giant dinosaur roared its grinding, predatory war cry. It was similar to the trumpet of a charging bull elephant punctuated by the territorial roar of a male lion, with both parts put through a chainsaw noise filter.

This was now harmoniously accompanied by the newly grown mouths of sharp teeth that had sprouted from the obsidian-colored regenerated skin on its left flank. The pairs of tooth lips screamed in short bursts simultaneously with the longer predatory roar of the monster's head, the eerily human lips sometimes smiling cruelly in between shrieks.

Very few who heard this unholy cacophony maintained clean underwear; instant fear flooded even the strongest minds. The sanity of many snapped that much more as the unfathomable cries penetrated a deeper, subconscious level of fear. It was a level of fright that most people do not realize they still possess: that mind-crippling fear of the unknown, of things beyond the breadth of our knowledge and the scope of our imaginations. Fear humanity's ancestors knew daily, whether from ignorance of the way things worked or because the insane myths and legends were true. The sort of fear all who remained in the ruined, burning financial district were all too aware of.

Stupefied and crippled by this phobic phenomenon, many people were trampled as Nautilus Rex plowed over them like frozen blades of grass and ran straight into the side of the 345 building. The monster's down-turned head, with its keratin crown of thorns and reinforced helmet of a skull, punched through the already crumbling face of the ruined structure. The floors above the new impact point collapsed and fell apart with a tremendous noise as debris rained down on the daikaiju's head.

Withdrawing from the destroyed target before being buried in rubble, the Nautilus Rex swung its body around 180 degrees and slashed its thick, scaly tail through the smoldering remains next door. One of the stunned choppers had crashed into this building and continued on, slicing deep into the structure's west side and cutting through most of the center supports of the building's framework. This essentially severed its inanimate spine.

The beast finished its half-circle spin and faced the decimated structure once again, just in time to watch it pitch forward. In a flurry of motion, the stretching coils that were its arms whipped about in a thrashing fury, obliterating and batting away all rubble that threatened to fall on the thing's head. Chunks of concrete and steel were later found as far as five miles away from the defensive maneuver.

Even with the flailing of tentacles, the toppling building still managed to pummel the young kaiju into the ground. It hit the decimated street with an audible groan, like an old dog laying down on a hardwood floor. Then it laid there helplessly as crumbling floors of the building piled up on top of the monster. The dust cloud created in the collapsing mess soon cleared, revealing the kaiju's already rising form.

Its left side exploded again as three of the remaining five Apaches swooped in firing more Hydras. It cried out in agony, but when the smoke cleared, its smooth, new flesh remained unscathed. A few of the extra appendages had been blown apart, but instantly healed over with the shiny, regenerative tissue. Otherwise, the rockets only pissed it off.

With a crackling boom, the electromagnetic pulse-like bolt erupted from its throat and instantly arced towards the fleeing vehicles. Only one managed to avoid it, banking to the left sharply and taking cover between two tall buildings, the electric streaks finding windows and concrete instead. The other two were hit directly, instantly losing power and bursting in flames as gravity ripped them out of the sky and pulled them down into two office buildings below. Explosions further ripped the buildings apart moments later as mangled remains sparked and burned. With a rapid-fire bellow almost like a laugh, the beast turned its head back to where it had last seen the evading warbird.

Suddenly, the chopper shot past Nautilus' horned head, streaking through the air in a burning, smoking ball, and burying itself into one of the buildings already burning. The creature looked up in the direction the fastball had come from to see the Terror Griffin flapping its giant wings above the remnants of 345. Its beak opened wide as a cry of victory tore from its throat, followed by an ungodly wail from the newly formed, screaming orifice decorating its freshly healed patch of ass skin.

Roaring in response, the Nautilus Rex turned towards San Francisco Bay. Then it was off, charging in the bright sunlight down California Street until it ran into the huge hotel at the end of the street. Momentum, tentacles, and brute strength spelled the end for the hotel as monster met building and the building lost, crumbling easily as the Hidora Neo creation continued on. The kaiju then leapt up over the Ferry house building, taking its clock tower with it as the titanic creature splashed into the bay.

Waves of displaced water doused the waterfronts on all sides of the bay like mini tsunamis, flash flooding the city streets nearest the shore. Then the beast was gone, concentric circles expanding out from where it entered the bay being the only evidence it had submerged.

Meanwhile, the Terror Griffin had flown up and up into the sky, disappearing into a giant cotton ball cloud that was threatening to block out the sun for a time. The two remaining Apaches began to give chase from their position in the sky but turned and flew back towards the way they had originally come, returning to base with tactical info the brass was very interested in learning from the pilots firsthand. This effectively spared the pilots' lives, much to their unspoken delight.

The behemoths' rampage was over. The chaos, however, continued as the city began to pull itself back to its feet. And the unspoken question looming over everyone's minds was the obvious one.

When would they be back?

END

GONO'S HUNT

Cody Bratsch

The kaiju Gono started to stir from his deep sleep. He let out several heavy breaths and growling groans as his senses became more alert to the environment around him. This and the increase of the cortisol hormone received overnight while sleeping provided Gono with more energy, wiped away the beast's drowsy fatigue, and forced him awake. His yellow reptilian eyes twitched for a few moments before shutting once more as the four-legged monster started to rise. Once he was on his feet, the giant Komodo dragon-like kaiju with leathery, marine blue-colored skin let out a loud, roar-like yawn.

Gono gazed about at his surroundings, which included a large forest that wrapped around the clearing he had slept in. He then looked up to see the sky was almost completely clear, being mostly blue with only a few stray clouds here and there. The light of the sun shining over all of creation even glistened slightly off Gono's single row of clear yellow, needle-like spikes. They started at the top of Gono's head, went down his back, and extended to his tail where they started to get smaller. The leathery-skinned Gono sniffed the air, flicked his tongue, and listened closely to everything. He wanted to test his basic senses and instincts as part of his wake-up routine.

There have been many theories and studies by mankind as to what exactly a kaiju's full instincts and intelligence were and how far they stretched. At first one would think a kaiju's instincts would basically be more attuned to those of the smaller animals they resembled to differing capacities. However, constant contact with kaiju over the years in one way or another has suggested different possibilities as to how intelligent they were. Such deferring accounts, studies, and beliefs have led to many a debate over the years about kaiju's instincts and capacities for intelligence. Did their instincts carry them? Or, did they have enough free will and cognizance that they could actually be sentient and thus independent of their basic animal instincts?

With the quick reactions and knowledge of their world some kaiju seemed to have, people wondered if it went further than that. It made them wonder if maybe some kaiju managed to somehow, someway develop an ESP-like awareness of their environment. Would they be aware of a tiny dragonfly or perhaps a human being was right next to their foot, even if they couldn't see them?

With the way Gono was reacting at that moment, some would probably think he had an environmental awareness that reached unusual lengths. It was like he could smell everything around him or even well beyond the shores of the island he stood upon; and could hear just as far. Plus, although Gono may have only had two eyes, his reflexes and response time was so fast it seemed as if he had many more such organs all over his giant reptilian form. Was he truly so aware of everything going on around him to the extent that it appeared? Did he and possibly other kaiju truly have this psychic (or quasi-psychic) ability to know all that may be going on around them?

Kaiju were certainly a fascinating class of creatures in every respect and this reptilian beast was no exception.

The aquatic-looking fins on the side of Gono's head ever so lightly twitched. The monster had gotten a very basic lay of the land from the assessment of his heightened senses and instincts. Not only was it reaffirmed he was still on the island he'd fell asleep on the night before, but that he was no longer alone on said atoll. There were now at least five other kaiju on there with Gono.

There were three smaller creatures clustered together, possibly a family group; one larger beast further away, and another large one that was closer to Gono. The biggest kaiju seemed to be keeping towards the outer rim of the island, while the three smaller ones were heading for a river in the center. This also happened to be where the second biggest monster was, most likely getting a drink. Also, it was very likely that the smaller creatures were on their way there to quench their thirst as well. From all he had gathered, Gono felt it was probably best for him to head for that part of the river too.

In addition to getting a drink for himself, Gono also had the potential to find a meal big enough to sustain him for the day. Should the monstrous lizard of titanic proportions decide to do this, he knew he would go straight for the big kaiju at the river. It would be a suitable meal, was closer than the other large beast by this point, and probably easier to take down. Gono was forty meters tall, -- sixty when he stood up in his hind legs -- with rather sharp talons and a mouth full of Tyrannosaurus-like teeth to aid him. Plus, Gono had other resources he could call on in a bid to take down the bigger kaiju, which made him unafraid of confronting it in battle.

After thinking about it for a moment, Gono decided he

was thirsty and hungry enough that he would venture down to the river. The reptilian giant started making his way out of his clearing and through the vast forest that covered a good chunk of the island. He didn't stop to look at any sights the verdant wilderness had to offer, nor was he careful about any trees he might smash along the way. The monster didn't care about how beautiful his surroundings may have been or preserving the integrity of the woodlands. Gono just wanted to get to the river and take his meal.

Gono stopped only once to sniff the air while also flicking out his long, yellow forked tongue. Like the species of lizard this kaiju bore a strong resemblance to (the Komodo dragon), he too could detect odors in the air with his oral muscle. Whenever Gono flicked it out, his tongue would pick up particles in the air, after which Gono would retract it to the roof of his mouth. Here the scents on the tongue made contact with what is called the Jacobson's organ, which analyzes the odors to help determine exactly what they were and where they came from. Having this fascinating natural ability in addition to a sniffer that would make any dog jealous made Gono an even more effective hunter.

The creature now knew for certain he was on the right path and thus slightly sped up his approach. Once Gono got closer to the river, he would slow down again and go into full-on hunt mode. Like with the majority of kaiju who walked on land, Gono's feet caused the earth to shake and rumble like the tremor of a tiny earthquake. The massive reptile hardly seemed to notice these mini-quakes himself, however, as was the case for most kaiju when it came to their own thundering footsteps. The lizard-kaiju kept on moving, hoping that his feet, nor anything else, would give his presence away as he continued his trek to the river.

He cared not about whatever plant life or animal life his mighty feet or larger body might crush under his girth. Gono didn't have time for any of that, only being concerned with getting at the bigger game on the island. Such prospects were becoming all too real when the saurian giant suddenly froze. His auditory senses had kicked in, telling him there were other kaiju close by and approaching at fast speeds. Gono had been so focused on his intended prey, he had been made almost completely blind to everything else around him -- a fault which many kaiju tended to get trapped in.

The reptilian monster stood poised and prepared for whatever he might have to face. Gono looked towards his eleven, ready for battle when... the three smaller kaiju popped into view. They burst from the forest's brush, running and squealing like death itself was after them. Being 20 meters in length, the purplish-pinkish, smooth-skinned creatures had pudgy bodies, four skinny legs, tiny feet, long thin tails, and lengthy serpentine necks. They also had big, bulbous yellow eyes, a single row of clear needles going down their backs, and Venus flytrap-like mouths.

All three needle-toothed creatures instantly skidded to a halt when they saw that they'd ran themselves right into the much bigger Gono. They may have cheated death once, but now it was staring them in the face in another form. The lizard-like kaiju emitted a reptilian hiss as he prepared to strike. The three Needle Teeths tried to evade their bigger rival, moving as fast as they possibly could.

96

While two of them managed to get away, the third wasn't so lucky. The jaws of the bigger kaiju clamped down upon the sides of this Needle Teeth's body, his many serrated fangs sinking deep into the purple-pink beast's flesh.

Gono was violent as could be, biting hard and ripping aggressively at the Needle Teeth's flesh. He also pressed one of his front feet down on the smaller creature's neck while using the other to slash his claws over his prey's body. Gono then brought his full body weight to bear on the Needle Teeth to help pin it down as he continued to bite. Finally, Gono lifted his front foot off the creature's neck only to stomp on its head, instantly squishing it and ending the Needle Teeth's life. Then the lizard-kaiju looked over at the remaining two Needle Teeth.

They stood close by, while still maintaining a respectable distance from Gono, looking uncertain and possibly even devastated that they had lost one of their own. The lizard-kaiju let out a warning hiss, which enticed the two remaining Needle Teeth to scurry away as fast as they could. Then Gono looked down at his kill, seeing all the tooth and claw marks he had left. He also looked to where the head used to be; a mash of blood and gore was left in its place. Even if the bigger kaiju hadn't resorted to such a brutal tactic, he would've certainly taken the smaller monster down just as easily through other means.

One such possible method could've been the acidic saliva that Gono expelled from his mouth. While to him it was just drool he secreted, it burned through just about anything else it came into contact with. That was clear by the growing size of the marks where Gono had bitten the now lifeless Needle Teeth. Gono contemplated just taking this carcass as his meal and being on his way, but quickly decided against it. There was a much bigger source of meat waiting for him at the river.

The reptilian kaiju decided he would go after that creature, kill it, eat it, and then come back for the smaller morsel to have as desert (assuming it was still there afterwards). Gono took one last look at his fallen prey before continuing to the river. It wasn't long after that the monster could actually smell and even taste the vegetation becoming more luscious. This told Gono he was coming up on the river, which made the beast slow his approach even more. Then the monster lizard used a fascinating gift of adaptation that evolution had felt so kind to bestow upon him.

The reptilian kaiju actually started to change the color of his skin to blend in more with the environment around him. In addition to this amazing display of physical camouflage, Gono also released scents from his pours that had been absorbed into his body while he was on the island. This disguised the beast's own scent in the hopes of giving him a better chance of getting in close to his prey. Many kaiju would seem to have some strange sense of environmental awareness, it was true. However, it wasn't uncommon for some of the lesser intelligent beasts to be tricked at least to some extent by such camouflage tactics.

Gono was obviously counting on such being the case in this situation and thus proceeded forward with that mindset. He already knew exactly where the other kaiju was without ever having to see it. The monstrous lizard didn't need to go straight to the water's edge, although he did anyway, looking across the stream and off to the left to see the other kaiju hunched over the riverside. This other kaiju, a female, was scooping up handfuls of water and bringing them up to her mouth to drink. Gono gazed at his intended prey with near absolute focus while still trying to be aware of the environment around him.

He took in all the physical details about this other creature, examining her closely to help come up with a plan of attack to take her down. This opposing kaiju was documented as Skearite. When standing up straight on her two dinosaur-like feet, she was 65 meters tall and had a somewhat rounded, almost barrel-shaped body. Her arms and legs were also rather thick, as was her long neck with a very bumpy pattern going across her rock-like, sickly yellow colored skin. Skearite's face appeared very gargoyle-like with orange, mammalian-esque eyes, and a full head of long brown hair with most strands coming down to her shoulders. She had long sharp talons on her hands and feet, along with white patches of fur on her elbows, knees, and chest. Her strange appearance was completed by a pair of large, jagged, deer-like antlers on her head.

Skearite was a very grotesque and frightening vision for certain. It wasn't helped by how prominently her vampire-like fangs were sticking out of her mouth, or by the small bump of a horn on her forehead. Such a sight would surely strike fear into the hearts of most human beings who looked upon the beast. But none of this kaiju's physical characteristics deterred Gono, who just kept looking on at the bigger beast with full malicious intent. He continued to observe Skearite from across the river, carefully examining every detail about her and the immediate environment she inhabited while still trying to think of a plan of attack.

The lizard-kaiju slightly tilted his head to the side as he watched the bizarre-looking Skearite continue to gulp down handfuls of water from the river. Kaiju often sought small uninhabited islands with fresh water sources like the one Skearite and Gono were now co-habiting in the hope of finding isolated solace from the rest of the world. Whether it was from constant conflict with the human population which covered most of the planet or conflict with other giant beasts, sometimes kaiju just needed a rest. Unfortunately, being the giant creatures kaiju happened to be usually tended to bring them into some sort of conflict no matter where they went. Whether they were looking for it or not, there always seemed to be a fight just waiting around the corner for these apex beasts of the planet.

Perhaps that was a curse that came with being a kaiju. No matter what personal needs or desires they may have had, it was forever their destinies to be creatures of combat because of the titanic giants they were. While that may have been the case in the grand scheme of things, in this instance Gono was just looking for breakfast. He thought he had figured out how to get it, and was preparing to make his move to try and strike his prey down in hopes of appeasing his appetite. Still camouflaged and still producing his disguising scent, Gono shifted his feet ever so slightly to prepare for attack.

As careful as Gono tried to be, however, the kaiju was unable to keep his feet from making at least the tiniest of scraping noises across the ground. Skearite's goblin-pointed ears twitched, having picked up the sound with her extra-sensitive hearing. She quickly snapped up her head and began to look around cautiously. Gono instantly stiffened into immobility, trying not to make any noises, even slowing his own breathing. The strange female kaiju stood up straight and looked around as she started to sniff the air.

Even though she couldn't see or smell anything out of the norm, Skearite had a strong suspicion that she wasn't alone. Whether it could be called kaiju intuition or paranoia, a lot of other giant monsters often displayed similarly cautious and alert feelings. It could even be called an essential part of the overall function of their extra sensitive awareness of their environment (assuming that was really a thing). Skearite would not easily let her guard down, nor would she return to her previous calm state until she was absolutely certain it was safe to do so. Gono knew this would be the case, having experienced it from other kaiju he'd fought in the past and had even felt such caution himself on occasion.

He would wait it out, though, having developed a rather large amount of patience from similar scenarios he had previously dealt with. Gono waited and gazed on as Skearite looked about and continued to sniff the air. It went on like this for four minutes, but it felt like hours to the hungry Gono. He tried to keep his tense feelings and hunger under control so as not to project them for the she-kaiju to sense. Finally, the odd beast Skearite turned away as she prepared to walk off and leave the area around the river.

Seeing that his intended prey was trying to escape, Gono quickly sprung through the air in an unbelievable display of agility. He'd actually managed to go sailing clear over the river all in his bid to pounce upon his prey before she could flee. Skearite turned to see the lizard-kaiju coming at her with claws outstretched and mouth opened wide. She released a bellowing roar as she raised her hands in an attempt to catch her foe. The impact of their collision sounded like several thousand battle tanks firing all at once as the two monsters went rolling across the ground.

After several moments of rolling, struggling, and wrestling, Skearite managed to stop herself and toss Gono to the side, making him roll further away. Gono then forced himself to stop and got back on all fours, taking a battle stance as Skearite rose to her feet. She glared at the reptilian kaiju and roared a warning for him to back down. Gono let out a hiss of refusal before charging forth at surprisingly quick speed that seemed to defy his size. Skearite barely had time to plant her feet and prepare herself for her quadrupedal opponent's leaping charge.

Lucky for Skearite she managed to get her hands up and catch the jaw-snapping, claw-slashing Gono and toss him into the river behind her with a swinging throw. When Skearite turned to look, Gono was already out of the water, glaring at the bipedal monster with enraged eyes. Skearite responded with a roar as orbs of red light manifested in the palm of her hands, seemingly from out of nowhere. They grew in mass until they took up the entirety of Skearite's palms, after which she tossed them at the reptilian creature before her. Gono quickly leapt over them as fast as he could, making them just barely miss, skimming the ends of his feet and tail.

Gono landed just as the duo orbs hit the ground behind him, igniting massive explosions. The four-legged kaiju looked back to see the towers of fire and smoke climbing into the air as burning pieces of debris and embers flew all over the place. Gono then looked back to Skearite and bellowed in defiance before his eyes lit up in a green glow. This was followed by the monster releasing what looked like a wave of green fire from his mouth. Skearite screamed out in pain from the intense heat of the flames as she started to stumble backwards.

Gono ceased fire and rushed at Skearite before leaping into the air, slamming his body against Skearite's as he dug his claws into her. He then bit into the female monster's left shoulder, clamping his jaws down as hard as he could. Skearite screamed loudly as she started to club her free arm across Gono's body. She switched between these blows and scratching her claws up and down Gono's back. This caused an intense pain in the quadrupedal beast which forced the weakening of his bite, allowing Skearite to toss him aside.

Gono was sent crashing into and sliding across the ground but amazingly managed to get up only a moment later. He still looked noticeably slower this time around, however. Skearite started to stomp towards her smaller foe to press her attack. However, the long-haired kaiju suddenly stopped and yelped as she felt a burning pain where she'd been bitten. Skearite brought her hand up to her shoulder but stopped short of touching it when she saw the smoke hissing from her open wound. The acidic nature of Gono's saliva was well in effect and caused a perfect distraction for said monster to take advantage of.

Gono ran up to his adversary, though not as fast as

before, but still managed to slam his head into Skearite's stomach with enough force to knock her down. Skearite tumbled onto her back, letting out a hollering roar as Gono pounced down upon her. At first, he bit into Skearite's neck, but the odd-looking monster quickly shook herself free of the reptile's bite before he could clamp his jaws. Gono would then start slashing his claws across Skearite's face, neck, and chest while occasionally trying to bite into her neck once more. Every time Gono would get a bite, however, Skearite would quickly shake him off before he got a chance to clamp his jaws properly.

The she-kaiju kept alternating between closed fists and open-handed swings meant to either slap Gono or slash her claws across his hide. The two monsters of titanic proportions kept on wrestling for several moments like the wild and vicious animals they were deep down inside. Eventually it got to the point where Skearite was able to get herself rolling despite Gono having her pinned down previously. They went tumbling for a few seconds before Skearite managed to roll up onto her two feet and sling her foe up onto her shoulders. Skearite then roared out as she pressed Gono over her head, ignoring his cries of protest, before she tossed him through the air.

Gono went sailing a good dozen meters, crying out before crashing to the ground in a heap. His body twitched a few times before he finally started to move on his own a moment later. He then gingerly rolled onto his belly before he tried pushing himself up onto his feet. Before he had a chance to get back up all the way, Gono faced a bombardment of red energy orbs from Skearite. Gono cried out each time he was struck with an explosion-inducing orb, the multiple bursts of force and fire leaving many a mark across his exterior.

When Skearite ceased fire, she ran up and kicked her foot into Gono's face, knocking him onto his back. The earth shook greatly as it had several other times throughout this battle of epic proportions. The reptilian beast bellowed in anguish but was cut off by Skearite's foot stomping down on his chest. She then roared angrily down into the lizard's face before she started swinging her fists across his features. Skearite got in about seven, stone-crushing blows across Gono's face before he managed to shoot a blaze of green fire up into his adversary's own monstrous countenance.

Skearite shrieked in agony as she threw her hands over her burning face, despite exposing them to Gono's flames as well. The strange creature started to titter back, but while she was in mid-step, Gono wrapped his tail around her ankle and pulled as hard as he could. Skearite ended up crashing into the ground, making the earthquake while her body left an imprint in the sediment where she fell. Gono rolled onto his belly and rushed at Skearite as she started to slowly sit up. Her eyes widened in alarm when she saw her foe was up and coming at her full steam ahead.

Gono bit down hard on Skearite's right forearm before shaking his head wildly and thrashing about like a rabid dog, trying to do as much damage as possible. Although Skearite was in pain, she forced herself up to a knee and eventually got back on her feet.

Then she started to shake and swing her arm in a desperate attempt to get Gono to release his bite. This was easier said than done, for no matter how much she shook, thrashed, and swung her arm around, the gargoyle-like kaiju couldn't get her limb free. It even seemed like her smaller opponent was biting down harder while also bringing up his front claws to do more damage to his foe's trapped arm.

As was expected, the immense pain that Skearite was already going through intensified thanks to Gono's added efforts. On top of that was the burning sensation of Gono's acid saliva, which had burnt Skearite every other time she'd been bitten as well. The female kaiju was desperate for an out and tried desperately to think of one for herself. Finally, Skearite brought her right arm high into the air, thus lifting Gono off the ground and leaving his hanging body exposed to attack. The gargoyle-like creature roared like a titanic crocodile before she started slamming her left fist into Gono's body.

Skearite got in several good hits on different parts of the lizard-kaiju's body before creating an orb in her left hand. She then tossed said orb into her opponent's saurian form, leading to typically explosive results. The new blast wound left in Gono's body forced the four-legged monster to release his bite and he started falling back to the ground. In mid-fall, the lizard-kaiju was met with a mighty left uppercut to his lower jaw from Skearite, which nearly knocked him silly. However, Gono managed to keep himself awake and focused; thus, he was able to land safely on his feet.

Gono examined the new bleeding wound in his side while Skearite was examining the still burning bite mark on her arm. Both monsters were in a lot of pain from the injuries they'd sustained throughout this fight, but they were also very angry. In fact, they were downright furious as could be and ready to take it out on each other in the worst possible way.

The snarling Gono struck first, rushing at Skearite and slashing at her with his front claws. The quadrupedal beast got in several good swipes before he suffered several massive punches into his exposed underbelly and a right uppercut, all from Skearite.

Then the she-beast rushed forth with a knee to Gono's face before grabbing him by the throat, lifting him up, and kneeing him in the gut. Skearite then looked her adversary in the face before biting into his shoulder. Gono shrieked out as blood flowed like a stream from the freshly bitten wound. The bite only lasted two seconds before Skearite pulled away. Then, still holding her opponent by the throat, lifted her adversary high into the air. Skearite then slammed Gono into the earth, making it break beneath him while the rest of the area around them trembled as if subject to a massive earthquake.

Skearite didn't let go of her enemy's throat but instead lifted him up again and slammed him down into a different part of the ground. She repeated the process once more, this time trying to put as much into her choke-slam as she could muster, wanting Gono to feel every last iota of the force. The collision of a huge mass of flesh against the earth's crust in such a violent way resulted in the most severe quake yet.

Gono's body left a bigger impression in the ground than any he or Skearite had previously left during their entire fight. And he was feeling it, too. All Gono could do now was let out a groan of agony and just barely move before being forced to stop because he was in so much pain.

The gargoyle-like kaiju roared out, already declaring her victory over Gono; that she'd won despite the fact that her opponent was still breathing. Skearite was about to end it, though, for the kaiju brought up her foot with full intent to stomp it down on the fallen Gono's head. She let her raised heel hover in mid-air for a bit before stomping it down with all her might.

Surely this would be the final nail in the coffin for Gono, for there was no possible way his head would be able to withstand such a vicious move from such an enraged monster. That would have proven true if the lizard-kaiju hadn't managed to roll out of the way at the very last second.

Gono managed to escape the fatal blow, rolling off to the side and onto his feet just as Skearite's foot came smashing down into the ground where his head once was. How Gono was able to still move so swiftly after such a beating was anyone's guess. Skearite certainly thought he was done for and was shocked as can be that she hadn't dealt the killing blow to end this no-holds-barred scuffle. Her hesitation would cost her, however, when Gono turned his sights on her foot and engulfed Skearite's entire leg in his green fire. As the female monster screamed out in pain, the lizard-kaiju aimed his mighty flames upward into her chest and face.

Gono then actually spat a glob of his saliva up into Skearite's gargoyle-like visage with marksman-like precision. The acidic nature of the monster's spit kicked in immediately, making Skearite scream louder than ever as she reached her hands up and grabbed at her burning and melting features.

Gono rushed up and swung his tail against his

adversary's ribs, nearly knocking all the breath out of her body. As Skearite reached her hands down towards her mid-section, Gono quickly swung his tail forth, slapping it across her face. He didn't let up on his attack, instead swinging his tail across Skearite's head three more times before turning to spew more of his green fire.

The searing emerald flame engulfed most of the gargoyle-like monster's upper body, burning hotter than the pit of a volcano. Gono roared out before swinging his tail into the side of his opponent's body with the same skyscraper-crushing force as before. Skearite groaned as she clutched desperately at her ribs, hoping beyond hope they weren't shattered. Seeing that his foe was in a lot of pain and having trouble standing, Gono rushed forth, slamming his body against Skearite's. The force sent the bipedal creature falling onto her back as she let out an agonized moan.

Skearite's mournful calls were met with deaf ears as Gono pounced down upon her and fired his wave of green flames into her face at point blank range. The female kaiju shrieked and howled out as she tried thrashing to get herself free. Pain and fear gripped Skearite tightly in her last moments before the flames overtook her and ended her life. The fallen monster's hands fell and her entire body went limp to confirm Gono's victory. He looked down at the face of his opponent for a moment, observing that her features had been greatly deformed from being burned and melted.

As a final act of contempt, Gono bit into his dead opponent's neck and yanked off a piece of meat. He then tossed it into the air before catching it in his mouth again and consuming it whole. Gono then raised his head into the sky and let out a bellowing roar to signal that he'd won the fight, something a lot of kaiju tended to do. Perhaps such acts of pride were eternally wired into every giant beast of mighty magnitude that human civilization labeled a kaiju. Whether that was the case or not, there was no denying that the victorious Gono had certainly earned his display of dominance after the great battle he'd been through.

Then Gono remembered he wasn't the only kaiju on the island, at least not the last time he checked. The saurian titan quickly looked around in every direction as he sniffed the air and flicked his tongue. It seemed that the biggest kaiju's scent trailed off back to the sea, the beast having apparently left. Gono's pride was telling him at that moment that he could probably take the big one on after how well he fared against Skearite. He was thankful he wouldn't have to find out, though, since his previous battle had taken a great toll on him.

Gono turned and sniffed in the direction he'd come from, where he'd left that Needle Teeth carcass before. The scent seemed to have gotten further away, the body apparently having been dragged off. Most likely it had been taken by the other two Needle Teeth. For what purpose they did this, it was hard to say, as was a lot of things kaiju did. Was it done to ensure the fallen Needle Teeth wasn't devoured by Gono? Was it possibly also to give their fallen comrade something akin to a proper burial?

Or was it for a darker, more sickening reason? Was it so they could devour the dead kaiju themselves in a cannibalistic display? Either way, Gono wasn't worried about it – certainly not with the proverbial buffet he had before him. The kaiju looked down upon the dead body of Skearite, savoring how great it was going to be to fill his stomach. Gono flicked out his tongue just once before he started biting down into the flesh of his large meal.

The mighty lizard-kaiju would most likely end up laying down to rest after he was done eating his fill. Then he would probably move on to other islands for whatever varying reasons. Until then, Gono took bite after bloody bite of the raw, dead, meaty flesh of the monster he'd conquered, greedily savoring each piece he devoured with aplomb.

END

HARVEST TIME

Neil Riebe

The humans called them Melgorthians. "Melgorthians" meant nothing to Noregon. He preferred "reptile men." That name fit because they were the same size as humans and stood on two legs, just like humans. Like reptiles, they had scales and snake-like fangs in their mouths. They also had nostril slits instead of noses, sharp cheeks, and sunken eyes. Their faces looked something like a skull, so "skull-face reptile men" would be a more accurate name, but "reptile men" worked fine.

The reptile men were lean, hardy creatures. Their skintight black garments had ridges along the sides of the arms and legs. Some had gold ridges and the rest had blue.

Noregon laid down on the shore of an island and watched them herd humans. One reptile man stood at the top of the stairs to a white marble building. Through the building's opening was a statue of a bearded human. Above the statue, these symbols were etched into the wall:

IN THIS TEMPLE AS IN THE HEARTS OF THE PEOPLE FOR WHOM HE SAVED THE UNION THE MEMORY OF ABRAHAM LINCOLN IS ENSHRINED FOREVER.

The reptile man at the top of stairs had silver ridges on his black garments instead of gold or blue. He also had silver emblems on his collar. The reptilian stood with his

112

fists on his hips as he observed the herding. His demeanor suggested that he was the leader.

The humans were leaders, too. Noregon could tell by two things. One, their outer coverings were clean and showed no sign of fading. The colors were those of granite and the ocean, particularly the deeper, colder parts of the sea. Bold and cheerless. The other thing was their faces. Human faces were like a primate's. They told you everything. These humans were sullen and resentful. They were unaccustomed to being told what to do. And they were afraid. Very, very afraid.

One of the females started sobbing. She dropped to her knees before one of the reptile men with the blue ridges. Then she pleaded, pressing her hands to her heart and then spread them out wide.

"Oh, please! Please! Please!" she wept. Those were the sounds he heard distinctly.

The reptile man struck her with his baton. One sharp crack.

The woman slumped onto the ground. It was a quick, clean kill. She died before she felt the blow.

Noregon respected the reptile man for that. In the animal kingdom a quick kill was a rare thing. A preferred thing. Too often killing was a painful process.

The humans on the far side of the herd stirred anxiously at some commotion going on over by another white marble building. This structure was not as ornate as the temple and had tall, narrow windows. Noregon raised his head just a bit to get a better look at what was happening.

A human leader exited from the side of the building with the tall, narrow windows. This leader still had his

113

guardians. The guardians formed a tight, protective circle around him as he slinked toward a machine parked close to the building.

The commotion caught the reptile men's attention.

The guardians aimed their weapons toward the reptile men, signaling the reptiles to keep back.

One reptile man walked toward the circle of guardians. The guardians barked at him. It sounded like, "Back! Back! Stay back!" Their bark reminded Noregon of a chirping bird. When he wanted to keep a threatening animal away, he let out a bellow that shook the leaves out of the trees. That was pretty good, considering he was an herbivore.

The reptile man stopped, snapped his fingers at the armed humans and their charge, and directed them to join the herd with a pointed finger. This simple gesture carried more authority than the guardians' "Back! Back! Back!"

The guardians slinked faster toward the machine. One opened the side of the device for the human they were protecting. They cooed encouraging notes to him. "Hurry! Hurry! Get in!"

Before anyone could get into the machine, another reptile man – one whom the guardians were not watching -- touched the pavement with his baton. A surge of electrical current flowed through the tarmac and up into the humans' legs. The guardians and their charge dropped to the ground. It was as if their bones had turned to jelly. Gasps rang out from the herd.

The reptile man who had approached the guardians closed the distance between them and removed the weapons from their limp grasp. The human leader harangued his protectors. As soon as the reptile touched him, the human started sobbing and harangued his guardians even more fiercely.

If Noregon were one of that human's guardians, he would have bitten him. Noregon never let another creature browbeat him, even if he liked the creature. He might make an exception if he had done something stupid, but then he often didn't realize he had done something stupid until long after he had bitten someone for browbeating him. That was the problem with being dull witted.

A reptile man with gold ridges on his uniform thumped several humans on the shoulder with his baton and then pointed at the guardians and their sobbing charge. The humans understood what to do. They shuffled over and dragged the guardians and their charge back to the herd.

The reptile man with the silver ridges watched their work with a keen eye. Satisfied with the size of his herd, he touched a device that was strapped to his wrist.

Giant humming machines lowered from the sky, casting their shadows on the clearing. The machines were as black as the reptile men's' garments, but they did not have the same plucky shine. Their dark hues had a more foreboding nature.

Noregon got up on all fours to get the best view. Would the humans attack the reptile men? Would they bolt from the clearing? Almost anything could happen at this desperate moment.

The machines hovered overhead and lowered their ramps into the herd.

The humans made a variety of sounds -- muttering, crying, shouting. Noregon sensed the energy build-up. He became excited and started to cross the reservoir that separated the island from the clearing.

The reptile man atop the stairs was alright with him watching from the island. Once Noregon stepped into the water, however, the reptilian thrust his baton toward the latter to get his attention and then pointed back toward the atoll.

The reptile men had controlled Noregon's mind once. He had broken their spell over him and they had never been able to control him since. It was amusing to see this slight creature behaving as though he could still tell Noregon what to do.

Noregon snorted at the reptile man. That alerted the humans that he was in the area. They looked up at him, screamed, and broke ranks from the herd.

Noregon roared, thrilled by the chaos he had caused.

The reptile men signaled the humans to stop running with upraised hands. Humans flowed past them and ran down the passages between the buildings. The reptile men wearing blue ridges on their garments aimed their batons at the fleeing humans. Bolts of electricity shot out from the batons. The electric bolts struck the closest human, and then branched out to the next closest human, and the next and the next. Their horrible screams were enough to frighten the others to shrink back into the clearing.

With a roar, Noregon congratulated the reptile men for their resourcefulness. The humans outnumbered them by a hundred to one. Yet they took control of their herd more effectively than the humans could control their stampeding cattle.

Then the reptile men showed they could still deal with Noregon.

Smaller, sphere-shaped devices separated from the big hovering machines and floated toward Noregon. The spheres emitted a high-pitched noise that set his teeth on edge. The metal in his osteoderms resonated the sound, allowing it to reverberate through his organs. His stomach felt ready to vomit. His heartbeat to the brink of bursting. His head ached.

Noregon backed up, turned around, and lumbered toward the south shore. The spheres dogged him all the way. He crossed the river to the mainland and headed toward the coast to get away from them. He got out of the range of the humming when he reached the ocean.

He lingered there to catch his breath. The confrontation with the reptile men spoiled his curiosity in the herd's fate. Besides, the reptiles would probably do what they always have done: They would force the humans into their hovering machines and then the apparatuses would take the humans up into the sky.

When he felt better, he loped along the shore heading north. Three waterborne tackles lay beached in the shallow water. These were fighting machines. The burn marks on the devices showed that they had fought the reptiles and lost.

Noregon growled at the waterborne machines in case there were still humans inside who wanted to fight. Nothing stirred from within the hulls. They were dead.

He then proceeded up the beach. Sea gulls circled overhead. Noregon sidetracked inland to trot through the houses. He left a trail of crushed lumber.

The area was deserted. Almost. A dog barked at him, and he stopped to face the animal.

The canine was large from a human standpoint, but from Noregon's the mammal was tiny. Yet, the dog stood his ground on his owner's front lawn. Noregon understood each bark perfectly.

Stay off my owner's territory! Stay off!

The dog growled to show he meant business. Noregon replied with a snort. Your owner is gone.

The dog gave him a worried look and then glanced back at the house. The front door was open. No one stirred inside. Deep down, the dog knew Noregon was right, but he clung onto his hope and resumed barking.

Noregon was glad he wasn't domesticated. Humans were fragile and lived short lives. He shivered at the thought of being in the dog's place. Who would take care of him then?

Luckily, Noregon did not have to worry about it. He was a giant in the animal kingdom and could fend for himself. His body metabolized iron, creating a form of natural steel. His blood deposited the bio-steel into his osteoderms. On sunny days his osteoderms shined like a knight's armor. Many a kaiju predator broke tooth and claw while trying to prey upon him. None had succeeded in cracking his metallic shell. Few have beaten him in battle and most important of all, he has survived every encounter.

As for the dog, who could say what would happen to him?

It was a terrible thing to be domesticated.

Noregon put the animal out of his mind and trotted up the road, pulverizing the pavement as he went. His footfalls echoed for miles.

That night he slept in the wetlands. For breakfast he gulped the tall grass growing out of the mud. Sated, he resumed his northerly march.

Up ahead he could see the concrete jungle erected by humankind. He bound along a highway and skidded to a halt amongst the cornucopia of buildings. Buildings and more buildings. Every which way he turned. Buildings! It was Kaiju Christmas.

Noregon romped through shopping malls, flipped rooves, and flattened vehicles. Brick and mortar, steel and glass, plaster and wood, it was so much fun to break. He grabbed a bridge with his mouth, pulled it from its roots, and swung it about, smashing storefronts, gas stations, and restaurants. With his prize still in his mouth, Noregon strutted down the road and into the narrow passages between the high rises. He set the gnarled remains of the bridge atop a roof. Noregon was 180 meters long and 60 meters in height. He was big, but these dandies were five times taller.

The armored kaiju charged down the street and smashed into a skyscraper, bursting out the other side in a glittering shower of broken glass. Amazingly, the building still stood, which was fine. He rammed into it from another direction. This time the structure fell into a neighboring skyscraper with a thunderous crash. Gray clouds of cinder billowed up out of the wreckage.

Noregon roared with joy.   He leapt head-first into another high-rise. The building shook from the impact.

His body sank halfway in. His hind legs and tail dangled over the street. Using his forepaws, he burrowed into the building like a worm in a tree trunk, climbing up, up, up. Near the top he popped his head out to check out the view.

His burrowing had compromised the structure. It collapsed, and its falling mass sent tremors through the city. When Noregon hit bottom, he crawled out of the heap of ruins and roared again, exhilarated by the fall.

The best part was that he had the whole city to himself. There were no sirens. No screaming hordes. No fighting machines. No competing kaiju. It was important to savor this moment because it was hard to find a place where there was no one else around. Nature abhorred a vacuum, however, so soon other animals would replace the humans.

Noregon rolled in the rubble, kicking his feet in the air. He paused to watch the clouds float through the warm sky and then rolled some more, grinding the concrete to powder. When he trundled back onto his feet, his gleaming armor was covered in a film of dust. The cinder clouds left his throat parched.

Through the haze, he trudged toward the smell of water, where he found an enormous brown river. There was a teal-colored statue of a human female out on an island.

Noregon had seen humans place replicas of themselves in fields to scare away birds. This statue was big enough to be used against kaiju. Maybe that was what it was for, to scare away kaiju. It held a torch up in the air. Humans had used torches to drive away predators. And it faced the water, the direction where a kaiju would come. So, yes, that had to be it.

Noregon crossed the river to the island to get a closer look at the statue. It would be fun to knock it down, but it might be more useful leaving it be. The figure didn't scare him, but it might scare others. There was a lot of city left to destroy and he wanted to save it for the next time he was in the mood to play.

He headed inland where the continent was greener and found another area where the reptile men had herded humans. It was in a large parking lot. Humans tended to drop their possessions while boarding the black flying machines. The lot was littered with their things. That's how he figured out this was a herding area. Noregon did not know what the items were, but they included articles of clothing, several wallets and purses, a handful of phones, and one doll. It laid on its back with its arms raised, as if it were reaching out for the child that had loved it.

The next town had been destroyed by a kaiju. Noregon didn't recognize whose tracks he found leading into the municipality. It was evident, however, that the beast could breathe fire, as the buildings had all been burned down.

Noregon felt territorial over the lost hamlet. Now that the humans weren't around to lay claim to the buildings, he wanted them for himself.

At noon the following day he stopped at a tree line bordering a cattle farm. The cows gave him a resentful eye, as though he had something to do with their loss of the humans that took care of them. They showed their indignation by grazing further away from him.

Indifferent to the bovines' attitude toward him, Noregon started cropping the trees of their sweet leaves and crunchy branches. In mid-chomp a thought struck him: One day, all the buildings will be destroyed. Panic rose up inside him.

Here he had been smashing buildings as though they would be back like the flowers in spring, forgetting that the humans built them. At the rate the reptile men were harvesting humans, there will be no one to rebuild the edifices he had smashed. That went for the buildings the other kaiju smashed, too.

Noregon wandered out into the countryside, bereft over what to do. On a hillside he spotted a young couple trudging along, holding hands as they walked. Each had a pack on their backs stuffed with provisions. One was a male; the other was female.

Perfect! This was what he needed.

He galloped up to them. They saw him coming and ran.

Noregon slowed down so he wouldn't step on them. He roared at them to wait. Don't run. You need to breed! Quickly! Before you go extinct. I will protect you! I will protect your offspring!

No matter how carefully he enunciated his growls and grunts, they did not understand. He had to let them go before they dropped from heart failure.

Depressed, Noregon dragged his tail behind him as he walked away.

At least there was a chance they would breed. Maybe their offspring would survive without his help. Or, maybe, he had frightened the couple too much and they were now infertile because of him.

Noregon was tempted to check on them but he would not be able to tell one way or another if they could still breed. He would have to let Nature take its course.

Later that day he found a town that was in pristine condition.

Noregon decided to guard it for future use.

Then he changed his mind. The city with the statue was a better place to guard because it had many more – and better – buildings.

Noregon turned back for the coast. However, the shoreline was a long ways away. It would take days to get there. By then the city could be destroyed, which meant he would have to come back here and by the time he did that, this town could be destroyed.

It would be better to guard what he had, meager as it was. He laid down outside the town and watched for other kaiju.

Eventually his bowels wanted relief. Noregon did not dare risk leaving the town, however. It could be smashed by the time he got back. He waited until his bowels were ready to burst. Checking the landscape first for incoming marauders, he loped into the hills, dug a pit with his forepaws, positioned his posterior, and unloaded his burden to great relief. While he completed his nature call, he peered over the hills to be sure the town was still there.

It was. Finished, he buried his dung with his hind feet and rushed back to his town, where he settled down for a long, long vigil.

That night Noregon had a nightmare. Kaiju from all over the world rose up out of the brown river. The teal-colored statue hopped down from her pedestal.

123

Brandishing her torch, she drove them away, but there were so many that one slipped by. As they rushed the giant lady in increasing numbers, she could not keep up. The kaiju invaded his city, smashed his buildings with sinister delight. His statue threw aside her torch, sat upon the pedestal, dropped her face into her hands, and wept.

Noregon woke up with a start. He immediately checked the status of his town.

It was still there. He was glad, but it took a long time before his heart stopped pounding.

At dawn Noregon heard the buzzing sound of insect wings. Staying put, he looked toward the hills and forests. In the pale light, he saw nothing. As the sun rose, shedding more light upon the landscape, he still saw nothing. Yet, he sensed someone else was nearby.

Noregon then heard a faint creak and a pop. A long stretch of silence passed. Then another faint, creaking sound reached his ears. It was difficult to figure out what the noise was. It sounded like a tree branch being bent. If a kaiju was nearby, it would bend more than a single branch when it walked through the trees. So, it couldn't be anything of that nature.

Hence, Noregon calmed down. The air turned more pleasant as the sun climbed higher in the sky. The creaking noise returned, this time occurring more often and coming from inside the town. The sound was clearer now, and it was not coming from any tree.

Noregon turned around and there in the suburb was Golgotha, the giant praying mantis. Her legs made the creaking noise. The mantis was about to pierce the roof of a house with her forelimb. Ever since she was a nymph, she had an appetite for humans, and she was here to feed. Her triangular head spun toward him when he spotted her. She turned around, raised her forelegs with their lethal barbs high in the air, flapped her wings, and hissed savagely. The third eye between her two main compound eyes glowed like a jewel. Her third eye was her most powerful weapon, as it could fire an energy beam.

This was the worst possible creature that could have discovered his town. Golgotha was an insect, so her mind was alien. She communicated by emitting odors. Grunts, growls, snorts, and roars – the universal language of vertebrates – meant nothing to her. Even the hiss she emitted was not a word. She was not saying anything but merely posturing to make herself appear dangerous. There was no possible way for him to convince her to leave. He would have to fight her, which would result in destruction of the buildings.

Noregon roared back, baring his teeth to show he was dangerous, too. He slammed his tail on the ground. The reverberation caused Golgotha to flinch. She stopped buzzing her wings, lowered her forelimbs part way, and canted her head in thought.

Noregon slammed the ground harder to show if she forced him to fight, she would be facing an opponent who was much heavier than her. Weight was an important factor in combat, as lighter kaiju risked breaking their bones fighting heavier opponents.

Golgotha hissed again. This time it seemed she was testing her opposition, to see what he would do. Noregon held still, just to make her think. Golgotha remained still, too, save for her antennae, which swiveled.

125

They faced each other, frozen in their stances. Golgotha cocked her head in a different direction. She was still thinking, which was good. Noregon remained patient, letting the tension build. Golgotha took one tentative step forward. Noregon coiled back and leapt up into the air. He came down with a crash whose echo hammered across the countryside. The reverberation cracked the windows in the nearby houses and clouds of dust puffed up for a half mile all around.

Golgotha stumbled backwards and then took off, flying toward the west.

Noregon watched her until he could no longer see her. He exhaled in relief. His armor saved the day. The bio steel in his armored plates made him five times heavier than any other kaiju his size. The thump on the ground he had made was enough to convince the giant mantis that her gracile limbs would be snapped if he fell on her. Making her think helped, too. Thinking was useful, but too much caused one to believe an opponent was stronger than it actually was.

To be sure Golgotha had not wrecked any of the buildings, Noregon circled the town. They all appeared to be intact. Completing his inspection, he proceeded to lay down in his usual spot. The rest of the afternoon was beautiful. Enormous clouds loomed over the horizon, bigger than mountains. The highest cloud had a flat top. As the day waned, the air pressure dropped. The white clouds took on an angry color. Lightning flickered. Thunder murmured in the distance. The wind picked up.

Noregon could sense what was coming. He galloped out into the field and stood between his beloved buildings and the oncoming storm. Even though he knew it was futile, he roared at the storm to go away.

The storm kept coming, turning the sky black in the process. Violent bolts of lightning flashed. The winds, wet with rain, turned fierce. They became hot, and then cold. Up above the clouds swirled.

Noregon wailed, begging the storm to stop. Then the swirling clouds spun into a funnel and touched down several miles away. It was a tornado!

As the funnel drew closer, Noregon stood his ground for as long as he could before seeking shelter in the hills. The freight-train roar of the tornado ripped through the town. To Noregon, the sounds of the buildings being torn apart were like the cries of his children, begging to be saved.

When it was all over, rainwater dripped into puddles. The soil and plants released a moist, fragrant scent. The clouds broke, unveiling the night. A full moon shone over the land. Noregon climbed out of the hills and beheld his town. It was in ruins.

Gone forever.

***

Noregon gave up on trying to preserve towns. The only option left was to save humans from extinction. For that he needed allies. He headed west, toward the mountains, to search for the kaiju pterosaurs known as the Flock that roosted there. He scaled many ranges until he found Flock droppings.

The Flock were the most intelligent kaiju on Earth. They were armed with a sharp keel that protruded from their chests. Their favorite tactic was to ram their keels into their opponents. The keels could split a kaiju's skull, although the Flock had never been able to crack Noregon's bio-steel armor. As flying creatures, they could destroy the reptile men's airborne machines.

The droppings were dry. He scraped them with his forepaw to work up an odor. Once he got the droppings' scent, he was able to locate a Flock colony. The group was roosting in the mountains on a stretch of land the humans called Vancouver Island. It was a beautiful place, bristling with pines.

A half dozen Flock juveniles were down on the coast. They appeared to be admiring their reflections in the crisp, blue water. Then one of them snapped its head into the water and pulled back with a fish wriggling in its mouth.

Adults circled overhead. Noregon was able to approach the youngsters since he was an herbivore.

The juveniles were ten meters tall. Fur covered their bodies and scales covered their limbs and faces. They were white in color with pink wing tips. Their beaks were large like a toucan's, and they had a sail atop their heads. Presently they had their sails folded down.

Noregon spoke to them with grunts and snorts, offering them a chance to go on a raid against the reptile men. He promised to protect them against the reptile men's energy weapons. The juveniles were leery. He grunted, telling them that the reptile men were good to eat, better than humans.

The one male youngster in the group cawed, "How would you know, plant eater?

His sisters stared at Noregon intently, waiting for an explanation.

Noregon was stumped. "Because…" He paused to think and then grunted, "The reptile men are stronger than the humans. That means less fat to ruin the flavor of the meat."

The juveniles cackled. Fat makes meat taste good, one of them clucked. Another cawed plant eater in the same tone one would say, "You dummy!"

They all cawed, chanting, "Plant eater! Plant eater!"

Noregon grunted further, challenging them to give reptile men a try. "Be brave! Eat new things."

The juveniles exchanged glances. Noregon could tell they were discussing with their telepathy. When they came to a decision, a female grabbed a fish out of the water and plopped it at Noregon's feet. The juveniles were striking a deal. If he proved his bravery by eating this fish, they would prove their bravery by eating a reptile man.

Noregon thought that was unfair. He offered them meat. They ate meat. He ate plants. They should offer him a new kind of plant.

The juveniles went back to talking amongst themselves with their minds. Before they could come to a decision, a Flock matriarch landed amongst the juveniles, scattering them. She stood fifty meters in height.

The matriarch introduced herself by hissing her name: Razor Beak. With a name like that, it was clear she was also issuing a warning.

Noregon introduced himself with a growl: The Mighty One, Heavy of Foot and Sharp of Nose. That was the name he had given himself. He emphasized his weight by thumping his tail, startling the birds in the trees.

Razor Beak explained in a series of clucks that the matriarchs decide when and where the juveniles conduct raids. The adult Flock members used raids to teach their young how to fight. The matriarchs had already made up their minds that the reptile men were too dangerous for this purpose. So, they continued to raid human settlements instead.

Noregon countered her argument with a series of grunts and snorts. The humans were dying out. Soon there will be no more humans.

Who would you raid then, Noregon grunted, the reptile men?

Razor Beak narrowed her eyes at him, wondering why he should care.

Noregon lowered his head, signaling that he was willing to submit himself to a telepathic probe. Razor Beak used her telepathy to find the truth. She learned that when he was in a playful mood, he destroyed buildings. Humans were the only ones who could rebuild the structures. If they became extinct, the world's supply of buildings would run out.

Noregon asked her with several grunts if she hadn't noticed it was getting difficult to find any humans. Razor Beak admitted that she had. Even so, while searching his mind she found that he was friends with Super Allosaurus. Super Allosaurus had tried to eat her. She could not trust him.

Noregon sighed. His breath exhaled in raspy gusts. You are looking for an excuse to be difficult, he growled.

She scrutinized him for a while and then clucked, Come back tomorrow.

Razor Beak then flew away to join the other matriarchs.

At dawn Noregon returned to the same spot where he had met the juveniles. Razor Beak was waiting for him. She announced the matriarchs' decision with several clucks and a series of chitters. The matriarchs agreed that Noregon was right. Even though kaiju and humans have been enemies, many kaiju had become dependent upon the humans. Noregon needed their buildings for recreation. The Flock needed human warriors to train their offspring. And others enjoyed human flesh as a delicacy. With that thought Razor Beak called out to one other kaiju who was present.

Golgotha, the giant mantis, rose up from her hiding place in the woods and stepped out onto the coast. This was too good to be true! Noregon grunted, asking if Golgotha was really going to help.

Razor Beak bowed her head, signaling that this was true. The matriarchs had used their telepathy to communicate with Golgotha. They learned from her that she was also having trouble finding humans. Razor Beak's Flock, even though they were experiencing the same difficulty, assumed there had to be humans somewhere. Humans numbered in the billions. Who could imagine them going extinct? Noregon earned respect from the Flock and the mantis for being the first to recognize this problem.

The reptile men had been rounding up humans in a city not far from the island. They had been doing this for some time. The Flock avoided the area because the reptiles had built a settlement in the city. The settlement was heavily armed. Razor Beak suggested if they destroyed this settlement, the rounding up process should cease and the humans in that area would have a chance to replenish their numbers.

Noregon wanted to go at once but Razor Beak told him to wait and dispatched a scout to the settlement to be sure it was still in operation. When the scout returned, she was out of breath. She had taken a beating. The reptile men had shot her many times with their energy beams. There were burn marks marring her white fur and scales.

The scout confirmed that, yes, the reptile bipeds were still using the settlement to corral humans by the thousands. She used her telepathy to pass her memories of what she saw to Noregon, Razor Beak, and Golgotha. The reptiles used an island in a harbor to gather the humans. This atoll was a sheet of pavement where the humans docked their watercraft, although there were no such vessels in sight.

The island was connected to the mainland by two bridges, one on either side of the isle. Each bridge had a gate to restrict access between the island and mainland. It was an excellent place to herd humans. The scout's memories showed that the reptiles had erected gun towers on the mainland, three west of the island and four on the other side. Further up the coast were four large black structures flanked by two under construction. Their ominous architecture made them stand out from the human-constructed buildings.

Razor Beak showed Noregon and Golgotha old memories of the reptile settlement, showing that the settlement had grown bigger from the last time the Flock had seen it. The kaiju agreed that if they destroyed this base of operations, they would save hundreds of thousands of humans. They might even save the humans from extinction.

Noregon was ready to go, but the reptile men were on alert.The scout suggested that they wait until the reptile men lowered their guard. The matriarchs decided to wait three days. Noregon could attack the settlement right away, if he wanted, but he would be heading out alone. He needed someone to destroy the flying machines, however so he reluctantly waited.

Noregon remained on the coast and munched pine trees. The juveniles were fascinated by his eating habits. They did not understand how anyone could survive without meat or, for that matter.

One of them perched atop his back and spotted something tasty stuck in the grooves of his armored plates. It cawed, Lice!

Excited, the juveniles flocked onto his back. Like a rhino on an African plain, Noregon kept munching while the juveniles pulled out the giant lice from between his armor plates and gobbled them up. They scratched along the grooves for the parasites' eggs, digging out old skin, lice droppings, and other detritus. No longer did the juveniles call him Plant Eater. Instead, Noregon became lovingly known as Lice Bringer.

Every morning, the young members of the Flock flew down from their roosts to see if he had any more lice. One female in particular was first to visit him and was the last to leave before nightfall. Her Flock did not give her a name because she had no distinguishing characteristics nor had she accomplished any notable feats. Since lice were her favorite food, Noregon named her Lice Eater. She liked it, and subsequently became his friend.

On the day of the attack, Razor Beak told Noregon to go on ahead, as he was the slowest. The Flock and the mantis would catch up once he attacked.

Noregon lumbered down the coast, heading south. Lice Eater accompanied him, against the wishes of her mother. She could not be dissuaded. Lice Eater was hooked on lice like a kid on candy. She expected him to attract more of the oversized parasites.

Lice Eater rode on Noregon's back. He grunted to her, advising the young flying kaiju that he did not know how he had found the last batch of lice. He could not guarantee he would find more.

Lice Eater chittered at him, telling him not to worry. The lice would find him.

Noregon reached the southernmost tip of the island. It faced the harbor, where there were many islands. The atoll he was heading toward was deep in the harbor's belly. In the distance he and Lice Eater could see flying machines descending from the sky. Another harvest was in progress.

With a grunt, Noregon forewarned Lice Eater he was going into the water. She hopped off his back and fluttered down to the ground. He lumbered into the endless stream. It was too difficult for him to swim because of his weight, but he could hold his breath for a long time. He walked along the seabed towards his destination, and upon approaching it he stopped to make sure no one saw him coming. He then crept forward and hunkered down among the sunken ships.

Noregon skulked forward a little further and laid down among the shipwrecks, pausing for a reaction. He was mimicking what Super Allosaurus would do when he was hunting prey: creep forward and then crouch. Creep forward and then crouch. When close enough -- attack! Since the reptile men had not responded Noregon assumed he was doing it right although his fat, pillar-like legs lacked the feline grace of Super Allosaurus.

When Noregon arrived at the island, he noted that reptile men with blue ridges on their uniforms were standing watch on the piers. This was the moment to attack!

He leapt for the surface and crashed into a grid made of a see-through material. Noregon did not notice this transparent barrier until he bashed into it. The grid covered the whole bay.

The reptiles spun around. Seeing that their lattice held, they motioned to their comrades to proceed with the harvest.

Undaunted, Noregon leapt again. This time his spear-pointed snout got caught in the net. He wriggled to get himself loose. Slowly, his snout slipped from the grid. Before he slid completely free a reptile guard touched a device that was attached to his wrist. The lattice emitted a hum and magnetically pulled Noregon back into its grip.

The armored kaiju twisted side to side but couldn't get loose. His lungs ached for relief. He had been in the water for a long time already, and if he did not break loose soon, he would drown. Noregon banged on the grid with his forepaw. It seemed to have been made of material that was as durable as his body armor.

Lice Eater flapped overhead. He did not expect her to follow him all this way. Nevertheless, she did, and the young flying monster looked distressed. She feared for his life.

Because he knew she looked up to him, Noregon doubled his determination. The armored beast balled his paw into a fist and hammered the grid until he smashed through the barrier. He then broke the surface of the water with a thunderous roar.

The humans awaiting to be crowded into the flying machines screamed. They stampeded toward the bridges on the far side of the island while the guards near Noregon tried to flee from him. This proved futile as the armored kaiju trampled the bipedal reptiles underfoot like fleas beneath a steamroller.

The gun towers opened fire on him. His armor withstood their fusillade, however. Noregon lumbered down the island, an unstoppable force. He drove the bipeds in his midst, humans and reptilians alike, toward the bridges. Lice Eater landed on his back and cawed in praise of his might.

At the gates, the reptile guards fired arcs of electricity from their batons, felling the humans coming toward them like wheat. The humans that had been struck by the electric bolts shook uncontrollably, with many rolling off the bridge. Unless those guards were destroyed, the humans would not be able to escape the island.

While Noregon considered the best approach for an attack, Golgotha flew into view. The giant insect buzzed over the city on the mainland, landed behind the eastern gate, and started snagging reptiles on the barbs of her forelimbs. She then stuffed the otherworldly creatures into her mandibles. The humans on the eastern bridge poured toward the western gate, terrified of the mantis. They crushed the people who were already on the western bridge, and more bodies fell into the water.

Then the gun towers intensified their fire. Their beams zinged dangerously close to Lice Eater. Taking that as a direct challenge, she flew toward the closest tower. It adjusted its sights from Noregon to her and shot the flying kaiju down with one searing blast. She squawked in alarm and fell into the water. The wounded juvenile kaiju clung to the grid, but her grip was slipping. She would drown without help.

Noregon looked from the humans to Lice Eater. Who should he help? Out of impulse, he decided to save Lice Eater first. Noregon trotted a few steps toward one side of the island then galloped over to the other and dove into the water. His massive weight busted the grid and washed Lice Eater onto the shore.

He climbed out of the water through the fresh hole he had made in the grid to check on her. Lice Eater laid on her side like a drenched butterfly. The flesh on her right arm, shoulder, and chest bubbled from the searing wound she had sustained. She looked up and cawed to show that she still had the strength to live. The whimpering sound her cry made also told Noregon she no longer had the strength to fight, either.

So long as she survived was all that mattered, however. Noregon proceeded to knock down the towers on the western shore and ripped the gate from the western bridge. He backed up so the humans could flee to the mainland. They gushed through the exit like a flood.

For the first time the reptile men were in a state of panic. Their herd of humans were scattering like ants. As the reptiles tried to stem the tide, Golgotha flew down, grabbed them, and devoured them.

Noregon searched for the Flock. They should have been here by now. The sky was clear, however; not a single pterosaur was in sight.

The flying machines fired energy beams at Golgotha and deployed spheres that emitted high-frequency sound waves toward Noregon. Noregon experienced the same symptoms as others caught in this ultra-sound field: Rapid heart rate. Queasy stomach. Aching head.

Golgotha retaliated against the flying machines with her own energy-based distance weapon. Her beam pierced the furthest vessel in the distance and. an explosion burst from the top of the craft. It dropped into the harbor, sending a plume of water up into the air. The water rained down, drenching the shores on either side of the harbor. The remaining two machines ascended straight up into the sky and out of sight.

Noregon wailed to the insectoid kaiju for help. It did no good, however. Golgotha communicated by scent, not sound. She resumed her search for more reptile bipeds, oblivious to his suffering.

Frustrated, Noregon dove back into the water where the piercing hum could not reach him. From the bottom of the harbor he trudged around the island. The flying machine that Golgotha had felled had created a third opening in the grid. He used it to reach the eastern shore. The alien machines were waiting for him there and they spewed the deadly combo of their energy beams and piercing sound waves.

Noregon collapsed under the blistering attack. His stomach lurched in prelude to vomiting its contents. He then panted before his eyes slowly closed. Noregon laid in a heap of bio-steel armor and weary limbs.

The spheres silenced their hum and the turrets ceased fire. Noregon knew the alien machines were smart. He had moments before they detected his ruse. Quickly, he got up onto his feet and spun around. His tail swept a gun tower off its foundation and sent it hurtling at the spheres. The objects separated, allowing the wreckage to fly through their ranks. It startled Golgotha when it crashed near her. She knew Noregon was her ally, so she assumed the wreckage came from the spheres and fired her ray at them. The devices exploded upon being struck, scattering metal fragments across the harbor.

After toppling the remaining towers, Noregon marched toward the alien buildings. To his right, the sides of a high rise lowered into the ground to reveal a bipedal figure encased in black armor. The figure stood a hundred meters in height. The face was smooth with no mouth or organs for hearing and smelling, at least none that were apparent. The eyes were a deeper shade of black and square-shaped with rounded corners.

The gigantic figure came to life with a subtle jerk and a soft hum. Its footsteps made a heavy, clanking noise as it strode forward and stopped between Noregon and the alien buildings. The creature smelled of oil and the tangy scent of warm alloys instead of flesh and blood. A machine man. That was what it must have been.

It pointed a black metallic finger at Noregon. Even though the metal biped did not speak, its gesture emoted with as much force as a shout. It was if the metal creature said, "You! Stop!" It ordered the kaiju trespasser to leave by pointing toward the harbor.

Noregon bellowed at the machine man as a final warning to step aside, and not pausing to give the machine a chance to leave, he charged. The machine man was as lithe as its builders. It dropped to one knee, caught Noregon by the chin, rose him up, and slammed the heel of its other hand into Noregon's unarmored chest. The move was accomplished in smooth, sweeping motions.

Noregon flopped onto his back, kicking dust off the pavement for several city blocks. The reverberation caught Golgotha's attention. She spun around, spotted the machine man, and reared up, hissing and fluttering her wings. The machine ignored her and assumed another combative stance, waiting patiently for Noregon.

Noregon coughed. His bruised sternum ached. He flailed on his back, helpless.

Golgotha fired her energy beam at the machine man from her third eye. The titanic automaton stood up, turned on its heel toward her, and fired an energy beam back from its forearm. Her beam warmed the metal on the machine man's chest to a bright orange color, but his retaliatory ray punched through her exoskeleton. The mammoth mantis's life juices spurted from the opening. Golgotha scrambled behind a row of tall buildings. From there she poked her head out to see what else the machine monster could do before getting back into the fray.

Machine Man spread his feet and hands, getting back into his combative stance while waiting with the patience of stone for Noregon to get back up. Once the sting from the blow eased, Noregon rolled back onto his feet and bellowed to show he was still full of fight.

Lice Eater cawed Lice Bringer! to show she believed in him.

Not wanting to disappoint her, Noregon charged. Machine Man delivered a series of kicks and chops with the sides of his hands. Noregon rolled away, bruised but eager for more. He charged again. Machine Man, with skilled precision, delivered another series of blows which ended with him holding Noregon up in the air by the throat. An aperture opened in the palm of his right hand. A sunburst of energy blew out of the opening, struck Noregon in the gut, and carried him across the docks. He crashed into a red, eight-story building, bringing the whole structure down into a heap of bricks.

Smoke wisped from the scorched scales on Noregon's belly. Angry, he roared, yet he was not sure how he was going to pull off the next charge. He had further to run this time and he was getting tired.

However, he quickly realized that the extra distance might work in his favor. Pushing himself to the fullest, Noregon barreled down the dock like a charging rhino. When his momentum reached its peak, he leapt into the air. Machine Man braced for the attack, but instead of leaping on top of the automaton, Noregon came crashing down onto the ground. The pavement turned to dust under his weight as he smashed into the dock. The concussion knocked Machine Man off his feet.

Both monsters raced to get back up. Noregon won that race, spun around, and swept the machine creature off its feet with his tail. Before Machine Man could rise, Noregon hammered him with his tail and then sprinted away, spun, and charged. He smashed into Machine Man, ramming the metal biped into the tallest of the alien buildings. Structure and man-machine collapsed into a pile of debris.

Noregon staggered back. His lungs puffed for air. His limbs ached. This was it. His vitality was spent.

But his opponent was down. Momentarily, anyway.

Machine Man rose up out of the wreckage. The metal plate on his chest that Golgotha had shot with her ray cooled to its original color. After all the effort both monsters had spent, the gigantic android remained unharmed and ready.

Noregon groaned. Machine Man strode forward to deliver another series of blows. Dispirited, Noregon was about willing to run.

Then Machine Man stopped. He became confused on which direction he should invest his attention as he looked from the left to the right. Picking a track, he raised his arm to fire his destructive beam. Before he did, Razor Beak flew over him, ramming her keel into the side of his head. No sooner had he recovered from the blow then the Flock matriarchs took their turns ramming into his head with their own keels. They attacked from different directions to keep Machine Man off balance. The impacts of their keels caused sparks to flash from his armored head.

Seeing her opportunity, Golgotha flew out from behind cover and fired her energy beam into the weakened metal. Her ray punched through the alien alloy, setting the machine's innards ablaze.

The excitement helped Noregon find his second wind. He charged into Machine Man, bringing the metal man down. Noregon stomped on top of the humanoid machine and his armored plates broke off the android's chassis.

Golgotha hovered nearby. Her jeweled lens glowed, ready to fire. Noregon promptly got out of her way.

Golgotha traced her beam up and down the machine man's body, finding exposed synthetic organs. Explosions rippled from head to toe, culminating into a single report. The detonation engulfed the remaining alien buildings. They too died with a bang and a flash of brilliant light. Metal fragments rained down like confetti.

The battle was won. The settlement was destroyed. Noregon roared and tossed his tail up in celebration.

Lice Eater cawed, Lice Bringer! Lice Bringer!

She became even more excited when her mother landed beside her. Razor Beak also landed there to check on her progeny. Lice Eater's mother gently picked up the injured juvenile in her beak and joined the matriarchs on their flight back to the mountains. Razor Beak gave Noregon a narrowed-eye glare before taking off.

Noregon was initially unsure why she was angry with him. Then he remembered his promise to protect the juveniles from the reptile men's weapons. Well, Lice Eater survived. As far as he was concerned, he had fulfilled his promise.

Golgotha hovered over him and released an odor that reminded him of the scent of flowers. She then flew away. Noregon understood that she had spoken to him. He did not know what the odor meant but it must have said something nice.

Alone yet satisfied with the day's work, the mighty armored kaiju trekked from the ruined settlement to the undamaged section of the city. He could see the humans scattering in the distance. Noregon roared at them, encouraging them to be fruitful and multiply.

143

And to build more buildings.

END

HERE WE GO! FIGHT!

Kane Gilmour

Editor's Note: This story was originally featured in Tim Marquitz's anthology _MECH: Age of Steel_ from Ragnarok Publications. Wild Hunt Press is proud to reprint it here with the editor's and author's permission!

Transparent acid rain spurted from pale green clouds surrounding the low mountains on the horizon of the base. Captain Justin Macumber looked out at the threatening storm through an armored two-foot-thick block of ballistic liquiglass that served as a viewport in the nano-metal wall of the craft. He sneered at the boiling clouds with their deadly spray of corrosive moisture. He and his crew of the _S.S. Nagai_ knew all too well what the oncoming storm clouds signified.

Yet another attack from the _Verengeretti._

The swirling clouds billowed towards the base. Except for their pea-soup coloration, they looked for all the world like a typical typhoon swarming over the hills from the South China Sea, which was just thirty-five miles west, as the crow flew. But Macumber knew what they were. A small valley was nestled just past the first line of the Zambales Mountains, between the shore and Mount Pinatubo. Its surface had been blasted to the consistency of glowing uranium glass, following battle after battle. The storm had started above the valley, and not out at sea. Much like all the storms in the last bloody eighteen years had. Pinatubo, and the five-mile radius around the volcano, had a different name now.

Zero Point.

Ever since the Verengeretti had first arrived in a turbulent fever of natural disasters and epic Cyclopean creatures with tangles of tentacles and insatiable appetites for concrete and human beings. There wasn't very much left of the man-made composite or the men who had made it these days, but still the invaders came, in wave after dreadful wave.

No one on Earth knew why the cephalopod creatures had chosen to invade the planet with an entry point into the human dimension over the island of Luzon, in the region formerly known as the nation of the Philippines. They hadn't been able to communicate with the creatures in any way. Even the name – *Verengeretti* -- had been given to the creatures by an Italian xenobiologist. They had no idea what the creatures might call themselves. But as for why they had come to Luzon, Captain Macumber had been stationed on the humid island long enough to study its tumultuous history. He had his own theory about the place.

It was cursed.

For centuries before the invasion, the island had been home to devastating tropical storms, destruction from tsunamis, human wars, earthquakes from the clash of two subduction zones straddling either side of the mountains like sardines in a pressure tin, and the biggest volcanic eruptions of the 20th, 21st, and 22nd centuries.

The island was the homeland of apocalyptic destruction.

"Mr. Pekkarin, status please," Macumber called, stepping back from the two-foot-thick viewing port and returning to his command chair at the side of the room.

Pekkarin did not glance in his direction -- no one on the bridge did. They all wore helmets that completely covered their heads, and the visors on the front faceplates were all digitally darkened on the exterior. On the insides, they would be viewing multiple data images that mimicked the curved television screens of the 21st century, showing all the views outside the craft far better than the natural viewport Macumber had just utilized. But the captain liked to use his own eyes sometimes, as opposed to relying solely on technology.

Despite his head being obscured from view in his helmet, Pekkarin had clearly heard his captain, though, and the young man replied through the inner-ear auditory system. This made it sound to Macumber as if the ensign's response was just a thought in his own head.

"No movement yet, sir."

The captain clambered into his gel chair, allowing the seat to envelop him. The others in the room -- six of them -- were all cocooned in their own chairs, reclined as if sleeping in beds. Robotic arms gently lowered Macumber's own helmet onto his head, snugging the locking mechanism in place. Neo-metal shells closed over his limbs like several tiny coffins. They hissed and filled with astro-gel that would absorb any and all impacts to the bridge, or to his body. The seat reclined, and he felt the sway as his body moved backward. Once his seat was fully activated, the zero-G compensators would keep him effectively weightless in his gel

147

container; even if the ship were to roll repeatedly, he would feel as if his body remained level.

Unless one of the squids bashed the ship hard enough to breach it, that is.

He'd seen that kind of mess before, and the results were not pretty. But now wasn't the time to mentally revisit the horrors of the war, and he chided himself with a gentle shake of his head for allowing his thoughts to drift. The chair moved with his body, the gel sluicing around him to accommodate his new position.

The view before his eyes remained dark. The digital and optical systems would remain dormant until he told them to activate with a verbal command. That was how he liked it. The calm before the storm. He would stay still in his gel swaddle, his head shrouded in darkness, waiting for Pekkarin to inform him of First Movement. It wasn't quite meditation for Macumber, just a chance to rest his eyes.

"Here we go," Pekkarin said though his earpiece.

"Activate," Macumber mumbled into his helmet.

His retinas stung briefly from the instant brightness of the screens leaping to life all around his eyes. He blinked twice, and his vision resolved.

Several screens appeared before his eyes. Views in all directions around the craft were now on display. In the upper right of his periphery, he could see a zoomed view of the distant acid clouds. He turned his eyes up toward that screen, and its view expanded and intensified, filling his field of vision.

The screens all tracked eye movement and would anticipate what a viewer wanted to see more of, moving that image to center and enhancing it. The training for the program had been intense, but Macumber was now so used to the transition between twelve images and one that his mind no longer even registered the change. Thought and action were one. If anything, he found the eye strain on changing depth-of-field to his unaided eyes was more of a challenge these days.

Waving strands of spaghetti-like purple tentacles descended from the sky, the creature levitating by means human scientists had yet to ascertain. As Macumber watched, the beast dropped from the boiling cumulus clouds, its upper body descending after the army of waving tendrils and covered in armor like a brick-red balloon wrapped in angular overlapping blood vessels. The creature was clearly some kind of octopus or squid-like thing, but the Verengeretti were 200 feet tall, and instead of eight limbs, they had hundreds.

In the last two years, after the humans had finally started to fight back with brains instead of only brawn, the Verengeretti had upped their game, covering the upper bodies of their invader scouts with the thick, ropey armor that covered most of their bulbous head-bodies -- with the exceptions of the base under the tentacles and a single, sinister, angled eye slit on the front. The overall appearance always somehow reminded Macumber of a Japanese samurai helmet's faceplate. And the armor made the bastards that much harder to kill.

"Fight!" Macumber ordered, and Pekkarin sent the craft into action.

***

Rockets engaged, launching the *S.S. Nagai*, a Polonium-class mechanized battle chassis, into the sky, leaving the gray, neo-metal and asphalt launch pad behind. Officially a World Security Force battleship, the 300-foot-long vehicle was known to its crew by an alternate moniker: *King Raidizer*.

The massive flying ship resembled the metal Naval vessels of the 20th century. At least, it did until it reached its destination, when thrusters lifted it vertical to reveal that the top surface of the craft, which was bristling with gun emplacements and other armaments, was in fact the front of a huge, humanoid robot. Its feet were known as the "bow," and the head, where the bridge was located, was technically the "stern" of the vessel. To keep things simple in battle, those terms were still used when the craft was in its vertical orientation as well. Constructed entirely of modern materials, the outer shell looked like it was shiny, old-world metal, but parts of the structure were astro-gel or a viscous liquid that excelled at redistributing vibrations from impacts. Other parts of the hull were high tech arsenals of nanobots that could repair damage to the ship in mid-flight – or in mid-battle while in its robot mode.

Designed to be manned by a crew of 600 human sailors and officers, but officially rated for duty with a skeleton crew of just 200, Raidizer actually ran with a crew of just 170 people dispersed throughout the craft's body. Trained humans were just too hard to come by in a war that had lasted for far too long.

As Macumber watched the armored squid descend below the clouds, Raidizer rocketed toward the creature at a speed close to its maximum velocity, flying feet first. Impact would occur in seconds.

"Commencing SK attack," Pekkarin announced.

The attack was formally known as a "forward thrust plantar action," but like with most things in the WSF, the ensigns renamed it something simple that they could pronounce under the stress of combat. In this case, the *shitkicker* attack was comprised of hydraulic pistons re-angling Raidizer's feet from their normal, pointed-toe position in flight to a non-aerodynamic, flat-footed orientation. The stern thrusters were then engaged at the last second, smashing the soles of the huge robot's flat feet into the opponent in a rocket-assisted stomp.

A second after Pekkarin made the announcement, Macumber felt a vibration gently rock his body in the impact fluid of his command chair, and he knew they had delivered a wallop to the creature. He watched on a viewscreen as the hungry squid, its front armor buckled inward slightly from the collision, began to fly backward and away from Raidizer.

Macumber wouldn't let it get far, though.

"Pivot and prepare rockets one and two," he commanded.

"Aye, Sir," Ensign Callabera announced.

Callabera was one of two women on the bridge, and she served as the chief weapons expert on deck. Macumber heard the ensign quickly mutter to her weapons crews in the robot's left forearm. They controlled the hand and all its munitions, and they were ordered to form the hand into a fist while preparing to launch the missiles mounted in each of Raidizer's knuckles.

Pekkarin followed Macumber's first direction and brought the craft from its battleship mode into the vertical robot orientation. Rockets on all sides of the lower legs and its back kept Raidizer in a hover several hundred feet off the ground. From outside, the move looked both fluid and threatening, but Macumber knew the Verengeretti were not impressed by swagger.

"Fire one and two," he ordered.

Twin trails of smoke spiraled away from Raidizer's extended fist as the projectiles --100-pound air-to-surface Devastation-class missiles with rotary-drilling nanobot warheads capable of puncturing any known Earth substance -- launched and streaked across the sky, darting and re-angling left and right past the Verengeretti's horde of defensive tendrils. The missiles erupted against the armored surface of the creature's head, hitting close to the top of its helmet. Macumber observed as the destructive cloud of nanobots swarmed over the huge alien's protection, while smoke from the explosion that had deployed them temporarily rose up to obscure his view.

Before he could order a second strike, however, the squid's tentacles pulled in toward the swarm of black mechanized insects covering its body.

What is it doing now?

Macumber's job as the captain of the vessel was never as simple as just presenting the crew with orders. He had to out-think the alien Verengeretti, and this was made further challenging by the fact that the creatures never fought the same way twice -- they adapted. Or evolved. No one was sure.

The Verengeretti had been breaching the fabric of space-time from their dimension for years. Always one at a time, but always fighting differently. The fissure would seal as soon as one came through. All attempts to breach the fissure in reverse, with all manner of probes and weaponry, had ended in complete failure. All studies of the invaders' strange biology was thwarted by their tendency to melt into a watery sludge upon death. Shortly thereafter their liquid remains would evaporate into the atmosphere, leaving only known gasses and something acidic like hydrogen sulfide -- but which wasn't.

Science had utterly failed at finding the chink in the armor of the alien menace, so the surviving militaries of the planet had formed the World Security Force and ordered a new tack. If they couldn't figure out how to stop the extradimensional incursions from happening, they could at least create weapons with enough variety and brawn to brutalize each tentacled intruder as it breached the world.

Macumber watched the final ropey tendril retreat into the nanobot swarm. All he could see now was a dark cloud of the miniature robots. But as the last tentacle slipped inside the swarm, he saw the black cloud of penetrating nanobots ripple, like a wake left in water after the movement of a large mammal or fish beneath it.

But the ripple moved horizontally, across what would be the squid's bulk.

"Defensive measures!" he shouted, despite the lack of any need to.

He could speak in a soft whisper and the audio compensators would enhance his voice for the crew. Luckily it worked in reverse as well, and his shouted command would convey all the urgency of the message without the volume.

A grim smile crept over Macumber's face. The crew was so well trained that even before he had finished the second syllable of the order, Pekkarin was dropping Raidizer from the sky to the glinting, glass-coated foothills below them; while Callabera was simultaneously ordering her rocket crews to reload.

Lieutenant Rutledge, the ship's defensive armaments officer, ordered the radiation and proton shields up over the craft. "Shields. Launch chaff."

Macumber blinked, and his viewscreen retreated to the upper right corner of his vision. He glanced left to a view just ahead of Raidizer's broad, armament-covered chest. Then he watched as two three-foot-long metal rods were forcibly ejected like spinning torpedoes, flinging away from the robot in both directions like flipping drum-major batons.

Macumber switched cameras again with a blink, and he saw what he'd expected.

The Verengeretti had begun to spin at incomprehensible speeds inside the nanobot cloud, its tentacles pulling in to whip horizontally around its core. Suddenly, the spin ejected the drilling micro-robots away like the metal fragments in a grenade. The bot-swarm shot away from the creature in all directions -- much of it heading for Raidizer. Then the Verengeretti charged toward its attacker, following close on the heels of the spray of drilling insects, the squid's tentacles still whirling and ready to deliver a spinning battering of their own.

This is going to be close, Macumber thought. *Way too close.*

***

Raidizer hit the ground, the soles of its forty-foot-long feet mashing through the glazed glass and sand surface of the ground and driving deeply into the soil under the battle-scarred façade.

"Arms up," Macumber ordered, and Rutledge repeated the command to the defense teams throughout the chassis.

The defense teams knew their jobs. Raidizer bent at the knees, dropping one to the fractured ground and crossing the robot's forearms over its head to withstand the oncoming collision. As the flung nanobots embedded in Raidizer's hull its matte gray-and-white exterior scrambled to critical areas, both to dull the impact and to repair any damage sustained.

The repelled devastation bots approached first. While most of the nanobots followed the chaff off to either side, a good third of the swarm hit in a series of ballistic pings. Most followed their programming and ricocheted away from their mother ship. Some of them, damaged by contact with the enemy -- or perhaps somehow overwritten by the Verengeretti -- attacked Raidizer's hull with the same vigor they had just used on the squid. They would be neutralized soon enough, though, by the defensive bots roaming the ship's hull. The rotating ball of fury with the multitudes of electrically stinging tentacles barreling toward the ship was the true threat.

"Wait for it," Macumber said softly.

On the viewscreen, the spinning squid shifted to a forty-five-degree angle, its tentacles ceasing their whirl and instead leading the attack. The creature's sharp beak, located under the legs at its bottom, began snapping in anticipation of a tasty snack. Over the exterior audio systems, Macumber could hear the rhythmic clacking. Without the computer's dampening, each mandibular strike would sound like a peal of thunder.

"And... now. Axes deploy."

Macumber's command was repeated, and he felt the gentle sway in his chair. Raidizer dove forward to the ground in a somersault, the robot's hands reaching over its shoulders to the handles of two crossed axes mounted on its back—the lower hull when the vessel was in flight as a battleship. The handles were half the length of the ship, and the ends held massive, double-sided, curving blades, which were engineered from the same material as the drill bits in the nanobot swarm.

As the Verengeretti's fusillade of wavering purple appendages scattered at the sudden movement of Raidizer below them, the robot rolled and swung upward, slicing two deep gouges in the creature's underside. The cuts bit deeply on either side of the squid's snapping beak, spraying acidic blood and sending a caul-like membrane to splatter on the cracked, blackened ground.

Raidizer completed its roll crouched on its feet, then sprang up into the air, spinning as it did so, until the superstructure chest faced the back of the still-moving invader.

"Fire main guns."

Unlike earlier versions of the battle-chassis, Raidizer was designed first and foremost as a battleship, to be used in its horizontal configuration. The entire topside of the vessel – the front of the robot – was covered in 16-inch guns on swiveling turrets. Instead of the 50-caliber ammunition of old, the cannon fired plasma pulses that could core through mountains. Unfortunately, Macumber knew they couldn't penetrate the ropey Verengeretti armor. But enough sustained blasts could weaken the alien protection so that the axes could bite through. Or he could just keep out-maneuvering the beast, so Raidizer could keep swiping at the creature's unprotected underside.

The blitzkrieg assault of the plasma blasts peppered the rear of the beast's armored head-covering, pocking the cabled surface, but as Macumber had guessed, not penetrating it. The Verengeretti quickly recovered from the feigned vulnerability of the robot, and twirled hard, several of its purple appendages lashing out and seizing around Raidizer's upper left leg. Instantly a burst of electricity blasted out of the creature and sizzled through the proton shields, throwing off sparks in all directions.

"Sweep and launch chest measures," Macumber said, not perturbed by the invader's tentacles having grabbed hold of his ship.

Raidizer's arms swung inward, bringing the axes in a low downward sweep, neatly slicing through the attached tentacles and three others that were in the process of reaching for the leg. Their armor was strong, but the Verengeretti's uncovered flesh was no match for the giant robot's blades.

As soon as the sweep completed, and before the creature could recoil in pain, huge missiles embedded in Raidizer's chestplate launched at point-blank range. The ten-ton tritonal warheads produced a pressure wave that rocked Raidizer back and down onto its feet, while the squid -- unprepared for the blast – was hurled away to careen into the side of a low mountain. A plume of dust erupted into the air, even as the noise from the blast – muted to acceptable levels in the crewmembers' helmets – was replaced by the keening, chittering wail of the creature.

"We've hurt it," Callabera reported.

A younger, less experienced captain would have pressed the attack, rushing in to fire more rockets and swing Raidizer's axes like a madman. However, Macumber knew the fight was far from over. Now wasn't the time to press on; it was the time to assess damage and prepare for the next round.

"Status, Mr. Rutledge?"

"The shields held up pretty well, sir. Just a twenty percent dip from that blast. We'll have them back up soon."

Rutledge sounded confident, and Macumber was glad for it. The lieutenant was new aboard the ship, but very efficient. Still, it wasn't the craft's defensive measures Macumber was concerned about. It always came down to ordinance. If they ran out, it would be practically impossible to take the creature down with Raidizer's physical strikes. While the robot could land a hell of a punch, Macumber would need to call in the next battle chassis -- the *S.S. Yardley* -- if he ran out of missiles.

"Callabera?" Macumber prompted. On his viewscreen, the soil and dust of the Verengeretti's faceplant into the side of Mother Earth had yet to clear.

"Sir?"

Before Macumber could issue the order, he was already changing strategy, as a blurring wheel of demolition launched from the dust cloud. The Verengeretti had flung itself from the mountain like a vertical circular saw, its tendrils propelling it across the cracked ground like hundreds of insectoid appendages.

"Brace for 'im –"

He never got the chance to finish the shout. Raidizer was slammed by the whirling pinwheel of tentacles and the armored head attached to them. The blow was akin to receiving a cannonball to the gut. The giant robot was sent sprawling across the valley and mashing into the side of a craggy hillside, the head and shoulders embedded in the ravaged, glowing soil.

Even inside the gel-cushioned compartments for the bridge crew, Macumber could feel that hit. His body tingled as if he had personally received a punch. He knew that the ship would have received damage on that strike. More importantly, if the crews in the limbs hadn't been paying close attention to the viewscreens in their areas they would have been unprepared for the impact. Unprotected by gel, there would be injuries, and probably also casualties.

Rutledge was already pulling in damage reports from his defensive teams while, without needing to be told to do so, Pekkarin had ordered engineering to reverse thrust and pull them from the mountain. Raidizer was back standing on its feet before the Verengeretti had stopped rolling past them from its last strike.

The reports washed over Macumber. Twelve dead. Fifteen injured. Raidizer's right leg thrusters down. Shield damage. Medical teams rushing to the injured. Dwindling armaments. One ax lost. Cannon lost from the head.

The robot's movements would be limited with the leg thrusters gone. The captain did some instant calculations in his head and reached the same conclusion he'd heard in the tone of the voices of his crew as they reported in.

It was clear they wouldn't last until the Yardley arrived.

"Callabera, instruct your team to prepare our own spinning weapon."

***

At a blink, the viewscreen switched to a close-up of the robot's massive left forearm. The smooth gray and white surface was marred by what appeared to be a deep opening that ran along the top of the lower arm. The uninitiated might suspect it was a maintenance trench or something similar. In fact, it was an elaborate weapons system. Before Macumber's eyes, Raidizer's left hand mashed the end of its long ax handle deeply into the slot.

Simultaneously, Pekkarin had raised the arm to a position level with the ground, and another blink by Macumber showed that the spinning squid-creature had come to a stop half a mile further along the valley floor. Another blink brought Macumber's view back to the arm, as the ax stood upright in the slot and canted forward, like a gun pointing up at the sky. Raidizer's left hand swept forward and cocked the ax's handle backward, like an old gunslinger swiping back the hammer on a Colt .45. The giant bladed weapon moved backward to the end of the trench nearest the elbow and locked into place.

"Fire when ready," Macumber ordered.

The ax snapped forward as if it had been launched by a slingshot. The heavy double-sided blades moved forward and tumbled, whipping the tip of the handle out of the slot. The weapon thus spun through the air as an impenetrable wall of slicing, razor-edged death.

Before the ax reached its target – the Verengeretti were still moving slowly after its rolling attack – Macumber issued another order.

"Fire all missiles. I want smoke."

"All?" Callabera questioned.

"All. Then, tell your team to evacuate the fist."

Macumber could hear the soft gasp that someone -- he thought it was Rutledge -- made. They had never heard that order before, but they all knew exactly what it meant. It was a desperation play.

"Missiles away," Callabera reported.

Macumber watched a river of smoke pour off the front of Raidizer as hundreds of rockets trailed vapor and chem trails.

"Fire main guns, too."

The whirling, flipping ax cracked into the creature's visor slit, the blade embedding the weapon in the armor. However, Macumber could not determine if the flesh underneath had been punctured. Then the maelstrom of missiles impacted the Verengeretti repeatedly, throwing up a billowing black mushroom of smoke, just as he'd wanted. The firing guns on Raidizer's front were creating their own competing screen of gray smoke.

"Fist is ready," Callabera said.

Macumber could hear regret in her voice. "Launch it."

Even through the gel cushioning, the captain could feel the deep rumble shuddering through the giant robot as nuclear motors fired the building-sized, gray robot fist into the battle. The rockets severed the hand from the arm, just aft of the wrist, and the clenched fist resembled an old zeppelin followed by a trail of green flame as it accelerated. A cone of vapor formed behind it as it broke the sound barrier, its tell-tale boom coming just a second later.

Then the massive projectile was lost to view through the cyclone of smoke.

Two seconds later, the eruption of noise -- a thunderous boom of impact and the fingernails-on-blackboard squeal of pain from the alien squid -- was even too loud for the audio dampeners. The result was a bowel-loosening feedback shriek, before the emergency audio settings killed all exterior sound.

Everyone waited in silence, hoping that this fight was over. Hoping the menace from another dimension had finally been silenced, as their audio feeds had been, so they might have a brief reprieve while the creature's tentacles liquefied into the radioactive soil. The tempest of black and gray smoke was dissipating, and a smaller cloud of dirt-brown unfurled within it. Macumber realized the fist-strike had driven the squid into the hill beyond the smoke blizzard, and they were seeing displaced dust and dirt from the ground.

"Pekkarin, can we get some altitude?" the captain asked.

Uncharacteristically, Pekkarin took some time to argue with engineering before he replied. "It will be dodgy, sir, but we should be able to maintain Raidizer orientation and achieve flight. We just won't have much maneuverability."

"That's fine. Take us up."

Macumber switched his viewscreens a few times, taking in the valley around him, as the massive war robot slowly rose into the sky. His view of the dissipating cloud was seen from above, as the robot moved into a less-than-graceful, wobbling hover.

"Movement, sir," Rutledge said, and when he said it, Macumber could hear pain in the man's voice.

He's injured, Macumber thought. And then he quickly forgot about his defense lieutenant. "Four hundred yards west of the smoke."

What?

Macumber switched his viewscreen with a blink, and then his eyes opened wide.

The Verengeretti was climbing up the side of a steep hill, some of its tentacles doing the work as others dragged limp behind it. The ax was still installed in the creature's face, the handle sticking upward like a strange, fancy hat.

It was the back of the creature that caught the captain's interest, though. The armored covering was dented inward in the exact shape of the knuckles of Raidizer's fist. The impact crater in the armor was so deep that Macumber estimated the squid's body would have been compressed by at least half inside the corded helmet.

Then he glanced at the creature's bottom, under the walking and dragging tentacles. Sure enough, the creature had a huge, purple embolism protruding downward from under the armor. It was a bubble of flesh that had been forcefully squeezed out of the invader's shell. Macumber had the idea that if he could pummel that bulge, he might actually rupture the creature in a manner similar to a water balloon.

The Verengeretti didn't appear inclined to give him the chance, though.

Turning and seeing the unsteady robot in the air, the massive squid crouched on its tentacles and launched itself off the side of the mountain, heading straight for Raidizer.

Pekkarin, in a move worthy of a promotion and a medal, dropped giant robot from the air, and brought it backward -- as if it intended to fall on its back -- before he whipped the legs over in a twist. This move brought Raidizer into a crouch on the ground, resting on its feet, the right hand, and the left forearm (now missing its hand).

The squid adjusted its course in mid-flight, so the move accomplished little in the way of evasion.

"Kick and full stern thrust!" Macumber shouted.

Just as the Verengeretti's tentacles wrapped around Raidizer's ankles, the robot thrust one leg backward, connecting with the side of the creature's helmet. Then the thrusters launched both robot and monster backward through the air.

But the loss of ground from which to maneuver was a disadvantage for Raidizer now. The squid used its tentacle to scramble up the robot's back towards its shoulders, where the tentacles wrapped around the head and blasted it with untold millions of amps of electrical discharge.

Damage reports rushed in as the electrical systems weathered the assault. The impact gel on the bridge would also keep the crew safe from the electrical attack should stray lightning bolts find their way past Raidizer's protected outer shell. Macumber was once again more concerned for his support teams in the robot's limbs.

Then an explosion shook the entire structure, and alarms rang out around the ship. The hull had been ruptured.

"Evasive thrash!" Macumber shouted.

Pekkarin relayed the order while Raidizer began to flail its limbs and twist like an epileptic in a berserker rage, trying to fling the squid-like creature from its back. Macumber felt a lurch in his stomach, indicating that the combination of the hull breach and the Verengeretti's electrical discharge had done the unthinkable. Their thruster engines had been knocked out. King Raidizer and the squid were plummeting from the sky.

***

The tangled mass of alien flesh and new-age ferro-organic battleship mashed into the ground with enough thrashing force to send shockwaves throughout the Philippine isles -- not the first time that the cursed land had suffered Richter scale shocks in excess of "7."

"Get us loose, and get us up," Macumber urged.

"Rutledge is dead, sir," Pekkarin's voice came.

Macumber felt a steady sway in his captain's cocoon, indicating the ensign was rolling and flailing Raidizer's limbs in an attempt to disentangle them from the persistent squid.

"Ensign Tubo, take over defense," Macumber ordered, without even considering who should replace the lieutenant.

Mary Tubongbanua was the second woman on the bridge, and like all of them, she had already proven herself in battle many times. There would be time to mourn Rutledge and worry about proper promotions later... if they survived this fight.

"Aye, sir," Tubo replied.

As both 'Tubo' and 'Tubongbanua' were proper Filipina surnames -- and related ones at that -- the ensign had suggested the abbreviated version when signing on with the crew.

Macumber's viewscreen showed Raidizer stagger to its feet. Without the thrusters, they wouldn't be able to take the battle to the sky, and returning to base would be a hassle, too. But between servos and smaller rockets, the robot could still function in battle mode, without the larger thrusters needed for flight.

They had exhausted all their weapons, and with this last tooth-rattling impact after plunging out of the ravaged sky, even the ax that had been lodged in the Verengeretti's eye slit was lost. Raidizer spread its feet in a fighting stance, and the right fist came up, ready for the next attack.

The squid was up on its tentacles, swaying from side to side. Macumber couldn't tell if the movement was a strategy, like a boxer's footwork, or the equivalent of a drunken stagger from the injuries the creature had already sustained. He did note that the protruding sack of flesh below the monster cephalopod's helmet had sprung a leak. The gash oozed a gelatinous substance on the ground, where the wavering tentacles danced in and out of large puddles of the goop.

"Do we have any ordinance left?" Macumber asked Callabera.

He knew he'd ordered them to fire out the guns and the missiles, but he also knew she was savvy enough to maybe have had something hidden up her sleeve.

After a brief pause, where she spoke to someone on her team, asking several times for clarification, she replied. Macumber could hear a strain of embarrassment in her voice.

"Ensign Wallach says he's got an experimental weapon we could try..."

"What is it?" Macumber asked, latching on to this faint sliver of hope.

"I don't really know, sir. I'll put him on."

With that, a screen jumped to Macumber's view containing a small, hairy man in grease-stained white overalls, who was rubbing his hands on an even greasier rag. Macumber wasn't sure if the man was trying to get the grease off his hands and onto the rag, or the other way around.

"Wallach," Macumber said. "What have you got?"

"The Action Missile, Captain," the man replied with a grin, obviously proud of his creation.

"What is it?"

"It's the middle knuckle of the Right Fist, sir. In place of a typical missile placement, we have what only appears to be a missile. Same color scheme and everything. But when launched, it springs forward thirty feet and locks into position when fully extended. It's more of an ejecting knuckle extension than a projectile."

When Macumber's face did not register any emotion, Wallach's grin slowly faded.

After a beat of silence, Macumber spoke again. "That's the stupidest fucking thing I've ever heard."

Wallach's smirk packed its bags and hopped a slow flight to cringing worry. The man's eyes enlarged, fearful for his life if he had wasted too much time to turn the tide of the battle, thus contributing to Raidizer's destruction or – worse – incurring Macumber's wrath.

"But what the hell," Macumber continued. "Prepare to deploy your Action Missile."

Wallach recovered his composure and nodded before his viewscreen switched off.

"Uh, how, exactly, sir?" Callabera asked.

"With extreme, rocket-assisted prejudice," the man said through gritted teeth.

"Aye, sir," Callabera responded, and Macumber heard several others on the bridge echo her enthusiastic sentiments.

The Verengeretti lunged forward, closing the distance, and Macumber ordered a kick. Raidizer took three running steps and launched into a flying sidekick that was minimally assisted by those few gyroscopic rockets still functioning. The impact sent the squid backward, and Raidizer – even injured as it was – landed on its feet, balanced and ready for the next strike.

"Pursue," Macumber ordered. "Multiple punches first. We'll save the secret weapon for a bit."

Pekkarin brought King Raidizer in closer, pursuing the recoiling alien creature. Like a martial artist in a sideways stance, the robot jabbed, right, right, right. Then it launched a right uppercut, the rocket-assisted arm bypassing the swirl of frantically defending tentacles and connecting once again with the creature's cracked and buckled armor.

"Visor. Go in for the kill and deploy Action Missile."

Pekkarin swung Raidizer's hand-less left arm, batting the squid over to the robot's right, where the remaining fist was already thrusting forward for the creature's faceplate. The knuckles of the fist pounded into the creature's face hard enough to send yet another jagged crack fracturing through the coiled armor.

"Now!"

"Action Missile deployed," Pekkarin responded.

The weapon, a thirty-foot-long brass knuckle equivalent, sprang forth and slipped through the angled crack in the creature's armor that served as a slotted visor. The Verengeretti's entire form shook and vibrated in a conniption of violence. This occurred until the frantically flailing tentacles dropped, and the dead weight of the creature tugged it backward. The Action Missile slurped out of the visor and trailed a sticky rope of plasm and ichor.

The squid creature fell backward and impacted the ground with a dull thump. It was only then that Macumber realized the outer audio had been restored at some point during the battle.

There was a hush on the bridge, as everyone waited to see if the Verengeretti would stir, but Macumber knew it was done for.

"Contact the *Yardley*. We're in no shape to take the next one."

"Aye, Sir. Already done," Tubo responded. "*Yardley* is twenty minutes out."

"Alright," Macumber said. "Let's peel it out of there."

Pekkarin maneuvered King Raidizer into position over the fallen monstrosity. The ship had received its unofficial nickname from the first battle they had survived with an armored Verengeretti. At the end of that fight, they had cracked the armor and pulled the squirming tentacled thing from its protection before stomping on the creature's face, turning its pulsating purple flesh into a lavender paste. Since that fight, the WSF had deemed all battle chassis should perform the action at the end of a fight -- just to make sure each invader was dead.

As Raidizer went about its grisly work, Macumber sighed. He was bone tired, but this was the job. The *Yardley* would relive them, and they would limp back to base for repairs, refueling, and re-arming -- in this case both figuratively and literally, as their mech required a new left fist.

As the giant robot placed a foot against one side of the jagged crack in the Verengeretti armor and pulled with its remaining hand, the ropey plating gave a metallic shriek, and Macumber knew that if he was standing outside -- and if he could withstand the ambient radiation -- he would be overcome instantly by the creature's acidic emissions as the raw stench of the dead alien would dissolve his innards.

"Stomp unnecessary, sir," Callabera notified him. "This one is already vaporizing. We must have hurt it worse than we thought."

The damned things always melted when they died, but the fact that this one was already going gooey told the captain that Callabera was correct. The embolism, Macumber remembered. *It was already dying.*

The creature had put up a pretty good fight at the end, regardless of how damaged it had been. Macumber could care less, though. The only thing this one's putrefaction meant that concerned him was a shortened clock on the appearance of the next dimensional incursion.

"Sonnofa –" Pekkarin began. "We have movement, sir."

Macumber was temporarily confused. The creature had already begun to decay and disincorporate. Then he rapidly blinked his eyes upward and to the left. The viewscreen shifted again in front of his tired eyes and Macumber was looking at the boiling clouds high above them. There he noticed that the tentacles of the next Verengeretti were already descending from cover.

Justin Macumber felt a wave of ennui crawl over his face. They were out of weapons. They were low on fuel. They had dead aboard the ship. King Raidizer had lost its axes and its left hand. And the Yardley...

"How long –?" Macumber started to ask.

"Fifteen minutes," Tubo was already replying.

The captain glanced upward again and saw the replacement Verengeretti had cleared the cloud cover and was rapidly descending, heading straight toward the injured robot and its exhausted crew. Pekkarin brought the robot upright, legs apart, torso twisted, injured stump back and right fist raised. Ready for battle.

The plummeting squid had an armored façade like the last one, but Macumber noted that the normally purple, fleshy, waving tentacles were also covered with linked, segmented, red armor plating. The creature's eye-slit on its helmet also looked altered. Macumber blinked twice, zooming in on it. The slit was covered in small octagonal stripes of the red armor, forming a mesh over the vulnerable area.

It would only be a matter of time until battle chassis captains could no longer out-think the Verengeretti or luck into wins. Each time one slipped into the atmosphere above Luzon, they brought enhancements or improved fighting tactics. Sooner or later, the alien squids would win.

The creature began rolling in its descent from the sky, once again mimicking the circular-saw motion of its predecessor, its red-covered tentacles whipping forward like a million vertical blades. This move was merely an opener, heralding more innovative attacks for later. Impact would take place in just a few seconds.

Eventually the Verengeretti variations and improvements would be all that was necessary to crush a battle chassis before the fight even began. When Macumber and the pilots of the other ships like the *Yardley* would have no more moves. No more innovations. No more ways to hurt the damn things.

But not today.

His crew was feeling the same sluggish reaction time he was. Macumber knew his job wasn't only to out-think the creatures or to shout orders. He had to be their rock,

172

even when every surviving soul aboard the ship was thinking this was the end. They would be thinking that they probably wouldn't last the ten minutes it would take for the *Yardley* to get into firing position.

But that wouldn't stop them from trying. They would kick. They would punch. They would use the ridiculous Action Missile. Macumber needed to show the crew that there was a reason their battle chassis, the *S.S. Nagai*, was more colloquially referred to as *King Raidizer*.

The rampaging ball of armored shell and slicing tentacles surged out of the sky like a meteor, and Ensign Pekkarin bent the Raidizer's knees, preparing to lunge upward.

"Here we go," Pekkarin announced, tension filling his voice.

Macumber sneered at the onslaught of the never-ending creatures. They would only get one response from him and Raidizer's crew:

"Fight!"

END

ROCK-EM SOCK-EM: A MASSIVE STORY

Alex Dumitru

Y'know, there are days when I actually kinda love this job. This might even turn out to be one of 'em, at this rate.

Harsh Nevada sunlight pours in through the lenses of my goggles. I can feel the heat on the outside of my suit and the sand and grit under my boots. It almost feels like I'm not 120 feet tall at the moment, and that I'm just out taking some sun. Except...

I duck and a claw swings over my head. This guy's problem is that he telegraphs. Makes everything real easy for me when a punch starts down in somebody's ankle instead of in their fist. But I guess not all Reptoids are created equal. This one burrowed up outta the sand about six hours ago and has been making a line for old Viva Las Vegas ever since then. Was spotted by the satellites, a scramble call was put through to me and my crew in Monument City, and now here I am trading shots with an overgrown bearded dragon.

Leastways, that's what he looks like to me. The code name they laid on this fella is simply Nevada Rex; you know, because while my crew and I like to have fun with our jobs, the military doesn't.

He's short for a Giant Reptoid anyways. A little under my shoulder, making him probably 110 feet? 105? I can't

174

quite tell for sure since he seems to keep sorta hunched down and he's quick on his feet. His hide is a dirty scaly tan color and covered with bony spurs and spikes running from his nose to the twin tips of his tail. That's plenty long, even for a Reptoid, and I'm already getting tired of ducking that too. But overall, he doesn't look like he's gonna be much of a problem. Just another day at the office. Maybe Rosie and I can catch a show in the city afterwards.

"Keep focused, Hartley," George says in my ear. "We're here to work. Get in there and engage!"

He's always one to ruin my fun, but hell, I don't mind. It's always comforting for somebody to have your back.

I dig into the desert dirt and jam a right cross into Nevada's jaw. He takes it well, but I know the next look on anything's face when I've rattled the loose change around in their noggin. His response is to go for it harder, close the distance. Suddenly I'm wrapped up in an angry cactus and damn, I do believe we're on our way down. We slam into the sand and a cloud of dust flies up around us. I do my best to roll with it, but this sucker is bendy like a snake. He wraps around me and is trying to squeeze down, force the air out of me. Not today, pal.

I don't try to get up all the way, but just enough so that when I fall back down all of me goes onto him. Hard. My shoulder blades drive him down and sends plume of dust into the pristine blue desert sky. His grip loosens up. And with that loosening I'm free and rolling to my feet.

Okay, Rexy. What else ya got? The Reptoid is still on his back when the cloud settles, and I can see him clearly. Must be "press my advantage time." I check my wrist monitor. I haven't even run down my first bar on the

175

energy counter. It's definitely time to call this one an early day and go on back to the barn.

I run up and grab onto the tail that was giving me so much attitude earlier. Wrapping both my hands around it, I lift with my legs, not my back. Nevada Rex comes up like a bag at the end of a thick rope and I dig in. Sometimes you have to appreciate the little things, like a quick game of Kaiju Hurling.

Nevada Rex gains a new ability, if ever so briefly. Suddenly the big boy can fly. He loses the power fast though. His return to the earth is about as graceful as the bottom going out of a box of antique plates. He's on the ground and all over the place. Sorry, buddy, but only one of us is hitting the casinos tonight.

Then I realize how I've made a mild error. Looks like I done made him mad. He's up on his scaly feet, taking on a quadruped stance. I notice that he's even faster on the ground, coming at me like a freight train. Then we're back to the rolling and punching as the Reptoid rocket launches into me. I'm blocking a bunch of frantic hits from bony fists and slaps from the tail that was so recently a lever. Then, it looks for all the world like Nevada Rex is gagging on something. My instincts kick in around the same time I hear Dr. Venus Milosevek in my earpiece saying, "Move! It's about to- "

The patch of dirt where my head was hisses and bubbles as a stream of green slime burns and smokes down into it. Spits acid, huh? Haven't seen that one in a while.

Let's start again, from the top. I place a solid kick from my back into his head and he goes over hard. I lean back, put my weight on my shoulders for a second, then kip up. Impressive? Sure, it is. But try it when you're 12 stories tall. It's murder.

Rexy is reeling still as I close in and start laying on the punches. Sometimes I wish I could talk when I'm this big, but I'm not sure how good it would look on the nine o'clock news if I was cursin' up a blue streak while pounding down on a monster in the middle of nowhere, so maybe it's for the best.

Slowly, ever so slowly, the struggle stops. Then all that's left is the twitching. The burning red light in his eyes goes out and it flops to the sand. I lean back and kneel there, catching my breath. I check my meter. Halfway through bar four out of five. Maybe a new personal best? I won't know for sure until we actually run the numbers on power consumption back at the lab. I'm just grateful that the great and powerful Massive might actually be able to sleep with just bumps and bruises tonight, and in a nice hotel, not a hospital. One with better room service and definitely better company.

I hear George again in my ear, sounding as close to happy as he gets. "Good work, Hartley. I think we can call this one wrapped up. Go ahead and- krrcchhzzzk! Grzzt. Ffffffff...."

Say what now? I tap at my ear, wondering what the hell is causing all the bad reception, and then the line goes dead all the way. After that, I get the full package of no service, and all the readouts in my HUD go blank too. This is very, very not right... it's been almost 20 different monsters and a lot of fights in some weird places, but nowhere -- from the middle of the city to the depths of the bayou -- have I ever lost the signal from home base.

I feel the shadow before I see it, a cold feeling that at first I think is just nerves. Then I realize something other than me is thumping out here. I start to turn, trying to get up and look at the same time. I don't do it fast enough, though. Something hard hits me harder in the back of the head and I go straight down. How the hell did it get the drop on me like that? Must have burrowed up from under the ground while I was finishing off his buddy, and now he's here to get some old-fashioned kaiju revenge, huh? Well, don't worry, pal, I've got enough for-

Both of you? Aw hell... I look up and see two silhouettes against the blue sky. But something here isn't right. These things are not Reptoids. Aside from color, one red and the other blue, they're almost exactly identical. Both of them are almost 150 feet tall, at least. As my eyes clear they gleam in the sun, all glistening metal like a pair of sports cars. Robots, I realize, as they begin to step forward in perfect unison. I just got bushwhacked by two honest-to-god giant robots.

Their heads are blocky and are molded into the shape of angular faces with sloped brows and jutting jaws. Square shoulders come down into heavy arms with oversized fists. Their feet pound rectangles into the dirt pan underneath us and I read the words that seal the deal as I scramble to my feet, trying to get some distance between us. On the red one's waist, like a belt-buckle, is a plate that reads "ROCK-EM." Big blue has a twin to it that says "SOCK-EM."

For just a second, I honestly question if this is a bad dream. Then Rock-Em closes the distance again and plants his overlarge fist in my chest and knocks all the air outta me. He is very real. And so is the pain. My ribs scream, but I'm pretty sure none of them give. it's a close thing, though.

I'm reeling from the hit when I get reception back. My HUD reloads, but... something is off. This looks like something out of one of those old arcade games. On the left is my name with a bar underneath it, one that has already been partially depleted. On the right are two bars, both full as you please, under the name "Box." I hear the pick-up in my earpiece and get the familiar sensation of a voice in my head.

"Good afternoon, Massive. Quite a show you put on. Care for an encore?"

As an answer I plant a kick in Rock-Em's chest. As he adjusts, Sock-Em makes his first move on me and shoves me hard. It sucks all the force out of my kick and sends me sprawling, and I find myself scrambling to get back to my feet.

"Oh, splendid. This will be quite a treat. I've been looking forward to meeting you again. Especially on such fun terms."

The voice in my ear isn't calming. In fact, it's kind of nasal and even in my ear he sounds almost greasy. Like he comes from money but doesn't have any class. Nobody I'd ever be hanging out with, so what the heck is he talking about "meeting again?" And why does he actually sound pretty familiar? Before I can ask myself anymore questions, the robots are on me again.

I duck a blue fist and then a red one comes down on my back. I grunt through it and push myself into the outer shell of Rock-Em, trying for a tackle. But the thing has mass on me, and it just takes a half step backwards.

"Ooh, I felt that one, Gene. Good thing I put seatbelts in here, huh, Quincy?"

"Oh yeah, should never get into a vehicle without seatbelts. That's dangerous."

The second voice I'm sure I don't know. He's lower, sounds more mature. Doesn't have the odd whiny quality of the first but has the same cruelty as he punctuates his statement with wrapping the hydraulic hands of the blue robot around my shoulders and hurling me bodily.

Before I can even start to pick myself up, one of them does it for me. A bright red steel fist wraps around my throat and suddenly my feet are off the ground.

"And here I was worrying that you were over-engineering the modifications on our little babies, Quincy. Look how smooth the action on that was. Even better than the tests suggested it could be."

"Well, nothing's too good for you, bro."

I interrupt the lovefest with a swift kick in the ribs to Rock-Em. Gotta remind these two I'm still here, I guess. It turns out to be a bad idea. Pain rips through my foot. Normally when you kick somebody in the ribs, something gives out. Your brain just naturally responds and says, "Get that foot away from me," and lurches back. Looks like Rock-Em has no such reflex built into him and kicking him is just like kicking a fire hydrant. I'm pretty sure I just broke my toe.

Instead of just dropping me, Rock-Em drives his other fist into my stomach and sends me flying over the desert. I land hard, the pain in my foot sucking all the grace outta me. I stand up and the final nail goes into my coffin. I can barely put weight on it, let alone however many thousand tons I weigh right now. Red and Blue are closing in on me. There's nowhere to run, even if I could, and I don't know how far away help is. Or even if it's coming.

I square up. Time to even up those status bars.

The robots close and I start swinging. They do too. A hard blow opens up my lip and loosens teeth as I grapple with Big Red. I start trying to use brute strength, but nothing is keeping one from pummeling me while I handle the other.

I break away and land a punch on the chin of Rock-Em and feel that pain rip into my hand again, just as Sock-Em steps on my injured foot. I try to shout, but nothing happens because it hurts too much. Hands of steel latch onto me and throw me into another set of punches. My goggles crack and I can barely make out the readings on the HUD... not like they matter, though. All they would read is "OW," anyway. Or, maybe "SCREWED."

A giant red fist fills my vision and I'm back down on the ground. A split second later the pain hits me like the "boom!" after something breaks the sound barrier. I'm going down, really going down. I remember the last time I felt this bad. Brass King, Monument City. My rodeo clown attack.

The Doc had said it was a miracle I hadn't shattered every bone in my body when I tried that move. The field that shields me from the forces of gravity had given out, and only the secondary systems he'd installed after his disastrous first experiment had saved me.

"But they won't always," he said. "They're designed to keep you from flying apart at the seams, not to keep you fighting after the suit has run out of primary power. Next time, I don't care how it looks; but if you run out of power in the field again, you get out of there and drop back down to size."

He had almost shouted that last part, but I guess he had the right to be mad. He'd invented this suit and hadn't seen around every corner there was concerning the hazards of being this size. His first test had gone great. That is, until the power got interrupted by a short-circuit in the prototype suit and his spine had instantly snapped. The rest of the team, namely Venus and Rosa Lee, stuck with him while he recuperated, and started work on a second version that could keep the wearer together and still do the job of bringing the fight to giants on their own ground.

I never pretended to understand any of it. I was just an over-sized kid from Oklahoma that was dumb enough to say yes to the most dangerous job in the world. All I knew was that it was a job that needed doing, that I was better than nobody, and that Rosie was cute as all get out. So, I took it.

A few weeks after I got out of the hospital from the Brass King fight, Rosie and I went out for dinner. We figured after everything that had been going on lately, we deserved ourselves a date night. It was this incredible sushi place called Mifune's; it had a big samurai out front and everything. All was going pretty great when suddenly Rosie had gotten kinda serious. It moved over her face like she'd taken off a mask and I realized that maybe we had come out here for something other than good cuisine.

"What is it, babe?" I asked, not sure what else to say.

I knew full well that most guys sealed their own fate asking that, and that it should be on the tombstone of most relationships. But it's better than saying nothing and being sure it was gonna go downhill.

"Just… something I've been thinking about. And I talked to V about it too, but we haven't brought it up to George yet," she said.

I perked up a little. Rosie wouldn't bring up a relationship thing to the Doc, even if she might with Venus. So, it was all business, a Massive talk.

"And?"

She sighed.

"Have you ever thought about how long we can keep this up? You in the suit? Another monster like the last one? I mean, the things out there are just getting bigger. Like every time we take one down one way, the next one requires something totally different. Eventually… I'm not sure, but Massive will be what we need. And that could be the day I lose you…"

I reached across the little table and put my hand over hers. She always looked so small in comparison to me that sometimes I forgot that, more often than not, I was the one in our relationship that needed the protecting.

"So, you think someday we might find some other poor soul to wear that jumpsuit? Is that what we're talking about here?"

"Partially. But the candidate list is still pretty short, even with the kind of… celebrity status you've gotten."

I rolled my eyes, not needing to be reminded of my cult following. They had almost made things worse during that fight with Brass King by putting themselves in danger and taking my focus off the mission.

"The other part," Rosie continued, "is simply that being Massive might not be enough against one of these threats one day. V agrees with me that the kaiju are changing. Almost like they're evolving."

"Correct me if I'm wrong here, I was never that great in science, but, uh... doesn't that take a while?"

"In nature, yes. But nothing about the kaiju is natural. They're all about unbalance. Every test we've done, every dissection by the government, everything points to each one having similar DNA, but being utterly individual. A species where every single member is a unique creature with highly variable traits isn't a species at all. They're something--"

She suddenly stopped, looking up at the man who had just walked to our table. I hadn't noticed him 'til just then either. He was almost tall... or would have looked that way if he wasn't so pudgy. Not fat, just soft looking. He had a big nose and beady eyes behind thick, black-framed glasses. He had longish sandy-colored hair that was lank and brittle looking. And under all that was a get-up that in my opinion belonged more on a fifth grader than a grown man: cargo shorts, sandals, and a t-shirt with a bunch of superheroes on it. And he was just standing there. Grinning.

"Can I help you?" I asked. I made it sound as much like "Go away" as I could.

The man-boy grinned wider.

"Oh, wow. Not what I expected your voice to sound like, at all. Interesting," he said.

I had a bad feeling about where this was headed. The stranger stuck a limp hand out to me to shake. I observed it.

"My name's Box. Minton Box." He said it like I was supposed to know who that was. Then he saw that I didn't. "Ah. Right. No kids. You probably, uh… no."

"My friend and I were having dinner, do you mind coming back another time, Mr. Box?" I requested. *Maybe after the next Ice Age,* I thought.

"I just want a simple moment of your time, Mr. Hartley. Can I call you Eugene, or is it just Gene?"

This was getting creepier by the second. I had been on the news plenty of times as Massive, but never as… well, me. My anonymity has been a delicate thing, but it had help up to that point.

"See, I am the head of Outside the Box. We're a toy company. I'm also a… bit of a collector…" He was kinda smirking to himself as he said this.

Oh, god… here we go.

"No," I said. "Just, no. I don't know how you found me, where you think you get off approaching me in public like this, or what exactly you –"

Then it hits me. I've seen this guy before. I hadn't noticed his pudgy belly at first because he was holding a sign that read "HIT 'EM HARDER" and leading a gaggle of other idiot ducklings. He was the one who had actually waved at me while I tried to save them from Brass King.

"You!" My shout attracted the attention of the whole restaurant.

"Ah! So, you do recognize me!" he crowed.

And he's right. I do recognize him; I recognize that voice, I recognize the attitude.

I Googled him later, after I calmed down. He really is the head of that toy company. And he isn't just a toy collector. He is the toy collector. And these must be the shining stars of his collection. He also has an older brother named Quincy who is more reclusive and said to be even more of a weirdo and genius. Serves me right for being an only child, I guess…

I snap back to the present along with a rib. There's a huge steel foot on my chest. It's Rock-Em again – excuse me, Minton. That big jutting face is looking down at me again. Part of me swears I can see him behind those big yellow screens it calls eyes, but it's just in my mind.

"Yes, now I see it," he says in my ear. "Even through the rather considerable swelling, I can see that recognition on your face. You do remember me."

The robot straightens and brings the foot up. I react as fast as I can and manage to catch the robotic limb. Everything I've got is all it takes to hold it back.

"All you had to do was listen, you know? I could have made you rich. Like, stupid rich. Like, me rich."

The foot finally presses down enough to touch my chest, and my grip slips. The pressure is unbelievable, sort of like a car slipping off the jack. I can't breathe. I'm just pinned. Everything hurts.

"Rich enough to figure out where you're going to be."

He lifts his foot and uses the other to kick me across the desert again. I roll right towards the waiting feet of Sock-Em.

"Rich enough to find out who you are."

The big blue robot plants a kick that sends me rolling back to his brother. I'm also pretty sure he just broke my nose.

"Rich enough to get my hands on two robots from a defunct Japanese mecha-defense project!" Box shouts in my ear.

He points one of the giant fists at me and something horrifying happens. Plates slide back and missiles raise themselves out. Lots of them, each with a shiny red paintjob.

With a fiery screech of jets, the missiles come flying out at me. The last thing I see before they strike is my wrist meter as I raise my arms. I've got two bars left when they're launched; I watch it flicker to one. Then they hit.

It can't be described. Not unless you have ever been hit by ten cars at once, then thrown under a train, then set on fire. The explosion simultaneously presses me down and into the dirt while also raising me up with the force. And once the ringing is gone from my ears, and all that's left is pain. I can still hear him laughing.

"I could have given you that! All you had to do was play ball, let me make you into the ultimate kaiju toy line. All you would have had to do is be the icon I wanted you to be! We could be fighting these monsters together, instead of making me use these on you."

As he speaks, he's stalking closer, his metal feet thumping over and over as he makes his way into the crater I lay at the center of. I can't see it anymore since the goggles are broke, but I can hear the pinging noise in my ear and feel the weight on me as the gravity fields around me give. I'm on reserve. Helpless. A wrong move is all it takes now, but I can barely move at all.

"But no... you had to tell me I was stupid. You had me thrown out. You. Made. Me. Look... small."

He lifts his foot up again and this time I can't do anything as he brings it down on my leg. I feel the bone snap, and everything turns red. I scream past the hold that the expansion field has on my vocal cords. It echoes through the desert and down into my mind. The other robot is looming up behind Minton; the fabulous Box brothers are about to finish the job of killing Massive…

I stop thinking about all this. I only want to think of Rosie; I had so many plans, so many things we were gonna do. I wanted to retire from this soon, like she and I had talked about that night. Get a ranch somewhere, raise horses, and never see another animal bigger than that ever again. But that's all over now, before it started.

"Gah! What the hell?"

I'm jolted awake by Quincy's lower, more measured voice going into hysterics. I look up through bloodied eyes and see… a miracle. A regular, blue-eyed, scaly miracle.

Sock-Em thrashes around, with Rock-Em turning to look. On his back, still ready to go another ten rounds, is Nevada Rex. The dragon screeches and tears at the robot's head, its oversized meat mallet hands unable to reach back to peel the monster off. Sparks begin to fly from around the neck of the metal head as Rex digs his needle-like teeth into it. Claws frantically rake at the steel, ripping gashes into the pristine paint job and making agonizing screeches like nails on the world's biggest chalkboard.

"You- what the- you get off my brother!" Minton screams and raises his other fist.

More missile platforms slide out, and he looks like he's trying to get a bead on just Rexy.

"Minty, no! It's too clo –"

His bro gets cut off in the screech of feedback as he's hit with some of the same flavor of hell I've been treated to this afternoon. Sock-Em lurches back, Nevada Rex wrapping his tail around the thick metal legs. The robots are designed for slow, deliberate beatdowns, but they're rendered ungainly and clumsy in the face of a swift opponent, even one this small.

Rock-Em stomps back and tries to grab at Rex but suddenly one of the big blue fists swinging around connects hard with his metallic jaw. Sparks fly and the glass from the red robot's left eye explodes outward in a shower of glittering shards. The fist has left a huge dent I could never have managed, but I'm satisfied to see it anyway.

"Quincy, I'm trying to help! don't punch *me!*"

"I wasn't! Those missiles knocked out my guidance unit -- I'm on automatic defense protocols!"

Nevada Rex roars in triumph as he leans back his horned head and vomits up a gout of burning green acid sludge onto Sock-Em's steel skull. I can't do anything to shut out the screams as the robot head burns, then buckles, then collapses. The metal colossus teeters for a second then falls back on the Reptoid riding it, smashing Nevada Rex in a crunch that leaves no question that, even posthumously, Quincy has done me the favor of finishing him off.

The red giant in front of me is motionless. Stunned.

"Q-Quincy...?"

It's so quiet that I can hear the jets from a mile off, and so does "Minty." The cavalry is coming.

The robot turns, trying to look at me, standing over the wreckage of his brother. The movements are mechanical, precise. But the com-link between me and the robot is still up. All I can hear is the hyper-ventilating breaths of someone about to break down hard -- whimpering, mewling, sniffling. Then, with a screech, the robot stands straight, arches back, and erupts into a jet-powered ascent straight up, leaving a pillar of smoke, and me, behind it.

I watch the robotic giant arc off into the sky. The jets pass over me and hare off in pursuit. Choppers are incoming too, whup-whup-whupping over the desert. My radio goes back down. I'm all alone in my head. I can feel myself going into shock, feel the blackout coming. But before it does, I squeeze my hand into a fist.

I don't know where you think you're goin,' Box. But wherever it is, I'm gonna find out. I'm gonna find you this time.

I promise...

MASSIVE WILL RETURN...

END

SMASH OR BE SMASHED: BLUE KING'S SECOND GIG

Christofer Nigro

Overtown, Miami, Florida

"I can't believe you had us hide out here in *this* shit hole, *tipo!*" Melvin Perez griped loudly to his long-time friend and literal partner-in-crime, Gil Garcia. "If you wanted to run from Iron City to Florida, couldn't you at least have picked Sarasota?"

"Hey, get off my case, will you, man?" Gil retorted firmly. Then he slumped back down on the small one-person bed provided by their cheap motel. "We couldn't stay in Iron Town[1] with those lawsuits on our ass after you smooshed a bunch of civilians while defending it from that kaiju, now could we? Or, would you have preferred to give back almost everything we earned to pay for that? And besides, didn't some kaiju thrash Sarasota last month anyway?"

Melvin walked over to his friend's bed and jutted an index finger in his face. "It was Fort Lauderdale! Now, let me correct you on a few things here, bro! First up, I

---

[1] Residents of Iron City, Missouri often refer to it interchangeably by its proper name and "Iron Town" or simply "The Town," due to its status as a small city. And here you thought this was an editing error on the part of the author, didn't you? Hah!

was the one fighting for my life as Blue King, not you. I told you I wasn't experienced with fighting giant monsters but no-o-o-ooo, you had to insist I do it anyway! If I could give you this pendant that lets me transform into that blue super-giant, I would see how well you could avoid stepping on cars and knocking over buildings when a giant creature is tryin' to gut *your* ass! This whole bright idea after I got saddled with the jewel was yours, man!"

"I didn't say it was easy for you! You mostly did good out there, I guess. And will you get that finger out of my face?"

"And what's this shit about 'we' when it comes to earning that 20 mil? You know, the millions of papers we now have to throw away because of those lawsuits? I was the one getting cut and slashed by Mokkadon's claws or whatever the hell you call those things it had for hands!"

Gil moved his friend's finger away from his scruffy countenance as gently as possible, as he did not want to risk provoking an escalation of hostilities.

"Look, man, like you said, the whole deal was my brainstorm. I've always been the brains in this partnership, and that idea was solid. It's just that… okay, you got a bit clumsy your first time out. So, now we got us a little setback."

Melvin swatted his friend on the back of the head, a frequent act of his that Gil found thoroughly annoying. He had resolved to say something about that eventually but decided now was not the ideal time.

"A 'little' setback? I earned us 20 mil and a pardon! Now we owe almost that much in lawsuits! On top of that, our pardon makes no major difference 'cause your next plan was flying the coop instead of trying to work things out with Mayor Pryce. So, now we got criminal records again as fugitives from the law! Why do I ever listen to your *loco* plans?"

"Because most of the time they tend to work out in the long run! And this one will too! There was no way we were gonna get out of paying off those lawsuits by pleading with the mayor. We just need time to plan without being hounded and thrown in the joint. This way we can find a way to earn back twice the lawsuit costs."

"And how are we gonna be solvent 'til then? And couldn't you have gotten us better than such a dive of a motel in *this* area of Miami to chill in?"

Gil tried to smile. "I'll answer the second one first. It's because we gotta keep a low profile. If I rented us a place at Hilton's finest in a ritzy area, we would be picked up by the end of the day. Here we can blend in among… you know, others of our usual vocation. And the answer to the first question ties into this one: We can get back to our old job of pushing some good product. Don't worry, I got it all covered, bro!"

"Pushing product? You mean drugs. Like we didn't almost get killed five times already doing that. And the last time it was because you thought it was a brilliant idea to skim off the take." [Using an exaggerated imitation of Gil's voice] "'Calm down, bro, they're not gonna notice such a tiny amount missing…' you said, just like the *estúpido* you are!"

Gil had now had enough of this and stood up to make a stand as he argued his case. "Okay, I underestimated the accuracy of their measuring gadgets just a bit. I'm man enough to admit I make mistakes now and then. Just like you stepped on all those buildings and civilians while playing hero. Shit happens, man."

Melvin looked out the second floor window and grimaced at the urban decay that punctuated the street outside their two-story bargain basement motel. He then moved his fingers across the smooth surface of the sapphire-hued triangular pendant around his neck – a gift from the gods intended for someone very different from Melvin Perez – and began pondering whether it had truly been worth stealing.

Here I thought we would be "living the life" for good after so many years of struggle when I snatched this pendant from the guy who was supposed to get it. I mean, I earned us 20 million for fighting off Mokkadon! And now we lost mostly all of that because I was so damn clumsy my first time out. I'll never admit it to him, but it really wasn't all Gil's fault. And his plan was solid, like he said. And yeah, doing the Blue King thing is risky; but is it any less risky than dealing drugs and all the other things we had to do to survive on the streets through the years?

"And look, dude," Gil continued, "here in Overtown you even have an art museum close by that has your name on it. Ha. Ha."

Melvin felt another urge to slap his friend over his ill-conceived attempt at levity but resisted the temptation (this time, anyway). They had much more serious concerns to deal with for the nonce.

"Okay, we can sell that product for a while, until another kaiju attack happens close by. But, we're totally new to Miami. We have no contacts here."

"You mean *you* have no contacts here. My brainstorming never stops, and I already told you I had that covered. I got us a network down in Columbia through a cousin on my dad's side of the family. He's gonna hook us up good with product.

"In the meantime, don't worry so much, brah. I'm sure another one of those giant bastards will attack some nearby city again before too long. Kaiju attacks are one of the few reliable things in this world besides homicide, cancer, drug addiction, taxes, and death. Ha!"

Melvin shook his head. "Alright. So, when do we start?"

"Tonight, man! We meet to pick up the product down at the corner of North West 5th and 6th, and..."

As fate would have it, once again the TV playing in the background had its volume automatically raised while an alert was flashed by the Emergency Broadcasting System. The loud, piercing, and familiar sound was enough to interrupt the conversation and cause both men to turn their ears to the screen.

"This is an alert from the Emergency Broadcasting System. It has been confirmed that the 50-meter-tall Milo Mouse robot designed for future display at the Eisner Center in downtown Orlando has suffered a malfunction and has run amok in the city. The robot is not only designed for entertainment purposes but is equipped with destructive combat capabilities to enable it to defend Eisner World and its other international amusement parks from any possible kaiju threat. Residents are now being evacuated by the city government, but the Global Defense Agency may take over 24 hours to send a combat squadron to deal with the threat due to the mass kaiju incursion now ensuing across the planet. Stand by for further updates."

"Aleluya!" Gil exclaimed while jumping up and down excitedly on his bed. "Man, this is it! This is our opportunity to get back in the black!"

Melvin glared at his friend with his familiar wary expression. "What do you mean? We've got that deal you set up for us tonight from your cuz, am-I-rite?"

"The hell with that deal! A way better offer just got dropped into our laps! Orlando is only like three hours away by car, and I can get us there faster by using some of our stash to charter a private plane from Miami International! In the meantime, I'm gonna contact Eisner's reps and offer Blue King's services to them! You're gonna flatten that giant robot and save them all the lawsuits the company would rack up!"

Melvin's jaw dropped. "I would tell you that you've gotta be kidding. But I know you better than that by now."

"Ha! Pack a few things, and get ready to rumble, *mi amigo!*"

***

Orlando, Florida, several hours later

Melvin Perez stood roughly eight blocks away from the Eisner Center. He was directly in the trajectory of the renegade Milo Mouse – whom the fast-moving online press had already dubbed "Mechani-Mouse." He looked down at the sapphire-like jewel hanging on a silvery chain from his neck for reassurance. He then poked his right ear a few times, to make certain the long-range communications earbud given him by Gil was in working order.

"Can you hear me, man?" Melvin said aloud, trying to speak over the screams of numerous people and the frequent honking of horns as civilians fled the area on foot or in vehicles.

"Loud and clear, brah," Gil's voice crackled into his friend's auditory canal. "These earbud thingies that Eisner gave us are top notch!"

Melvin stepped aside and cursed as a large man fleeing the scene on foot almost knocked him down. *Lucky for that ignorant* hombre *that I'm on a schedule here.*

"Are you sure those Eisner suits agreed to your 40 mil request? I mean, that sounds a bit steep even for rich 'mo 'fo-s like them."

"They totally agreed! That's actually lots less than the lawsuits and lost revenue from their theme park they would take, not to mention the beating they'd get in the stock market, if that robo-mouse of theirs thrashes all of Orlando and wipes out thousands of folks along with the architecture."

"Okay, alright! Anyway, what makes you so certain this little device in my ear will grow with me when I become Blue King? I mean, when I transform my clothing gets replaced, my cellphone and bling vanishes, and only this necklace that gives me the power grows big along with me."

"Just trust me on this one, okay? You said the gods made that jewelry of yours, *si?* Well, if they're powerful enough to make something that can create giant people and axes and shit, they gotta be able to make little devices grow too, especially when you totally need them. I just got a feelin' about this. Trust the brains of our little team here, okay?"

The brains? More like the ass *of the team.*

"Okay, okay! Just keep in mind that I can't talk back to you when I become Blue King. For some reason I'm mute when I change into the big super-guy. But you said the last time you could 'hear' me scream in pain in your head? Like, with psychic waves of some sort? I'll try to communicate with you that way, but don't' be surprised if it doesn't work."

"Word! As long as you can still hear me through that earbud, which I'm confident will grow real big along with you, then you can receive my on-the-spot advice. I'm watching everything from about half a mile away from our room on the Hyatt Regency's 20th floor. I can't see you as a regular guy with these new military-grade binocs, but once you get big –"

"Yeah, yeah, I know. Okay, I have to pay attention now, 'cause that giant robot should be here any..."

Melvin's words were cut off as a series of thunderous sounds rattled the very earth he stood on, almost making him lose his balance. The streetwise thug heard louder screams and saw cars from a two-block radius abruptly picking up speed. It was a mere split second before he realized that those rumbling sounds were the footsteps of the rapidly approaching giant Milo Mouse robot.

The fact that the jewel hanging in front of his sternum began to emit an intense azure radiance was the final confirmation... and a major source of relief.

"Gil, the jewel is glowing! So, you were right when you said it would react to a robotic kaiju the same as the flesh and blood type. Thank Jesus."

"Hey, I told ya that you need to listen to my wisdom more often. I figured the gods wouldn't be that picky. But get ready, 'cause I see that mother coming into view, and it's crazy big! It's kinda silly looking, though. So, how dangerous can it really be, right?"

Melvin looked upwards as the glow of his jewel intensified and the robotic titan came into view a few blocks distant.

The giant automaton was expertly molded to resemble the world-famous cartoon character Milo Mouse, a beloved figure of children and young-hearted adults since the early 20th century. The gargantuan robot had a grayish cast to its entire form, as it was cleverly designed to resemble the classic version of Milo that appeared in Eisner's early black and white cinema shorts.

Its arms, covered in Milo's distinctive gloves, were very well designed and moved with a degree of articulation that belied its nature as a clunky anthropomorphic machine. It was built with the perfection of Eisner's human-sized automatons, which were skillfully designed to resemble real-life personages that had entertained (and unnerved) generations on the stages of its theme parks. The optical sensors of the robot flashed an intermittent series of green and mauve lights as it scanned its nearby surroundings.

The frankly comical-looking mechanical monstrosity soon let it be known that its rogue status made it anything *but* a joke, however, as its powerfully built arms casually reached out and smashed clear through the center of two large buildings. This move showered the streets with debris that snuffed out the lives of a few fleeing pedestrians in bloody fashion.

Additionally, a number of vehicles that attempted to flee the vicinity by going around its enormous feet (which were wearing recreations of Milo's black booties) were stomped into flattened shards of metal with acts of seemingly malicious intent. Melvin cringed as he pondered the equally flattened bits of human anatomy that were crushed invisibly within those compressed wreckages.

The robot then stopped its forward trek, opened its mouth via hinges that enabled its lower jaw to slide downwards, and its loud oral speaker system emitted an amplified, patented greeting in the recorded voice of the actor known for providing Milo's speech in Eisner's more recent cartoons: "Hello, boys and girls! This is Milo Mouse, and I welcome you! Can we be friends?"

You have got *to be kidding me.*

Those were the final thoughts to stream through Melvin's mind while he was in human form. As soon as the robot resumed its forward pace, it came close enough to fully activate the god-jewel around the mercenary's neck.

A brilliant flash of azure radiance enveloped Melvin's comparatively tiny form and quickly expanded in size to encase a half a block radius in four directions. The robot stopped in its tracks and its optical lights began flashing with an enhanced quickness as its AI system struggled to make sense of the unexpected surge of light and energy.

The uber-brilliant flash quickly receded back into the glowing jewel to reveal the 45-meter tall, cerulean-costumed form of the kyodai known as the Blue King – whose power was under the control of Melvin Perez, the mercenary now being paid big bucks to stop the bizarre automaton's rampage.

The giant warrior of fortune barely had time to raise his arms to revel in the sense of power he felt following the transformation when a sudden distraction hit him. It was Gil's voice, transmitting into Blue King's giant ear that was hidden under the giant's cowl.

"Bro, can you still hear me? That damn light that comes with your change almost blinded me, as usual! Oh, wait, you can't talk. Alright, if you can't send me mind messages at will, give me a thumb's up so I can tell if you're receiving this."

Blue King complied – sort of – by extending his middle finger in place of an upturned thumb.

"Um, thanks, that was close enough. Glad you can hear me. But pay attention now! You're about to rumble!"

Blue King stood his ground as the Mechani-Mouse's sensors scanned the presence of the giant interloper that was suddenly barring its path. The robot's mouth opened again, and its loudspeaker uttered another statement in Milo's familiar cartoon voice.

"Hello there, friend! Welcome to Eisner World! Can we be friends?"

Blue King raised his hands in a gesture of incredulity. *Huh? I just can't take this thing seriously!*

That attitude changed a moment later when a high-powered "stinger" missile was launched from a portal in the robot's mouth. Its high speed and advanced computer guidance system combined with the automaton's close distance to enable the projectile to strike the kyodai's left shoulder before he could react. The missile exploded on impact and a spray of blood spurted from the resulting flesh wound. The sudden pain and impact caused the giant mercenary to fall back against a nearby Gold Dome Bank, causing half the multi-story structure to collapse.

"Aw, man!" Gil shouted into his own earbud. "You were supposed to be careful about not adding to the infrastructure damage, dude! And be careful, that robot has some serious ammo!"

Geez, I hope mi amigo *is alright. I saw all the blood and that looked painful even for him in his giant form. Dude does have some serious* bolas *to be out there like that. But hey, the brains of this team are obviously important too.*

Gil received Blue King's reply as a gargantuan hand rose from the rubble of what used to be the Gold Dome Bank and once again flipped him the bird.

"Aaargh, that hurt!"

"Dude, I heard you! Or, 'sensed' you! Or, whatever you call it when you talk in my head instead of my ears!"

"You did? I guess I just have to put 'feeling' into it to make it work, like when I holler in pain."

And I also have to learn to shield my thoughts, so Gil doesn't "hear" everything I'm thinking. And it looks like it worked, as he would have said something about it if he picked that up. In the meantime, I better work on picking myself up.

Blue King pushed his massive form out of the crushed portion of the bank building. He soon was on his feet again, but his hand immediately went to the bleeding tear on his left shoulder. It was already healing, and healing fast, but it was still painfully throbbing.

The kyodai released a psychic howl of rage that caused Gil and the few pedestrians remaining in the area to instinctively cover their ears as if they heard a piercing audible sound. He then rushed at his mechanical opponent and delivered a powerful side kick to its barrel-shaped chest. A loud metallic "clang" was heard as the automaton moved back a few feet. It seemed otherwise intact save for a small dent in its solid steel sternum, however.

Blue King followed that move up with throwing a punch towards the robot's globe-shaped nose. Much to his surprise, the mecha-Milo's arm rotated with jet-like speed so that its open gloved hand caught and intercepted the giant's intended blow. The hydraulic system in the robot's arms neatly absorbed an impact strong enough to shatter the upper portion of a skyscraper with no discernible damage.

"Oh-oh," he heard Gil's voice say through his earbud. "Eisner has some *really* good engineers!"

A second later the robot tightened its mechanized grip to exert a vice-like pressure on the kyodai's hand.

Aaahg! This thing has one hell of a grip! I think it's actually crushing my fist!

Blue King attempted to pry the robot's sausage-shaped metal fingers from his hand, but they proved resistant to his best efforts. Within seconds he was down on his knees as he felt the ultra-dense bones of his giant hand beginning to crack.

"Mel, now that you're down there grab its legs and make it fall!" Gil shouted through the ear communicators. "Do it, man! Hurry!"

Thanks to his incredible reaction time in kyodai form, Blue King did precisely as his friend's electronic message demanded with due speed. He wrapped his free muscular arm around the automaton's legs and pulled towards himself with all his considerable might. As hoped for, the robot's sturdy pogo-stick-like legs were successfully wrested out from under it. The 50-meter metal monstrosity went crashing down to the street, a move that created a seismic disruption which shattered building and car windows over a two-block radius. It also left a nearly four-meter-deep crater in the asphalt.

As was also hoped for, the fall caused the robot to release its clutch on Blue King's hand. The azure-clad giant quickly stood to his full titanic height and waved his hand to ease the pain. The wound on his shoulder was about 85% closed and no longer oozing blood, and he anticipated the small fractures inflicted upon the bones of his hand to heal just as quickly.

"Maybe that metal pendajo *won't be able to get up again."*

"Um… I wouldn't count on that, bro. Head's up!"

Blue King raised his cowled face to see that Eisner's engineering crew had skills beyond even the credit Gil had previously given them. With a sudden jerky motion, the robot's upper body slid upwards into what resembled a sitting position. A second later it pressed its hands into the street, and with powerful push it aided the strong motors in its legs into moving the gargantuan automated cartoon star back up onto its booted feet.

204

Ooohh... man!

The automaton's mouth slid open again and its speaker system released a melodious, sing-song message: "That wasn't very nice, young man. If you hit others, then you have to be pun – iiii – ssshhhh – ed!"

With that spoken, another stinger missile was projected from a turret hidden in the robot's mouth.

"Dude, look out –!"

But Blue King needed no warning from his friend this time. The cerulean-clothed giant quickly rolled onto the street to dodge the fast-moving projectile, albeit barely. The evaded missile instead smashed into a building a block away, blowing its upper ten floors to mortar smithereens.

"Another building gone! Mel, you gotta be careful there!"

"Excuse me for being more concerned about those damn missiles hitting me *instead of the buildings!"*

Upon getting back to his feet Blue King resolved to go on the offensive in an aggressive manner. He extended his right arm and focused an intense mental command. The ornately decorated metal gauntlet covering his right forearm seemed to liquify, flow up into his hand, and re-solidify as a fierce-looking, silvery battle axe.

"Oh yeah!" Gil shouted into his earbud. "Now Milo is gonna get his *axe* kicked! Bwah-hah!"

Blue King ran towards the friendly-looking but deadly giant automaton and swung his gleaming double blade at its smiling face. *I gotta try and demolish whatever part of it holds the AI system. Might as well start with the head.*

The mechanized Milo Mouse once again twisted its arm upwards at nearly blinding speed. The automated limb intercepted Blue King's swipe, and the axe embedded about a quarter of the way into its metal framework. Needless to say, the arm wasn't severed and the swing was successfully halted.

Oh, c'mon now!

"Mel! Pull the axe out before it can –"

Gil's command was cut off as the robot's free arm socked the kyodai in his masked face. The impact knocked Blue King off his feet, causing him to let go of the still embedded axe and go crashing down onto the street and crushing a few parked cars as if they were tinfoil boxes.

"Ohhh!. Coldcocked by Milo Mouse!" Gil hollered into the communicator. "That's gotta be embarrassing, man! Now, get back on your feet and redeem yourself!"

The giant shook his head to clear his vision and shake off the pain. The giant nose concealed by his azure mask felt as if it were broken, and he was sure he could taste blood in his mouth.

Time... for a new strategy.

Mel's colossal alter-ego sat up, raised his right hand, and focused another mental command at the axe whose metal was psychically attuned to his brainwaves. The bladed weapon shook where it was entrenched in the alloy of the robot's right arm for a few seconds. It then forcefully detached of its own accord and flew back into the hand of its owner and commander.

"Naughty boys get no toys!" the Milo mechanoid decreed just before launching another missile.

This time, though, Blue King was prepared for such a move. He used his amazing reflexes to swing his axe and successfully deflect the six-meter-long projectile. It exploded in mid-air several meters away to no effect.

That move clearly excited Gil. "Yeah! The Red Sox have a new recruit, brah!"

That robot's AI makes it seriously fast. I need to fake it out by doing the unexpected.

Blue King jumped back to his feet and again charged the robot with the handle of his axe held by both hands. He attempted a feint towards the mechanoid's face, and again its arm moved to block. The giant mercenary stopped in mid-lunge, however. He pulled the axe back and swung at the robot's barrel-shaped belly while its arm covered its face. The razor-sharp blade sliced neatly through the reinforced steel hull of the automaton's lower abdomen. Sparks spewed out the tear from the damaged circuitry within as bronze lubricating oil seeped out.

"Boo-yaah! Hit 'im again, Mel!"

"Like I need you to tell me that!"

"Just sayin', man. You know, like when you scream the obvious at a boxing match! Or, a street fight!"

The sapphire-clothed kyodai had stopped paying attention to his friend's spiel over a second ago. He lifted the axe again and prepared to "fool" the robot's sophisticated sensors with another ruse. This time, however, the Milo monstrosity did the unexpected by extending its left arm and trudging forward with surprising suddenness. It was clear that its AI determined the axe to be a serious threat and its intention was to snatch the weapon from its opponent's grip.

No, you don't! Thankfully, Blue King's reflexes were just fast enough that he was able to swing back his axe a split second before the robot could grasp its handle. The giant then executed a sweeping side kick with his leg that knocked the automaton's left arm aside. He then used his right hand to swing his axe back into the same gash he had already rent in the robot's metallic gut.

A fireworks-like cascade of sparks and sizzling sounds emanated from the now much larger tear in Milo's lower hull while more of the oil-like fluid spattered out onto the street. The robot's eyes began emitting mauve flares with great rapidity and its mouth opened to release a loud screeching sound from its speaker system. Its arms whirled about in a haphazard fashion while the mechanical monstrosity took several steps backwards.

"Naughty… naughty… naughty…!" it began repeating as Blue King backed away from its powerful flailing limbs and raised his axe again.

When he determined that its internal systems were sufficiently "shocked" to prevent it from bringing its AI-enhanced reflexes to bear in a defensive fashion, Blue King attacked. The cerulean-clad titan leapt forward and swung the blade at the automaton's head. He was holding the handle with two hands to put maximum strength behind the swipe, and it paid off. The axe vertically sliced the robot's head in half.

The left section of the bifurcated, big-eared metallic cranium detached and fell to the street behind it with a loud clanging sound. Sparks sputtered from a series of exposed wires from the still extant right side of the head, and what remained of the mouth rapidly opened and closed on its broken hinge. It was clearly suffering from a shattered central control box that did indeed house its AI system.

It's a good thing Eisner's engineers weren't too *innovative in the design.*

The giant mechanical Milo Mouse's arms whirled around at blurring speed for a few moments before halting with a whining screech. The robot then went still on its feet, with just a few sparks continuing to pop from the severed wires protruding out what remained of its head unit. A short-lived shower of the automaton's oleaginous lubricant spewed out the top of the spliced head like a small geyser before all was motionless.

"Whoa-ho! That was a cut above the rest, dude!"

"Geez. You deserve the axe yourself for that one, bro."

"Hah. Hah! We in the black, man! And all you had to do was ruin the childhood of millions of kids across the world! Hah!"

With that completed, the axe liquified again and re-formed into the gauntlet surrounding Blue King's right forearm. The giant mercenary then turned and ran down a side street wide enough to fit his immense form as the tingling glow in his chest-embedded jewel signaled that his reversion to the tiny human form of Melvin Perez was imminent. A blinding sapphire-colored flash of light briefly shined brighter than the late afternoon sunlight to mark – and conceal – the amazing transformation that spontaneously occurred whenever the kaiju threat at hand was definitively resolved.

***

Several hours later, Melvin and Gil sat on the dingy beds in their dingy Overtown motel room as they looked at a large stack of unmarked greenbacks in a suitcase.

"Count it, man!" Gil said in an elated fashion. "Over 20 mil left to us after I wired the rest to City Hall in Iron Town to cover the lawsuits. And Mayor Pryce was impressed enough to let our pardon stand. We're in the clear! And this is all ours, about 15 and a half mil for each of us. Another two bouts or so as Blue King, and we can both retire for life at 36! And with the mass kaiju attacks going on in the world right now, opportunities for that will abound! Imagine how much we could get if you take on and defeat Megadrak himself!"[2]

"Forget *that*, man!" Melvin retorted as he flipped a stack of money through his fingers. "I ain't taking on Megadrak! Let the Global Defense Agency handle that one, 'cause no one could pay *me* enough. But there has to be a few others that won't be too big a deal…"

Melvin's statement was interrupted as an ominous-sounding jingle played on Gil's cellphone. He couldn't help noticing how his partner-in-crime frowned so deeply at the name that appeared on the Caller ID. Gil hesitated for a few seconds, as if contemplating whether to decline the call. He then seemed to think better of it and swiped the "answer" button on the touchscreen.

---

[2] Megadrak is the alpha daikaiju of the DragonStorm Universe. To see him in all his destructive glory check out this author's novels *Megadrak Book 1: Beast of the Apocalypse* and *Megadrak Book 2: Tokyo Screams*.

"Hey, Paco! What's up, man?"

His tone strongly suggested a lack of sincerity to those words. The fact that he trembled as he spoke made this all the clearer to a concerned Melvin.

"Look, guy, I swear I didn't mean to duck the deal. Something really important came up. Like life or death, man! Huh? Look, I hope you're just trying to be a smartass by saying that. Right?"

Then it fully occurred to Melvin what was going down. Or, rather, what was *about* to go down.

"C'mon, man, you can't mean that!" Gil continued, growing even more tense. "We're family! I understand that the big man is pissed off, but you know I would never duck out on things for no good reason! I'm telling you the truth! Something really important did come up...! Hello? You there?" Gil dropped the phone and looked at Melvin as his mocha complexion actually seemed to go pale. "Oh, man..."

"Pendajo, I am so going to kill you!" Melvin shouted. "You didn't bother to call your cuz and let him know we couldn't make the product pick up Thursday night so that he could have time to replace us, did you?"

"It slipped my mind, okay? When the better deal with the robot came along, I tried to focus on that. What kind of businessman would I be if I don't know how to prioritize?"

Melvin's eyelids shut tightly. "Jesus. H. Christ. You damned fool. Just tell me how much we owe the big man to make this right. One mil? Two?"

Gil grinned in trepidation. "Um... the pick-up we missed was worth almost 15 mil."

"Seriously, man? *Seriously?* That's most of what we got left between the two of us after paying off Iron Town! They're gonna come after us for this!"

"Uh, yeah, bro, they are. And that means we have to get way the hell out of Florida until we can find us another gig to pay off my cousin's contacts."

Melvin gritted his teeth to the point of cracking the enamel. "Jesus. H. *Christ!*"

And so it went...

END

THE SHISA AND THE DRAGON

Nathan Marchand

Author's Note: If this story seems familiar, that's because it should. While serving as co-host for Season One of Kaijuvision Radio, a podcast I created with Brian Scherschel, I came across a little-known legend while researching Okinawan religion and culture for the episode on *Godzilla vs. Mechagodzilla* (1974). I couldn't help but connect it to the explosive climax of that film. (I highly recommend listening to that episode to hear about all the mind-blowing things I discovered about Okinawa that add many layers to what on the surface seems like a simple film). Anyway, this story was inspired in large part by both that legend and, to a much lesser extent, that underestimated G-film. Enjoy!

Dread flooded the village of Madanbashi. Every door and window was locked, but these barriers were as paper before a tiger, as the debris of a dozen destroyed houses illustrated. The wind itself was silent and still. Stray dogs cowered under wagons. Even the sun hid behind gray clouds in fear.

Three people stood between the village and the beach at Naha Port Bay. Standing with regal poise on wobbly knees was King Eiji, whose red robe and golden crown distinguished him from his companions. A small lion-dog *shisa* statue dangled from his neck. Next to him stood Natsu, his *kikoe-ōgimi*, an old priestess with a hunched back pressing against her white robes. Sunken eyes

213

peeked from behind a headband that blended into her long, thinning hair. Prayer beads and a *magatama* stone dangled from each wrist. She leaned against a small dark-haired boy named Chiga. His face betrayed a stoic reverence, for he – a barefoot urchin clothed in rags – was in the presence of Ryukyuan royalty.

"It is madness for me to face Shidoragon alone!" said the king, staring at the colorless ocean.

The old woman bent slightly and whispered in Chiga's ear.

"The priestess Natsu reminds the king he has always trusted in her visions," the boy said. "Why is this any different?"

"Your dreams never advised me to confront a foe like this!" replied the king.

Natsu whispered in Chiga's ear again.

"The priestess Natsu says it is time to trust in something greater than her. This is a battle the king must begin if he is to save his people."

"Using this… trinket from a Chinese emissary?" the agitated king retorted while clutching the lion-dog necklace between his fingers and thumb as he fired a glare at the old woman and the boy.

The *kikoe-ōgimi* whispered once more to Chiga.

"The priestess Natsu says the king is only required to believe in Shisasama," relayed the boy.

King Eiji sighed. "Help me with my unbelief," he said under his breath.

If the old crone heard him – he was sure she had – she didn't react. Was this apathy or encouragement? Either way, the king breathed deeply, calling upon his martial arts training to calm himself.

He then walked forward.

His slippers sank into the cold sand with each timid step. Sunlight pierced the thick clouds, and a subtle shadow crept from the mountainous cliff-face overlooking the beach. It followed the king, and his heart quickened. Sweat glistened upon his forehead. He gripped the lion-dog *shisa* necklace around his neck as though it were his queen's hand. Waves licked gently at the shore, darkening it, the air thick with salt. It was a painting of perfect tranquility.

Until a black head broke through the now cerulean ocean and bellowed.

King Eiji froze as if turned to stone.

The head swam toward the shore, a long ebony body cutting through the water's surface with a row of spikes. The king blinked. A bearded snout and a crown of horns fully emerged as Shidoragon reached the shallows. The dragon's eyes locked with Eiji's. Tiny legs whipped the serpent's body through frothing water until he loomed as a defiant ruler. Shidoragon lifted his head high and opened a mouth full of fangs to emit a hiss louder than a rushing river.

King Eiji was paralyzed.

Two little words exclaimed by a child punched through his horror: "The *shisa*!"

A surge of courage shot through the king, whose hand tore the necklace off and raised it toward the dragon.

A roar, deep and guttural, thundered from the tiny figurine. King Eiji felt his innards shake. The ground quaked under his feet. Even Shidoragon lurched back, trembling.

The statue's eyes flared red.

215

Suddenly, the king's grip loosened as the effigy became heavier. He placed it on the ground and the sand began undulating from an invisible energy.

The *shisa* was growing.

King Eiji panicked and ran, not stopping until he rejoined Natsu and Chiga. He turned and saw that what was once small was now a towering scarlet creature with a thick mane and a tuft of fiery hair on its tail.

"Shisasama." The name fell quietly and deliberately from Natsu's lips. Both the king and Chiga eyed the old woman with surprise.

The lion-dog's ears stood erect, lips curling back to reveal sharp ivory teeth as it snarled at Shidoragon.

The dragon hissed.

Instantly, Shisasama dug his clawed feet into the sand and pounced at Shidoragon, the serpent springing out of the way. The lion-dog landed in the shallows, splashing water across the beach and making the king wish he'd brought his umbrella.

The creatures turned to face each other. Shidoragon opened his mouth. Shisasama hunched to pounce again. The serpent spat a green venom from his bared fangs at the lion-dog's face. Shisasama yelped, pawing at the acid in his burning eyes. Seizing the opening, Shidoragon lunged at his foe. Though blinded, Shisasama somehow sensed the dragon's attack and swatted Shidoragon's head, knocking the serpent sideways.

Instinctively, Shisasama splashed water in his face in a desperate effort to wash out the venom. Shidoragon, having recovered from the blow, crawled toward the distracted lion-dog. Before the king or his companions could shout warnings, the serpent wrapped itself around

Shisasama's body. The lion-dog's yelps quieted as the dragon's coils constricted, squeezing the air from his throat.

Shisasama buckled, falling to the ground with a thunderous thud. Shidoragon's head slithered around the lion-dog's shoulders. He bared his fangs again and plunged them into Shisasama's neck. The lion-dog's body went limp as the serpent injected his poison. A shadow fell as a cloud obscured the sun.

"No... no!" exclaimed King Eiji, falling to his knees.

For a moment – a brief moment – his gaze met the eyes of Shisasama, which now looked like dying embers. They spoke no words nor made any sounds, and yet the lion-dog heard the king's plea.

Shisasama's eyes brightened. He forced his legs to straighten. Shidoragon's bite loosened. Then, with one last burst of willpower, the lion-dog threw his body back with his hind legs, smashing himself and the coiling serpent against the cliff-face. A hiss of air escaped the sea-dragon's mouth as his fangs unclamped from Shisasama's neck. With Shidoragon's coils loosened, he unwrapped the dragon from his body and threw the rattled serpent aside.

Chiga cheered.

A long-lost smile cracked upon King Eiji's face, but it was erased when Shisasama collapsed and Shidoragon stirred.

The fight was not over.

The lion-dog stood groggily, his blazing eyes locked on the sea serpent, who was preparing to strike. Ichor-like blood trickled down Shisasama's forelegs, almost blending into his crimson fur. He stepped sideways

217

toward the cliff-face, stumbling. Red drops speckled the sand.

Shidoragon hissed.

Shisasama growled.

The sea-dragon sprang.

The lion-dog reflexively slapped the serpent's face. Stunned, Shidoragon coiled his body, looking like a living rope, and poised to strike again. Summoning his last ounces of supernatural strength, Shisasama inhaled, the wind howling through his nostrils and his chest swelling to the point of bursting.

Shidoragon bared his fangs and lunged.

Shisasama opened his mouth and roared.

Thunder shot from the lion-dog's maw. He shook the earth beneath the feet of King Eiji and his companions. They covered their ears in a desperate effort to shield against deafness.

The king dropped to one knee. He looked up and saw a wave of distorted air shooting from Shisasama's mouth and crashing into Shidoragon, launching the dragon backward and slamming him against the cliff-face. The reptilian monster squealed in agony, unable to move. Cracks crawled across the mountain, crisscrossing in intricate webs. Only then did the lion-dog hush -- his roar replaced by the rumble of an avalanche. The peak of the cliff-face crumbled and great boulders rained down upon Shidoragon. The serpent, confused by the noise, vanished in a cloud of dust and sand.

Silence.

King Eiji, Chiga, and Natsu uncovered their ears and watched in amazement.

The cloud dissipated to reveal Shidoragon buried under boulders up to his forelegs.

Shisasama, staggering as he approached, walked toward his fallen foe. The dragon's eyes were closed. Blood trickled from his mouth. The lion-dog nudged the serpent's head with his paw. He seemed stiff as a corpse.

A reluctant smile returned to King Eiji's face.

Shisasama turned away from Shidoragon.

The dragon's eyes suddenly opened.

The king's cry of warning shot from his mouth as a gasp.

The serpent's jaws clamped onto the lion-dog's back heel. Shisasama groaned in painful shock. He looked over his shoulder and scowled. With a flick of his foot, he threw the serpent back, where it squirmed in desperation, clawing at the crimson sand.

The two creatures' gazes met for an instance. Shisasama's eyes flared a fiery red. With that, the lion-dog kicked the cliff-face with both hind legs. Another boulder fell from the now jagged peak and crushed Shidoragon's head. A red puddle formed around it as the rumble echoed down the beach.

The shadows of clouds receded like a black tide. Sunlight raced along the shore until it touched everything in sight.

King Eiji was finally able to breathe again. He heard quiet laughter from Chiga and Natsu behind him. This was instantly replaced by loud footfalls. He looked toward the destroyed mountain. Shisasama, slowly regaining his stately gait, was walking toward them. The king lurched back in fear, but it vanished in his awe of the creature that once hung around his neck.

The lion-dog stopped and sat down, his tail erect with its tuft of fur curling around and touching his back. His eyes flashed in the sun, nearly blinding the king and his companions. When they'd blinked away the white spots obscuring their vision, they saw a huge indentation the size of a ship in the sand. At the center something glinted. King Eiji, undaunted, ran toward it. As he approached, he came upon a small *shisa* necklace. He slowly, reverently knelt and picked up the statue by its chain. Staring into its tiny eyes, he walked back to Chiga and Natsu.

"Shisasama has saved us!" he said upon rejoining them.

Natsu leaned over to Chiga and whispered in his ear. He nodded.

"No," the boy said. "The priestess Natsu says it was Ryukyu's king who saved the islands."

King Eiji furrowed his brow. "How? I could do nothing but watch as the monsters battled."

Natsu whispered in Chiga's ear once more. The boy pursed his lips in intense concentration as the old priestess spoke to him for a long moment.

The king heard his heartbeats echo in his chest.

Finally, Natsu straightened as best as her old body would allow, and the boy proclaimed, "The priestess Natsu says the king's faith animated the statue and strengthened Shisasama throughout the battle. Did you not sense the connection the guardian lion made with you? Though it wavered at times, it was your belief that compelled Shisasama to fight the sea dragon, to accomplish what Ryukyu's king desired but was powerless to do. Without this, the battle could not begin let alone be fought."

King Eiji stared at the little figurine laying in the palm of his hand as Chiga relayed Natsu's words. It felt heavier now, if only a little. Heavy with a heretofore unknowable power. He found comfort in this. As Chiga finished, the king hung the statue around his neck, the tiny lion-dog dangling in front of his heart.

"Then I proclaim that every house in Ryukyu shall have a *shisa* statue erected at its entrance in remembrance of this day of deliverance," he began, his royal stature returning. "May the Ryukyu people and their king always trust the guardian lions to protect them against evil. So long as the *shisa* remain, Ryukyu will always have hope in the midst of monsters."

"It shall be done, my king," replied Chiga, bowing.

A smile crinkled Natsu's wrinkly face.

"Come," the king said as he stepped between the boy and old woman, putting a hand on their shoulders. "Let us celebrate with the people."

END

DEMONIC MAELSTROM IN THE PHILIPPINE SEA

Andrew Nguyen

The Western Pacific Ocean
June 9th, 202X
8:00 a.m.

While there are many means of travel across the world, the oceans remain one of the most vital. Through the four great oceans of the world flow the goods and people in enormous numbers that allow global civilization to function. Within those waters of the world live an endless variety of plant and animal life that strive to flourish despite the interactions of humanity.

Sadly, as with all areas of the world that are touched by humanity, the oceans have been a war zone. This is ironic in the largest body of water on the globe, the Pacific Ocean, for in the 20th century, some of the greatest naval wars in history occurred in these waters. During the Cold War and in the early years of the 21st century, the Pacific was a flashpoint in a conflict that had the capability of destroying the entire world.

Sometimes the ocean strikes back, however. For hidden deep beneath the dark waters of the Pacific lay entities that managed to survive from the time of the destruction of the dinosaurs -- and other climactic world destroying events -- to the present day. A few of those entities had even awoken from time to time to plague the

221

oceans and the mysterious parts of the world. Those events that the few humans who had witnessed them were passed on until they became legends. However, all legends are based on a seed of truth.

Down in the darkest depths of the Pacific, a living mass slipped through the crushing pressure with ease. Its size was enough to cause a kraken to shy away at its approach. If human eyes could penetrate far enough to see the beast, it would chill a person to the bone. Some of its features were similar to known animals, while others seemed to be from the underworld. Although the entity feasted upon other animals it also consumed energy from sources not considered natural, in fact it and others like it were also capable of drawing power upon sources of energy that were the source of the most horrific weapons known to mankind

In fact, up until the mid-20th century, they resided in the darkest depths of the ocean and earth, where they drew upon the power of the molten secretions of the Earth. However, when the planet's inhabitants unleashed the power of the sun for horrific purposes, these atomic emanations drew the creatures up towards the surface of the earth and affected them in ways considered unnatural.

For this particular entity, it had suddenly stumbled upon what one could consider a buffet; for over the span of a few weeks; it had been hunting objects in the water that resembled the outline of metal fish to the creature's perception. In addition to feasting upon their metallic corpses, the creature also feasted upon the "metal hearts" of the steel fish, which somehow gave it more power than feasting upon normal prey. And it was about to stumble upon another feast.

Scanning with both its eyes and ears the creature soon spotted another metal fish that was sailing much closer to the surface. Trailing behind the prey was a smaller object that seemed to be the fish's offspring. The creature silently ascended to the same level as that of its metallic quarry while also gradually increasing its speed, its large bulk and massive fish-like tail propelling it along.

However, the fish somehow detected the entity's approach, to which it silently turned and confronted its predator. Snarling at its prey, the creature warily focused on its target while waiting for it to make its next move. That came a moment later when the metal fish emitted a powerful sound.

Roaring at what had just happened, the creature suddenly surged forward before thrusting out with an enormous four-fingered claw. The fish tried to evade but the creature rapidly latched on with both hands, with which it ripped deeply into the fish's metal skin. Once the gigantic entity had its prey fully within its grasp, it heard sounds from within metal fish that roused it into a frenzied state. It then tore into its prey with renewed vigor.

The metallic fish rapidly gave way under the assault of its attacker. Already several sections of the sub had been torn off and were quickly being crumbled under the incredible pressure of the Pacific Ocean. The remaining sections of the sub soon disintegrated under the combined assault of the creature and of the aforementioned water pressure.

Despite nearly being crushed, the reactor still pulsed with energy but that would not last long as the creature began to quickly swim down after it. Once the creature reached the reactor, a trail of energy seemed to transfer from the reactor to the entity. Within seconds, the reactor died and instantly crumpled like a squeezed tin can in the deep dark depths of the Pacific.

As for the entity itself, the energy transferring from the metal heart of the prey that the entity destroyed caused it to glow for several moments, illuminating the deep darkness of the ocean.

For any human eyes that had managed to see it, the creature had features that seemed a horrific mismatch of animals that are known on Earth. The entity's head resembled that of an alligator with eyes as black as that of a shark while gills were noticeable on its neck. Though the creature had four legs, the two forward limbs had features that combined a mix of feet and arms. Each of the four legs had small protrusions that pointed outward from the beast's skin. At first its tail resembled that of a normal one but towards its edge, one could see details found on fish. Its skin seemed to have scales and bumps on different sections of the body.

Letting out a satisfied howl as if finishing a sumptuous meal, its eyes seemed to burn red for a moment before they disappeared back into black again. The creature was snarling in annoyance at its inability to find any other immediate prey before it disappeared back into the darkness of the Pacific Ocean.

Camp H.M. Smith
June 11th, 202X.
6:00 p.m.

Located in the middle of the Pacific Ocean, the 50th state of the United States has had a long and complicated history with war and the Pacific Ocean. Annexed in 1898, it served as a waypoint between the U.S. and the overseas territories of Guam and the Philippines. In May 1940, Hawaii gained further importance when President Franklin Delano Roosevelt relocated the United States Pacific Fleet to Pearl Harbor on the Hawaiian island of Oahu. It entered immortality on December 7th, 1941 when the Imperial Japanese Navy launched a surprise attack on the base and the U.S. Pacific Fleet.

The next day, the United States declared war on Japan and the two nations waged one of the greatest naval wars in the 20th century, which ended in an atomic nightmare unleashed on Japan. While the two main fleets in the Pacific, the 3rd and 7th, were not located in Hawaii, it still served as the main headquarters of U.S. Pacific Command. It was thus the main U.S. theater command in the event of conflict with today's great Asian power, the People's Republic of China.

Looking towards Pearl Harbor, Admiral Horner, commander of U.S. Indo-Pacific Command (INDO-PACCOM) pondered the notes for the meeting. Although he had managed to do as well as anyone could under the circumstances, the losses of the preceding weeks had stunned everyone in the United States Navy, until the present conflict was considered the safest branch of the

military; certainly when compared to the Army and Air
Force.

A knock on the door interrupted the admiral's
thoughts, to which he responded, "Enter."

An aide walked in, to which the admiral inquired,
"Have the others arrived?"

The aide nodded. "Yes, sir, they're waiting in the main
conference room and we have established
communications links with Yokosuka."

Horner nodded and departed to the conference room
with his aide directly behind him. Within minutes the
admiral arrived in the main conference hall where several
other military officers were engaged in quiet
conversations with each other.

Other personnel present included intelligence officials
from both the military and the CIA, the latter of which
stood out in their business suits in comparison to the
former's uniforms. Once they noticed his arrival,
everyone stood at instant attention before Horner
signaled the officers to take their seats. As they did so
several aides moved to the walls around the room, which
retracted to show screens already filling with maps. Once
everything was in order the meeting began.

The commander of U.S. INDO-PACCOM looked at
the faces of his fellow officers before he began to speak.

"Thank you all for coming, we have much ground to
cover and little time to waste." As several maps of the
western Pacific appeared on the walls behind him,
Horner continued. "Right now, we are at a stalemate in
the Western Pacific. While we have had several
successes, the situation is tenuous." He paused for a
moment to give his words maximum impact. "National

Command Authority has given us a firm directive to develop an option to turn the situation to our advantage."

With that he resumed his seat while his chief of staff stood up to speak to the room while pointing to the maps on the walls.

"On all fronts, we have managed to halt or slow down the Chinese advance, although the cost has been high. In turn, our attempts to try to regain any territory has proven unsuccessful." Pausing for a moment to take a sip from his cup of water, the chief of staff then highlighted the maps showing smaller sections of Asia. "In Southeast Asia, we have already attempted a counter-offensive with reinforcement from the Atlantic Fleet, but the gains have been modest and have encountered heavy resistance. For the central Pacific, the PLA is rapidly fortifying Taiwan and Okinawa."

Although it was familiar information, the news was enough to sober everyone, for they had long been used to the U.S. military being the dominant power on the planet. Despite the war on terror, the U.S. had trained for a potential match with other great powers. However, training and experiencing it first-hand were two different things. Already the U.S. Navy had suffered the loss of one of its legendary aircraft carriers in the conflict's early stages.

Looking at the faces of his fellow officers, Horner paused for a moment before he announced to the room, "After careful consideration of the information, we have decided to commence with a push towards the Central Pacific again." Standing up to point at the main map behind him, he continued. "By doing so, we will draw Chinese forces away from the south while relieving pressure on our allies there. Furthermore, if we do succeed, it will divide Chinese forces while assisting Japan and South Korea."

The room nodded grimly in agreement before his subordinate commanders began to stand up and deliver their reports on their own commands.

First up was Vice-Admiral Maxwell, the commander of the U.S. 3rd fleet, "The carriers are already past Wake Island and the Expeditionary Strike Groups are a day behind them. My subs are already gathering southeast of Iwo Jima and we're awaiting the arrival of the rest of the fleet."

Next was Vice Admiral Howard, Maxwell's counterpart in the U.S. 7th fleet, the frontline fleet in the war, "Right now we're barely holding the line with our remaining resources." His voice then turned grim as he continued to speak. "While 65 to 70 percent of my forces are back up to strength, the remainder are either too badly damaged or destroyed. Our immediate problem is clearing the obstacles that the PLAN seeded in the harbors in Japan and Guam. Once clear, the 7th fleet will be able to engage."

All winced at the news before the two Japanese military officers alongside Howard began to speak.

First up was the commander of the Japanese Maritime Self Defense Force (JMSDF), Admiral Okawara. "As you see on this map, half of my fleet has allocated forces to defending western Japan from both North Korea and China." Pausing his briefing to look over additional information, the admiral resumed his report. "In conjunction with your 7th fleet, we have attempted to clear out the mines that the PLAN has laid in our harbors.

Hopefully, we should remove the last of them before the attack begins. In addition, we have completed repairs and resupply of the *Kaga* and *Izumo*, thus making them available."

General Nishizawa of the Japanese Air Self Defense Force (JASDF) then presented his own report to the audience. "Right now, the JASDF along with your air force have achieved a temporary stalemate, but we are barely holding the line. To help counter the bombardments from Chinese missiles, we have relocated our anti-air defenses to protect the airfields without compromising key installations or our cities."

General Robinson, commander of U.S. Pacific Air Forces (PACAF), was the last to present his information, although perhaps it was the most vital. "We've been transferring forces from home to our forward operating bases although it has proven difficult to the missile attacks which limit the airbases available and the number of planes we will have on hand. Furthermore, due to the constant combat and its scale, we are operating at a disadvantage in resources. Provided we use our assets judiciously we should be able to operate freely in this operation."

Horner nodded at the news before announcing to the room, "We're preparing to present this information to the president but based on your information, we should expect the operation to begin in several days."

Maxwell raised his hand at the request to which Horner acknowledged before he spoke his question. "Sir, what about the mysterious object that has been prowling the battle area? Are there any countermeasures to deal with it?"

All the other officers nodded. Horner agreed with them, for he too had thoughts about the object that had been prowling the central Pacific.

That was when one of the CIA officials in the back of the room began to speak. "Based on the information gathered by the CIA and our allies, we believe that the object attacks ships with a particular focus on those that have nuclear reactors. In response, we've recommended to the Joint Chiefs to reinforce U.S. INDO-PACCOM with additional ASW assets. Finally, based on what information we could gather, it seems the object responds to use of active sonar. If our ships keep to using their passive sonar systems, they should be able to engage the object while avoiding immediate retaliation."

Horner nodded in agreement before he added, "We've already undertaken those measures partially in response to the Chinese submarine threat." Pausing for a moment to signal that the meeting was wrapping up, the admiral then announced, "Report back to your commands and ensure that they're ready to move out the moment that we receive the order from Washington."

All nodded at the order and saluted the admiral before they departed from the room in quiet conversations. Watching them go before turning to the map, Horner quietly wondered the age-old question that commanders wondered on the eve of battle: How many of these men would he ever see again?

Nanjing, China
June 14th, 202X.
1:00 p.m.

Walking along the hallway towards the main conference room at the headquarters of Eastern Theater Command, People's Liberation Army Air Force (PLAAF) General Cheng had one eye on the path to his destination with another peering eye out the windows that displayed the city below him. While one may thank that it would be a hazard, to Cheng it was no problem, as he already knew his destination. To him, looking outside at the city from time to time -- even if only a peek -- served to strengthen his resolve for the task at hand. That was because this city had a dark history in the mid-20th century that had seared itself into the soul of every Chinese.

Inside, the commanders of the Eastern and Northeastern Theater Commands were in conversations with their staffs. When they all saw Cheng and his own staff arrive, the main generals of the theater commands snapped to attention while their staffs took their respective places, some sitting at the side of their commanding officers while others alongside the respective screens that surrounded the circular hall.

Pausing for a moment to observe the entire room around him, Cheng began the briefing. "Alright, gentlemen, we have much ground to cover, so let us get going. First off, I bring congratulations from and the gratitude for the success of the war. Hopefully what we discuss here will help bring the conflict to an end and complete the restoration of honor to our country and our people."

His aide then described the overall situation. "As you can see on the main map, we are at a stalemate with the United States and its allies. After a successful wave of initial operations, enemy resistance has stiffened, and our advances have slowed on all fronts. Fortunately, we have repulsed every attempt by the enemy to retake ground. In initial combat operations as well as in defense, the enemy has suffered heavy losses."

The aide then turned to nod silently one of the intelligence officers

That officer, a colonel, walked over to the map, which was soon highlighted with potential enemy concentrations.

"Based on multiple sources," he said, "we have identified these main enemy groups. In the south, we have identified two U.S. carriers in the area with another joining them shortly, as well as additional air force units arriving in the area. In the central pacific, we have detected a large reinforcement of planes and ships, including multiple aircraft carriers."

After pausing for a moment, the colonel wrapped up his briefing by stating, "We believe that the Americans will attempt another offensive. Although the south is of concern due to our vital holdings there, an attack in the central pacific is also of concern due to the targets. However, it may present opportunities for a decisive victory."

Cheng then spoke up again. "As you can see with the information presented, our enemies plan to move against us. Based on the information presented, the central military council has released assets to us to use to meet this upcoming threat."

As he spoke those words, several smaller images appeared on the map, detailing the movement of ships, planes, and more importantly, radar, missiles, and satellites. The general then turned to the officers who represented the Eastern and Northeastern Theater commands.

"Provide status report and plans to meet this attack."

General Yingchang, the commander of the Eastern Theater Command and thus the point command of a conflict with Taiwan and the southern Japanese islands presented his information first. "Right now, we have been fortifying our positions on Taiwan, Diaoyu, and Okinawa. The focus has been on anti-air defenses and surface to surface missiles. The Eastern Sea Fleet already has its submarines west of our positions. We have also intensified our air activities in order to delay their preparations and to find more information."

General Dehuai, the commander of the Northeastern Theater Command was next to present his report. "We are also undertaking similar measures. Our air units have been conducting aggressive attacks in the region of South Korea and Japan. Furthermore, the Northern Seas fleet has kept up the pressure with attacks on their supply lines and blockading the ports. Right now, we are looking at additional assets that we can release to Eastern Theater Command."

Cheng nodded at the news of his subordinates before he spoke again, "Thank you for the information. It shows that you have been taking the measure of our foes seriously." He then observed his subordinates before he spoke again. "The Central Military Commission will need to review these plans, but you should expect a quick approval."

The others nodded in agreement at the news that Cheng had said. but then Yingchang signaled with a small hand wave before he asked, "Comrade General, I do have a concern to voice here." When Cheng silently nodded for him to continue, the general said, "About the recent rash of submarines and ships mysteriously sunk. Do we have a contingency should the cause of this appear?"

The room erupted in murmurs as they digested what Yingchang had said.

To that, Cheng agreed before he said, "Ensure that both the East Sea and North Sea fleets of the People's Liberation Army Navy (PLAN) have adequate countermeasures in place. In turn, the Central Military Council will provide additional resources to deal with this mysterious entity that has been plaguing our shores. Right now, we must focus on the enemy that we are facing."

The general then took a on a dark humorous tone. "Don't forget that the entity has also destroyed their ships, as well." The room erupted in grim laughter at that for a moment before he addressed the assembled officers. "Right now, we are at a critical stage where we must make one gargantuan effort to secure victory. If we succeed, we will have undone the years of humiliation that they have inflicted on us for so long. Our people and our ancestors watch us this very moment. Let us prove worthy of them."

With that, the meeting ended as the general and his staff departed the conference room. The rest followed them out, all in hushed tones as they pondered the gravity of the task. Either way this went, they would be making history in a matter much like what Japan did, or even greater than what it had done, at the beginning of the last century.

Philippine Sea
June 19th, 202X.
9:00 a.m.

The deeper one descended into the ocean, the darker the color seemed to be. Although it remained blue, it seemed to turn almost black due to the inability of light to penetrate to the watery depths. However, there were sections of the ocean that possessed a hue as dark as that of space itself. The source of such anomalies was most often natural, although there were exceptions.

One such exception floated in the deep darkness of the Pacific. At times, if the creature were sighted, it would lead one to believe that the entity was dead. However, it was very much alive; and though asleep, its senses were very much active. These were soon assaulted from a variety of different sources. Blackish-red eyes opened and moved as if receiving an irritating sound. The creature snarled, its mood a mix of annoyance and hunger, before it began to move towards the closest source of potential foes.

East Sea Fleet Headquarters
Ningbo, China

Although they all wore different uniforms and operated under different flags, the commanders on the opposing side in this conflict often conducted similar activities and operated in similar environments when conducting operations against each other. The respective lead commanders were in their shore-based headquarters watching the battle on large overhead screens. Their respective staffs were busy attending to their duties as they attempted to deal with the chaos of battle even if they were not involved in the actual fighting.

Sensing the gravity of the hour that faced them all, the personnel at headquarters all had grim and resolute expressions on their faces. Only their training and the culture in which they grew up provided the difference in what the commanders felt as the battle unfolded.

Watching as the PLAAF and the PLAN move out to counter the enemy, Cheng felt a sense of pride as his forces exchanged fire with their foes. Although it was still early in the battle, he and everyone else in the room could see their forces fighting well. In the air and depending on the situation, both sides were at a stalemate. Even then, it was in China's favor as it took more time than necessary for the U.S. and its allies to destroy individual Chinese fighters. It was a similar situation in the ocean as groups of warships exchanged missile fire with their counterparts. While their respective air defenses mitigated the damage, the PLAN scored an early success with concentrated fire from sea and air against one of the prized U.S. carrier groups.

Despite the apparent success, there had been some setbacks. With the drawdown of forces surrounding Japan in order to meet the U.S. Navy's advance, the combined U.S. 7th fleet and JSDF had cleared the blockade around the islands and elements were now racing towards the 3rd fleet. Furthermore, reports began arriving of U.S. submarines having successes in fighting through the ASW groups and inflicting damage, although it was still within projections.

Suddenly, one of the radar operators, who had been quietly listening in on his headphones, turned to the commanders and said "Sir, one of our *Type 039A* class submarines (NATO codename *Yuan*) has disappeared." Before anyone could ask, the operator pulled up information on one of the larger screens. "This was the position of our submarine before it disappeared."

The commanders looked at the information for several moments before Admiral Shan, the commander of the East Sea Fleet, said to the others, "So far we've detected no enemy units within close proximity."

Cheng and the other commanders nodded at his statement as they thought of their options before Shan turned to point at one of the screens. He said, "Send in this task group and order other units to be on the alert."

The communications officers nodded and began transmitting the orders as Shan headed back to join his fellow officers. All shared the same concern of what they had just encountered and its potential meaning.

Camp H.M. Smith
Hawaii
June 18th, 202X

Watching the exact events playing out on a large screen halfway across the world, Admiral Horner and his subordinates also had identical looks of deep concentration on their faces. Compared to their Chinese counterparts, the faces of the American commanders and their allies revealed their tension and worry as their forces engaged the Chinese. Though the battle seemed to be progressing their way, it was at too slow a pace. They had successes as the 7th fleet and the JMSDF had broken clear of the blockade around Japan and were heading to meet the northern elements of the 3rd fleet west of Iwo Jima. Furthermore, U.S. submarines had managed to penetrate the Chinese ASW patrol line and had inflicted damage, though already at the cost of one *Virginia*-class submarine.

Despite the successes of the submarines, the surface battle remained stalemated as both fleets exchanged missile fire with each other. As for the air battle, it was a balancing act; if the U.S. and her allies flew over neutral territory, they held their ground against the PLAAF. However, if they advanced towards the Chinese forces, they had a more difficult fight as Chinese anti-air defenses joined the battle. Already Carrier Strike Group 8, centered on the U.S.S. *Harry S. Truman*, was withdrawing as the aircraft carrier. That craft had suffered grievous damage, including a devastating hit from a DF-21. The sight of the damaged carrier reminded the command staff of the loss of the U.S.S. *Ronald*

Reagan and the near sinking of the U.S.S. *Carl Vinson* earlier in the war.

A communications officer broke their thoughts as he yelled, "Sir, we just intercepted a communique to one of the Chinese surface groups and one of their submarines!" The officer pulled up a section of the map before he continued, "They are heading to these coordinates."

Horner looked at the map, then whispered to the others, "We don't have any units in the area, correct?" Several of his comrades present nodded in agreement as they turned back to look at the screen and any forces closest to the designated area.

Horner closed his eyes for a moment before opening them again and issuing an order. "Signal the subs and the air units to head to those coordinates. Find out what is going on there."

The officer nodded before he transmitted the directive as Horner joined his fellow commanders with one eye on the overall battle and the other on the impending direct collision between the two sides.

Task Group 234:
550 miles southeast of Okinawa

Steaming rapidly towards the coordinates provided by their superiors, the ships of the Task group, consisting of a Type 54A frigate (NATO codename *Jiangkai II*) and three Type 56A corvettes (NATO codename *Jiangdao*), warily searched the seas ahead for any potential threats. Overhead, several Harbin Z-6C ASW helicopters and long-range J-11 fighters flew air cover, while underneath a Type 93 class nuclear submarine (NATO codename

239

Shang) scouted ahead for any threats or potential targets. While the crews of the assembled forces were mystified at the orders due to the location of the coordinates in the proximity to that of their enemies, they nevertheless carried them out in a professional manner.

Creeping forward in the darkness of the ocean, the *Shang* swept the area in front of it with its passive sonar. Thus far, they had not found anything out of the ordinary. That, however, did not lessen the tension of the crew as they dealt with a potential new threat in addition to the present danger from the Americans and their allies. Most of them still felt that they were out on a wild goose chase that increased their chances of dying. They were correct on their eventual fate, but wrong on its cause.

That cause showed itself as one of the sonar operators spotted an object that seemed to be moving towards them. Both the captain and the XO rushed to the station to see for themselves for several minutes before the captain yelled out the order for battle stations, while the XO ordered the communications officers to relay the information to the awaiting ships and planes. Once the message was sent, the captain of the *Shang* ordered the submarine's sonar to begin active pinging, a decision that proved a fatal mistake.

Silently eying the large metal "fish" in front of it, the creature snarled as he sensed potential prey to hunt. Blinking for several moments while making small movements with its long snout, the monster spotted several more potential quarries as it tracked its present target. Suddenly, the creature roared as a sound repeatedly began to emit from the target. The monster reacted by instantly sprinting forward, one of its arms grasping onto the metal skin.

The *Shang* immediately fired a torpedo at the oncoming hostile, but the explosive projectile had no time to arm before it slammed into the creature's skin and broke in half. Like the others that had gone before, the Chinese submarine crumbled under the attack by the creature, its titanium hull torn apart like paper. Within seconds the submarine retrograded into several pieces with its nuclear reactor falling into the sea before its attacker grasped it with its left claw-like foot.

Feasting on the nuclear reactor, the creature let out a roar of victory before it picked up several different sounds occurring all around it. Bellowing in anger at the interruption of its meal, the creature rushed towards the source of the new sounds. It wasn't long before it spotted several small objects heading towards it. Before the monster moved onto the new targets, several Chinese Yu-7 torpedoes slammed into it. These were followed by a salvo of ASW rockets. Momentarily stunned, the monster roared with apoplectic fury before ascending rapidly to the surface.

After surrounding the roiling area of the ocean, the Chinese task group fired away with all its ASW weapons while overhead the air units prepared to provide support. As the ships attempted to reload their weapons, the water began churning even more violently, forcing them into evasive action while delaying their attempt to rearm. Before the ships could take countermeasures, a huge shape leapt high out of the water before descending right onto the *Jiangkai II* frigate.

Before the horrified eyes of the other ships and planes, the vessel broke in half under the creature's tremendous weight. This was followed by an explosion that destroyed the remains of the doomed ship. Pushing their engines to full power, the *Jiangdao* corvettes resumed firing with the aircraft and helicopters joining in with their own missiles and torpedoes.

The creature roared furiously before it swam towards the Chinese warships. Its black eyes narrowed on the targets in front of it while its huge bulk and fish-like tail left an enormous wake in the water. The distance was quickly closed between them, and before the ships could attempt to evade, the monster reached with one of its limbs towards a *Jiangdao* corvette. While the two other corvettes and planes attempted to assist the stricken vessel, the creature pulled the first ship towards it. The aquatic beast then tore the corvette apart with its front limbs and alligator-shaped mouth as if it were tinfoil.

Seeing that they could do no more, the two remaining Chinese ships began to flee at flank speed with the air support covering their withdrawal. However, the firepower was ineffective and the monster rapidly closed in. It repeated the process of tearing the second corvette apart with its forward limbs and jaw.

Fortunately, the third corvette managed to escape at flank speed while their unfortunate comrades on its doomed counterpart were killed. After finishing off its victim, the monster rose above the water as if standing on its two rear legs before bellowing a challenge to its aerial assailants.

U.S.S. Hampton
630 miles southwest of Okinawa

The submarines U.S.S. *Hampton* and U.S.S. *Olympia* crept toward the area, when they picked up the creature as it attacked the Chinese task group. Silently ascending to the surface, they relayed the information to the orbiting P-3 Orion and their F-15E Strike Eagle escort before they descended back down into the ocean. There they resumed course to their target, their crews tense as they listened in on the destruction of the Chinese force. It was the enormous roars that they heard over their sonar systems that convinced the crews that there was another threat, one perhaps even more dangerous than their compeers on the Chinese side.

On the *Hampton*, its captain looked pensively at the sonar screens before he made his grim decision.

"Get the range to the target, arm weapons, and order engineering to go to full power for the reactor. he commanded. Make sure the *Olympia* does the same and signal the air units for support."

His fellow officers nodded grimly and within seconds the *Los Angeles*-class submarine was primed for action. While the XO nodded to the sonar personnel, the captain waited grimly as the ping went out, followed by the roar of the entity that they had encountered.

Upon hearing the range, the captain issued what he hoped was not his final order.

"Match bearings and shoot."

The *Hampton* and the *Olympia* rumbled for a moment as they each fired four Mark 48 torpedoes, immediately cutting the wires and allowing the torpedoes to use their own sonar. While the fish sped on towards the target, the two submarines immediately accelerated to flank speed and attempted to head to the surface while launching decoys to distract the target from pursuit.

Roaring with a fearsome furor as it spotted the torpedoes heading its way, the creature accelerated its speed. However, the torpedoes' onboard sensors kept track of the target and soon found their marks. The monster did dodge two of the pursuing projectiles, which self-destructed after their sensors could not regain targeting lock.

Enraged by the attack, the creature suddenly sprinted forward, its eyes blinking several times as it tried to gain a glimpse of its targets through the bubbles generated by the decoys. More Mark 50 torpedoes quickly dropped into the water in front of the sea beast before heading straight towards it.

Bellowing in rage at the resistance that it encountered, the creature seemed to increase its speed further despite the hail of explosions surrounding it. Inevitably the torpedo attacks only delayed the monster, and it soon caught up with the two *Los Angeles*-class subs, its front limbs already stretching out to grasp them in its vice-like clutches.

The *Olympia*, which was further ahead, managed to dodge the monster's attack -- although it was a close one. Releasing several more decoys, the *Olympia* resumed flank speed as she attempted to escape from the creature's grasp. Its sister vessel was not so lucky as the creature's right arm grabbed into the *Hampton's* stern, almost crushing it instantly.

After spiraling downward and out of control, the submarine released several more decoys while pinging away with its active sonar in order to occupy the beast's attention. As the *Olympia* and the Orions observed, the creature destroyed the *Hampton* and absorbed the nuclear energy from the submarine's reactor.

The aquatic monstrosity snarled as it attempted to sense more targets in its vicinity. These it soon found. Snarling for a movement as if attempting to ascertain its quarry, the monster's alligator-shaped mouth turned into what would resemble a glee before it suddenly ascended before heading east by northeast towards a large batch of prey.

Flying overhead above the water, the Orions kept track of the creature's advance through their sonar buoys. They soon realized that they had much reason for concern. The pilot of one of the Orions immediately transmitted a warning.

Camp H.M. Smith
Hawaii

Pandemonium broke out in the main command center as the news came in from the Orions. While their subordinates scrambled to deal with this new potential threat, Horner and his fellow commanders considered their options, which were not good. While their forces held their ground, the pressure was piling on them and now an unknown threat was stalking their vessels.

Looking at the recent information, Horner turned to his fellow commanders and queried, "What's status of the fleet?"

"Gerald R. Ford has reported in," Maxwell replied. "The escorts for the *Truman* have detached from her and are heading back to the main force. The remaining carriers are continuing the attack, but their air units have suffered losses and are now at a stalemate.

"Right now, the amphibious carriers are doing what they can," Howard added, "but with the limited capabilities of the F-35Bs Lightning II and of the amphibious ships themselves, they too are getting stretched. As for the JMSDF, they are reporting the same issue with their fighters on the *Kaga* and *Izumo*."

Grimly looking at the information, Robinson said, "Right now the air units are holding their own, but they have suffered losses and despite the countermeasures taken, Guam and Iwo Jima have been hit. So far, our airfields in Japan have escaped serious damage, but the aircraft losses there are also a cause of concern."

Wincing at the information, Horner turned to look back at the main map as he considered his options. On the one hand, he had a known threat in the form of the People's Liberation Army; on the other, he had an unknown foe – one which appeared to be devoid of human control -- heading straight for his forces.

After pondering the matter for a moment, the admiral made up his mind and turned to one of the communication officers with a command "Signal our forces of the approaching object. And signal the Chinese of the situation. Hopefully, they may at least back off on hearing this."

The subordinates proceeded to transmit the orders while Horner and the rest turned to watch the mysterious entity heading toward the nearest forces. All were wondering what the hell they had stumbled upon.

Carrier Strike Group 3
700 miles southwest of Iwo Jima

It was fortunate that Carrier Strike Group 3 (CSG-3), which centered on the *John C. Stennis*, had gained some breathing space when they received the information from the Orions and Pearl Harbor. When the group's commander read the news, it took several critical moments for him and his staff to comprehend it. Soon CSG-3 was heading north to link up with reinforcements while its ships rapidly launched a new wave of aircraft into the sky.

Already a squadron of four destroyers was closing in to assist CSG-3, boosting its immediate firepower. It was none too soon as the sonar picked up the monster heading straight for them. While vectoring in aircraft, the ships combined with the escorts to form a barrier between the *Stennis* and the mysterious foe.

Sensing the presence of multiple different targets, the creature blinked its eyes and let out a small grunt before increasing its speed. Suddenly, the monster picked up the sight of several Mark 50 and Mark 54 torpedoes heading its way, to which it growled before heading on a collision course. In several seconds, the torpedoes found their target, surrounding the aquatic beast in a wave of explosions.

Although the creature was not injured, it angrily ascended to the surface, breaching with a huge plume of sea water. Growling at the attack, the monster moved its enormous head around for several moments before seeing its foes, who were attempting to fall back. Raising its frontal limbs in an attack posture, the creature resumed his advance, eager for blood and death.

From the bridge of the *John C. Stennis*, the ship's command crew watched in horror as a monstrosity that seemed to be a nightmarish cross between several animal species on Earth headed towards them. It was only their training that kept them from falling apart --and only barely -- as they issued their orders. Within moments, the five-inch guns on the escorts began rapid firing onto the target with a wave of Mark 54 torpedoes following on behind them.

Meanwhile SH-60 Seahawk helicopters already in the air moved into position to drop their remaining Mark 54s before heading back to their ships for hasty rearmament. Those that were still on their vessels had armed themselves with any available weapon before taking off.

Orbiting above the carrier group, F/A-18E/Fs Super Hornets circled their monstrous mark as the E-2 Hawkeye issued targeting orders. Once all received their instructions, the Super Hornets targeted the creature with a mix of guided and dumb bombs before strafing with 20mm gunfire. Rapidly exhausting their weapons, most Super Hornets departed for the other carriers, or for Guam and Iwo Jima, to rearm. A few dived to the deck and headed towards the creature to try and lure the beast away from the fleet. While most escaped retaliation, a few were unlucky as the creature slashed them out of the sky with its forward limbs or by utilizing its own massive head as a colossal fly swatter.

While the firepower was impressive in terms of modern military weaponry, it did not stop the monster altogether, a sight that unnerved the human combatants. In rapid succession, the ships increased speed to flank while activating their CIWS systems.

Bellowing defiantly at the resistance it faced, the monster swiped away at its aerial foes before a mix of bombs and shells forced it beneath the surface. However, its foes were disappointed as the creature resumed its advance in the manner of a gigantic shark. With explosions occurring all over its back, the entity rapidly closed the distance to its prey as if sensing their fear.

The creature abruptly stopped for a moment, as if the resistance deterred it from advancing further. Without warning, it descended beneath the waves before it closed the remaining distance towards its target.

CSG-3's escorts frantically attempted to regain target lock with their sonar systems, but it was too late. A huge geyser of water developed below the *Ticonderoga*-class cruiser U.S.S. *Mobile Bay*. As the other ships watched in horror, the *Mobile Bay* seemed to lift out of the water before several spikes broke the ship in half.

As the remnants sank beneath the ocean, the destroyers and aircraft blazed away at the monster while it was distracted. All this succeeded in doing, however, was to drive the monster into a frenzy and draw its attention to the three onrushing Arleigh Burke-class destroyers. The creature roared in a primal rage at the resistance it encountered as it swam at high speed towards the closest destroyer. Before the ship could evade, the monster was already on top of the vessel, its huge bulk crushing the forward section of the ship. Seeing that discretion was the better part of valor, the remaining destroyers backed off while the aircraft confined their attacks to high-altitude runs, leaving the doomed warship to die.

The command crew of the *Stennis* watched in horror as their inhuman opponent picked off their escorts. With the remaining two destroyers closing in to regroup with the carrier, the three ships immediately headed to flank speed while the F/A-18E/Fs and other aircraft took position to cover the rear. The remaining escorts attempted to keep a constant stream of fire onto the target, but it was not as intense as before due to the need to conserve ammunition. As the distances inexorably closed, the men all wondered if their luck had run out.

Fortunately help arrived in the form of a hail of surface-to-surface missiles flying overhead from the north to slam directly on top of the monster. A rain of bombs soon followed on behind, the combined explosions strong enough to force the monster to emerge from the water. To the relief of CSG-3, they could see aircraft from their fellow carriers and land bases heading in on their radar screens, missiles, and guided bombs launching from them onto the target. Several minutes later, lookouts spotted the silhouette of the destroyer squadron steaming in from the northeast, as the ships covered in smoke from the firing of their missiles.

On the *Stennis's* bridge, the admiral and his staff observed the action when one of the communications officers signaled a message arriving from the *Ford*. The admiral of CSG-3 immediately headed to one of the intercoms to speak with his counterpart and brief him about CSG-3's status for several minutes before the admiral deactivated the console and turned to his staff.

"Signal all ships to head north at flank," the admiral said. "We're linking up with the *Ford* as well as two SAGs that are heading south to meet us."

The others nodded in full agreement and the captain contacted the bridge to relay the orders while everyone else turned back to the battle.

Swinging its frontal limbs and head in a wild manner, the monster continued to defend itself against its aerial assailants. However, its foes had resorted to engaging from a safe distance with their guided weapons, or from higher altitudes with their general weaponry despite the possibility of those armaments missing their target. It was only when the fighters closed in to use their 20mm guns that the monster could retaliate, as the wreckage of several fighters had already shown to the survivors. The constant aerial and missile bombardment gradually began to have an effect; as the monster focused onto the sky, the ships of CSG-3 escaped into the distance and out of visual sight of the creature with their air cover quickly moving to join them.

Snarling as its prey escaped, the monster suddenly dropped into the water after being buffeted by a salvo of bombs. After shaking off the effect, the beast raised its snout into the air to search again for any new assailants to fight. As its head turned towards the west, the creature's eyes blinked several times as if trying to see in the far distance before it began moving again.

Chinese task group 257
620 miles northeast of Taiwan

Looking warily from the bridge of the Type 52D destroyer (NATO codename *Luyang III*), the captain of the task group attempted to spot any potential hazards heading his way. It helped keep his mind focused as his task group headed northeast towards where an enemy carrier group had been involved in a ferocious firefight. Z-9C helicopters from the ships were already pinging on forward with their sonar while long range J-11s patrolled overhead. Two other task groups were following on behind him with the same measures in place in case they encountered opposition.

Suddenly, one of the intercoms began beeping, which the captain immediately answered. It was the XO who was in the ship's CDC.

"Sir, we've spotted an unidentified object heading straight for us," the subordinate officer said. He paused for a moment before he added, "Based on its location, the unidentified object was near the area where the enemy came under attack."

Wincing at the news, the captain replied, "Signal all ships to battle stations and request support."

His XO nodded in agreement and within minutes, the alarm bells rang loudly as the destroyer and its accompanying warships readied their weapons. Meanwhile, the Z-9Cs already in the air began to move off into the distance with the ships launching the rest in rapid succession with a mix of armaments.

Moving rapidly under the ocean's surface, the creature swung its head side-to-side as it searched for any potential prey. Exhaling air from its alligator-shaped mouth, the creature snarled as it sensed potential foes ahead, after which it switched its course toward the closest prey while increasing speed. Soon enough that resistance arrived as the monster spotted several small shapes in the water heading towards it. Bellowing out in anger at his foes, the monster charged head on and soon collided with the torpedoes, which exploded all around it. As it shook off the effects of the attack, the creature roared before it lunged forward through another hail of torpedoes that dropped all around it.

Though far off in the distance to the northeast, the Chinese task group saw explosions and waterspout-like disruptions, which seemed to be getting bigger as the task group closed the distance to the area. Watching the area through his binoculars, the captain of the *Luyang III* destroyer grimaced as several Z-9Cs dropped another round of ET52 torpedoes onto the area. He paled further when a wave of additional projectiles from the helicopters and an accompanying Yuan-class submarines forced the unidentified object to the surface, where it finally revealed its full horrific form to its human adversaries.

Sensing that he was about to give his final order, the Chinese captain yelled out. "All ships commence firing!"

East Sea Fleet Headquarters

On the main screen in the Eastern Sea Fleet headquarters, Cheng and his fellow commanders watched in stunned silence as their forces engaged a being that was unlike anything they had seen before on this planet. Despite the firepower hamming away at it, the creature advanced inexorably upon the Chinese task group. Soon the ships were blasting away at the target at point-blank range, even bringing their CIWS to bear. The air units were attacking the monster as well, although once they had used up their guided weapons, they had a difficult time. This was due to the need to get in close and not hit friendly forces during their attack runs on the target.

After observing the battle for several minutes, Shan turned to look at several smaller screens. before inquiring to his subordinates. "Status of enemy forces?" he inquired to his subordinates.

"The enemy forces have seemed to have fallen back," one of them replied. "We've only detected units that are on patrol. Two of the enemy carriers nearest to our forces have linked up and the others are moving closer to their location."

"We need to get the ships out of there," Shan lamented. "I need to send assistance but with the American fleet still a threat, it will be difficult. The only assistance available are the two additional groups that were moving in for support."

Cheng nodded in agreement with the admiral. "Divert what forces you can to assistance without weakening your defense. I will contact the premier and advise him of the situation."

"Once your lead forces have regrouped," Yingchang interjected, "signal them to fall back. The closer you can get to either Taiwan or Okinawa, the more air support we can provide you."

Shan nodded in acknowledgement before the officers dispersed. Cheng and his entourage immediately moved to a secure communications area to contact Beijing while his fellow officers transmitted orders to their forces.

Task Group 257

The Chinese task group was engaged the fight of its life against an enemy that they could never have imagined. Despite bringing heavy firepower to bear, the three ships and their smaller escorts could barely slow it down. Observing the movements of its foes, the creature suddenly lashed out with its left forward limb towards a *Jiangkai II* frigate that sailed too close. The monster seemed to throw its entire weight onto the ship's stern, which capsized the seemingly intact vessel in the manner of a seesaw. Once the titanic sea beast landed back in the water, the frigate seemed to right itself but then began to sink as its stern was smashed to pieces. In short order, the monster wrecked the superstructure of the vessel as the crew attempted to abandon ship, with most failing to escape.

Watching the last of their comrades brutally die before the creature headed straight for them, the *Luyang III* destroyer and the remaining *Jiangkai II* frigate let fly with every weapon in their respective arsenals. However, with the overall limited firepower at their disposal the creature immediately closed in on the ships before rising to its full height. Blinking its bulging eyes for several moments, the scaly beast rushed towards the destroyer and was about to smash its gigantic body against the ship when a hail of YJ-83 cruise missiles slammed into it.

The surprised crews of the warships turned to see aircraft over the horizon along with additional waves of missiles heading towards their foe. Seeing their chance, the two Chinese warships unleashed a defiant wave of firepower while departing the area at flank speed.

Consumed by explosions, the monster roared at the sight of its prey escaping. It attempted to pursue but the mix of missiles and torpedoes from the two warships prevented the creature from diving until the vessels receded off into the distance. The aquatic leviathan let out a loud bellow of victory as he saw no prey in sight before it dove back into the Pacific Ocean and disappeared beneath its dark depths.

Camp H.M. Smith
Hawaii

The main command center at Camp H.M. Smith was silent as they watched the combatants slowly disengage from each other. Some forces still traded fire with each other but everyone else seemed to be backing off. To the eyes of an observer, it seemed the fight had gone out of both combatants after the hell they had witnessed for the past several hours. Although peace and quiet had descended over the ocean, it was a tense accord that could change in an instant back to open warfare, a situation that kept everyone on guard.

Watching as the last of the fleet fall back to relative safety, the CO of U.S. INDO-PACCOM turned to ask a subordinate, "What are the casualty reports?"

The subordinate read off the reports from the battlefield, a figure that made the commanders in the room winch. The commander then addressed the question that was on everyone's mind. "As for the battle against the unidentified creature, we lost a cruiser, several destroyers, several aircraft, and two submarines."

"And that was only in several hours of combat against that thing," Horner noted. He then turned to his fellow officers and inquired, "Do we know if that thing is still alive?"

Maxwell took that question. "After the attack on the Chinese task group, the creature disappeared beneath the waves. We believe that the cumulative damage from both our forces and the Chinese may have injured it, but thus far we haven't found any trace."

"Alright then," Horner with a sigh. "Check on the status of all our forces. Right now, we also need to put together a report to send to Washington."

His fellow commanders all nodded and vacated the room. Maxwell then turned back to the main screen where the last of his forces and that of the Chinese had disengaged from each other. Closing his eyes for several moments, he opened them and contemplated the events of the last few hours before he headed back to his office.

Turning to look outside the window as he pondered what to say to Washington, Horner suddenly thought of the famous line from the play Hamlet that was was apt here, for even the most advanced science couldn't explain what they had just witnessed. Letting out a gulp of air at that dark thought, the commander of U.S. INDO-PACCOM contacted the Pentagon to deliver his report.

East Sea Fleet Headquarters
Ningbo, China

At almost the same time, the Chinese military command was also taking stock of what they had just witnessed. While his subordinates were checking on the status of their own commands, Cheng stared grimly at the main map which showed his forces and that of the enemy falling away from each other. While they did prevent their foes from taking the holdings that the PLA had secured earlier, the means that it had come about put a dark shadow on this "victory."

Though he was focused on the main screen, Cheng sensed the arrival of one of the aides with some information in hand.

Without turning to face his subordinate, the general asked quietly, "Do you have the report?"

The aide responded in the affirmative and handed the information for Cheng to read.

The general perused the document for several moments before he asked the pertinent question: "What about that unidentified creature?"

The aide cleared his throat before answering his superior. "Our scouts have been unable to find it. There have been no new attacks in the past few hours and the location of the vicinity where we last saw him is a deep area. When last seen, the creature seemed to be exhausted and slowing down due to the multiple wounds it received."

Cheng nodded and tried to take on a firm tone, but the news did not reassure him much. The general then looked around to see if there was anything else that was needed.

"Tell the others to gather all of the information they can," Cheng commanded. "I will be in my office."

With that, the general curtly headed out of the room, his mind struggling to grasp what he had seen. As he headed down the hallway, Cheng turned to look at several paintings of ancient Chinese history, some of them being displays of ancient dragons. The commanding officer shivered at the thought that those legends potentially had some validity.

Philippine Sea

In the deep darkness of the Pacific Ocean, fish and other aquatic life scattered as an enormous object seemed to inexorably sink to the ocean floor. In fact, the depth had reached the point where most other animals did not go any further due to the danger of being crushed by the incredible pressure. However, if one were to look very closely at the object, it would appear to be the carcass of an enormous animal of unknown taxonomy.

The seeming corpse suddenly displayed signs of life as its black eyes began to flicker. A moment later it opened its cavernous mouth and let out a snarl, bubbles escaping its mouth and floating upwards. The creature's four limbs began wriggling about, and moments later the creature's entire titanic form began to move as it returned to the darkness from whence it came. It would rest for now and regain its strength before unleashing its wrath on the world once more.

END

DRACO AZUL: DIVINE INTERVENTION

Andres Perez

Editor's Note: This yarn is an edited version of the story originally published in the anthology *Courage on Infinite Earths: A Kaiju vs. Cancer Anthology* from the Kaiju vs. Cancer charity label. It is an honor for Wild Hunt Press to receive permission from the author reprint it here!

It was a bright and cloudless day in the capital of Mexico. However, the sun was not shining on a city filled with peace and prosperity, but one tainted by an unspeakable reign of carnage. For the people of Mexico City, their world was collapsing all around them as a series of black, sludge-like entities appeared out of mysterious otherworldly portals in the center of town. The moment they entered this world their ferocious hunger forced them to consume every organic being in sight. As these things fed on everyone and everything, their mass grew larger, their yellow eyes glowed brighter, and their vicious teeth became sharper.

While the city's population attempted to escape the horror, the military endeavored to intervene. Unfortunately for the humans, the savage invaders had already grown too powerful for their weaponry. Dozens of bullets, missiles, and grenades were launched at the creatures, only to be proven ineffective as their gelatinous bodies were incapable of being harmed by solid objects and explosives. Every attack launched at the toothy blobs was retaliated with aggression and ferocity. By the time the invasion entered its second hour, the military had to set up a blockade to contain the threat. Sadly, it would take more than a few dozen tanks to hold these demons off.

If anyone outside this universe were to witness the calamity, they would most likely view this event as the end of days. However, in an ironic twist of fate, this sort of occurrence had been quite common to the people of Mexico. While these invaders were indeed a threat to the country, they were certainly not the *first*. It was this reason why a champion exists to dispel such evil.

Over 400 kilometers away in the mountainous region of Sierra Madre del Sur, inside a hidden cave, a metal giant laid in slumber. The metallic goliath's yellow eyes lit up and pierced through the darkness. Its body began to move. Standing 60 meters tall, the giant looked towards the entrance of its cave and took its first steps towards it.

Trailing the giant was an elongated crimson-colored scarf that wrapped around its neck. Its steps quickly picked up speed and within seconds the titan leaped out of the cave. The iron titan's blue and white armor glistened in the sunlight. Just as gravity began to take its toll, large metal wings sprouted from the giant's back and lifted it into the sky through jet propulsion. The metal warrior was now on its way towards Mexico City. This being was Mexico's, and the world's, last line of defense. Its name: Draco Azul!

An advanced machine far beyond any sort of human engineering, Draco Azul was given to the Maya civilization centuries ago by what the natives could only describe as "strangers from beyond the stars." These mysterious space Samaritans bestowed upon the Maya people this technological titan to serve as the planet's protector. For several generations, Draco Azul would protect the world from threats both native and extraterrestrial.

However, for reasons unknown, the blue behemoth stayed hidden from the world for the last 800 years, waiting until it was needed once again. In recent times, strange beasts called "Diablos" have threatened the safety of Mexico, which resulted in Draco Azul's resurrection. The ravenous creatures now attacking Mexico City were now the latest threat for Draco Azul to vanquish.

However, despite Draco Azul's awesome might, it still required a human spirit to fuel its power. Within the robot's heavily armored chassis was a mortal man, the most recent in a long line of pilots. Throughout history, generations of aeronauts had used Draco Azul as a weapon of justice. The latest individual to take up the mantle was Eric Martinez, a 28-year-old former educator that had reluctantly been tasked with the duty of piloting Draco Azul, having stumbled upon it during the Diablos' initial raid on Cancun.

Despite his lack of experience in fighting, Eric had become a very quick learner thanks in part to the AI system that ran the majority of Draco Azul's functions. This AI was Ekchuah, named by the Maya people after their god of travelers and journeys. In the case of this Ekchuah, he would guide previous pilots on a journey of dedication, bravery, and heroism. Out of respect for the people who first adopted Draco Azul, he took on the appearance of a Maya warrior via his hologram avatar.

It is through Ekchuah's assistance that helped Eric grow accustomed to Draco Azul's control mechanisms, an astounding system that allowed the robot's movements to follow his own. By standing on a platform while wearing the necessary bodysuit and accessories, Eric could feel the sensation of having the body of a god.

Through the visor on Eric's face as well as his bodysuit, he could experience Draco Azul's vision, its power... and its pain. Any time Draco Azul was damaged, Eric would feel an approximation of the blows given to his mech. Ekchuah once explained that this sensation was made to heighten the user's senses, as well as increase his urgency if Draco Azul was ever in critical condition. After all, how could you fight with one disabled arm if your natural body still thinks it could use two?

The cockpit Eric stood in also gave him the benefit of being in whatever position Draco Azul found itself thanks to its spherical design. If the mech were to fall on its back, Eric would find himself doing the same within his cockpit despite the rest of the mech laying down.

Whatever happened, the cockpit would remain parallel to the ground.

"How long until we get to Mexico City, coach?" said Eric, as he hovered over his platform facing forward in the same fashion as his flying robot.

The holographic representation of Ekchuah appeared next to Eric and activated a screen on the wall of the cockpit. Several statistics were displayed.

"At our speed, we'll be there in about 20 minutes. We could get there in ten, but it's gonna cost us more fuel."

"I see. How much would we have by then?"

"Depends on how we'll fight these things. We'll be okay if we stick to physical combat. Though if you plan to really dish out the pain, you'll only have enough left over for one big shot."

Draco Azul's systems ran on the electrostatic discharges provided by Earth's thunderstorms, with the mech's horn acting as an immense lightning rod. It had been a while since the giant last replenished its power due to the fact that thunderstorms weren't as common this time of year.

Eric paused for a moment, thinking about the immeasurable amount of suffering the victims of Mexico City must be experiencing.

"Alright, set boosters to full speed."

Ekchuah smiled, "That's what I wanted to hear, kid!"

Draco Azul's wings propelled the mech even faster than before -- from the speed of an air carrier to that of a jet fighter. As the robot passed each city, hundreds of men, women, and children alike could hear the azure goliath soar through the sky. To them, it was as if they were listening to the screech of a mighty dragon. They all knew that their mysterious hero was on the move, ready to save more unfortunate souls.

As Draco Azul approached the perimeters of the city, Eric saw a large swarm of the black monsters converging on one location. Others were attacking the tanks that reinforced the blockade. Eric's eyes darted all around the battlefield as he was making a dive.

"Hey coach, find the best place to land."

"Already on it!"

In mere seconds, red and green dots appeared in Eric's field of vision. Many of the green points were centered around a spot Eric recognized from his childhood. Around this collection was a ring of red dots closing in.

"The red points are the enemies; I've counted 86 of them. The green ones are the civilians still inside the area. As you can see many of the enemies are near the blockades, most likely trying to escape. However, a large group of them are circling around the biggest gathering of civilians. Which is—"

"The Basilica of Guadalupe!"

"Yeah. You familiar with it?"

"Of course! It's practically the holiest place in the Americas! No wonder everyone's there."

"All the more reason to land there and, hopefully, attract the vermin at the blockade."

"You don't have to tell me twice!"

"Of course not, kid. Now, let's show these bastards who's boss!"

Eric aimed his mech feet-first at the group of the black creatures farthest from the basilica. He knew he wasn't going to let these demons hurt any more people. Draco Azul landed with a thunderous boom as the ground beneath its feet caved in, crushing the monsters beneath the metal giant into black puddles. Nearly every remaining creature turned around to face their challenger. Their eyes glowed intensely as they all screamed in unison.

The invaders started crawling towards the mech. Eric held up his arms, as did Draco Azul in unison, showing off its razor-sharp arm blades. As the swarm approached, he took a few steps back so as to bring the battle farther away from the basilica. He could see through his mech's telescopic vision that the church was in the clear. The young pilot breathed a slight sigh of relief. With one hand, he performed the sign of the cross.

"Hm, never pegged you as the religious type," Ekchuah proclaimed with a hint of amused curiosity.

Eric rarely, if ever, practiced his mother's Catholicism once he reached his teens, but that did not mean that he didn't believe in the existence of a higher power. And with the recent appearance of aliens, robots, and demons, he figured anything was possible. So, if there was a god up there, he thanked the Lord that the people were safe… for now. Eric opened his eyes, focused and ready to fight.

"Let's do this!"

Draco Azul rushed towards the approaching horrors. Many of them assimilated into one another to form larger blobs of slime. They all came at the mech like huge black whips, barbed with thousands of sharp teeth. This did not deter Eric as he swung his arms at each of these assailing masses, cleaving all of them in two. In the process, he had also stepped on the smaller monsters like the vermin they were.

Draco Azul paused as soon as it ran through the army. The goliath quickly turned around, it's back facing the basilica. The mech was now the only thing standing between the monsters and the majority of the survivors.

To Eric's shock, he noticed that his attacks left no lasting damage on the strange life forms. The monsters slowly reformed and had begun to assimilate into a single, giant abomination. Even the creatures within the crater Draco Azul made with its landing were joining in. As were the reinforcements from the perimeter of the border. Sweat poured down Eric's head. He turned to his A.I. companion.

"This ain't good."

"Good? Since when was it ever good?"

"Got a point there. Any suggestions?"

"Well, we could use our strongest move, but I can't guarantee it'll wipe them all out in one fell swoop. But we still have another ace up our sleeve: the Draco Kick!"

Eric's eyes widened in shock.

"What?"

Ekchuah smirked, as if he was excited by his own plan.

"Rather than risk blasting our opponent into a million pieces, we'll electrocute the whole thing from the inside out!"

"B-but I dunno if I can do that yet!"

"Trust me, kid, you got what it takes."

The smile on Ekchuah's face somewhat alleviated Eric's concerns. His mentor was always demanding, but at the same time understanding of the pilot's limitations as a fighter. Before he accidentally stumbled across Ekchuah and Draco Azul, Eric Martinez was merely a high school teacher in southern California. Getting into confrontations, let alone actual fights, was the last thing he ever wanted. However, all it took was a trip to Cancun, and a lot of bad luck, which landed him in a position that required him to change his pacifistic outlook on life. He had learned to throw caution to the wind and fight for what he felt was right!

As the newly assimilated beast howled into the sky, Eric thought about the people hiding in the basilica and how they must be praying for mercy. He thought about the Mexican soldiers fighting to protect the blockade from what few creatures remained at the perimeter. He thought about the countless people already killed. Most importantly, he thought about how far this destruction would spread if he were to fail. With a newfound sense of vengeance burning within, Eric knew that his only option was to face the invader.

The singular entity had finished its metamorphosis. Its body no longer had an intangible appearance but rather a solid structure. It had grown arms, legs, and a head in an attempt to imitate its opponent. However, it had twisted and contorted its body into an animalistic form, complete with a lengthy barbed tail. Its hunched back was rigid with spines, identical to teeth. In fact, its whole body was covered with them! Its head, torso, limbs, and tail were adorned with those razor-sharp protrusions. The beast opened its three glowing eyes and focused them on Draco Azul. Eric remained undeterred and raised his fists once more.

Ekchuah chuckled to himself. "Heh, it may be bigger, but now it made itself one giant target. Makes our job a whole lot easier. Keep its attention on you, kid, and wait until I give the signal."

"Got it, coach!"

The beast slammed its hands to the ground and began to charge at the blue robot. The monster lunged at the mech bearing every one of its teeth and claws. With perfect timing, Draco Azul countered with an uppercut into the creature's mouth with its blade slicing through its torso in the process. The monster fell on its back, only for it to restlessly get back up.

Draco Azul retaliated with several more jabs and swings. However, once the blade-wielding mech stepped back Eric noticed that every gash on the demon's body slowly reformed to its original shape. The intrepid pilot was *really* ticked off now.

"Well, that rules out a beat down," an annoyed Eric stated.

"Yeah, but at least we know it's not as tough as it looks. Continue to hold it off!"

Just then the beast's central eye glowed fiercely as its head finished healing. With an intense roar, the monster fired a concentrated beam of yellow energy at Draco Azul. Eric quickly placed his hands up and endured the full force of the blast. He knew that if he moved away from his spot, the basilica was as good as gone. Suddenly, Eric heard Ekchuah's voice.

"Eric, look out!"

Eric peaked from beyond his robot's arms and witnessed numerous claws coming at him from both sides. Draco Azul leapt backwards just as the two sets of talons closed in on each other like a Venus fly trap. Eric was exhausted. The pilot had never reacted that fast before in his life. He looked up and noticed that the attacking claws came from the monster's chest, which had morphed into a sideways mouth. Had he not moved out of the way at the last possible second, things could've gotten ugly. Ekchuah then created a map of the war zone and displayed it on Eric's visor.

"We're a lot closer to the church now. Take extra caution!" the hologram advised in a stern tone.

Eric realized that things had to end here and now. Just as the beast was about to attack, Draco Azul made the first move and started rushing towards the monster. The creature screeched as it prepared for another assault. However, this time the machine leaped over the beast. Once Draco Azul landed behind it, the monster turned around -- only for it to realize that its opponent's scarf was now wrapped around it.

With Eric's diversion successful, he made his mech grab its scarf and pull the monster towards him and further away from the Basilica. The creature then dug its feet and tail into the ground as it struggled to free its arms and legs. With quick thinking, Eric had Draco Azul activate its wings once more. The moment they sprung forth from its back, the mech blasted off into the air.

The lassoed beast was yanked out from the ground and was now trailing behind the metal titan. In desperation, the monster made its body intangible and began traveling up Draco Azul's scarf. In response, Ekchuah flashed a warning on Eric's visor with footage from the mech's external cameras.

"Heads up, kid!"

With quick thinking, Eric made Draco Azul dive straight downward while loosening his scarf's grip on his opponent. With its body still forced into an upwards projection, the invader completely slid off the mech's scarf. Eventually, gravity started working against the abomination. The beast flailed its tentacles in all directions in a failed attempt to grab onto anything to stop its descent.

At this point, it had all but abandoned its solid form save for its head. After a few seconds, the monster smashed into the middle of the city, creating another massive crater. Within the massive puddle of black sludge, its horrific head reformed and roared in anger. Now every single creature that was once trying to escape the area was heading towards the larger entity. As the last of the invaders assimilated into the main beast, the head looked all around for its enemy.

Suddenly, a bright light shined overhead. The invader looked up and saw crackling arcs of electricity. Miles above the monster, Draco Azul was summoning forth the last of its expendable energy! Bolts of lightning surged from his horn. The mecha-warrior then raised its right knee and transferred the energy into its leg.

"Now, kid! Bring the pain!"

Draco Azul's wings activated their reverse thrusters and blasted the giant robot downward foot first. While the mech was descending towards the monster, Eric began to recite the name of his hidden ace, activating it in the process.

"Dracoooo…"

The giant's robotic boot that was once surging with lightning was now enveloped by the glow of the raw, concentrated power. Draco Azul's path of descent was now highlighted with sparks of excess lightning bursting from the its foot. Eric finished reciting his attack, which became his declaration of victory.

"Kiiiiiiiiiick!"

The beast had realized what was approaching, but it was too late. It hadn't finished fully assimilating back into a mobile form and there wasn't enough time to completely separate and escape the deep crater. Like a cornered animal, its only instinct was to fight back. The monster quickly created several tentacles adorned with as many teeth-spikes it could muster and launched them at Draco Azul.

Draco Azul's foot came crashing down on the monster's tentacles, each disintegrating within seconds. The mech landed a kick into the beast's face with all its might. The monster let out a loud but truncated screech before its reign of terror came to an end. Draco Azul's foot pierced through the creature's head and entered the deepest pit of the semi-solid monstrosity's gelatinous body.

By then the lighting had begun to evaporate the disgusting matter that composed the creature faster than it could create new appendages to fight back. Some pieces of the monster attempted to separate from the main body. Luckily, however, the energy from Draco Azul's attack expanded all throughout the deepening crater, taking with it every last bit of the black sludge.

Miles away, the residents of Mexico City had already begun to exit the Basilica. To their shock, they witnessed what seemed like an act of God, as they saw what looked like a massive bolt of lightning falling onto the demon that tried to kill them all. The resulting impact took down several more city blocks with it. Many had hoped this would bring an end to the disaster. Others hoped that their mysterious savior would be alright. Some tried to look away from the unimaginable levels of destruction that not even Mother Nature could create.

A few more seconds later, Eric recovered from the attack and managed to catch his breath. He opened his eyes and noticed that the area around him had widened up. The young aviator looked down and beheld the charred remains of the sludge that once threatened the very existence of North America. He quickly turned to Ekchuah.

"Any casualties?"

"Nope. You managed to get that thing far enough from the locals. See for yourself!"

Back at the Basilica men, women, and children all came outside after they heard the lightning's crackle subside. Their eyes lit up as they gazed upon the blue and white robot exiting the crater with its scarf billowing in the wind. They had all cheered, and some of them thanked God for blessing them with such a hero. Others quickly embraced their families and loved ones, grateful that they managed to survive the nightmare and lived to see another day.

Draco Azul's telescopic vision allowed Eric to confirm that the people were all right. He wished he could've avoided causing more damage to the city. Though at this point, he took whatever satisfaction he could get at a time like this. He let out a long sigh of relief.

"Whew! It's over. For now, at least."

"Don't celebrate too quickly, kid. Ya did good, but there's still the problem of that thing back there."

Eric was confused. What was Ekchuah talking about? He looked back at the pile of ashes that used to be the black creature. The holographic A.I. system brought up microscopic scans on Eric's visor. There the young man could see that within the ashes something survived.

"While the activity in that black matter subsided, its cells are still alive… somewhat."

"Dammit! Well, what can we do?"

Draco Azul approached the gray dust to take a closer look at it. The A.I.-driven hologram pondered as he attempted to determine its genetic makeup.

"Let's see… I tell ya, this thing's one tough nut to crack. I can't make heads or tails of it. It's like it –"

"Came from another world?"

This foreign voice sent a shock though Eric as he had never heard anyone other than Ekchuah within his cockpit.

"Gah!"

The pilot ripped the visor off his head and, to his surprise, he found the most bizarre figure standing mere

274

feet away from him and Ekchuah's hologram. The male figure was a head taller than him and had a slender build. The stranger wore a blue and orange coat and top hat, like a neon-colored 18th-century gentleman.

That alone was bizarre, but to top off this otherworldly sight was the figure's face. It appeared to be wearing a mask. The right half was white and had a toothy grin, while the other was black with a depressing frown. The being talked through the right half of his mask.

"I'm sorry, did I come at a bad time?"

Eric didn't pay attention to the stranger's smug apology. He was too freaked out to care.

"Who… what the hell are you?"

Meanwhile, Ekchuah's hologram waved his hand, activating the cockpit's defense mechanisms. The room's lights turned on and two mechanical arms ending in tasers extended from the walls.

"You better start talking, fella. One wrong move and you're done!"

The skeletal figure chuckled to himself and bowed towards the duo out of an ironic sense of courtesy.

"Heh heh heh. Oh, where are my manners? Allow me to introduce myself. I'm Augustine, though my victims call me the *Crooked Man*. I came here to assist you with that abomination you just faced, but it seemed you had a handle on things. So, I decided to sit back and watch you guys do your thing."

Ekchuah's hologram raised an eyebrow at the sarcastic Crooked Man.

"Hold on. You mean to tell me you've been *here* the whole time? How did I not pick you up? I can see everything here."

Eric stepped in between the Crooked Man and the holographic avatar of the mech's A.I. system.

"Unless... you chose not to let us see you."

The Crooked Man's crooked smile grew even more devilish.

"Bingo! This guy was definitely paying attention in class!"

Ekchuah rubbed his chin.

"So, you're from another dimension, eh? Shame my creators never filled me in on guys like you. Guess they never thought Earthlings would have to deal with extradimensional threats. Either that or they weren't aware of beings like you and that monster."

The Crooked Man now spoke from the frowning side of his face.

"Hey, don't you start comparing me to that mindless beast!"

Eric raised his voice in an attempt to show authority.

"Did you send that monster here? Are you responsible for all this?"

The Crooked Man switched back to talking through the smiling half.

"Hah! Pease. If I wanted to kill, maim, and torture an entire city I would've done it myself. Besides, killing mortals on a grand scale isn't really my style. I'm more of the Faustian kinda guy."

Eric and Ekchuah stood silent. The Crooked Man's eyes shifted back and forth between the two of them and decided to continue.

"Y'know the whole 'deal-with-the-devil' business? Yeah, that's my thing. And unfortunately, some interdimensional jackass is taking all that away from me! So, I and a mortal from a universe different from this one decided to find some people who can help deal with the problem."

Ekchuah crossed his arms and spoke.

"And you think Draco Azul can help you."

"Exactly! I'm fairly certain you guys got the chops. After all, you already took down one of the creature's children."

Eric's heart skipped a beat. "Children...?"

"Oh yeah, this thing's merely a piece of the real deal. Now, a calamity this large doesn't occur very often. So, if it's any consolation, this is the first time I've ever seen one personally. And I've been around for several centuries."

Ekchuah remained unenthused with the Crooked Man's demeanor.

"It's not. So, if we help you then our universe will be safe?"

"Yes, as well as the rest of reality. So, you, me, and everyone else can continue doing what we do best."

Another moment of silence passed. Eric and Ekchuah looked at each other. The hologram then approached the Crooked Man.

"How can we believe that anything you say is true?"

The Crooked Man closed his eyes and shrugged.

"Well, for starters, I already took care of the dust pile you left behind. So, you won't have to worry about that coming back."

Eric looked at Ekchuah. His holographic ally nodded and activated a monitor on the wall, displaying Draco Azul's POV camera. Indeed, every trace of the creature was gone. This confounded Eric.

"Where'd you put it?"

"Oh, don't worry about that. I sent it somewhere where it'll never bother anyone again. Now, I heard about your little 'fuel problem.' How about we make a deal? I refill your robot's tank, and you'll assist me in saving the multiverse!"

Ekchuah grew even more skeptical.

"And how exactly are you gonna do that?"

At that moment, the entire mech was enveloped in a shroud of black mist. The Crooked Man's eyes took on a reddish glow and he now spoke with a louder and echoing voice through both halves of his face.

"Oh, I thought you'd never ask!"

The entire room shook as if there was an earthquake. Eric grabbed onto the wall of his cockpit to keep himself from falling. Meanwhile, Ekchuah attempted to tase the Crooked Man, only for the electro-shock wires to phase harmlessly through him.

"Ha! Silly old program. Your tech may be impressive, but it's not enough to bring down the Crooked Man!" Augustine boasted.

The cockpit suddenly stopped shaking and loud thunderous booms could be heard outside. The Crooked Man's manner of speaking returned to normal.

"Ah, we're here!"

Eric and Ekchuah looked at the monitor as they saw that Draco Azul was now standing in a river with hundreds of lightning bolts covering the sky! The first of several bolts struck Draco Azul's lightning rod of a horn and the mech quickly began converting its energy into fuel. Eric was astounded by the sight.

"Where are we?"

The Crooked Man responded with great enthusiasm.

"This is the Catatumbo River in Venezuela, the best place for all your lightning needs! It was the best I could do on such short notice."

Within minutes, Draco Azul was fully restored to its full strength with enough left over to fill its extra reserves. Ekchuah still wasn't impressed.

"Big deal! We could've come here ourselves. What makes you think we could trust you?"

"Oh, you don't have to. You just need to hold up your end of the deal."

Eric stepped in. "But we never agreed to it!"

The Crooked Man grinned. "I know, and that's why I'm going to leave you stranded here, away from any other source of power with zero fuel, unless you agree to help me save the multiverse."

Eric and Ekchuah looked at each other with concern. With his back against the wall, Eric once more thought about the fate of his world. Ekchuah could read the contemplative look on his protégé's face. The holographic avatar nodded to him with assurance. Eric turned to face their vexing adversary.

"Alright, we'll do it. But once this is over, you'll send us back here right away!"

Ekchuah placed his hands on his hips and sighed. "You really are a crooked son of a bitch."

Augustine winked.

"Why, thank you. I do my best!"

As if on cue the cockpit started vibrating once more. The Crooked Man grew even more excited.

"Now, let's get down to business. Team Draco, prepare to ROLL OUT!"

An awkward silence took place between the three of them. Eric facepalmed as he couldn't believe he made

279

that reference at a time like this. At the same time, Ekchuah was completely lost. Their new ally grew annoyed with their reactions and shrugged.

"Hey, it's better than 'morphin' time,' am I right?"

Once Eric and Ekchuah collectively rolled their eyes at the Crooked Man's comments, the otherworldly phantom turned away from the two and began to talk to himself.

"Now, let's hope Bell got ahold of *her* favorite mech. If she did, we might actually survive this little escapade…"

END

Editor's Note: If you're interested in seeing where this story leads and where the sludge-like monsters came from, be sure to get yourself a copy of the multi-author crossover anthology *Courage on Infinite Earths: A Kaiju vs. Cancer Anthology*. All proceeds to that publication from the Kaiju vs. Cancer charity label go to St. Jude Children's Hospital to help wage war against childhood cancer! An earlier version of this story appeared there, along with many other super-hero stories from a variety of authors.

Had anyone been watching the sky over southern New Hampshire that night, it would have looked like a meteor entering Earth's atmosphere, burning briefly yet brightly as it hurtled towards the planet. It was not anything so large as a meteor though, and it was nowhere near so high in the sky as to have come from outer space. Just a mile or so above Nashua, the flaming globule had appeared out of nowhere, and it streaked through the air so quickly it was gone in a blink, landing with a sick thump in the soft mud alongside the Merrimack River, just over the state line in Tyngsboro, Massachusetts. The lump of organic matter was not sentient. It did not know it had traveled through a breech in the membrane separating realities to land on a planet in a different space-time from whence it came – a planet where monsters sometimes roamed and where monster hunters sometimes rose to the challenge.

No, the mass of tissues was incapable of anything resembling reason. It was not equipped to observe its surroundings. It could do only one thing automatically: grow. And to do that, it had to do one thing instinctively: feed!

THE TERROR THAT CAME TO TYNGSBORO

Kevin Heim

Saturday, September 15th, 2018, too early A.M. Too early for sane people to be awake and sitting in cars. Far too early for any kind of activity that isn't prefaced by coffee. I know this, because I'm fully dressed in the back seat of a Ford Transit and I haven't had any coffee yet. Since we have at least an hour's drive to get where we're going, there won't be any stops for coffee, either.

"Alright, let's run some red lights!" shouts Ark Gearheart with far too much enthusiasm for 4:12 in the morning.

He's joking, of course. We aren't legally allowed to run through intersections without stopping, even though we have a siren and a light bar. It's like on a tow truck; there to warn other traffic. And yes, sometimes we do have emergencies that we'll get to a little faster than the speed limits allow for, but we don't have First Responder status and we aren't paid by any city, county, or state (though Essex County was nice enough to give us a free base of operations in Pinkham, Massachusetts). Taskforce Ecto has more in common with repair services or exterminators than we do with fire fighters or law enforcement. In many ways we are exterminators, just highly specialized ones.

My name is Ivan Ronald Schablotski. Most people call me Ivan, pronounced the American way (EYE-vun). I joined Taskforce Ecto not just to capture ghosts, but to study them, and even help them when possible. My background with the paranormal goes all the way back to 1981, so I know a few things; but each of us brings something different to the table.

Sitting next to me is Hazel Dinkley, an archeology professor at Miskatonic University who came to believe in spirits after an incident involving her aunt, a devout skeptic. But really, that's not important right now. Dinkley and I both live in Salem, Massachusetts, but we spend more time in Arkham, Massachusetts, a real hotbed of supernatural activity. In most communities, people assume we just conduct dubious science experiments to investigate dubious hauntings, like those guys on TV. To some extent that's an accurate description of what we do too, but once we conclusively identify that a spirit of some kind is present, we actually do something about it.

Doctor Ark Gearheart lives in Rowley these days. He's something of an engineering savant. Electrical, chemical, mechanical, his proficiency with inventing and reinventing equipment to help us in our cause is astounding. He did some interesting work with ley lines a few years back too… let's just say that his mistakes are as epic as his successes. His girlfriend is Taskforce Ecto's liaison with the Environmental Protection Agency, so technically she's the enemy, but Ark and Kit look so cute together I can't be mad at her.

Kit Soony has gone on a few cases, to spot-check our safety standards, but there's no Kit with us today. Riding shotgun is Calvin Scarborough, a New Hampshire native that's been learning how to maintain the equipment from Ark. His real expertise is with the legends and lore of the paranormal in New England, though. Need to know the classification of a spook, specter, or ghost on the fly, or having trouble remembering what bait works best for Pukwudgies? Calvin is the man with the answers. He's also the equivalent of a labor union executive for the Taskforce, so in a roundabout way, it's his fault I am not full of coffee right now.

Though we don't all normally work in the same area, on weekends and holidays a skeleton crew stays at the Taskforce headquarters; another similarity between us and the fire department. This weekend we are the on-call paranormal investigators, and that means if an emergency pops up, we get to stagger out of bed and stumble into the car. All, that is, except for our fifth member, who serves as dispatcher. Scáth (pronounced "Skaw") Hazard had the night shift, so he was the one that took the call when it came in around 3:45 AM. If this was a slow day, I'd be taking the morning shift from him at six, but something tells me we won't be back by then.

It takes us 30 minutes to get to Tyngsboro, Massachusetts from Pinkham, an unincorporated village that should have dissolved and been absorbed by the surrounding cities of Middleton, Boxford, and North Andover decades ago. Two things keep Pinkham on the map; a lonely strip of commerce called the Pinkham Airfield, which provides us with an isolated hangar with which to conduct necessary experiments, and the Pinkham Reservoir, an artificial pond created for the purpose of scuttling explosives during World War Two, should a shipment become unstable during take-off or landing. The fact that Taskforce Ecto occupies one of the buildings adjacent to the reservoir has not been included on any maps to date.

Another six minutes gets us through the residential neighborhood where the call originated. Ark is trying to keep the car from falling into the many potholes peppering the streets, Calvin is on the phone with the caller, and I'm going through Scáth's texts for details on what we're looking for. So, it's Hazel that sees it first.

"It's in the trees!" she shouts, and we all look in different directions. Doesn't matter, as it's in all the trees, in all directions!

The tops of the trees, usually full of green leaves this time of year, were instead covered with dark grey, meaty lumps, connected to each other by webs of rope-like tendrils throughout the canopy and connecting the trees together with veiny membranes. It's hard to tell in this pre-dawn light, but I think the trees don't have any leaves left, and the whole thing looks like someone stretches a giant bat wing across the sky.

I'm sure it says something about our Smart Phone culture that all four of us just start trying to take pictures of it instead of discussing what it might be. I know I'm planning on texting a photo of it to Dispatch as soon as I get a decent shot. But flash or no flash, none of us can get a clear image of what we're looking at.

"Could this be some mutant moss or other parasite?" I wave towards the Merrimack Riverbank, which is only 50 feet east from us. "Remember when we found those contaminated turkeys a few years ago? There's a lot of hazardous waste in this water. Maybe we should contact the Clean River Project."

Ark points up at the fleshy canopy. "Let's make sure we know what we're talking about, before we determine who we're going to call. Scanners at the ready!"

He pulls a device out from under the driver's seat that looks like it was made from kitchen utensils and gets out of the car. The rest of us join him. Calvin has an EMF Detector and a Spirit Box in hand. Hazel enables an InfraRed camera/scanner app on her phone.

I walk over to a tree with a spectral analyzer and start checking out the bark, which is an ashen gray, not what I'd expect for September. I scrape a little off into a baggie and notice limp tendrils hanging down. They look like thick vines, but they smell awful; and when I approach one it reminds me more of entrails than any kind of plant.

"If this is a monster," I noted, "it's disgusting but really placid. Maybe it's not a threat? Beyond the danger of it falling on people, of course."

Calvin shakes his head but doesn't look up from his gadgets. "I don't think it's psycho-reactive, but the stench is foul. That alone makes it unsafe to let it stay in a place like this."

"Guys?" Hazel calls out, sounding repulsed by her findings. "Is that a bat stuck inside a vine? That's pretty gross!"

Hard to tell just by looking up, but she has Night Vision activated on her camera, so we can clearly see it displayed on the screen. Calvin switches to his own phone and starts wandering around. "There's a lot of wildlife caught in whatever this is. And I really don't think it's ectoplasm. It's too viscous and dark."

I touch a blob of it dribbling down a tree while wearing my chemical gloves. "Yeah, I've never seen grey ectoplasm before. And with the streaks of red and brown woven in, it looks more like a roadkill smoothie.

It's not tacky though. Maybe it's protoplasm? I thought it would stick to my hand or something."

Ark tweaks a dial on the box he's holding. "I wouldn't get too close, Ivan. I'm getting strong readings on the Giger Meter."

I jump back, flicking the junk off my glove, though there's not really any trace on it. "Is this shit radioactive? Did we bring hazmat suits?"

"No, not a Geiger-Counter. I use Dosimeters to check for radiation. This is my H R Giger Counter. It looks for proteins that didn't originate on Earth… and also traces of radiation. I made this after we fought those bugs under Sentinel Hill."

Two years ago, Ark, Calvin and I ran into some extraterrestrial life forms at a Holiday Inn in New Jersey. Shortly after that we found some chitinous aliens in Massachusetts, which is also when Hazel joined Taskforce Ecto. Actually, her University expedition discovered the alien pods and we were called in to help investigate. Gearheart never mentioned it after that, so I didn't realize he kept working on tools to help in case we have a close encounter for a third time.

Calvin starts heading back to the van for some Personal Protective Equipment we can wear when Hazel, in a surprisingly baritone voice, shouts, "Nope!" We all turn to look and see her dancing backwards away from one of the tendrils, which is snaking across the ground towards her. "Can somebody please shoot the monster? I think I'm going to be sick!"

None of us has anything on hand that shoots, but Calvin's already got the van's hatch open, so he pulls out his Soliton Collapser, a device used to disrupt the energy fields that spirits generate when they interact with the material world. He fires the emitter at the ropy mass following Hazel. The effect is immediate and violent; it responds by rearing up and thrashing at the air as it starts to sizzle where Calvin's beam hits it. Normally there is a phase shift when the soliton wave interacts with a psychic entity, and that either immobilizes the target or repels it, but this is an unprecedented reaction.

Suddenly the tentacle rises into the canopy, as do at least a dozen more I hadn't even noticed yet, all coming nearer to us. Several trees uproot as well, which makes no sense if the creature or creatures are in the trees. Turns out it's not in the trees; it is the trees!

A massive lump that resembles a grain silo made of intestinal lining reaches at least 50 feet into the air, with maybe a hundred limbs coming out of the top. Many of the tentacles are trees; or, rather they were trees, their roots hanging limp. It's already apparent that they used to be separate organisms, like the bats and squirrels, but are now part of a single creature, one that spreads over other living things only to assimilate them and expand its own mass. We can't see what may pass for a head, if anything, but it does roar at us so there must be a mouth, though what it is used for when the thing feeds by… mitosis I suppose, is a complete unknown.

"Run!" I'm not sure who yells it, but there's a good chance all four of us do.

The trees start coming down hard and fast, and it's only the creature's lack of sensory organs that saves us from being pummeled. The car, which was not fleeing in terror like the rest of us, is not so lucky. So, we hear the awful grinding of metal and see shrapnel fly past us in our efforts to escape.

When we reach the nearest houses, we stop running and turn to look at what we're really running from. It's so huge we have no real comparison for it. I'm still trying to think of a bad analogy, preferably something gross I can say to capture the moment, when it rolls over and starts using several of those trees as legs… and it starts wobbling around.

"It's learning how to walk," Hazel hypothesizes. "It won't be long before it's fully mobile."

"If it makes it to the river it could spread all the way to the coast!" Ark fumbles for his phone to take a picture now that we can see it for what it is. "This thing is like a giant loogie, and I think it's learning about biology through absorption of random genetic materials. If it is able to adapt into something viable, and figures out cellular mitosis, we could have a hundred of these things within a week!"

Calvin looks to me. "You're retired military. Can you call in an airstrike or something?"

"It doesn't really work that way, but I might be able to reach someone that can help." I dial a 10-digit number I'm not supposed to know while everyone else starts knocking on doors and blaring sirens to evacuate the community. When I hear the line pick up, I yell, "We have a Code Verdigris! Request Blue Jacket support immediately!"

***

I should probably explain a little about my military service. From 1990 to 2010 I was in a special branch of the United States military that is dedicated to "Unconventional Warfare." How special? It's so special, it doesn't even have an official name. Of course, that just leaves it to other people to call it something unofficial, so instead of having one name, it has several.

Some people think of us as being so elite that we're some kind of royalty among military forces, so they call us things like Majesty, Monarchy, the Royal Family, or even Escutcheon (that shield part of a Coat of Arms in old world heraldry) -- the joke being that royalty doesn't exist in the United States, and neither do we. My own word for it was the Ordnance, because they have the special resources that stay locked up until things get bad enough to need them. And if anyone heard me say I was in the Ordnance, they might think I meant the E.O.D.; Explosive Ordnance Disposal, which is part of the Navy.

It's also worth noting that I did not leave the Ordnance under ideal circumstances, so I don't exactly have any friends there.

***

Forty minutes after I placed the call, we are exiting a black helicopter on a short airstrip in front of a building marked as Hangar 18. Since the Ordnance doesn't officially exist it piggybacks off other military bases, always using a building with that name as its command center. This particular Hangar 18 is on the Portsmouth Naval Shipyard base off the coast of Kittery, Maine.

Ark Gearheart, Calvin Scarborough, and Hazel Dinkley are ushered into a debriefing room, where I'm sure they'll be forced to sign Non-Disclosure Agreements about what goes on here. I, on the other hand, get escorted to a guard shack next to a docked submarine. The sub's captain, a surly looking man three inches shorter than me and balding on top, looks me over and hands me back my retired military identity card. The disgust on his face as he does so is clearly evident.

"Petty Officer Schuh… I don't even care what your name is! Wanna tell me why you think you can order around the United States Navy?"

"Sir, I wasn't in the Navy, and neither are you. We have a kaiju-sized creature destroying Tyngsboro right now, and if it isn't taken care of right away, it could spread like a virus across New England." He looks about to say something loud, but I cut him off. "That's exactly what the Verdigris Protocols were put in place for, so don't act like I'm overstepping. Who do you think they were named for? I'm Code Name: Verdigris!"

I can tell he was offended that I wasn't respecting the officer/enlisted relationship, but my revelation shuts him up. Back in 2006 a kaiju escaped containment from a Hangar 18 at a French facility. That time the creature was some kind of amphibious insect/reptile hybrid. An adult of its species attacked a major US city and laid eggs, which hatched within days. A few eggs were recovered by French agents and stored in a cryogenic chamber, but when they thawed one out for study, it too hatched, and was found to be pregnant even as it grew to a height of over 160 feet in a matter of weeks. Upon reaching maturity, it too laid fertile eggs. Because of this feature it was identified as a gynomorph, or "Ginomorph" to avoid terminology confusion.

These eggs were also frozen, but the French had too many to maintain properly. My Ordnance unit was assigned to the *USS Lagos Island*, an amphibious assault ship, and we were sent to visit the facility to assist with removal or disposal of the eggs. While there, a power surge that probably had nothing to do with the coffee I spilled on a refrigeration unit power supply caused the unit to fail and a baby ginomorph got loose. We wound up pursuing it all along the Mediterranean coast, eventually destroying it by dropping it into Mount Vesuvius. The gino left a trail of destruction in its wake and as a result we had a pretty large clean up job.

Someone higher up than I ever met made the decision to create steps to ensure nothing like that ever happens on American soil, so a series of war machines, the Blue Jacket fleet, were created for rapid response. The procedures for deploying them were called the Verdigris Protocols. I didn't take it personally at first but having my call sign made synonymous with a colossal screw-up didn't do my reputation any favors.

"I know all about what a Code Verdigris is!" he shouts at me, inches from my face. "I'm the captain of the *USS Metropolis*. We know what we're doing. We took down a giant hellbeast in Michigan last Spring. You and your 'Taskforce' will give us whatever intel you have on the beast and get out of our way so we can do our jobs. Now move it!"

Captain Bolivar goes aboard the sub while I get unceremoniously pushed into the debriefing room where Scarborough, Dinkley, and Gearheart are already trying to explain what happened to two guys in black suits. Not

"MIB" suits, just black suits. Terms like 'alien life form', 'cross between a mighty sloar and the dark young of Shub-Niggurath', and 'it's not a tumor' fill the air as everyone strives to speak over everyone else. I sit down alongside them and wait for someone to ask me a question. I also hold my phone under the table and text Hazard the details. Honestly, I'm surprised no one made the effort to confiscate our phones or at least block cell reception. I have to remind myself this is really a shipyard run by the Navy, and aside from this building, there isn't much need for security.

As soon as we hear the *Metropolis* get underway, the men in black suits (but who aren't "Men In Black") stand up and tell us they have all they need. Clearly, they don't really care what we had to say and were only stalling us so we wouldn't interfere with the sub's deployment.

They start directing us towards the front gate when Calvin stops them. "You're going to give us a ride back to our car, aren't you?"

One of them reaches into an inside jacket pocket. Hazel reflexively shields her eyes with her left arm and shouts, "don't flashy-thing us!"

The man sighs and pulls out a twenty-dollar bill to hand to Calvin. "Call an Uber."

Ark is already arranging a ride for us. "Well, those guys are dicks. Didn't you used to have friends in the Men In Black?"

I shake my head and remember that even retired, I'm bound by certain clearance restrictions. "If I did, I don't remember."

***

Kit Soony is waiting for us at the gate. It's a tight fit but Calvin, Hazel, and I squeeze into the backseat of her Tartan Prancer. Ark obviously rides shotgun. It takes an hour to get back to Tyngsboro, making me miss the expediency of riding in a black helicopter. We've been gone for about 2 hours, and the foul kaiju never stopped growing in our absence. By now it dwarfs the houses and remaining trees, easily over 100 feet tall. Fortunately, we had also called Taskforce headquarters for more immediate back up, so as we're seeing the monster in daylight for the first time, we also see the second team of paranormal investigators that Hazard sent to replace us: Anna O'Rourke, Billie Harkness, George Dumas, and Scáth Hazard himself.

They have a van with them, a Ford E250. They filled it with spare equipment for us, but all four of the newcomers are already armed with heavy weapons. They do what they can to corral the kaiju away from the river. Billie has a flame thrower bigger than she is, but it seems to be doing a lot of damage to the phlegm monster, so more power to her!

We don't have a chance to get out of the car before the submarine surfaces. And I don't mean it breaks the surface of the water and sits 2/3rds submerged. I mean it pops out of the Merrimack River like a cork, soaring into the air...

... and transforms!

Yes, of course it transforms into a robot. What else would it possibly transform into? It was already a 360-foot-long warship capable of delivering tomahawk missiles, harpoon torpedoes, and CAPTOR mines. Now

294

it stands 180 feet tall, with two fully articulated legs, two fully articulated arms, and a roughly female-looking head. In fact, the robot somewhat resembles a feminine C-3PO robot from Star Wars. So maybe not "fully" articulated then, because it moves somewhat like C-3PO too.

Ark grins. "I get it now. *Metropolis*, like the Fritz Lang film." Then he shakes his head. "Wish I still had the G.E.A.R.Box. It may not be as tall as the muck monster, but it packed a punch."

"I wish you still had your car," I say while grabbing my spare Tillinghast Projector from Hazard's van. "Sorry, too soon?"

"Dude!" Calvin stops looking for a Soliton Collapser long enough to scold me. "Not cool!" Then he spins on Ark. "Wait, is that what we're calling it?" 'Muck Monster'? It reminds me of a species of procreative oozes called the Unclean."

"I've heard of those," I offer, hoping to provide useful information. "Abhoth was the first recorded Unclean, recorded as a noxious underground pool of living biological noxious sentience during the Hyperborean era, classifying it as either a titan or a god of putrescence. Some theories link it to the entities known as Ubbo-Sathla and Shub-Niggurath, but those unholy beings are believed to create life, while Abhoth generates obscene mockeries of life out of filth and doesn't usually let its creations leave the nest before reabsorbing them. I think other Unclean were spotted more recently; around Tokyo in the early 70s and in Arizona around the year 2000, so I guess some of its spawn managed to get away."

"The Arizona sighting wasn't an Unclean," grunts Gearheart while rummaging in the van for another flame

295

thrower. "The geological reports claimed it produced multicellular lifeforms independent of its central mass that could –"

"How about we argue this later, after we aren't about to die?" Calvin looks panicky, but that's just the face he makes when a conversation is getting away from him. "Selenium worked against the Arizona Protean, but fire was useless, so we already know this isn't the same thing. What can hurt Abhoth?"

I make an adjustment to the output of my Tillinghast Generator. "Abby should be hurt by intense radiation or psychic energy. We've already seen that fireworks too, but the fumes it puts off might kill us anyway."

Hazel digs through synchrotrons and cyclotrons looking for something to use while Ark, Calvin, and I debate nomenclature standards. Her own equipment contained a mystic artifact, and was in Ark's Transit when it was destroyed, and she doesn't have a backup. "Hey, are we going to get in the way of the fembot? I don't want to get caught in a 'friendly fire' situation."

She has a good point. Unlike the robots in a lot of cartoons and movies, this one isn't self-aware or piloted by one to five people. It has a crew of about 140 people inside it, all responsible for different tasks. Human communication from the control room to engineering where the legs are steered from can take several seconds, plus the hydraulics in the legs won't respond to new commands immediately. We might all be in real danger where we are.

"Let's all back up to the road, and only attack if it starts coming near the house."

Harkness yells over the sound of her flamethrower, "We need to keep it from getting to the water, too! We should split up!"

I head towards the river to join Billie and Scáth. My Tillinghast Projector doesn't seem to be doing as much to hurt the monster as the flame thrower is, but every bit helps. I see Ark on our side of 'Abby' as well.

Scáth Hazard looks to me. "They wouldn't launch a missile at it this close to a population, would they?"

"I hope not, but if the threat level is high enough, 'acceptable losses' is a thing."

Watching the mech engage in hand to hand combat with a gray and black lump that has no hands is uncomfortable, but with every strike I see Abby arranging more and more limbs with which to ensnare the arms of the combat robot... com-bot? What do they even call that thing? I try not to let this distract me, but even in the chaos of firing at the kaiju while dodging the... Fembot? Gynoid? Dot Matrix? Whatever its name, I can't stop thinking about it.

If they built a blow torch into its right arm, they could call it Lady Liberty. Since it's based on the robot in *Metropolis*, and it's a submarine, maybe it's called the Sub-Maria. I wince at that thought, though no one else heard it to judge me. I know a bad pun when I hear one, even in my own head.

Sub-Maria has moves. It's pretty slow, but at that scale I'm sure it's actually got thousands of parts moving really fast. Instead of hands, it has the propellers that provide thrust for the ship in water. Dark bloody meat sprays out of the monster with each blow, and the howling sounds grow. Abby may have no central nervous system of its own, but it absorbed an awful lot of plant and animal lives to get as big as it is, and it may be adapting. Its stumpy body seems to be stretching and compressing, heaving skyward with each renewed effort to affect a counterstrike against its enemy.

Scarborough yells something to us from the tree line, but we can't hear him. Ark gets a text and relays the message to us. "Calvin thinks the Ordnance has Abby's attention. We should evacuate!"

Scáth, Billie, and I nod in agreement and make our way around the far side of the monster. Like Anna, Hazel, and Calvin, we remain armed and facing the battle, at the ready. Only George Dumas and Kit Soony have retreated to the vehicles; Kit seems to be calling someone, probably the E.P.A. to inform them of the situation. Hopefully she's making us sound competent. George is… eating a three-layer cake. I don't know why he has a cake with him, but I hope he isn't too distracted to help if needed.

The Bar-Kays song "Soul Finger," as covered by the Blues Brothers, starts to sound from my work phone. I answer the call, which turns out to be Captain Bolivar. Somewhat flustered sounding, he's asking for advice. "You said your people took some scans of this thing. Did you find anything conclusive? We can't seem to find a weak spot to fire on and the Hel will only get a few shots off before the monster escapes to the river."

"You named your robot 'Hel'? And I thought 'Sub-Maria' was bad." I remember the spectral analyzer, still tethered to my belt. "We found it may be extradimensional, but not from a hell dimension. I think Gearheart detected alien DNA, but I'm not sure."

I ask Ark for clarification of his Giger Counter readings. "It's not from another planet; it's from another

298

plane of existence. Residual radiation from its passage through the membrane that separates our reality from its own still lingers in it, and it vibrates at…"

"Extradimensional vibrations? Sweet, I can use that! Thanks, Ark." I get back to the phone conversation. "Captain, do you have radar transmitters that can broadcast narrow beams of 1.21 gigawatts or higher?"

"No, we mostly use sonar for navigation."

"Even better! Can your sonar emitters ping at the Extremely High Frequency range?"

"No! Soundwaves at that high frequency would pass through most solid objects. It would be useless for navigation." I hear some background noise as someone else in the room talks to him. "But we do have a rail gun that hits those frequencies when it launches a projectile. I'll get them to weaponize the pulse." There's a long enough pause that I think the connection may have been lost. "Thank you for your help. Have the Taskforce clear the area. E.M.P. in 15 minutes. Five-mile radius should do it."

"That's our cue to skedaddle! Let's roll out!" I raise my hand over my head and gesture to the SUVs for emphasis. "We have ten minutes to get out of range of an E.M.P., so don't mind the potholes this time!"

To emphasize the point, Hel starts sounding an air raid siren and all our phones get messages to leave Tyngsboro. Those people who haven't already fled start flooding out of their homes in various stages of preparedness. It's still early on a Saturday and I've no doubt most of them managed to sleep through the mayhem so far.

We make it to the University of Massachusetts campus in Lowell and go to the top of the Fox building to watch what happens. It actually takes thirty minutes from when the phone call ended, but I appreciate the exaggeration. I have military grade stabilizing binoculars, but I still keep my sunglasses on when I look through them, just to be safe.

A spear-like missile shoots from Hel's... chest. I hope there's no media catching this part of the show, or the Navy will have a heck of a public relations nightmare to deal with. The projectile strikes the kaiju, which has reared up to a height of over 200 feet by this time. A blur in the air in front of the robot signifies the detonation of the E.M.P. The blur spreads, somehow enveloping the entire monster.

Then I see it is working. Unclean Abby starts to fade out of existence. The explosion wasn't meant as the attack; it was just clearing the rail gun cannon so the modified pulse could be fired. Once it hit, the Extremely High Frequency reacted with the vibrations within the creature that signified its origin in another dimension.

The experience appears to be painful, if the thrashing and screeching is any indication. Hel is knocked over, though only through reflexive lashing out with tree trunk tentacles, rather than any intentional retaliation. The robot lurches back to its feet but doesn't quite make it. It crawls back to the Merrimack River so it can resume its submarine features and escape the scene. Abby doesn't pursue the robot. It continues flailing for a good ten minutes, fading in and out of focus as it slowly phases out of reality.

I feel bad about this. I don't know where the monster came from, but I'm sure wherever it is now doesn't want it any more than we did. On the other hand, maybe it will return to face Abhoth, and the two will destroy each other, or at least keep each other too busy for any more Unclean to be generated for a while.

Now the real challenge begins: filing a claim for the extermination of a 200-foot-tall kaiju when we have no remains to prove its existence; and keeping the Ordnance out of the story; and to avoid getting stuck with responsibility for all the damage their E.M.P. caused. And I still haven't had any coffee!

Credits:
Ark Gearheart, G.E.A.R.Box - Michael Muscatell
Kit Soony - Charlene Carson
Calvin Scarborough, Soniton Collapser - Douglas Fisher
George Dumas - Neal Devlin
Hazel Dinkley - Sarah Michaud
Scáth Hazard - Aaron Oliver
Billie Harkness - Danielle Oliver
Anna O'Rourke - Beth Harrington
Ivan Ronald Schablotski / Agent Verdigris, Captain Bolivar, United States Ordnance Department, *USS Metropolis*, *USS Lagos Island*, Taskforce Ecto, Spectral Analyzer, H. R. Giger Counter, Ginomorph, Unclean Abby – Kevin Heim

END

MARUGRAH VS. PLAGUE

Zach Cole

Editor's Note: The following story is a self-contained excerpt from Zach's novel *Kaiju Epoch*, the debut appearance of his heroic kaiju Marugrah, which will soon be re-released in a new edition by Wild Hunt Press.

1

New York City

Normally having a population of eight million people, the Big Apple was now only populated by the hundreds of military soldiers surrounding Central Park where the monster from the stars was supposed to land. Central Park was an urban park opened in 1856 on 778 acres of city-owned land in middle-upper Manhattan. It was the most visited spot in the United States. On any other occasion, it would have been a beautiful place to hang out, but Sergeant Nick Huber knew this was no ordinary day. Today was the supposed beginning of the apocalypse.

He walked over to the man holding the Javelin, Private Jake Doland, who was watching the sky from their position on 59th street on the south side of the park. Everyone was skeptical about this whole idea. They were only going on information from a new agency created in the last few months. Kind of shady, if you asked him.

302

None of them had heard of the Creature Containment Unit before now. None of them believed in this whole mess going on, but the higher ups did. They were supposedly presented with proof upon the danger of the situation and his job was not to question orders given to him but to follow them.

I guess we will find out soon whether this shit is real, Huber thought, still skeptical. He watched the white fluffy clouds pass overhead through the bright blue sky.

"You really think it's coming, sir?" Doland asked.

"I'm not sure, private," Huber replied. "The CCU jerkwads seem to think it is."

"Yeah. I guess we will find out soon enough, huh?" Doland said, mirroring Huber's earlier assessment as he looked at his tactical watch. "It's almost the time they predicted the creature will land."

A thunderous crackling filled the air, followed by the sky lighting up blindingly bright. A flaming cylindrical object rocketed from the sky, landing in the Jacqueline Kennedy Onassis Reservoir fifteen meters from Huber's men. Water and earth exploded into the air, most of the former turning to steam from contact with the burning hot object. The shock wave from the object's landing uprooted trees and flung them away from the reservoir and down to the ground, giving Huber's team a better look at the destruction wrought. A few trees were flung over his team's head, making them drop to the ground.

When the men got back to their feet, they readied their guns, including Doland. Huber put a hand on Doland's shoulder, calming the man. The rocket contained within his Javelin was something cooked up by the CCU. Some kind of mind control device, they said. He had no idea if something like that would control a beast the size of the metal cylinder.

The steam dissipated, giving Huber a clear look at the pod laying in the now empty reservoir. The pod split down the middle, the two sides flinging away, revealing something so terrifying it made Huber stumble back a few steps.

The head of the creature that emerged from the pod looked like it was a flaming skull. It wasn't a human skull, however. The top of the bony cranium was a half circle piece of bone curving down to jagged, sharp teeth. The creature's jaw was the same, but thinner and more of an oval than a circle. It lacked any eyes or eye sockets that he could see. Its back was lined with spiked plates of overlapping armor, ending at the base of the creature's tail. White armor plates ran down from the monster's neck down to its crotch. Its arms were armored, with jagged spikes rising out of the beast's shoulders. Three spikes poked out of the creature's armored forearms.

The hands looked as if they burned red-hot, its four digits at the end twitching with energy. The black skin of its wrists looked as if they were melted away. A gigantic spike protruded from each of its elbows. The skin at the end of the tail also appeared as if it were melted away. Bone-white armor ran down the front of its legs, ending at its kneecap. The titanic beast's leg muscles were also chaotically arranged, its four toes looking like skeletal digits tipped with deadly claws and spikes protruding from its calf. The creature stood a towering 400 feet over the park.

The kaiju (that was the term the CCU was using for the monster) let out a deafening roar, making the men cringe and want to cover their ears. Huber figured it was probably heard for miles around. The men's faces twisted with terror, but they stood their ground, guns at the ready The kaiju lifted itself out of the cratered pond with one of its massive legs, which decimated one half of the Metropolitan Museum of Art as it landed.

Once the beast was clear of the pond, four Sikorsky UH-60 Black Hawk attack helicopters descended from the sky, raining down AGM-114 Hellfire laser guided missiles, 70 mm Hydra rockets, and AIM-92 Stinger air-to-air missiles upon the horrifying monstrosity. Huber was surprised that the beast didn't flinch at -- or even notice -- the missiles bombarding its body while standing in the almost flat site of the thirty-five-acre lower reservoir known as the Great Lawn. He was briefed that the creature would withstand them, but it seemed impossible to comprehend. Huber had seen the damage the missiles can do firsthand, as he was sometimes the one firing them. But here he was, watching the impossible.

The helicopters started swinging around, trying to get the kaiju to turn its back to Huber's team so they could fire the device at the back of its neck. The creature tracked the choppers with its head, somehow seeing them with no eyes, as it followed the annoying buzzing machines as they formed a line. The kaiju followed their lead, turning its body when it could no longer track them with its head. When the monster's back was to them, Huber tapped Doland on the shoulder. He knew what to do. The young soldier looked through the eye piece, targeting the back of the creature's neck. Once locked on, he pulled the trigger. The rocket erupted from the launcher with a hiss, skimming towards its target.

It slammed into the creature's armored neck, between a plate of armor and the back of the kaiju's flaming head where the monster's spine should be. The casing of the projectile split apart and flew away upon impact.

Huber toggled his throat mic. "Come in, command. This is Alpha Team. Objective complete."

"Roger that, Alpha Team," a woman's voice said through the mic. "Command out."

Huber looked up as the monster opened its mouth wide, letting loose a torrent of flame which struck the Black Hawk in the front of the line. The blaze must've ignited the chopper's fuel because it erupted into a ball of fire, plummeting to the ground and landing in a pile of uprooted trees, setting them on fire as well.

"Holy shit!" Doland exclaimed, reeling back in fright.

"What do we do now?" another man on Huber's team, who he knew as Lyngly, asked.

"Nothing. Our objective is complete. It's up to Beta Team now," Huber said. "We wait for further orders."

The Black Hawks spread out, forming a horizontal line and unleashing Gatling gunfire upon the kaiju. Two A-10 Thunderbolts passed overhead, raining down AIM-9 Sidewinder air-to-air missiles and AGM-65 Maverick missiles down on the monster's back, careful not to hit the portion of its neck where the black box resided. The monster roared angrily up at the jets as they passed over it. The kaiju lifted one of its massive legs, about to take a step, but suddenly froze. It shook its head back and forth like a wet dog shaking off water. But Huber knew that wasn't what the kaiju was doing. It threw its head back, letting out a high-pitched wail before grabbing its head with its massive fiery hands. The chain gunfire stopped.

The device is working, Huber realized. *They're getting inside its head!*

The creature cradled its seemingly skinless cranium, hunching over. Huber felt hopeful that they would be able to stop this monster with a relatively small loss of life; the four men aboard the Black Hawk that erupted in flames were most definitely dead.

The feeling lasted only a few moments before it all drained away.

The monster pulled its hands away from its head and stood up straight. It roared in what looked to Huber like victory. It then lashed out with one of its hands, striking a Black Hawk that came foolishly close. Huber watched in horror as the helicopter plummeted to the ground where it was crushed under the giant's foot. The two remaining Black Hawks opened fire with their Gatling guns once again, further annoying the behemoth. It let loose a torrent of fire from its mouth, destroying another Black Hawk.

Perhaps in an attempt to save the remaining helicopter, three M1A2 Abrams main battle tanks rolled into the park from the north side, crushing tree branches beneath their treads as they weaved their way inside while firing 120 mm rounds at the kaiju's chest. The monster looked down at the small annoyances with rage. It did, in fact, allow the Black Hawk to escape safely. The kaiju walked around the reservoir, stomping its way toward the tanks firing at it.

And Beta Team.

That was when the A-10 Thunderbolts returned, firing more Sidewinders and Mavericks at the beast and eliciting a cheer from Huber's men. But the missiles just made the beast angrier. It jumped up. The kaiju caught one of the Thunderbolts in its massive, agape maw, seemingly swallowing the plane whole. The earth was decimated with trees being uprooted and crumbling beneath its feet after the creature's massive weight slammed back into it. The monster spat out the plane, hacking it at the three battle tanks who tried to move out of the way, but not fast enough. Two of the three tanks were damaged by the lougied jet, making them easy for the kaiju to crush them underfoot.

The remaining tank made its way back out of the park through the mess of trees and slipped in between the buildings fringing the north side of the park. The kaiju let out an angry growl as it charged toward the buildings.

"That thing is going to decimate Beta Team!" Doland yelled.

The woman who served as command's voice came through Huber's earpiece. "Command to all ground teams. Fire everything you have at the kaiju. Aim for its legs. Maybe you can cripple it."

"Affirmative," he said into his mic, turning toward his men while hefting up a M32 rotary grenade launcher. "You heard the lady! Move! We need to help them!"

Huber weaved his way around uprooted trees, past Central Park Lake, across the decimated Great Lawn, past the reservoir, all the way to the north end as the kaiju decimated the buildings fringing it. Huber and his men were exhausted once they reached it; they all carried heavy hitting weapons, rocket launchers, and grenade launchers as well, which didn't make the run any easier for them.

They raised their weapons, firing at the creature's armored back and legs as it swung its massive hands back and forth, decimating stone and melting metal to push its way into the street in pursuit of the retreating tank. The monster was a half mile into the city from the park when Huber's team started firing. The kaiju continued its rampage before noticing the rockets and grenades peppering its back and legs. It whirled around, sighting in on the five men launching artillery. The skull-headed beast let out an ear-splitting roar that made the men cringe.

Huber gasped in horror as flames erupted from the monster's gullet, washing over the quintet of soldiers. They didn't even have time to scream before they ceased to exist, their bodies turned to ash.

2

Washington, D.C.

Marugrah watched the big screen in the front of the military control room that showed satellite footage of Central Park. From there he could see men gathered on the north and south sides of the green. A flash of light momentarily obscured their vision before a fiery object landed in the reservoir. After a few moments, the pod split apart, revealing the Vexnoxtuque -- the kaiju -- the Plagueonians sent as their harbinger. He was unable to tell what species it was before the Plagueonians experimented upon it. Marugrah watched as the kaiju stepped out of the empty reservoir and onto the Great Lawn, helicopters swooping around it and firing missiles at the giant beast. It turned its back to Alpha Team, allowing them to fire the device at the back of the creature's head.

Marugrah adjusted the black metal headband on his head. The band would allow the diminutive reptilian alien to access the kaiju's mind and battle it for control over its body. Once he won, he would be able to control the monster and use it against its makers. He had only done it once before. It was difficult, but Marugrah believed he could get it done. Depending on the species...

"Come in, command. This is Alpha Team. Objective complete," a male voice came through the headband, the screen identifying the speaker as Sergeant Nick Huber along with background information about the man.

"Copy that, Alpha Team. Command out," Christina Angel, leader of Gamma Team, said. She turned to Marugrah. "Your time to shine."

Marugrah looked around the room at the people standing in it. From Marudon, his Queen, to Will, a human he could actually call his friend even with their... strained relationship. Will gave him a smile and a nod, boosting his confidence level a little more. The alien activated the device mentally, connecting him to the kaiju's mind.

He slipped out of his mind and into the kaiju's, feeling the creature's rage and bloodlust toward humanity. He came face-to-ugly-face with the monster, which looked oddly familiar to him but at the same time not.

Who are you? the creature mentally queried, his skull-like mouth not moving as it spoke and tilted to the side.

I am Marugrah, guardian of the Queen of... the reptilian alien started.

"Maruia. You are a Maruian?"

Marugrah's eyes widened as a familiar sensation enveloped him... one indicative of a killer. Of a destroyer of worlds. Of his world. The creature before him was a Plagueonian.

Who are you? Marugrah asked.

I am Plague, prince of Plagueonia. Destroyer of worlds. Like yours, Maruian, the creature said. *Maybe you'd recognize me better like this.*

The kaiju's appearance shifted from the monster in New York to a more familiar form. His head looked vaguely humanoid, standing like a human on two armored back legs. But it wasn't like the armor on his kaiju form. It was silver with symbols carved into it. He wore the same armor all over his body, a red cape fluttering behind him. A curved helmet sat atop his head, framing his black eyes, flat nose, and wicked, sharp-toothed smile.

I recognize you just by your name, monster. It's impossible that you're alive. You died. I killed you myself.

Yes, I remember that. The alterations to my body were the only way to save my life. By becoming one of our repulsive Vexnoxtuque, I was granted regenerative abilities that saved my life. It is disgusting but it has allowed me to continue conquering worlds like this ball of dirt I am now on.

I won't allow you to conquer this planet.

Plague let out a cackle. *You think you can take over my mind? I saw you do that on Anterkia. You're not doing that this time. Goodbye, Maruian.*

With a wave of Plague's four-digit hand, Marugrah was thrown out of Plague's mind violently. He grabbed his head, letting out a high-pitched squeal of pain. His brain felt like it was on fire, a burst of agony that soon faded to a dull headache.

"Maru!" he heard Will yell as his mind slipped from New York to his body in Washington D.C., making him open his eyes. Will and his other friends/allies Ashley, Aaron, Nicole, Jamie, Walt, Marudon, and Angel stood over him as he laid on his back on the carpeted floor of the control room.

"Are you in control?" Angel asked as he stood up from the floor.

If I were in control, I would not be laying on the ground, Marugrah snapped.

What happened? Will asked via their telepathic rapport.

What happened was that thing in New York is a Plagueonian I thought I [had] killed a long time ago. I was wrong, it seems. He was saved by being turned into a Vexnoxtuque.

Marudon looked stunned, probably realizing who he was talking about. *You don't mean...?*

Yes. Plague.

"Sounds like a Batman villain's name," Aaron retorted.

He is indeed a villain, but not of this Batman's, Marugrah explained. *He is a villain of the galaxy. And mine. Plague was the prince of the Plagueonian race, son of the Plagueonian Queen. I thought I [had] killed him at the battle for Anterkia. However, he must have been recovered and saved by being turned into the monster you see on the screen.*

Marugrah turned toward the big screen displaying the satellite footage of New York. Plague jumped into the sky, snatching a jet in his jaws before falling back to the ground. He then spat the aircraft out at the tanks that entered the park, destroying two of them.

"So, that is their harbinger... one of their own," Lance Cole, head of the CCU, said while stepping into the glow of the screen from the shadows, watching Plague's rampage and appearing a little too interested in the revelation.

It would seem so, yes, Marugrah replied, a little bit annoyed at the man's interest.

"What the hell are we supposed to do about it now? You guys got a spare giant robot around we can use to fight it?" Nicole asked sarcastically.

"That would be awesome," Jamie whispered, but Maru heard it perfectly.

"No, we don't have a giant robot, as convenient as that would be," Cole said solemnly. "All we can really do is throw everything we have in our arsenal at it, hoping to injure it or slow it down."

"Even nuclear options?" Will asked.

"If it comes to that, yes."

Marugrah looked up to see Will cringe at the words. He searched his human friend's mind, finding information on atomic bombs and nuclear weaponry, seeing their destructive power. They might be enough to kill Plague but at the cost of New York City... and any of the military troops that were stationed there.

"Command to all ground teams," Angel said into her headset. "Fire everything you have at the kaiju. Aim for its legs. Maybe you can cripple it."

Marugrah heard the doubt in her last sentence. She didn't believe they could really cripple it. And neither did Marugrah.

Affirmatives came in through the screen. Marugrah looked to the monitor, seeing Plague making his way into the city as he followed the retreating soldiers. The squadron that were responsible for firing the black box device at Plague were running through the park toward the monster. Once they reached him, they fired their weapons at the kaiju only to be doused with fire and reduced to piles of ash and melted metal.

"This is a losing battle," Walt said, a defeated look on his face.

Marugrah knew he was right. There was no known way to kill a Vexnoxtuque other than another kaiju. And they didn't have one of those, let alone the technology to make one of their own. But the small reptilian alien was desperate enough to do just that, no matter how disgusting of a thought it was. It was the only way to stop the giant creatures. A plan started formulating in his mind, but it would only work when the Plagueonians arrived. And even then, it might be too late.

"I'm gonna be sick," Ashley groaned, burying her face in Will's chest.

He put his arms around her, doing his best to offer comfort. He ushered her out of the room and out of Marugrah's sight.

What are you thinking? Marudon asked, keeping her voice telepathically limited to Marugrah's mind.

I'm thinking that he is right. This is a losing battle. We have no way of stopping Plague or any of the other Vexnoxtuque in their arsenal, Marugrah replied, masking his real thoughts.

You may be right, but we still have a few more Anterkian neural interface boxes. If another Vexnoxtuque falls from the sky, we can take control of it.

We could, but we aren't guaranteed access. Like me with Plague, we could be thrown out of their heads. Not to mention, Plague could decimate a few cities before then as well.

Frantic chatter flooded from the screen into Marugrah's ears. They were losing horribly against the monster devastating the city.

Burned alive.

Crushed within their war machines or under Plague's colossal feet.

Dying.

"Half of our ground troops have been annihilated. More air support is inbound," a man at a console reported.

"Shit. *Half?* How many troops did you guys send out there?" Aaron asked, astonished.

"We sent 400, including the men in the helicopters and tanks," Cole replied.

"So, this monster, Plague, has killed 200 people so far, that quickly?"

"Yeah... and the number is climbing. Anyone that gets in its way are killed. We may want to review our remaining options." Cole nodded to Angel, who knew what he was implying.

Remaining options? Marugrah asked while watching Angel walk away and pull out a phone. *You're talking about nuclear weapons.*

"Something of the same power, yes. It may be the only way we can stop the kaiju."

At the cost of your own city!

"It's a price we have to pay for the sake of humanity."

Is that what you plan on doing with every Vexnoxtuque that falls from the sky? Drop an atomic bomb on it?

"If it kills them and saves us from being eradicated, I will do what I think is necessary."

You're a fool, Cole.

"A fool with no other options and is looking out for his species. At least *I am* fighting for my planet instead of fleeing it and bringing that trouble on another world."

Cole gave Marugrah a stern look. The diminutive alien started growling, and he was about to attack the man but was stopped by Marudon's hand on his scaly shoulder. Marugrah looked into her green eyes, calming himself in them. Cole gave him a squinty-eyed look before turning back to the screen, hands behind his back.

Marugrah was seeing a new side to the man. A cold side. But it didn't mean Cole wasn't right. Marugrah ran as his homeworld was ravaged. If he would have stayed, his people may have stood a chance of stopping the Plagueonians on Maruia, and Earth would have been spared from the destruction now being wrought. Will and his other human friends were only here because Marugrah and Marudon were. Or were they?

"Everything is under way, sir," Angel said as she walked back into the room. "A bomber will be there within the hour."

"Good," Cole replied. "Let's hope it works. We'll hit it with MOABs before we resort to the nuclear option, Maru. I know you are not familiar with the weapon. MOAB stands for Massive Ordinance Air Blast, the largest non-nuclear weapon in the U.S. arsenal. It's a vacuum bomb equivalent to eleven tons of TNT that basically melts everything within a one-mile radius. The weapon is a fuel-air explosive, meaning it will detonate before hitting its target, creating a thermobaric wave of force and heat. It's close to a nuke in destructive power."

Aaron let out a disgusted sigh as he made his way out of the control room with Walt, Jamie, and Nicole following him. Marugrah took one last look at Cole's cold eyes before following them out, Marudon on his short tail.

"Can you believe this shit?" Aaron asked as they walked into the hallway.

"You mean, sacrificing New York City to stop an unstoppable monster?" Will enquired, disgust mixed with determination on his face. "I mean, the city has been evacuated. And they'll pull the remaining soldiers out of the city. It'll just be the monster and buildings. I don't like it any more than anyone else but if they can kill the kaiju, then why stop them? We have who-knows-how-many-more on the way."

"He's right," Ashley agreed. "New York can be rebuilt."

The destruction isn't going to be just limited to New York, either, Marugrah chimed in psychically.

"The whole world could be destroyed if they don't at least *try* to stop Plague," Walt said.

"Do we at least agree that it makes us all sick to our stomachs?" Aaron asked.

Everyone in the room nodded their heads.

"Good."

3

New York City

Jason Keen flew the B-2 Spirit stealth bomber toward the target, the city of New York racing towards him in his windshield. He looked to his right where his co-pilot and mission commander, Cody Stewart, sat. Jason gave his partner a nod as they approached the area where the kaiju code-named "Plague" was on a rampage. The fiery-headed titan was carving a path of destruction through the theater district from the now demolished Central Park as it pushed its way south, heading who-knows-where. After ridding the north side of soldiers, the monster headed back through Central Park to the south side.

It looked to Keen that it was heading down the coast. Toward Washington D.C.

If the creature was smart enough, it could have slipped into the waterways surrounding New York and make its way along the coast from there. Maybe it just liked to cause destruction? Maybe it was afraid of water? Or maybe it really was just dumb.

Keen didn't know anything about the monster or what it wanted and didn't care. His only job was to drop a MOAB on its ugly flaming head, erasing it from existence. He flicked a switch, opening the bay doors on the bottom of the triangular craft. Another flick of a switch released the MOAB. The deadly payload fell from the bomber's belly, landing on the monster's head and detonating with a powerful force. Keen didn't feel any of its effects as he was tens of thousands of feet above the ground when it detonated.

The pilot guided the bomber around in a half circle, coming around for a look. A mile-wide radius around where the MOAB had dropped was smoldering ash. Buildings laid in blackened ruins. The air burnt. No sign of Plague, though. It was like the creature was vaporized by the bomb.

Then, the blackened husks of toppled buildings shifted and parted as the monster rose from under them, unharmed. It seemingly roared up at Keen, looking very pissed off and probably sounded the same way. The pilot was too far up for the monster to reach him, so he wasn't too worried. Then a big gray blur sped past his craft, startling him.

"What the hell was that?" Stewart asked.

"No idea. All I saw was a blur," Keen said.

The aviator circled around, looking for the object. He didn't see anything... until he did. Keen could scarcely believe what he saw. He was looking at what seemed to be a flying saucer. A disk spun around a circular gray orb with alien carvings all over it.

"What in God's name is that?" Stewart asked.

"It looks like a UFO," Keen said, flying around the object.

The mysterious craft seemed to spot them and a red dot on the gray orb's hull sighted in on the bomber. Keen pulled away from the object, the radar showing it on his ass.

"Shit! It's following us!" Stewart yelled.

"I can see that," Keen growled.

He then pushed the bomber to its top speed of 630 miles per hour in an attempt to shake it off using evasive maneuvers, but the thing kept up. The craft shuddered from an impact as alarms rang throughout. They had been hit.

But hit by what? A missile? A bullet? What did the thing chasing them even use as a weapon?

Keen had a million questions about the object that was following them, but he didn't think anyone could provide a satisfactory answer. Or that he'd survive to ask them.

A second impact rocked the bomber. He checked the displays after seeing that the thrusters were damaged and failing. They were going down.

Keen fought with the controls, losing an already lost battle. Stewart screamed as the view out the windshield changed from blue sky to tall gray buildings. Keen frantically fought to pull the craft up when they suddenly stopped in midair, 350 feet from the ground.

They were spun around, and the hapless pilot caught a glimpse of massive burning digits before coming face-to-face with the flaming skulled monster Plague. When Stewart squealed in fright, Keen unashamedly joined him.

The kaiju opened its massive maw, letting loose a loud roar that made the men quit their screaming and cover their ears. When they pulled their hands away, they were covered in blood. The creature's roar had burst their eardrums, so they weren't able to hear the order from command to eject.

Plague watched the tiny humans quiver in fear before opening his mouth again and letting loose a stream of fire upon the craft which exploded in the kaiju's already burning hands.

4

Washington, D.C.

"Are you shitting me? It shrugged off the Mother of All Bombs and destroyed the bomber?" Angel enquired, shocked at the event that transpired in just minutes.

"It had help. Zoom in on that object above the creature," Cole said, pointing to an aberration on the feed.

Just as Cole commanded, the screen zoomed in on the object hovering just a hundred feet above Plague. The thing was a gray sphere with a ring of metal spinning around it. A red circle was the only blemish on the symbol-covered hull's smooth surface.

"Is that...?" Ashley started, but never finished her sentence.

"A UFO... a flying saucer," Will said in awe.

It looked much like the spaceships that nut jobs claim to spot all the time, but he doubted that they saw this exact same craft. Probably crafts of similar design, though.

It was not just any flying saucer, however. It was a Plagueonian research vessel that monitors the Vexnoxtuque's vitals and provides it with energy if it cannot find a food source.

We need to seize that vessel, Marugrah said telepathically, looking a little more excited than he should.

"Why not just blow it up?" Cole asked, turning his attention away from the screen and toward the three-foot-tall alien lizard-dragon.

You saw how ineffective your MOAB was on the Vexnoxtuque. You will have no further luck with the orb. It has a high-grade shield protecting it, not to mention it will shoot anything that approaches it or Plague now that it has arrived.

"So, what? You want me to drop a team on the thing, infiltrate it, and disable its shields?"

No. Just me.

"Why would I do that?"

Because I am the only one that can fly my ship, which has cloaking capabilities. That is the only thing that will be able to get even remotely close to that vessel. Like I said, anything else will be shot from the sky. Anything they can see, at least.

Will watched in horror as Cole considered the idea. The plan was dangerous, and he suspected Marugrah had an ulterior motive for entering that ship. What it was, he had no idea. Revenge, maybe?

"You make a convincing case, Marugrah," Cole said. "Sergeant Hlad will escort you to your ship."

The big man stepped forward, running a giant hand through the short white hair atop his head.

"Maru, are you sure about this?" Will asked his alien friend.

It may be the only way to stop Plague, Marugrah told him.

Will looked into the alien reptilian's lizard-like eyes, seeing nothing but the truth in them. Marugrah gave him his best smile since he lacked the face muscles to make a human-like beam. He gave Marugrah a smile of his own in return, approving of the mission. If he had a way to stop Plague, they had to try it. The young man didn't want to see his planet and everyone he loved fall to the alien invaders.

"Fine, fine," Will said. "If it'll stop Plague, we'll try it."

Marugrah nodded and followed the giant of a man out of the control room. Will thought on it a moment before joining them in the elevator at the end of the hallway. They went down until the door opened up into a basement. Hlad flipped a switch to reveal a big object sitting in the middle of the room, covered with a black tarp. Hlad walked over to the object and pulled the tarp off it, revealing a gold, oval-shaped craft covered in alien symbols. Will felt those ciphers were very different than the ones on the Plagueonian craft; they somehow seemed less... sinister.

Marugrah bounced over to it, running his hands across the shiny hull. Will laughed as his lizard-like friend seemingly hugged the ship. Maru gave him a squinty-eyed look, shutting him up. The reptilian alien tapped a section near the middle of the craft. A panel appeared and Maru typed in a code. The door swung upwards, revealing an interior which was nothing more than a silver space with a rack that looked to adorn some kind of gun.

"I believe you will find everything is in working order," Hlad said.

Maru climbed inside the small ship, moving out of sight. A beeping sound suddenly became audible as Will watched the hatch. He didn't know what Maru was doing in there, but he figured he was checking out the ship's vitals.

You are correct. Everything is in working order, Maru said, returning to Will's view and hopping out of the vessel.

"Good. We didn't touch the craft after we brought it here," Hlad explained. "Marudon took some stuff out of some crates that were in here but that was about it."

Are these the devices she made?

"Yeah. She made them from stuff aboard the ship."

Alright, how do I fly this out of here?

Hlad hit a button next to the light switch. A hatch at the far end of the basement opened.

Ah. That's how, Maru said, climbing back into the ship.

"Wait, you're going by yourself?" Will asked.

Of course, I am.

"Let me go with you."

No, Will. This task is very dangerous, and I don't want to see you hurt… or worse. Ashley would be very displeased with me if that happened.

"I know the risks involved and I don't care. I want to help. I'm not going to just sit idly by while the world goes to shit. If there's something I can do, I want to do it."

I admire your enthusiasm about fighting the invading force, but this isn't a job for a human.

"Too bad. I'm coming with you."

Before Maru could protest, Will slid into the small craft obviously built for three-foot-tall alien lizards. The ship was maybe five feet tall and ten feet long. Maru gave him an angry look before heading toward the cockpit with what Will could only guess was an exasperated gasp.

"Wait a second," Hlad said, walking toward the ship. He took off his Kevlar vest, removing a gun from the holster attached to the vest's chest, and handed it to Will. "Take it."

Will took the protective raiment and put it on the best he could in the small space for his six-foot height.

"This too," Hlad said, second guessing the decision to remove the handgun and gave him the 9mm M9 Baretta and two spare magazines.

Will took the gun hesitantly, sliding it back in the holster attached to the vest on his chest.

The gun must have some sentimental value to the man, Will thought.

It's not like it'll do any good, Marugrah scoffed.

"It'll have to do. Thanks, Sergeant," Will said.

Hlad nodded and closed the hatch. Maru soon had the ship hovering off the ground. Will shuffled toward the cockpit, hunched over as he couldn't stand up fully in the little vessel. He watched as they ascended into the sky and sped toward New York at Mach 3, the fastest they could safely go through without killing themselves.

"Are we cloaked?" Will asked.

Yep. We cloaked before I even exited the CCU building, Marugrah mentally replied.

"How long until we reach New York?"

About ten minutes.

"Awesome."

We are heading toward one of the many thousands of the invaders' ships, as well as one of their ultimate weapons. How is any of that awesome?

"Sarcasm, dude. I don't find this scenario awesome at all."

Oh. I haven't quite mastered reading human seriousness or sarcasticness yet.

"So I've noticed."

They spent the ride to New York City in silence. Plague was almost out of the city, heading south through Chinatown, back the way Will and Maru had just come from.

Where the hell is it going? Will wondered.

His task is to eliminate this country's leader, Marugrah answered Will's mental question.

"So, its headed for D.C. That's an even better reason to stop it here and now."

Will's friends were in that city and he'd be damned if he let this creature go there and put them in danger as it rampaged towards the White House to kill the President.

Agreed.

Marugrah guided the ship to the miniature gray Saturn-shaped craft that hovered over the kaiju charging through the city. Will almost expected a laser bolt to shoot out of the red eye adorning the smooth gray surface of the sphere like it did with the B2 bomber, but none came. It seemed the cloaking that covered the ship was doing its job.

Maru gently docked the craft to the top of the gray sphere, careful not to alert them to their presence. He hopped from his seat behind the controls and made a shooing motion with his small clawed hands, an indication for Will to scoot to the back of the cargo bay. Maru came in, putting a hand on the ship's floor. A light traced a rectangular section at this spot and lifted up to reveal the shiny gray symbol-covered hull of the Plagueonian ship beneath. He put his hand on the gray surface, opening another hatch that revealed a glowing gold walkway beyond it.

Hand me that gun over there, Maru said, pointing at the rack beside Will.

Will plucked the small weapon and handed it to Maru. The scaly alien took it and jumped through the hatch in the floor. Will dropped down next, drawing the Barretta from the chest holster on his vest and holding it like his dad taught him to when they used to hunt together when he was a kid.

"Okay, where to now, boss?" Will asked with a smirk, sweeping the eight-and-a-half-foot-tall and six-foot-wide hallway.

Just follow me, Maru replied, annoyed as he swept his gun in the same manner.

The little alien led Will down the hallway, coming upon a door. He put his hand on it, which caused it to slide into the wall to reveal an elevator door.

"What's this?"

A lift that will take us to the center of the ship, where we need to be.

Maru stepped onto the lift, with Will following suit. They rode it down for a minute before it stopped, and the door slid open. As it did so, Maru fired a shot, hitting an eight-foot armored creature directly between the eyes. Will did not get a good look at the creature before Maru literally blasted its head off. They stepped out of the lift tube and into what looked like a laboratory, sweeping the area with their weapons.

Hit that red button on the side of the lift.

Will complied, hitting the button with a closed fist while staying near the lift. He shifted his gaze to the creatures in the room. They wore some sort of weird-looking white clothing. They had bald, circular heads with wide human-shaped but pure black eyes. Their noses were nothing more than two thin slits and their mouths were just lipless lines stretched into a frown of horror with razor sharp teeth.

He couldn't see the creatures' bodies, but he knew they were probably very powerful. Their arms looked about as thick as a human arm, ending in four sharp digits. It was quite clear to the young human that they could eviscerate him with a single swipe. Their legs were equally thick with a more dog-like than human structure that ended in four digits on their feet. They didn't look like soldiers, but more like scientists.

Will found it a bit humorous that the "warmongers" were afraid of just two creatures smaller than them. There were at least twenty Plagueonians in the lab. They could easily overtake Maru and Will but instead they cowered in fear of them.

Definitely scientists.

As for the room, it looked to span the whole circumference of the orb's middle section. It was full of lab tables, monitors, and scary-looking devices hanging from the ceiling ten-feet above them.

Who is the head scientist? Maru asked telepathically, forcefully thrusting his gun toward the crowd of aliens.

A Plagueonian with an intricately designed cloak stepped forward.

"I am," the creature said, his voice deep and menacing but clearly scared out of its mind.

Prep a table, Maru demanded while training his gun on the creature.

"What? Are you crazy? These stations are for creating Vexnoxtuque," the Plagueonian said, horror written all over his face.

"Maru, what the hell?" Will said, just as horrified as the Plagueonian. "I thought we were stopping Plague by blowing the shit out of this place."

I'm sorry, Will. I lied to Cole. The only way to stop Plague is to become what he is, Marugrah said, head down in shame for lying.

Will ground his teeth together in frustration. He didn't want to lose his friend, but he didn't want to lose the world either. Or his friends in D.C., whom the rampaging monster beneath them was now heading towards. Maru looked at him, sensing his frustration. The alien reptile's eyes were full of sorrow at his friend's pain.

"Fine, do it," Will said, turning away from Maru.

He turned back again to see Maru jumping up on one of the tables, gun still in his hand. Some of the Plagueonians were relaxing until Will brought up his own gun, and they tensed up again. The head scientist brought down a tool that that was obviously an injector, which was hanging from the ceiling. The alien scientist plunged the needle into Maru's arm and depressed the trigger. Green fluid surged through the cord attached to the room's ceiling, through the futuristic looking injector gun, and into Marugrah.

His body seized as the fluid entered his body, doing who-knows-what to his physiology. Well, Will did know what was happening to his friend. He was being turned into a kaiju. A Vexnoxtuque. Could he fight whatever the Plagueonians used to control the giant creatures? Did they even use anything to control the giants? Will had no idea how that worked.

Will... get out of here, Maru said, looking and "sounding" a bit woozy. *Take the ship and go back to D.C.*

"How the hell am I supposed to fly it out of here? I know nothing of flying a spaceship." Will sounded confused and clearly did not want to leave his friend to deal with this alone.

It will adjust itself to accommodate any life form in the driver's seat.

Maru was grinding his teeth as he mentally explained this. Whatever was being injected into him was working its way through his body and it obviously hurt a lot.

Now go!

Will turned to the lift, putting a hand on the door but nothing happened.

"You have to release the lift lock," one of the Plagueonians said.

Will was momentarily puzzled as to why the alien would help him. He quickly ignored his confusion and hit the red button on the side of the tubular structure that was the lift. The door immediately opened. Will jumped to the side as three armed Plagueonians in silver armor and some sort of black fibered undersuit rushed out of the lift, their weapons pointed at Maru.

Will darted behind the side of the lift tube, effectively concealing himself from their line of sight and peeking around at the action.

Spikes seemingly exploded from the skin on Maru's head, knees, elbow, the end of his tail, and the sides of his back. His muscles rippled unnaturally under his scaly crimson skin. And he was a good foot taller.

While the Plagueonian soldiers were busy watching Maru's transformation in horror, Will slipped around the lift's perimeter and into the entrance. The lift door closed as Maru let out a scary, foreboding roar that was unlike anything Will had ever heard from the alien lizard before. His stomach lurched as the lift ascended, opening at the walkway they first arrived at. He walked back the way they came, finding the opening they jumped down from... and a Plagueonian soldier looking up at the portal with his weapon raised.

Will raised his own weapon, aiming at the creature's helmeted head. He squeezed the trigger, firing off three shots that just ricocheted off its metallic headdress. The Plagueonian turned toward him, probably pissed off. It was hard to tell with the alien's eyes being behind a black visor. But by the way it bared its teeth, Will could tell he was pretty mad.

The alien soldier raised his weapon, a futuristic-looking rifle not unlike Maru's, toward Will, inciting the latter to swiftly squeeze off another shot without aiming. The bullet entered the alien's skull through its slitted nose and out the back of its gray head, spraying purple gore. The guard's body dropped in a heap under the hatch.

Will walked over to the trapdoor, looking up at it from two-and-a-half feet away from his face. He knew he couldn't make that jump; he wasn't much of an athlete. The young man looked down at the body by his feet and an idea immediately came to mind.

The young man holstered his gun and stepped up on the giant's silver armored chest, which raised him two feet off the gold walkway. He crouched down low and jumped. Will caught the sides of the hatch, but his fingers fell free from the smooth surface. He repeated the act until he was able to catch the sides and pull himself up. The smell of smoke and burning metal greeted his nostrils as he pulled himself up onto the surface of the sphere.

Will next pulled himself up through Maru's ship's hatch as the sphere beneath him shuddered from within. He quickly crouch ran toward the ship's cockpit, squeezing his way into the tiny seat that immediately adjusted to his much bigger size than its usual pilot.

"Biometric signature required," a computerized female voice said as a panel popped up beside what looked like the flight controls, a U-shaped steering wheel device.

He put his hand on the panel, information flooding his brain as the ship's A.I. told him how to drive it. Will worked his fingers across the craft's controls, disengaging the gravity tether Maru engaged to keep them linked together with the Plagueonian ship. He then pulled on the flight wheel pulled away from the gray spherical ship moments before it exploded from the inside and falling behind the rampaging monster in the city below.

5

New York City

Will watched from 700-feet up in the air as the kaiju known as Plague approached the wreckage of the crashed Plagueonian sphere that landed in the Civic Center. The titanic monster inspected the wreckage, reeling back as a creature half his size sprang from it and unleashed a blast of some sort of fiery green breath into his face. Plague stumbled back, destroying a big red building as the creature that attacked him landed on its five-digit, black claw tipped feet.

The new monster's saurian head looked up at his opponent, green eyes blazing, his armor-laden brows that stretched back to its horn-crested head furrowed, and his sharp teeth bared. The crimson-scaled creature's nostrils flared in anger, a horn protruding from its nose at the end of its squared snout. A small horn protruded from the monster's forehead.

Jagged armored plates with green glowing spirals lined the smaller kaiju's back, starting at the back of the monster's head and ending at the base of its tail. Three large bony jagged spikes protruded from each side in between the middle four plates.

A giant armored plate adorned the kaiju's broad chest, glowing spirals reaching out from a green jewel on the middle of the carapace. More armored plates reached down from the chest plate, ending at the bottom of the base of its tail. The scaly posterior appendage was decorated with two glowing green, squared spirals on each side.

His shoulders were armored with plates running down to its elbow where a bundle of spikes protruded. Its forearms were armored as well, and they possessed a semi-concealed chamber that extended down to the kaiju's wrists. These limbs ended in armored, four-digit hands tipped with razor-sharp, black claws.

The legs were as heavily armored as the rest of the kaiju's body, plates of armor running up his thighs from the knees, which a giant spike protruded from. A tail wrapped in bony bands of armor whipped around behind the creature, the appendage rippling with unnatural muscles and ending in a club-like structure with three spikes.

Will recognized the creature. The maroon color of his flesh and the dragon-like appearance was all he could recognize of what once was his three-foot-tall friend. The monster standing before Plague was Marugrah.

Plague recovered, staring at the smaller but still growing kaiju standing before him. It was now quite clear what caused the Plagueonian ship to explode from within. Plague roared, letting loose a torrent of fire from his maw that enveloped Marugrah.

Once the flames faded, Marugrah stood smoldering but unharmed, thanks to his new heavily armored body. The maroon-scaled kaiju let loose another blast of his green heat ray, striking Plague in the chest and throwing the larger creature back into a big white rectangular building with the Verizon logo on it. The titan with the skull-like head demolished some weird X-shaped edifices as he fell through the Verizon building.

While Plague struggled with his bulk, Marugrah inspected his new body. He looked at his hands, his body, and his legs. Satisfied with what he saw, he let out what Will could only guess as being a war cry before he pounced on his larger foe, clawing at the larger kaiju's armored chest. Plague grabbed Marugrah by the waist, searing his armored flesh with fiery hands, as he rose to his feet and tossed the smaller kaiju across the city. Marugrah tumbled through the decimated Civic Center, past Canal Street, and coming to a stop in lower Manhattan.

Marugrah crawled out of the ruins of a few blocks of city, about 300 feet tall now. Whatever was in that serum he was injected with was making him grow rapidly. He roared defiantly at the flaming monster charging through untold miles of concrete and steel toward him. Marugrah then charged himself, running at Plague on his new thick, stocky legs. Marugrah turned his body, lashing out at Plague with his long club-tipped tail. The club hit Plague in his flaming face, throwing the kaiju to the ground of Little Italy with a yelp.

Maru grabbed the armored plates on Plague's back, pulling the larger creature to his knees. Plague tried to reach back and grab Maru to no avail. One of his hands released its grip on Plague's armored back and a bony spike erupted from the chamber on his forearm. Marugrah plunged the barb into Plague's unarmored side, eliciting a cry of pain from the killing machine.

Plague swung his arm around, striking Marugrah in the side of the head. He stumbled back as Plague's tail wrapped around his leg and pulled him off his feet. Marugrah fell on his armored back, crushing buildings beneath his mass. Plague got to his feet, the hole in his side leaking black blood. The partly skeletal kaiju then leaned down and grasped Marugrah's throat with his hands. Marugrah gurgled, unable to breathe.

Not wanting to see his friend die, Will engaged the ship's weapon systems. He targeted Plague's back, pulling the trigger on the flight wheel. Twin streams of yellow lasers erupted from the front of the oval craft, striking Plague's head. The kaiju put his hands to his head, trying to block the annoying lasers. Will let go of the trigger as a warning icon blinked on the heads-up display This indicated that the lasers were out of juice and needed to recharge. Plague removed his hands, looking to the sky for the source of the annoyance but found nothing as the ship was still cloaked.

The distraction was enough for the now 400-foot Marugrah to catch his breath and push the Plagueonian kaiju off him and get to his feet. Plague got to his feet as well and then shoulder-charged its opponent. Marugrah side-stepped the charging monster, grabbing the biggest spike on Plague's shoulder as he passed. Plague didn't even try to stop, and the spike was ripped from his shoulder in a spray of ebony blood, a tangle of sinews and veins dangling from the bottom of the broken bone. Plague fell to the ground, crying out in agony as he landed on his stomach atop the former New York Police Department HQ.

With ebony-colored blood gushing from his wounded shoulder Plague tried to get to his feet, but Marugrah was already on top of him. He grabbed at the plates lining Plague's back, peeling them away as his fire-headed adversary squealed with anguish. Once he removed most of the plates, he raised the spike he pulled from Plague's arm and plunged it into the kaiju's back.

The observing Will guessed that Maru was probably estimating where the creature's heart was. Plague squirmed and wailed until the partly skeletal kaiju finally fell still.

Plague, the giant destroyer of worlds, was dead. Just like that.

The battle went so fast that Will could hardly believe it was really over after the Plagueonian kaiju had seemed invincible an hour or so ago when he first arrived. Marugrah threw his head to the sky and roared in victory.

A squadron of jets then descended from the sky, firing at the last monster standing.

"No!" Will yelled. "He's on our side!"

"Opening com channels," the A.I. said.

"Circling around for another pass," one of the pilots of the four F-22 Raptors that came out of nowhere said over his comm system. "Aim for the creature's legs."

"No! Disengage!" Will hollered. "He's on our side."

"What the hell is a kid doing on the radio?" the same pilot wondered aloud. "This is a military channel; get off the radio!"

"William? Is that you?" Angel's voice came over the comm.

The pilots stayed silent upon hearing Command's voice.

"Yeah, it's me," Will said. "Don't shoot. That's Marugrah. I repeat, that creature is Marugrah."

"But how?" Angel asked.

"I'll explain once I return to HQ. Just don't fire at him, please. He's in enough pain already."

"Alright. All units, stand down."

"Roger that, Command," another pilot said.

Will could tell the air soldier was holding back his anger at being told to abandon fighting something he obviously thought was a threat.

Will sat back in his seat relieved as the F-22s broke away. Marugrah, seeing the jets leaving, followed the path of destruction from his fight with Plague back to the decimated Verizon building and the weird X-shaped structures. He moved past them, heading for the waterway. The crimson kaiju stepped into it, the water sloshing up to his knees.

Seeing no other way around or just not caring, Marugrah plowed clear through the Brooklyn Bridge, one of the oldest suspension bridges in the United States. He made his way along the channel to the Upper Bay and then the Lower Bay before slipping into the ocean depths, where he would wait for the next kaiju to show its ugly face.

Seeing that Marugrah was gone, Will piloted the ship away from the decimated city of New York and back towards Washington, D.C. to his friends and allies. After a ten-minute ride at Mach 3, he located the CCU HQ and landed on its roof. No one could see the cloaked ship, so Will didn't think it was a problem. He found the roof door, taking it down to the top floor that the command room was on. Will walked in and everyone in the room turned toward him.

"Where the hell have you been?" Ashley said, her face a mask of anger.

"Um, well... in a spaceship," Will replied.

Ashley's response was a literal slap to the face. "I was worried about you. You just disappeared. You didn't even tell us where you went. You could have been killed infiltrating that ship."

Will rubbed the side of his face where a red handprint was forming. "Yeah, yeah. It was a bit of a dick move. I'm sorry. I'm fine. Plus, I got to see a kaiju fight."

"Speaking of which, what happened to Marugrah?" Cole asked while stepping forward. "You said that giant red dragon was him."

"Yeah… he turned himself into a Vexnoxtuque," Will said.

He did what? That fool! Marudon fumed telepathically while audibly letting out an angry squawk. *There is no way he can fight the effects that the serum will have on his mind.*

"Are you saying that the green stuff they pumped into him will drive him crazy?" Will queried.

Yes, that is what I am saying. Though it is possible that he could fight the effects, now that I think of it. Plague seemed to have been able to. But that could have been because he was always a crazy lunatic.

"Maru looked like he lost it there for a moment when he was finishing off Plague," Will noted after remembering the way Marugrah slowly killed Plague, as if he enjoyed the kaiju's suffering.

"So, he may turn against us?" Cole asked.

"Let's hope he doesn't," Will rejoined. "He's the only chance we have at getting through this thing alive."

END

PART 2: ESSAYS

KAIJU FROM KOREA AND TITANS FROM TAIWAN: THE OTHER ASIATIC GIANT MONSTERS

John LeMay

"Hey, kaiju-fans! It looks like Godzilla has another cinematic rival in me, huh?" Collective fandom response: "Nah."

To the best of my knowledge, it was Japanese special effects technicians that pioneered the famous suitmation technique to bring giant monsters (i.e., daikaiju) to life. This happened first not in *Godzilla* (1954), but in several other predating productions. Nikkatsu's *Gōketsu Jiraiya* (1921) with a giant toad and snake may have been the first. Then there was *King Kong Made in Japan* (1933), *The Giant Buddha Statue's Travel Through the Country* (1934), and *King Kong Appears in Edo* (1938). But that's not what I'm here to talk about.

Regardless of the fact that Japan was famous for suitmation monsters throughout the Showa Era (1926-1989[3]), there were many other suitmation monsters all across Asia during this time. The two best known are from Korea: *Yongary, Monster from the Deep* (1967) and *Pulgasari* (1985). Contrary to popular belief though, 1967's Yongary wasn't even the first non-Japanese giant monster.

The first may have been a 1961 version of the Pulgasari legend called *Bulgasari*. Though it's still

---

[3] This editor considers the official Toho Showa Era for its daikaiju eiga film series to be 1955-1978, from *Godzilla Raids Again* to *The War in Space*. *Godzilla* (1954) did indeed technically occur in the Showa Era, obviously, but since that debut appearance of The Big G has been part of the Showa, Heisei, and all Millennium Era G-film series – including films with kaiju but sans Godzilla that were produced during that era, and later established to be in continuity – I have personally considered it distinct from yet part of all of these continuities (Toho's Millennium Series consisted of six films with five separate continuities, all of which had only the basic events of the first G-film in common as a launching point). I consider *Godzilla 1985* (American title) to be the first of the Heisei Series continuity. Of course, different authors will divide the eras based on different criteria, including on an actual historical basis rather than strict film continuity, and that's perfectly fine. – CN

unconfirmed if this was a real film, advertising materials exist for it in the form of several posters (and an official listing on the Korean Movie Database). The film was allegedly shot in color and directed by Myeong-je Kim, a real Korean director with many credits to his name. The story was set during the Goryeo Dynasty and focused on a martial artist. The man is murdered and reborn as Bulgasari, the iron eating monster, which goes off on a quest for revenge. The theory is that the film was lost as a side effect of war.

The next Korean monster to grace the silver screen still wasn't Yongary, though. Beating Yongary to theaters by a few months on June 30, 1967 was *Space Monster Wangmagwi*, a combination of the King Kong story coupled with a space monster. The film, shot in black and white, focuses on a South Korean Air Force pilot, Oh Jeong-hwan, on the day of his wedding. Unfortunately for him, he and his fiancé, Ahn Hee, scheduled their wedding on the day that aliens decide to invade Earth. Worse yet, the space-ape kaiju Wangmawgi has eyes for Ahn Hee and scoops her up in the palm of his hand, carrying her with him as he destroys Seoul. The action that follows is apparently pretty aimless, as Wangmagwi wanders about the flaming city having run-ins with various Korean comedians and TV personalities. When the monster finally leaves the city the military battles it in the countryside.

Can Wangmagwi stomp out the kaiju competition in Japan? Kaiju fandom's simultaneous response: "Nah."

This little seen film – outside of South Korea where 50,000 people went to see it – is notable for a spot in the *Guinness Book of World Records*. Up until the production of 1982's *Ghandi*, it was *Space Monster Wangmagwi* that held the record for most extras used in one film: 157,000 screaming South Koreans. Supposedly a print of the film has been found and is currently being restored[4]. A toy company even made a figurine of the monster.

---

[4] Update: *Space Monster Wangmagwi* has been released to DVD in 2023 and to Blu-ray in 2024 by SRS Cinema. It is also available to

Far East Entertainment, who had invested a bit more effort into their Yongary movie, tried to stop *Space Monster Wangmagwi's* release with a lawsuit. Despite not being the first Korean monster movie that year, *Yongary* has since managed to go down as the more memorable of the two. It even secured a TV broadcast in the U.S., something *Space Monster Wangmagwi* didn't.

Yongary's story begins with a nuclear test in the Middle East's Goma Desert that somehow manages to awaken the ancient monster Yongary in South Korea. At first thought to be a series of earthquakes, the monster reveals itself when it bursts from the ground and begins attacking Seoul. Officials debate how to kill the kaiju but fear destroying their own landmarks in the process. A young boy named Eicho becomes sympathetic to the monster and beseeches the government not to kill him. However, his efforts are in vain and Yongary eventually succumbs to the military via an ammonia compound created by scientists.

Essentially, *Yongary* combined most of the elements that made Japanese daikaiju popular at the time. He had the basic form of Godzilla but also carried over the Gamera franchise's child-friendly aspect. Actually, in the Korean version, the film's ending dialogue reveals something lost in translation in the U.S. version. As it turns out, Yongary is not dead as the U.S. dub implies. The monster was merely rendered unconscious, and there

stream on Midnight Pulp as of 2025, which can be done via Amazon Prime. – CN are plans to launch Yongary into space like the original *Gamera* movie's Plan Z.

Speaking of being lost in translation, the Korean version of *Yongary* is lost. Today only 48 minutes of the original Korean version have been salvaged. As it turns out, the original Korean print was loaned out never to be returned. Today the AIP English dubbed version is the only complete print. But don't worry, there are no missing scenes. The movie wasn't even re-edited for the U.S. Therefore, English-speaking viewers aren't missing anything, but the original Korean fans are. If they want to watch a complete version of the film (with altered English dialogue, mind you) they must watch a Korean subtitled print of the English version!

In 1969 Taiwan got into the kaiju game. Their inspiration wasn't the Godzilla movies, however, but Toei's 1966 movie *The Magic Serpent* (another adaptation of *Gōketsu Jiraiya*). The film seemed to have inspired a whole subgenre of ninja/monster mashup movies. The first, that I know of anyway, is thanks to Kevin Derendorf who covers it in his wonderful book *Kaiju for Hipsters*. The movie is called *Feng Shen Bang*, and features SPFX from Gamera effects technicians Masao Yagi, Michio Mikami, and Toru Suzuki. Among their creations are a traditional Chinese dragon, an ogre, and mutant sea people based on fish, shrimp, turtles, and crabs. Produced in 1970 was *Young Flying Hero*, which in bootleg circles has been retitled as *Return of the Magic Serpent* to imply that it is a sequel to Toei's film from 1966.

In 1971 came *The Founding of the Ming Dynasty*, also from Taiwan. The effects sequences from this film were done by the staff of Japan's Tsuburaya Productions, and this footage would be cannibalized into at least two other films. Most die-hard kaiju-fans may recall footage of an ogre battling an albino gorilla in a movie called *The Fairy and the Devil* (1982). We'll get to *Fairy and the Devil* later, but for now let's just say it was a Franken-movie ala *Thunder of Gigantic Serpent* (1987).

The Founding of the Ming Dynasty is quite the epic, with a run time of 111 minutes. I won't even begin to try and describe the storyline, and besides, you just want to know about the monsters, right? Well, it's got monsters alright! We'll start with the two dragons, one green and one gold. The green one has Rodan's roar and the gold one has Godzilla's. The two puppets best resemble Manda from *Atragon* (1963) and also project fire and missiles from their mouths! The fight is a gnarly one, taking place in the air and under the water and is definitely worth your viewing pleasure. Among the film's other monsters are a huge ogre reminiscent of Daiei's Daimajin and an albino gorilla that resembles (but also predates) the one from Tsuburaya's *The Ivory Ape* (1980). When the white ape fails to prevail against this demon, the golden dragon from earlier returns to tackle it.

In 1973 came another film from South Korea, *Hippie Carnage*. It is another of those dubious lost films that we can't prove the existence of. Supposedly it was inspired by *Godzilla vs. Hedorah* (American title: *Godzilla vs. The Smog Monster*) and *Godzilla vs. Megalon* in that an inventor's giant robot battles monsters spawned by pollution. Specifically, the story is set on Cheju Island where pollution spawns three monsters. These monsters then terrorize the island, populated mostly by hippies. An inventor, his daughter, and their magical maid (some sort of witch) combine their talents to create a giant robot to battle the beasts. Supposedly there was not only a Korean print (lost in a flood) but even a U.S. print meant for television made by Crown International Pictures (also lost).

Thailand likewise got into the kaiju game in 1973 via Sompote Sands, a former student of Eiji Tsuburaya. Sands took what he learned from Tsuburaya back to Thailand where he started Chaiyo Studios. His first kaiju-film was *Tah Tien*, about giant statues which come to life and fight. Sands then approached the late Eiji Tsuburaya's son, Noboru, about co-producing movies together in Thailand. Noboru said yes, and though these movies were interesting at the time, they later proved disastrous for Tsuburaya – more on that later.

The first of these movies was a big screen adaptation of Tsuburaya's TV series *Jumborg Ace*. In *Jumborg Ace and Giant* (1974), the leftover statue suits from *Tah Tien* team with Jumborg Ace to battle aliens. Next up that same year was the better known *6 Ultra Brothers vs. the Monster Army*. In that film, all the then current Ultra Brothers (sans Leo) team up with monkey deity Hanuman to battle five kaiju left over from various Tsuburaya TV series – so not quite a monster army. Though Sand's partnership with Tsuburaya ended, the next year he illegally used Toei's *Kamen Rider* franchise for *Hanuman and the Seven Riders*. Sands would later claim that he helped Eiji Tsuburaya invent Ultraman in 1966 and also claimed that he owned all distribution rights to Ultraman outside of Japan! Sadly, this whole dispute was not settled until recent years.

Though it took them long enough, in 1975 China finally got into the giant monster game -- just as the heyday of that genre was ending in Japan. They produced the superhero vs. giant monster movie *Infra-Man*, which was even released to the U.S. theatrically. It was followed in 1977 by a movie that had jumped on the 1976 *King Kong* remake bandwagon entitled *Mighty Peking Man*. Korea preceded this with their own take on King Kong titled *A*P*E* for legal reasons.

While kaiju movies were for the most part dormant in Japan until *The Return of Godzilla* (1984)[5], other Asian countries produced them sporadically in the interim. Taiwan produced another in 1976 called *War God*. In that film giant aliens attack Hong Kong until they are driven away by a protective statue. *Prince of the Dragon King* (1977) and *The Fairy and the Devil* (1982) were both monster movies, even if said monsters were borrowed from *The Founding of the Ming Dynasty*. Even Sompote Sands produced more monster movies in Thailand during this time, though some of his fare was starting to deviate into the "giant animals on the loose" genre popularized by *Jaws* (1975).

The years 1984 and 1985 would see the releases of two of the most notorious non-Japanese kaiju movies. The first was Taiwan's *King of Snake* (1984), which infamously evolved into the Franken-movie *Thunder of*

---

[5] The Japanese title of *Godzilla 1985*, which was released that eponymous year in the USA by New World Pictures. – CN

Gigantic Serpent (1987). *King of Snake* is a bizarre child's film that tonally could be considered two different movies.

Plot A revolves around scientists trying to retrieve a stolen growth device from a crime syndicate (and is quite violent). Plot B revolves around a young girl and her pet snake, Mosler, who grew to gigantic proportions due to the stolen growth device. Eventually the plots collide when the girl is kidnapped by the crime syndicate and Mosler, now kaiju-sized, must rescue her. In the process Mosler destroys most of Hong Kong. In 1987, even more violent footage was added in with actor Pierre Kirby by Godfrey Ho in the version known as *Thunder of Gigantic Serpent* – the version most kaiju-fans have seen.

Even more notorious was 1985's *Pulgasari*, not for the film itself, which is well done; but for how it was made. It all began with North Korean dictator Kim Jong Il, who was a huge Godzilla fan. He was also a fan of South Korean film director Shin Sang-ok, whom he had kidnapped several years prior to and had been forcing to direct films for him. Naturally, Shin was Il's number one choice for his own kaiju epic. Invited to the production with the promise of "an unlimited budget" was also Toho special effects director Teruyoshi Nakano and Godzilla suit performer Kenpachiro Satsuma, set to play the new monster.

In the story, a village suffers famine during the Koryo Dynasty in North Korea at the hands of an oppressive king. When the king learns of an uprising, he imprisons several of the villagers, among them blacksmith Takuse. In his last moment of life, Takuse fashions a small figure of the mythical Pulgasari and hopes it will take revenge

351

on the king and defend the villagers. When his daughter Ami comes into the possession of the figure, she stores it in her sewing kit. When she accidentally pricks her finger and bleeds on the doll, it comes to life.

The tiny Pulgasari begins feeding on iron and grows bigger with each passing day. Eventually the monster becomes the main force behind a people's army to take down the king. To combat the monster, the king enlists the evil General Fuan. Believing the blacksmith's spirit to be in the monster, General Fuan has a priestess perform an exorcism on the beast and it becomes disoriented and falls into a large pit dug to trap it. Ami sneaks into the camp and frees the monster by spilling more of her blood. Pulgasari revives and treks to the king's castle where he kills the despot.

Does Pulgasari look like someone – or some*thing* – you want to piss off by telling him that he's a poor alternative to Japanese kaiju?

However, once the battle is over, Pulgasari's hunger for iron takes over and the villagers must begin feeding him all their farming tools. Their pet monster has now become a huge problem himself. Ami tricks Pulgasari into eating her inside a large, iron bell which causes the monster to randomly turn into a statue and then explode. The form of the baby Pulgasari emerges from the rubble and uses its life force to revive Ami.

Supposedly, the twist ending with Pulgasari becoming a burden to his people is an allegory for capitalism on Kim Jong Il's part. The idea is that capitalism seems alluring at first, but then becomes problematic once the reality sets in. The director, on the other hand, is said to view Pulgasari as an allegory for Kim Jong Il! As for director Shin, he eventually escaped North Korea and fled to the United States for a time.

Like the Japanese giant monsters, other Asiatic kaiju-films continued to be produced in the 1990s and into the next century with movies such as *Reptilian* (1999/2001)[6], *Garuda* (2004), and *Dragon Wars* (2007). So, in summary, if you lament the fact that you've already seen

---

[6] *Reptilian* is the American direct to home video and TV release title of *Yonggary*, or more specifically, the 2001 version with a supposedly "altered plot and updated special effects" (according to Wikipedia) that was was re-released in Korea as *Yonggary: 2001 Upgrade Edition* (or sometimes simply *Yonggary 2001*). As its Korean title suggests, the film was a (very unsuccessful) attempt to reboot/re-imagine Korea's most well-known kaiju. Also according to Wikipedia, the original version of this movie has not been released to home video or TV in any market to date. – CN

every Japanese Giant Monster movie, give these other Asian kaiju-films a try. There are plenty to choose from.

END

GODZILLA VS. THE LEGENDARY WOLFMAN: THE AMAZING, MYSTERIOUS FAN FILM

D.G. Valdron

If Toho had teamed with Universal Pictures or Hammer Studios, this *might* have been the result!

The end of the Showa Era was hard on Godzilla. In the 1950s and 1960s they'd struck gold with Godzilla as an embodiment of terror. Through its later run in the 1970s, however, the franchise was clearly running out of steam, and Toho was visibly struggling to find a new direction.

Godzilla (1954) was a naked embodiment of the atom bomb, and through his next few movies he was a nightmarish force of nature. Even *King Kong vs. Godzilla* (1962), which had strong comedic elements, showed Godzilla as a lethal engine of destruction.

Of course, all the giant monsters of the 1950s and early 1960s were destroyers. But that formula went stale fast. None of the other monsters came back for sequels, and by 1960, in most places the genre had exhausted itself. Only Toho managed to prolong it by changing the formula with a brilliant stroke – instead of one monster, why not have two, fighting each other? In short order, Godzilla fought Anguirus (*Godzilla Raids Again* [1955]); threw down on a celebrity, King Kong; and attacked the beloved Mothra and her offspring.

But the thing was, you couldn't just repeat yourself, at least not too much; you had to keep going to new places. Which meant you had to keep adding more monsters, and bigger and better monsters. This led to *Ghidorah, The Three-Headed Monster* (1964) and its effective sequel, *Godzilla vs. Monster Zero* (1965); and eventually culminated in *Destroy All Monsters* (1968). During this time, Godzilla transitioned from force for destruction to something like a hero; if not an actual friend to humanity, at least a protector of the Earth from darker forces.

Partly this had to do with the evolution of what Godzilla represented – the Atom Bomb. The first few Godzilla movies embodied naked terror of nuclear weapons: he was the bomb incarnate, and his subsequent movies can be seen as struggles to cope with that.

Godzilla Raids Again (1955) has Japan helplessly caught between two nuclear monsters and their Cold War. Godzilla's bout with Kong reflect a warmer, lighter view of the Americans. *Godzilla vs. Mothra* (or, *Mothra vs. Godzilla*, if one prefers the Japanese title that gave Mothra top billing; 1964) features a more confident Japan, recovering and perhaps restraining Godzilla. But Godzilla is always nuclear destruction... in the beginning.

As the '60s wore on, however, Japan began to invest more and more heavily in nuclear power and rely more on nuclear deterrence. Eventually, over 25% of Japan's electricity came from nuclear power plants. And with that, as the Japanese embraced the atom, as nuclear power became valued and a source of pride, Godzilla got friendlier and more benign. He became a symbol of Japanese courage and resolve.

Indeed, the metaphor extended. In *Godzilla vs The Smog Monster* (a.k.a., *Godzilla vs. Hedorah* [1971]) and *Godzilla vs Gigan* (1972), the enemy in both cases is pollution. So, these are movies about clean nuclear power winning out over smog and pollution. It's notable that the first of these movies bucked the trend of multi-monster-fests, but the second immediately went back to that by-then conventional trope with a four-monster melee. Arguably, Toho and the audience were very conscious of a focused message. But not a terribly successful one.

So, Godzilla went the Gamera route, literally becoming friend to children – he's positively benign in *Godzilla vs Megalon* (1973) (and his appearances later that year in the Toho kyodai TV series *Zone Fighter, the Meteor Man*). But by this time, the formula was literally exhausted, there were no more variations; they'd painted themselves into a corner and were all out of ideas. *Godzilla vs Mechagodzilla* (1974) is a mélange of robot doubles, *Planet of the Apes*, and spy adventure. And the follow up, *Terror of Mechagodzilla* (1975)? More of the same. The franchise ends with a whimper in '75 – a mere two years before *Star Wars Episode IV: A New Hope* (it was just "*Star Wars*" back then) comes out and literally rewrites the genre.

Which is why *Godzilla vs. The Legendary Wolfman* is so interesting on so many levels. It's because someone had come up with a way to make Godzilla interesting again, to simultaneously bring Godzilla back to his roots, and to come up with a new spin.

And it wasn't even Toho, which is the most amazing part. *Godzilla vs. The Legendary Wolfman* is a fan film from 1983, created by Shizuo Nakajima, a former Toho employee working in effects. Nakajima was apparently on the crew for the two Showa Mechagodzilla movies. A check of the Internet Movie Database [IMDb] does not list him for anything else but this film.

Nakajima was able to recruit several people who had worked on the Showa Godzilla series, or who would work on the Heisei series. Together, they had access to plans, designs, and materials, and began to make their own short kaiju-film centering around a giant Wolfman. This included the building of miniature sets, special effects, an impressive Baragon costume, and an even more impressive Godzilla suit, as well as different variations of the titular Wolfman.

That's what we know for sure. After that, things get dicey. It looks like Nakajima and his friends started their venture in the 1970s or possibly as late as 1979, working with Super8, or 16 mm, or possibly even both formats at different times for different films. Initially, they did at least two, possibly more, shorts or incomplete films featuring a different, earlier version of their Wolfman; and respectively, a version of Baragon and a Godzilla suit resembling the one from *Mothra vs. Godzilla*.

But as they went on, they got more ambitious, and in 1983, built a new Godzilla suit modeled after the one from *King Kong vs. Godzilla* and an elegant Wolfman. They were also quite impressed with werewolf films like *The Howling* and *An American Werewolf in London* (both 1981) and replicated those effects on a human scale. There are reports that they were working on it into the 1980s.

Apparently, they were well on their way towards doing a full-length Godzilla film, until Toho stepped in. Or, perhaps they did. Or, perhaps they merely shot enough footage for one. The stories are all over the place as to exactly what they did, how much they did, and how far they got.

But they got something done. If you check YouTube and other streaming sources, you can find as much as fifteen or twenty minutes of different footage from their projects. After being little more than a rumour for years, interest peaked when fans started tracking down Nakajima, and clips began to appear online and at G-Fest conventions, beginning about 2012. Nakajima was flattered by the attention and announced his intent to release a completed feature, possibly incorporating some of the earlier shorter subjects. According to Nakajima, there are ten hours of raw footage. This led to interest reaching a peak in 2016-2017. Sadly, the feature has failed to materialize, or at least to be released to the public to date (mid-2019 at this writing). This should be no surprise given the recent success of both the Legendary and Shin versions of Godzilla, as this film treads hard on those toes.

So, it's not clear whether it now exists as a completed hidden film, or simply a pile of shorts and footage waiting to be assembled, or something less coherent.

There was a time when I thought it was all a peculiar hoax, one of those strange rumours that floats around. But the footage is there, it's clearly genuine, and not traceable to any other mundane source.

So, what's the story?

Well, there does seem to be a thorough line or consistent pattern of scenes in a lot of videos, with some variation. There's also a handful of unique scenes here and there which seem to fit into the narrative. So, applying some guesswork, I have fit the existing bits and pieces into the following narrative.

***

THE PLOT: In Egypt, a Japanese archeologist explores a cave which leads to a mysterious tomb. Following the passageway, he comes to a hidden room, filled with statues of bestial wolfmen. He retrieves a small sarcophagus or upright statue, the head of which resembles a cat or a short, muzzled canine. There, he becomes possessed by the beast's spirit.

Returning home, and right in front of his terrified wife, he begins a painful mutation into a wolfman, in transformations equivalent to *The Howling* or *An American Werewolf in London*. His clothes tear, he becomes hairy and monstrous, and his features become bestial as his face transforms. Civilians show up, and he attacks them. He is shot by plainclothes policemen without effect. Carrying his unconscious bride from his home, he is confronted by a squadron of police or military, but they are unable to stop him.

As the transformation proceeds, he grows to kaiju size, resembling a Gargantua, and later still his covering of hair turns gray, perhaps through exposure to radiation, or possibly the mystical effects of his possession (I lean to mystical, as his clothes seem to grow along with him). The Wolfman, still somewhat human, stumbles across Baragon at a burning refinery, and the two battle. Subsequently, the Wolfman, his coat having turned white, has his first encounter with Godzilla.

The Wolfman continues to mutate, eventually losing all human features and becoming a white-furred, long-eared demon. He is pursued by the Japanese Self Defense Force [JSDF], initially attacking with tanks and firearms.

361

Later, they use a helicopter to lure the creature within range of its Maser Tanks. The sustained barrages of the masers bring the creature down, leaving it thrashing on the ground.

Meanwhile, other detachments of the JSDF mount a sustained, but ultimately futile, attack upon Godzilla, as he devastates a military base. Relentlessly, Godzilla advances on the city, and we see an evacuation to shelters in progress. Temporarily, Godzilla is deterred by power lines.

Afterwards, scientists studying the strange Beast statue taken from the temple are visited by mysterious men in casual suits, presumably secret agents, to initiate a last-ditch plan to try to send the Wolfman against Godzilla.

The plan works, as the Wolfman searches out Godzilla and attacks. At first, it appears that the Wolfman is quickly defeated, but the creature later recovers and comes back looking for a rematch. The two then engage in an epic battle to the death.

The next scene features the secret agents desperately running a police roadblock, clearly attempting to enter the evacuation zone and presumably moving towards the scene of the battle. The police give chase, but the agents fire a bazooka to drive them off.

Meanwhile, the Wolfman pursues Godzilla. Lacking the raw power to take on the King of the Monsters, but clearly faster, the Wolfman stalks and harasses him through the countryside, flinging boulders at the frustrated Kaiju King. This proves fruitless, as eventually Godzilla's raw power gives him the upper hand, and the Wolfman falls once again.

We cut to a train at night, and the wife of the Wolfman, or the wife of the man who became the Wolfman, is sitting alone in one of the cars looking very pensive. The train stops and the passengers evacuate in terror, as Godzilla is approaching. The military can do no more than track Godzilla's movements by following him with a helicopter. As his wife screams, the Wolfman rouses with renewed fury, perhaps sensing the danger to his mate, and returns to the battle.

Cut to the mysterious statue, out in the open with clouds streaming past it, indicating that the idol is clearly some sort of supernatural beacon. The Wolfman is fighting with renewed strength and vigour, able to lift Godzilla off the ground! The battle extends into the night. Who will win?

***

STORY CAVEATS: Now, a couple of caveats. I am basically going off the footage and scenes available from YouTube, and roughly following the order of scenes found in the Walter Belcher upload, or at least the first 24 of that 36 minutes. The last twelve minutes seem to repeat a bit.

Overall, this is an approximation of what the story is. We don't have the full film, and we don't have a complete script. It's not clear that Nakajima actually has a completed script, or if he does, how well those early shorts/incompletes and the ten hours of footage would suit that screenplay. If he had a script, there may be gaps and scenes that were never filmed, and whatever gets finally cobbled together may be different than what we have seen in the sample footage.

There does seem to be a logical progression and linkage to many of the scenes – obviously the transformation comes first, the military confrontations with the Wolfman and Godzilla respectively have their own internal logic, the battles between the Wolfman and Godzilla clearly follow that and have a discernible structure of the Wolfman pursuing and harassing Godzilla and getting beaten down for it, leading to a final renewal and perhaps triumph.

The character of the wife from the transformation scene shows up in train sequences, so we can assume that there was an underlying narrative purpose to her being on the train, and it probably fits in later. The stuff with the statue was probably meant to be significant. So, I think you can work out the narrative, or at least a workable narrative, and even draw some conclusions about characterization and dramatic approach.

I seem to remember the scene or scenes in the mysterious temple where the Beast Spirit possesses the man, but this last time I looked I can't find them. It's clearly implied from later scenes of the statue that this is not a "bitten by a werewolf" infection, but rather a supernatural possession. The frequent title "Legendary Wolfman" implies that this isn't a regular wolfman, but some sort of mythological creature or beast deity.

Most compilations seem to start with the transformation scene, into a dark-haired, torn-shirted, Oliver Reed-style wolfman, and then jump from there straight into the big, white-furred monster. I think that's a hard transition.

On YouTube, there's a three minute "Baragon vs the Wolfman" sequence by Nakajima, where Baragon battles an intermediate giant version of the Wolfman. He's still wearing clothes and has ape-like features, but his hair is gray. So, I'm assuming this is a transitional form, and this is part of the narrative. In reality, this was a separate, earlier short, but Nakajima did state that he intended to use some of the earlier shorts, or earlier incomplete films. And it does fit in reasonably well.

Not available on YouTube is the short or incomplete film of the earlier version of the Wolfman fighting the earlier Godzilla suit. If you watch the available scenes closely, you'll see that both versions of the suit are used in different scenes. There are photographs of the earlier version of the Wolfman duking it out with Godzilla. In the photos, he looks like the version that fights Baragon, except that his fur appears white. Was he maybe continuing to evolve into his final form here?

So, on the principle of throwing the kitchen sink, I am assuming that there was an earlier, unsuccessful encounter of the transitional Wolfman with Godzilla, before he reaches his final form. But I think it's not unreasonable.

As to the secret agents, I'm not really sure that's what they are. They look and act like regular guys having an adventure, so they may be free agents – journalists, archeologists, or just guys with a mission. On the other hand, they seem to have access to a lab, to bazookas, and even show up in military establishments. On the other hand, they have to run a roadblock and brave a police chase.

***

THE REVIEW: First comment – Holy Cow!!! That is one amazingly good Godzilla suit. Both known suits are terrific, as they're dead ringers for the official Toho suits, to the extent that some people are convinced that they're the actual King-Goji and Mosu-Goji Toho suits [from *King Kong vs. Godzilla* and *Godzilla vs. Mothra,* respectively]. They are not, however – these suits tended to decay fast, and there's no chance that the '60s era suits survived in any kind of condition into the late '70s-early '80s. These are new ones. Not only does Godzilla look good, but his tail moves fluidly, his jaws move, and he's got atomic breath and glowing dorsal spines (yes, I know that's effects). The point is that this feels exactly like the real thing. The suits, by the way, were the creation of Fuyuki Shinada, who went on to the design work for *Godzilla, Mothra, King Ghidorah: Giant Monsters All Out Attack* (a.k.a., *GMK*, 2001), among other things.

Second comment: – Holy Cow!!! That is a brilliant Wolfman suit. It is really well done; in some scenes we see the mouth move and various facial expressions. Overall, the suit is elegant and beautiful, and amazingly, it allows the actor within to move freely and fluidly. Considering some of the messes that Toho was foisting off on us during its decline (King Caesar, I'm looking at you). This is an amazing suit, and well-acted physically... although I'm not sure that the Wolfman is entirely a wolfman (i.e., werewolf) per se, as the mysterious statue looks more cat-like, and the Wolfman tends to make cat noises when he's fighting. Perhaps he's more a legendary beast than either wolfman or a catman?

366

The Baragon suit in the "Baragon vs. The Wolfman" short doesn't quite measure up to the Godzilla and the Wolfman costumes. It's not bad by any means, but it's a rather free interpretation of Baragon: the ears are much larger, practically resembling wings; and the underside of the suit's neck in some ways clearly makes it look like a costume. So, kind of imperfect. And this is unfair, but the transitional kaiju Wolfman that fights Baragon... looks a bit tosh, being more Gargantua-like or ape-like. I forgive that, however, as they were still working on it.

Overall, the miniature work and the effects are very impressive. This is first class stuff. And yeah, there's some tosh stuff in there. But not much of it. This was a group of people who were inspired by and working towards the early '60s stuff, and not Toho's lazier '70s output.

There are clear call backs – scenes of Godzilla at electrical power lines reminiscent of those from earlier movies. In particular, there are several bits from the battle scenes between the Wolfman and Godzilla that are pretty much lifts from *King Kong vs. Godzilla*. Now, I think to some extent, it would be hard to avoid some resemblance, as in both Godzilla is fighting a humanoid rather than his more typical reptilian foes. Humanoids are going to do humanoid stuff, so there's that. On the other hand, some of it probably is a lift, but I'll let it pass.

The action sequences are well done, and the kaiju characterizations are effective. Particularly Godzilla, as this version of the Big G exudes menace. In many shots, the camera is slowed down slightly, adding a feeling of ponderous mass. Godzilla's motions are controlled. In most of his scenes, Godzilla comes across as genuinely dangerous, a relentless destroyer of anything in his path, and all the more fearsome because that path is so random.

This is a Godzilla of the 1950s and early 1960s, a friend to nothing and no one. He is simply a force of nature, indifferent to almost anything and everything, no more benign than a hurricane. The battle with the Japanese armed forces underscores his power; there's really nothing to do but get out of the way.

In contrast, the Wolfman isn't nearly so implacable. At points, he's almost a comic figure – as when he follows after and keeps trying to grab a helicopter, or when the masers give him a hotfoot, causing him to dance around. There's just a trace of a human quality to the Wolfman, but mostly, he's an animal – he growls, he wanders. It's when he battles Godzilla again and again that we see something like human perseverance. If Godzilla is a force of nature, then the Wolfman is a personality; if not a human personality, then some kind of animal persona.

This dichotomy works effectively and helps them to bounce off against each other quite well. The kaiju of the Showa Era didn't always come across as personalities. Sometimes that was just the design limitations of the suits – it's hard to be expressive under a hundred pounds of monster costume – and partly slack direction or writing. But here it comes across strongly.

And there is another thing that helps this movie transcend the works of the later Showa: the human factor. The early transformation scenes, reminiscent as they are of *The Howling*, really set a tone of darker, edgier horror that casts a welcome shadow over what comes next. I could see them feeling a bit out of place, but I'd argue that they're not.

Here's the thing – the Wolfman is a *kaiju*, sort of like King Kong and King Caesar, although arguably this costume is better than either of those. But he's not just a kaiju. The movie establishes that he is a human being; he is a man, he has a wife, he loves his wife, he has a normal life... and something utterly terrible happens to him and keeps happening to him. As the white, furry demon towers over trees, we never quite forget that there is a person trapped in there somehow.

That is a quality, of lost, trapped, cursed humanity that King Caesar never has – he is simply a supernatural guardian monster. Caesar wakes up, does his job, and goes back to sleep. Kong has more personality, but he is basically a big, tough, angry ape. The Wolfman contains a tragic lost soul. That's why the transformation scene belongs there, to let us know that this is a person. We get reminders of that in the reappearance of his wife on the train, the mysterious statue, and the fact that the Wolfman seems to respond to both.

It brings the movie back to human levels, something I'm not sure I've really felt since those scenes in *Godzilla vs. Mothra*, where a group of school children are trapped and hiding from Godzilla. Here, it's a little more adult – no children in obvious danger, but human tragedy affecting a man and his wife. Werewolf tales have always been intimate, personal stories. Werewolf stories are about the werewolf endangering the people closest to them, the people around them, the beast intruding into the safe world.

Crossing a werewolf story with Godzilla pays unexpected dividends. That personal story, that intimate human tragedy, highlights the menace of Godzilla. He is

369

not just a big implacable force of nature stomping around anymore. Well, he is still that, of course, but I think that there's a little more here in this film. Reminded of the human dimension, and human tragedy, the intimacy of the werewolf story... it brings it subtly home to us that Godzilla is not just a remote menace; he kills people. People die in Godzilla's path – the soldiers die, the civilians on the train will die.

Another interesting aspect is the supernatural. The Showa series tended towards science fiction elements – aliens, robots, mutants, cyborgs, extraterrestrial monsters, pollution monsters. There weren't that many mystical elements. Sometimes it was ridiculous sci-fi, but it was mainly sci-fi. King Caesar, really, is the only significant one I can think of other than Mothra, her dark counterpart Battra, and largely unseen quantities like Orochi and Bagan[7]. So, the use of mystical/supernatural elements, the temple, the statue with clearly supernatural effects, the possession, et al. makes for an intriguing departure

---

[7] Bagan is a bipedal dragon-like kaiju who, like King Caesar, hails from actual Asian mythology. Different versions of him were slated to be pitted against both Godzilla and Mothra onscreen by Toho, but all such plans were ultimately scuttled. The version finally settled on by Toho appeared in the completed screenplay for the aborted film *Mothra vs. Bagan*, where the latter took the role of a planetary protector bent on destroying humanity to save the biosphere, only to be opposed by Mothra, who is humanity's protector. Elements of the script found its way into the Heisei Series film *Godzilla and Mothra: The Battle for Earth* (1992), with Battra taking over the role of Bagan. The only time this version of Bagan was ever seen was as the final boss faced by Godzilla in the 1992 video game *Super Godzilla* for Super Nintendo. – CN

from the normal run. It gives a sense of something more going on, and it is more... spooky at times.

In what seems to be the penultimate parts, there are cuts to both the wife and the statue. So, there is an interesting ambiguity there. The Wolfman has already been defeated several times, and twice in his final form by Godzilla. But in the final battle, he is renewed and fights with strength and ferocity, perhaps to victory. Is it the supernatural influence, or is it the human inside fighting for love of his wife that gives the Wolfman his new edge? There is an interesting, and perhaps intentional, ambiguity at play here.

Now perhaps I am making too much of all of this. After all, the scenes I have watched are fragmentary, and they are in Japanese. So, I am admittedly reading a lot between the lines, and a lot between the scenes. I don't know, and honestly, I do not believe that Nakajima and his friends really intended to push the nuance this deep. Further, I do not think that they explored, or would have explored, these themes overtly or heavily handed. They wanted to make a kaiju movie, that is all.

But here's the thing: Even a little bit of a certain spice can change the flavour of soup. You do not need to ladle in a cup of the stuff 'till it's overpowering. But a little dash, a suggestion, an element, can make a subtle difference. It can take something which is bland and familiar and make it delicious and different, while still being clearly recognizably what we are used to.

And I do think that in returning to the early, implacably menacing Godzilla, in introducing a kaiju-sized wolfman with more personality than we have seen in ages, in introducing elements of human tragedy and the supernatural, Nakajima and his friends managed to make one of the best and one of the most imaginative and affecting Godzilla films in a decade or more.

So, if you're a Godzilla fan, I really suggest you check out this affectionate and heartwarming tribute.

***

LINKS: And where do you go to find it? (**Editor's note:** Each of these links were active as of July 2019.)

Wikizilla: There are a handful of text sources and stills on the Internet, including subreddits and threads in chat forums. The most comprehensive history, with some of the best photographs, is Wikizilla. Check this out.

https://wikizilla.org/wiki/Wolfman_vs._Godzilla

"A History of Godzilla vs Wolfman." If you're more video-oriented, there is a decent little Colton Review right here. It's a bit snarky at one point, but it's a decent overview.

https://www.youtube.com/watch?v=I3wAc-j-N88

"Behind the Scenes of the Lost Film Godzilla vs the Wolfman" from Walter Belcher, is a little misleading. There is no actual behind the scenes footage. What we have is 36 minutes of the existing footage, most of which lines up in a narrative order, or at least the first 24 minutes. This is the closest single video to the narrative I describe, although the Egyptian Temple and Baragon battle bits are missing. The last third seems to mostly be a repeat of things we've seen before, so possibly Belcher's compiling the same or similar scenes from a different source.

One of the unique scenes in the last third is the army attacking the Wolfman with conventional rifles and tanks – in the earlier version of this scene featured in the first third, they use the masers. In reconstructing my plot, I have put them together: conventional attack on the Wolfman, followed by masers. But possibly, according to this edit, maybe what's intended is that after defeating Godzilla and wandering off, the JSDF finally takes the Wolfman down with silver bullets or conventional armaments. Overall, essential viewing!

https://www.youtube.com/watch?v=nyCTUlANYOw

GODZILLA VS. WOLFMAN a.k.a. (Japanese characters) (Special Edit Ver.). This is a fourteen-minute compilation. But what makes it significant is the minute of opening footage featuring a Japanese archeologist exploring a ruined Egyptian temple and encountering a chamber filled with statues of wolfmen. Clearly this is intended to be the man who becomes possessed by the beast spirit and transforms into a wolfman back in Japan. So, it is a unique scene, and I have opted to include that in my plot synopsis.

Oddly, the transformation footage is not included in this version. Instead, after a title flash of the Wolfman,

the scenes go to Godzilla attacking the city, and then to
the scenes of the Masers vs. the Wolfman. The battle
between Godzilla and the Wolfman is also edited and
sequenced differently from the Belcher version.

https://www.youtube.com/watch?v=Y7QVhn6cGzg

"Baragon vs the Wolfman" is a three-minute
segment, or possibly the entire film, depicting an earlier
version of the Wolfman, a decent iteration of Baragon,
and a pretty good miniature refinery set and effects.
Overall, it's not bad, so I opted to include it in my plot
synopsis.

https://www.youtube.com/watch?v=Oa3Mb4g7DxM

**"Especial Godzilla vs. Legendary Beast Wolfman
Loquendo"** A six-minute Spanish language YouTube
video. Half documentary discussion, half scenes. The
scenes are video recorded off a television screen, which
is peculiar. It does contain shots that I have not seen
elsewhere. Most notably, this footage consists of brief
additional scenes where the human-sized Wolfman
attacks another man and advances on plain clothes police
detectives, only to be shot by them.

https://www.youtube.com/watch?v=nka2GscN8p8

"Godzilla vs the Wolfman Fanmade Film 1983"
Twenty-five minutes in length, and mostly similar in content and arrangement to the Belcher version, but without the duplication of footage. It includes the conventional weapons military assault on the Wolfman as the closing footage. The consistency of arrangement in these and other versions suggests that maybe the sequence reflects Nakajima's intended narrative.

https://www.youtube.com/watch?v=sTF7enxTlhU

"Scenes from The Lost Film Godzilla Vs. The Wolfman" from Felicia Bearsley. This is an hour-long compilation of scenes, but it appears that there is a fair bit of redundancy or repetition, so I can't say that there is any new material here not seen elsewhere. There doesn't seem to be a narrative structure, and things do not seem to flow in any kind of order. For instance, the human-sized transformation scene occurs in three different places through the hour. So, either that is just inserted randomly as it came up, or Bearsley was trying to do some sort of flashback. If she is trying to arrange the scenes in some kind of narrative line, it may be a little too complicated to follow.

https://www.youtube.com/watch?v=rbh_lB7JBfA

"Godzilla vs. the Wolfman, Fan Made Intro and Surviving Footage" is a nineteen-minute edit from Zacc Wylde Holland. It's adulterated, the intro is actually three or four minutes composed of shots from the original *Godzilla*, along with other werewolf movies – you will recognise Lon Chaney Jr. – with a title. The actual scenes run about fifteen minutes, grouped together and separated by title cards. As a bonus, the last two minutes are genuine behind the scenes footage from the "human-sized Wolfman" scenes.

https://www.youtube.com/watch?v=Q0XNrHrmNU0

Godzilla vs. Wolfman Behind the Scenes - "A state of the film photography" Three minutes of actual behind the scenes footage, this time from the *Godzilla vs. The Legendary Wolfman* fight scene, so we see the actors in suit with crew.

https://www.youtube.com/watch?v=EQ8RD8vPcXg

"Godzilla vs. the Wolfman KAIJU MOMENTS #14" This is a fan film of a fan film. A four-minute animated bit, where the Wolfman emerges and ultimately defeats Godzilla. The creator made a follow up where Godzilla wins. I'm speechless.

https://www.youtube.com/watch?v=cZ1QKMBTg7o

There are a few other YouTube videos of *Godzilla vs. The Legendary Wolfman*, some as long as fifteen minutes, some three or four, and others only a minute or so. They can be compilations, edits of specific scenes or battles, or trailers. But I do not think that there is anything else that we haven't already seen elsewhere.

END

MATTEL'S 24-INCH SHOGUN WARRIORS: GIANT MEMORIES

Christofer Nigro

Ah, the 1970s. Not only is that bygone decade known for its pioneering and awesome TV shows and films, but it's also well known for having the coolest toys and action figure lines of any other decade before or since. We had awesome toy companies like Mego, Kenner, and Mattel – the last one being of main concern to this article – churning out cool stuff by the boatload. Action figure/playset lines based on popular movie and TV franchises of the decade like *Planet of the Apes*, the *Six Million Dollar Man*, *Evel Knieval* (with working miniature motorcycles!), and every major (and a few minor) Marvel and DC super-heroes reigned supreme on the shelves of toy stores and playrooms at home.

And, of course, the decade capped off with the ultra-popular and extensive line of *Star Wars* figures, ships/vehicles, and playsets that every kid (including yours truly) ravenously coveted. Original character creations for the toy lines like the popular Stretch Armstrong also ruled the racks at the fondly remembered Toys R' Us and proved its selling power when Kenner soon came out with monstrous elastic nemeses like Stretch Monster and Stretch X-Ray (yes, his thing was a transparent body with viscera clearly visible), and then followed by rival lines of stretchable versions of popular super-heroes (including the first ever figure of the actual stretching hero Plastic Man).

Then… there were the Shogun Warriors. Mattel was the toy manufacturer with the license to sell different lines of these giant mechs from Japanese comic books and anime in America, and they certainly aimed to please. And nothing among the assortment of Shogun Warrior toys pleased more than the Jumbo Mahinder line (as it was known in Japan) of 24-inch action figures. Yes, you read that right: 24 *inches*. That's two feet tall to those who can do basic math, making them perhaps the largest set of action figures ever. They looked as awesome as they sound and everything about them just got cooler from there.

Therein lies the fond childhood memories of collecting this line of the Shogun Warriors. I wasn't able to finagle my family to get me all of them, but I did manage to acquire a few and my memories of those are among the highlights of my childhood nerd love for all things gigantic and monstrous and/or super-heroic.

As I recall, there were three distinct "waves" of these 24-inch Shogun Warrior figures, with one unusual outlier trailing the final of these waves. I'll get to that one, worry not. Most importantly is the fact that we got some cool Toho kaiju crossover action in this line that were nothing less than the stuff that nerd dreams are made of.

These toys made the Shogun Warriors explosively popular in the U.S. for a brief few years before a combination of the *Star Wars* craze and vocal public safety concerns about toys that fired small plastic projectiles came along and did them in. It was quite a ride while it lasted, though, and in addition to this toy

line we had an all-too brief comic book series from
Marvel at the same time in the late 1970s. It's a shame
we didn't have a pop chart hit called "Shogun Fever" or
something like that.

The first wave of these giant toys was around circa
1977 or thereabouts, and they featured a trio of Shoguns:
Mazinga (yes, we Americans called him Mazinga rather
than the more proper Mazinger), Raydeen, and Dragun.
The last of these three was the first one I got, as I thought
Dragun looked the most unique with his scarlet finish.
This contrasted with the other two, which were adorned
in mostly blues, grays, and blacks; I considered this motif
to be drab in comparison to the crimson guy. Dragun also
came equipped with an arsenal of projectable weaponry
that was the stuff of concerned parents' nightmares, but
nothing less than way cool to the kids who collected
them.

This guy had a rather clunky "star shooter" strapped to
one arm that could project giant-sized plastic shuriken,
and this toy came with several of them in three different
colors. A lever was on the back of the star shooter that
you pulled left to right or something like that to fire one
shuriken at a time. This was fraught with problems
because I found it maddeningly difficult to make that
adjustable strap just tight enough to keep the device from
falling upside down on the red guy's arm. After a while
the frustration became so great that I ended up
accidentally breaking the adjustable strap in my
endeavors to get it to fit just right. Luckily, my Uncle
Pete came to the rescue and created a tighter strap for me
out of thick tape, and the star shooter always stayed in

place then. My uncle was obviously a more competent craftsman by far than the designers for Mattel.

With the Warrior's other fist, you could insert one of several small battle axes – also in three different colors – that came with the toy. The pushing of a small lever enabled Dragun to hurl them up to several feet forward. I recall thinking the axes were cooler and easier to use as weapons than the star shooter.

Mazinga and Dragun, cool and powerful as can be.

As one may imagine, I couldn't wait to convince some of my neighborhood friends to buy Raydeen and Mazinga so between us we would have all three and could thus play out adventures with the full team. Of

382

course, few things in life go as planned, and I remember turning red in the face (that being an apt color here) when a few of my friends, upon seeing my Dragun figure, decided they were both going to get that one instead of Mazinga or Raydeen.

Yeah, that sucked. And of course, my protestations about how not fun such redundancy would be elicited the expected "You can't tell them what to do! Stop trying to tell them which ones they can get!" lectures from my family. This was not surprising since they weren't the ones having their fun spoiled, so they could afford that righteous posturing instead of being the selfish little brat that I was. As it turned out one of my friends did end up getting Mazinga, though none ever got Raydeen. I remember taking a liking to the Mazinga figure's coolness and realized I would eventually want to have that one too. After all, if my friends could play the redundancy game, then what the hell, I could too, right?

As I would later learn, Mazinga was cooler by a few levels of magnitude than Dragun. What this figure lacked in terms of colorful armor compared to the axe-throwing Warrior he more than made up for with versatility of weaponry and user-friendliness. This toy came with a bunch of miniature white and red plastic missiles that could be loaded three at a time in a trifecta of small launching units in his right hand. Three levers were present that could be pushed to fire this trio of separately armed missiles, either one at a time or all of them simultaneously. None of the other toys in the line could ever match that level of cool functionality. Even better were slots on his legs where you could store six missiles on each, so you would always have some handy no matter where you and Mazinga went.

The figure was rounded out by two red plastic swords that fit in convenient sheathes near either side of his hips (or what passed for them). Each blade could be unsheathed and fit firmly into the Warrior's clenched left fist. I remember how cool I thought that was. To top it off, the original version of the figure had a miniature removable spaceship (or "brainship") embedded in his cranium that could be used as a separate toy. This figure was worth every penny it must have cost back then (sellers on eBay are currently asking for $400.00 to get an intact figure of this guy).

I never did get to see the Raydeen figure save for briefly getting my hands on a display item at a toy store. For the record, this figure was also very impressive to behold. His main weapon was a bunch of avian-shaped attack craft that could be fired (one at a time) from his diaphragm. One of his arms had a shield with a nasty-looking blade that did nothing except look cool; his other arm had axe-like blades on either side of the wrist, and the arm could be launched at the press of a button. The launching fist motif would be a recurring one for the entire line, pretty much whenever a toy designer couldn't think of any other functional weapon they could create and make work with plastic and spring-loaded action. One of the cool things about the Raydeen figure that is still often overlooked is how he resembled a condor-like bird of prey when viewed from the side.

My plans to try and convince another of my friends in the 'hood to get the Raydeen figure were curtailed when the second wave of 24-inch Shogun Warriors were released in America by Mattel the following year. It was another trio, and one of them was nothing less than an exceedingly rare thing in life that seemed too good to be true... but wasn't. I'll get to that one in a moment.

A new adjective-enhanced version of Mazinga, easily the most popular of the original three, was released as *Great* Mazinga for that second wave. A newcomer to the trio was a relatively mediocre addition called Gaiking, this one decked out with a mostly yellow color motif (more on him below). But the third part of this new wave was the unbelievably awesome crown jewel of the set: we got a nearly 24-inch-high figure of the King of the Monsters himself, Godzilla! Yes, Toho gave Mattel the license to sell this toy to American buyers, and you can imagine the buildings I knocked down to get my hands on this.

The Godzilla figure looked basically the way he was supposed to, but the manufacturers didn't exactly go out of their way to provide meticulous detail. A good example was the figure's simplistic dorsal plates on his back, like something you would see on a dinosaur from *The Flintstones*. The figure was a lizard-like green rather than the brownish-gray of the Showa Era version of the Kaiju King, who had just recently finished that era's set of films which recast him as a giant super-hero. His mug was rather ugly and seemed to more resemble one of those Reptoid aliens you see in UFO accounts rather than any version of the Big G we saw onscreen. His feet were on wheels much like the rest of the Jumbo Mahinder Warriors line, and his tail was all too detachable.

Since Mattel didn't want to incorporate battery-operated functions like lights and sounds into these toys (a very wasted opportunity), Godzilla was given the typical launchable fist. I was a total terror with that fist, by the way, and I would frequently piss off family members by launching it at noses or the back of one's head. It didn't hit hard enough to cause injury, but it certainly made you shout and jump if you didn't expect to be hit square in the face or on the noggin with it.

His only other functional attribute was a red lever on the back of his head that could be used to project a forked tongue from his mouth that had flames painted on it. I suppose this lazy accessory was designed to be seen as either a flickering tongue (since when did Godzilla ever have that?) or interpreted as the spewing of flame (at the time, many American G-fans and semi-G-Fans mistakenly considered the Big G an upchucker of fire rather than beams of concentrated radiation), whatever the owner may prefer during any given play session.

Up from the depths! Or, at least from the toy shelves...

Better yet, I was able to convince another friend to buy Gaiking, but only after a bit of drama where he insisted that he wanted to get Mazinga like our other friend did. Once he got Gaiking, there was an all-too brief time when we had a lot of fun enacting play battles and team-ups between the three Warriors. Interestingly enough, the memorable commercials advertising these jumbo figures painted Godzilla in an ambiguous way by declaring, "Is he friend or foe? You decide!"

The party quickly ended after my friend with Gaiking discovered how easily one of its two functional weapons could break. Besides the typical launching left fist, the horned yellow Warrior had a body that resembled a huge sinister face. The eyes of this "face" were actually launching units for two small plastic missiles that could be projected by a cheap side-to-side lever located in back of the figure. As mentioned, this rather easily broke one day when the three of us were having the time of our lives conducting a faux three-way battle. We turned it over to my grandfather, who was good at fixing anything that broke, but he noted that because the broken lever was made of cheap plastic he was unable to simply wield it back together as he could have if Mattel had used metal parts.

With the party over, I soon talked my family into getting me a Great Mazinga figure. I assumed that added adjective made this second version better than the first. Unfortunately, the figure had a few inexplicable re-designs that made it quite the opposite. One worthwhile alteration was the reduction in size of the chest emblem. The original version had two protruding points which were just looking forward to puncturing someone's eye. That change was no big deal to me. What was a big deal was the number of missile-holding leg slots being reduced by half. Moreover, the brainship was no longer a separate detachable toy. It could be yanked out with some effort, but this non-functional version had no front section!

Why this particular change? It's not like the brainship was easy to swallow unless you were a kid who could open his mouth and throat wider than a cottonmouth.

This little craft also had no dangerous parts or launchable weaponry. I remember how let down I felt with Great Mazinga for failing to live up to the addition to his name. I even wondered if it was some type of ruse to make you think a watered down version of the toy was actually something more. Sadly, it worked in my case (*giving the bird to Mattel for their effrontery*).

The third wave came out a year after this, and it was by far the least exciting of the three. Great Mazinga and Gaiking were still part of the trio, but now Godzilla was replaced by a third mech called Daimos. I never actually had or saw this figure save once briefly as a display item in a toy store. At this point in time the Shogun Warrior craze had run its course, and the 24-inch Mahinder figure line was breathing its last as it was supplanted by the *Star Wars* toy-collecting frenzy, along with other popular figure lines of the time such as the Micronauts.

In short, Daimos was a most lackluster addition to the line that served to demonstrate how it was running out of steam more than anything else. Other than the tired and uber-generic launching fist, this Warrior's arsenal consisted of nothing more than two big, bulky missiles that could be launched one at a time from each of his... legs? Um, okay. Even more silly was the fact that these missiles were not made of plastic but something that looked and felt like foam rubber. This final member of the Big 5 was clearly made to placate the child safety crowd, and though this toy succeeded in not killing any kids it did manage to kill the line of Jumbo Mahinder Shogun Warrior figures.

Now for that previously mentioned outlier. This one was another dream for kaiju-fans and another figure

Mattel got out of its licensing deal with Toho. That was nothing less than a very cool-looking Rodan figure. I never had it, but I do remember seeing and marveling over it at a toy store. This large figure was rendered with great fidelity to detail, and never did the Kaiju of the Sky look better and larger-than-life in toy form – and large it most certainly was with nearly a three-foot wingspan! Interestingly, the red color scheme was indicative of the Fire Rodan incarnation that was still over a decade away from its debut in the film *Godzilla vs. Mechagodzilla 2*.

The Mattel Rodan figure's functionality was based around the fact that the toy was essentially a moveable plastic puppet whose strings were literally rubber bands. There were openings in the back where you could insert your fingers and use them to make Rodan move his head, mouth, and wings. I recall the box mentioning that you could make him "squawk," but I have no idea how that worked since like the rest of the Mahinder line this toy had no battery-operated features.

One more interesting thing to note about Mattel's Rodan figure. Despite being a component of Mattel's licensed Toho products, the figure was never marketed as part of the Mahinder Shogun Warriors line. Instead, he was listed on the box as being part of Mattel's "World's Greatest Monsters" set. This line of toys evidently began and ended with the Rodan figure, however. This is only speculation, but likely the toy was produced and marketed separately from the Shogun Warriors line because at the time the 24-inch figures were in the process of being phased out.

**The sky's greatest warrior enters the toy market!
Woohoo!**

After this, Mattel came out with a smaller and still rather cool line of die-cast metal Shogun Warriors that could be disassembled and reassembled as fighter craft or spaceships, beating the soon-to-be-popular Transformers toy line at its very successful game by a few years. The then-popular Micronauts line of toys already had a lock on that sort of modular functionality, and this new line of Warrior figures failed to recoup the loss that the franchise suffered to the superior popularity of the *Star Wars* toy line and competition from would-be upstarts like *Battlestar Galactica*. Not only that, but the smaller diecast line was hit particularly hard by the child safety voices of the time, and this resulted in new editions with much less functionality (read: small plastic projectile weapons incapable of blowing up a building but more than capable of taking out an eye or blocking an esophagus) than their predecessors.

By the time the 1970s were over, Mattel's once thriving Shogun Warriors line of action figures was likewise on its way out. By the time I was in middle school, the colorful toy line had gone the way of disco. However, it didn't fade away without leaving some truly unforgettable memories of being one of the coolest things to come out of one of the coolest decades to be a kid.

END

PART 3: ART

The following section contains samples of kaiju artwork from artists who are quite obviously fans of the genre. This will serve the dual purpose of helping them to promote their work and providing some awesome visual bonus eye candy to you, the reader.

Chimera vs. Bubbles

Art: John Opal

Noregon

Art: Neil Riebe

Ogopogo vs. Giant Eel

Art: Brion Haloway

**The story behind this battle is featured in Wild Hunt Press'
anthology *Duel of the Monsters* Vol. 1. Get it to see these two,
plus several other pairs of monsters, throw down in bloody
combat!**

Blue King

Art: Frank Parr

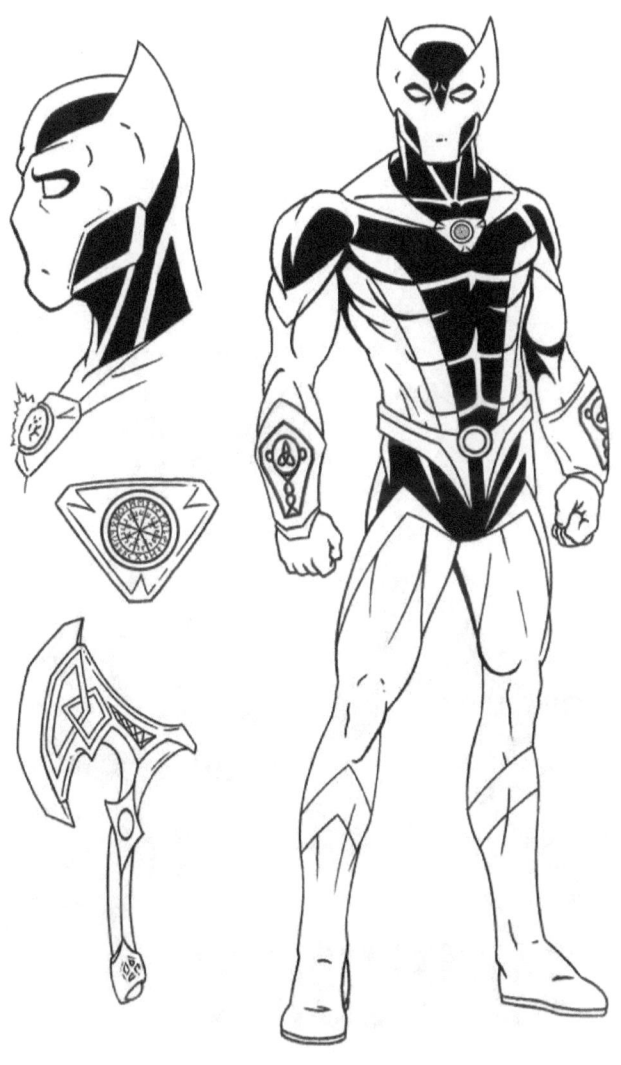

Marugrah

Art: Garayann

MARUGRAH

Plague

Art: GabeTKezilla

Marugrah

and

Plague

Art: Ray Fromm

ABOUT THE AUTHORS

Matthew (Matt) Dennion lives in New Jersey with his wife and two daughters. Matt works primarily as a teacher of students with autism and an SLE (Structured Learning Experience) Coordinator. He has loved giant monster and superhero stories his entire life. He began writing short stories for Black Coat Press and *G-Fan* magazine in 2007. In 2015 he began writing kaiju novels for Severed Press. His current works for Severed Press include *Chimera: Scourge of the Gods*; *Operation ROC*; *Atomic Rex*; *Polar Yeti*; *Atomic Rex: Wrath of the Polar Yeti*; *Kaiju Corps*; *Atomic Rex: Conquest of Chimera*; *Operation Megalodon*; and *Valley of the Dinosaurs*.

Matt has recently began writing comics books in collaboration with other creators. His comic works include *Draco Azul/Atomic Rex: Shadow of the Raptor* with Andres Perez and *Irokus x Atomic Rex: Avatars of the Apocalypse* Vol. 1 with Frank Parr and Wayne Smith. Matthew has a line of self-published novellas including *The Kaiju and the Crime Fighter and Other Tales* and *Raptor Tales: Heroes and Monsters*; he also edited and contributed to the mutli-author kaiju anthology *Gfantis vs. Guest Monsters*. He self-published the first edition of the anthology *Attack of the Kaiju Vol. 1: Age of Monsters* and he has short fiction in *Duel of the Monsters* Vol. 1 from Wild Hunt Press.

All of Matt's novels and comics are available on Amazon in print and digital formats and can be purchased on Amazon. Along with his friends Andres Perez and Chris Martinez, Matt has created the charity publishing venture Kaiju vs. Cancer, through which creators use their monsters and heroes to team with St. Jude Children's Research Hospital to battle childhood cancer. The first of these anthologies to be published was *Courage on Infinite Earths: A Kaiju vs. Cancer Anthology*.

Christopher Conde is a graphic designer from Massachusetts. Illustrating monsters became his interest after watching *Godzilla Against Mechagodzilla* at a young age. Nowadays, Chris designs work with the help of various organizations and companies, like Mattel. He is as the creator of the giant fish-in-a-suit-of-armor known as Bubbles, whose publication debut came in Matt Dennion's self-published kaiju anthology *Gfantis vs. Guest Monsters*.

Skip Peel, alias Galen Edward Peel Jr., is a longtime Florida-based writer now exploring more northerly climes with his wife Jill. A travel enthusiast, Japanophile*, one-time Disney Pirate, and inaugural staff for Repticon Reptile Shows, he holds a bachelor's in English and master's in Global Studies from Liberty University. He is the creator and author of the "Rex Summeral" series for *G-Fan* magazine that has appeared in over fifty installments during that publication's over 25-year history, as well as being featured in the *Daikaiju! Giant Monster Tales* anthology by Agog! Press. His first novel to be released on the market is *A Halloween Hymn,* a direct adaptation which inverses Charles Dickens' famous tale *A Christmas Carol* to tell the story of a charitable man tempted by three devils in the context of the modern American holiday of Halloween. Skip perpetually dreams of returning to Asia for humanitarian work, kissing his wife, and eating as much quality sashimi as is reasonably possible.

*親日

Zach Cole is the author of the novella *Tsuchigumo* (his debut work), *Kaiju Epoch*, and the Jeremy Walker Thriller series (beginning with *Blue Moon: A Jeremy Walker Thriller*) and is the mastermind behind the multi-author linear horror anthology *The Experiment* from Wild Hunt Press. He was born in Wooster, Ohio, beginning his love of monsters at the age of two after viewing *Mothra vs. Godzilla*. He became a writer around the age of ten, penning Godzilla stories and even comics containing his own monstrous creations. His love of books started with the *Goosebumps* series, reading anything that has to do with monsters, big or small. He lives in Wooster, Ohio.

John LeMay is the author of over a dozen books on film, history, and cryptozoology. His best known works in kaiju circles are *Kong Unmade: The Lost Films of Skull Island; The Big Book of Japanese Giant Monster Movies: The Lost Films;* and *Terror of the Lost Tokusatsu Films.* His most recent title is *Cowboys & Saurians: Dinosaurs and Prehistoric Beasts as Seen by the Pioneers*, a cryptozoological study on newspaper articles from the U.S. Pioneer Period on remnant dinosaur sightings.

Kane Gilmour is the international bestselling author of *The Crypt of Dracula*. He co-authored *Ragnarok* and *Omega*, the fourth and fifth novels in Jeremy Robinson's Jack Sigler/Chess Team series, and he's working on the final volume, *Kingdom*, as well. He also writes his own thriller novels, including the popular Jason Quinn novel *Resurrect*. His short stories have been published in *Dark Discoveries*, *Kaiju Rising* Volumes 1 and 2, *SNAFU: Survival of the Fittest*, and *MECH: Age of Steel*.

In addition to his novels, Kane wrote the sci-fi noir webcomic *Warbirds of Mars,* and Jeremy Robinson's comic-book adaptation of *Island 731*. He lives with his partner, her children, his children, a dog, and a cat in Vermont.

Visit him online at: www.kanegilmour.com.

D.G. Valdron is a renegade Canadian writer, former lawyer, journalist, teacher, carpenter, car thief, ne'er do well, professional student, and breeder of mutant cats. The guy just can't hold down a job. A long-time contributor to Christofer Nigro's website The Godzilla Saga, Den has also written esoteric articles about Edgar Rice Burroughs' creations and other pulp heroes. His novel, *The Mermaid's Tale*, was shortlisted for the Kevin Van Rooy Award. Other publications are *Lexx Unauthorized*; *Dawn of Cthulhu!*; *Bear Cavalry - the True (Not!) History of the Icelandic Bears*; *The Greatest Unauthorized Doctor Stories;* and *Giant Monsters Sing*

Sad Songs story collection. He is secretly working on an epic kaiju throwdown novel.

Born on May 15, 1991, in Washington state (where he still currently resides), **Cody Bratsch** has had a fascination with all sorts of creative ventures and forms of storytelling ever since he was a kid. Cody has watched and read a massive selection from them all and has come to adore a great many of them. His debut as a published author was in the short story anthology *Attack of the Kaiju Vol. 1: Age of Monsters*, and his work has also been featured in *Duel of the Monsters* Vol. 1 from Wild Hunt Press.

Neil Riebe has been a lifelong fan of Japanese giant monsters since seeing *King Kong vs Godzilla* back in the '70s. The three-part story "Godzilla vs Atragon", published in *G-Fan* issues #9 through #11, inspired him to write his multi-part Godzilla stories. These tales included "Godzilla vs Super Allosaurus", published in *G-Fan* issues #15 through #17; "Battle of Manazura Island", published in *G-Fan* #25; and "Rodana", published in *G-Fan* #42. After Toho asked *G-Fan* to cease publishing fan fiction based on their characters, Neil posted subsequent stories on FanFiction.net. While writing kaiju fan fiction, he also wrote an article for *Japanese Giants* #10 and the forewords to the *Gfantis vs Guest Monsters* anthology and John LeMay's *The Big Book of Japanese Giant Monster Movies Vol. 1: 1954-1982*.

Matt Dennion, author of the popular *Atomic Rex* novels, invited Neil to contribute a short story to his *Attack of the Kaiju Vol. 1: Age of Monsters* anthology. Since then Neil has switched from kaiju fan fiction to writing original kaiju stories. His latest kaiju novel is *I Shall Not Mate,* which can be found on Amazon.com. His next, *Vistakill,* should be released in early 2020, as well as an essay in the second edition of *The Big Book of Japanese Giant Monster Movies: The Lost Films*.

Kevin Heim was born in 1969 and began writing fiction shortly after he learned how to read – so, for almost ten years now. In 2012 he contributed two short stories to *Psychopomp*, a defunct ezine, which introduced his version of the Frankenstein Monster and his original character Ivan Ronald Schablotski, both of which have a small but mediocre fan base. Since then he has submitted stories for a number of Wild Hunt Press anthologies, including *Dorian Gray: Darker Shades* (2018); *Duel of the Monsters* Vol. 1 (2019); *Boogey Knights* Vol. 1; and *Mansion of the Macabre* Vol. 1 (the latter two upcoming in 2020 at this writing). His most notable achievements are having visited the Elvis American Diner in Jerusalem, Israel, and getting thrown out of St. Peter's Basilica in Vatican City, Rome. Kevin lives in Salem, Massachusetts, where he likes to dress up in costumes and pretend that fictional characters are real people.

Andres Perez is a Japan-based English teacher and aspiring film critic who makes movie, television, comic book, and video game reviews on his YouTube channel, *KaijuNoir*. He is also a freelance editor who has worked on other projects, such as the giant monster comic *Nagoraiar: Kingdom of the Monsters* as well as William Kearney's mythology-themed novel series *Gods' Wrath: Tournament of the Divine* from Wild Hunt Press.

Dustin Dreyling is an avid fan of science fiction and horror with a soft spot for all things kaiju. Originally hailing from White Bear Lake, Minnesota, he also likes proofreading novels, playing video games both old and new, and taking care of his planted freshwater aquariums. His first published story was featured in Zach Cole's linear horror anthology *The Experiment* from Wild Hunt Press, and his work can also be found in WHP's horror anthology *Duel of the Monsters* Vol. 1. His first novel, batch one of a kaiju horror series *Primordial Soup,* will be released in 2020 from Wild Hunt Press.

Alex Dumitru is from Northwest, Indiana, where he lives with his family and a very small dog. He was first inspired to write kaiju literature after becoming a fan of the *Ultraman* franchise from Tsuburaya Productions, and this inspired the creation of his own published kyodai character, Massive. His debut (and that of Massive) was in Matt Dennion's self-published edition of *Attack of the Kaiju Vol. 1: Age of Monsters*. Alex also made a major contribution to Zach Cole's linear horror anthology *The Experiment* from Wild Hunt Press, and his newest work can be found here and in *Duel of the Monsters* Vol. 1 from Wild Hunt.

Ever since watching his first G-film, *Godzilla vs. Monster Zero* in 1992, **Andrew Nguyen** has been a lifelong fan of the Godzilla series. This interest in the Godzilla film franchise has extended to other segments of Japanese entertainment, particularly Japanese animation, as well as military history due to the background behind the creation of the G-series. From a young age, Andrew has dabbled in writing, first on school projects and then posting on the website *Fanfiction.net*. In 2008, Andrew switched to writing articles for several websites that dealt with entertainment and military history, including book, movie, and game reviews. A long-time colleague of his, Neil Riebe, brought Andrew's attention to Christofer Nigro and Wild Hunt Press' continuation of the *Attack of the Kaiju* anthology series established by Matthew Dennion. Presently, Andrew is continuing to write on topics relating to either entertainment or history at websites including *Sci Fi Japan* and *Toho Kingdom*, and in the immediate future will have his first article published in *G-Fan* magazine.

Nathan Marchand is a young writer from northeastern Indiana. Homeschooled starting in first grade, he discovered his talent for writing in sixth grade English. He was given the assignment to write a "fanciful story," so he crafted one about his toys coming to life and fighting each other. He enjoyed it so much, he wrote many sequels (he still has them all… somewhere). He eventually expanded into writing other stories and genres. Nathan has wanted to write science fiction since his dad introduced him to the original *Star Trek* at age three.

Nathan attended Taylor University Fort Wayne, earning a B.A. in professional writing. Since graduation, he's worked as a reporter and freelancer. His first novel, _Pandora's Box_, was published in 2010 by Edge Science Fiction and Fantasy. He's also the co-creator of the ongoing fantasy book serial _Children of the Wells_ and the podcast Kaijuvision Radio. In 2011 he published the kaiju novella _Destroyer_, which he co-wrote with Natasha Hayden and Timothy Deal. He's now the host of The Monster Island Film Vault podcast (www.MonsterIslandFilmVault.com).

His literary influences include C.S. Lewis, J.R.R. Tolkien, Robert Heinlein, and Orson Scott Card. His favorite books are _The Lord of the Rings_ trilogy; C.S. Lewis' _Space Trilogy_; _The Chronicles of Narnia; Starship Troopers_; and _Ender's Game_.

When not writing, he enjoys other creative endeavors like photography, acting, videography, ballroom dancing, and occasionally saving the world. His website is: www.NathanJSMarchand.com.

Christofer Nigro has been a lifelong fan of fantastic fiction in all mediums, from cinema to TV to prose to comic books to board games to video games etc. This includes horror, sci-fi, superheroes, anime, tokusatsu, and pulp adventure. He has earned a bachelor's degree in English with a focus on creative writing. The public first saw his writing online with the original websites for _Warrenverse: The Amazing World of the Warren Comics Characters_ and _The Godzilla Saga_; he later reconstructed the MONSTAAH website with the permission and

413

blessing of its creator, Chuck Loridans (all three are slated for a refurbishment). He got his start as a published author with Black Coat Press in several of its annual *Tales of the Shadowmen* anthologies and has had short stories published by Sirens Call Publications, Pro Se Press, Pulp Empire, Grinning Skull Press, Horrified Press, and Local Hero Press.

He also contributed to Matt Dennion's self-published *Attack of the Kaiju Vol. 1: Age of Monsters* and Matt's charity anthology *Courage on Infinite Earths: A Kaiju vs. Cancer Anthology* to aid St. Jude Children's Research Hospital to battle childhood cancer. His first two kaiju novels *Dargolla: A Kaiju Nightmare* and *Megadrak: Beast of the Apocalypse,* were published by Severed Press. He established Wild Hunt Press in 2018 to continue publishing his work and those of other authors.

Also available

I Shall
Not
Mate

Neil
Riebe

The Flock's war with mankind has triggered their species to evolve. They hatch their first offspring with an armored hide and opposable thumbs. The Flock fears he will pollute the bloodline, but mankind sees his adaptions for what they are — an improvement. Both man and beast are out to destroy the baby kaiju. The race for survival is on.

Grab your copy on Amazon.com

Werewolf vs. Vampire
Yeti vs. Owlman
Mothman vs. Jersey Devil
Vampire vs. Killer Clown
and many more...

DUEL OF THE
MONSTERS
Volume 1

Cody Bratsch
Zach Cole
Matt Dennion
Dustin Dreyling
Alex Dumitru
Robert Galvin
Breyden Halverson
Kevin Heim
Christofer Nigro
Peter Rawlik
Tyler Shepard

Hot from Wild Hunt Press!

***Duel of the Monsters* Vol. 1 is the first edition of a new horror anthology series featuring short stories by multiple authors in the genre. Together they will show you exactly what happens when two monsters of a distinct type cross paths and knock heads! The gore will be great, and the terror will only escalate, as different groups of hapless humans face not one but two different monsters – who will then ultimately face off against each other!**

Miss this one at your peril! After all, why should the victims in these tales face the horror alone?

From D.G. Valdron!!

Also from D.G. Valdron!!

www.ingramcontent.com/pod-product-compliance
Lightning Source LLC
Chambersburg PA
CBHW051514250626
47156CB00001B/87